THE ROAD TO THE THIRD WORLD

THE ROAD TO THE THIRD WORLD

Conspiring to Destroy America

A Novel

Stephen R. Cafaro

iUniverse, Inc.

New York Lincoln Shanghai

The Road to the Third World

Conspiring to Destroy America

iUniverse books may be ordered through booksellers or by contacting:

iUniverse
2021 Pine Lake Road, Suite 100
Lincoln, NE 68512
www.iuniverse.com
1-800-Authors (1-800-288-4677)

Because of the dynamic nature of the Internet, any Web addresses or links contained in this book may have changed since publication and may no longer be valid.

This is a work of fiction. All of the characters, names, incidents, organizations, and dialogue in this novel are either the products of the author's imagination or are used fictitiously.

ISBN: 978-0-595-48226-9 (pbk)
ISBN: 978-0-595-60318-3 (ebk)

Printed in the United States of America

CHAPTER 1

▼

The elderly couple huddle together in a corner of their bullet riddled home. Their middle class house is boarded up to provide protection from unwelcome intruders. They stare blankly at a small static speaking television set. The listening volume of the set goes from near silence to a blasting crescendo, and the video jumps frames at a time reminiscent of a 1940's television viewing experience. It is the second decade of the 21st century, and time has not been kind to America.

The old man rises from his position of safety and hobbles over to the sporadic set to adjust the makeshift wire antenna. He moves the improvised metal hanger in various directions, but to no avail. Frustrated, he slaps the side of the set and suddenly the sound and scenes improve. "Humph" he mutters as he slowly moves back to the corner. He is bent over as he prepares to seat himself beside his wife. Suddenly, there is a loud cracking noise just as a large splinter of wood is dislodged from a wood covered window. The elderly lady looks up to view a pencil sized beam of new light that has invaded the darkened room. Momentarily, she smiles as she muses with her husband. "Another near miss, but we have more light and air conditioning."

The words were no sooner said when she felt the weight descend upon her. Her husband falls into her lap gasping for air and clutching his throat. She moves his hand to reveal the splinter lodged in his throat. She cringes as she prepares to remove the wood. Before she can assist, her husband faintly waves off the effort as he casts a directional glance at his upper body. The woman follows the gaze to reveal a bullet wound in his chest. She grows faint as she observes the flow of blood and hears the horrific sucking sound coming from the wound. She futilely cradles his head in her arms in a comforting motion. Within seconds, she feels his body stiffen just as he expels a final whoosh of air. A lone tear flows from her tired eyes and she gently rocks the dead body. She brushes the few remaining hairs on his balding forehead and gently lays his head on the floor.

She rises and shuffles to the bathroom where she opens a container bearing a hand written label—**Cyanide**. She grabs 2 capsules and pours a glass of water. Returning, she lifts her husbands head to her bosom. She again resumes the consoling rocking and gulps a drink of water to swallow the pills. Resigned to her fate, she awaits her final moments. She looks down at her husbands graying face and whispers "I'm coming to join you just as we discussed. It will be good to be away from this world. I'm surprised we lasted this long!" A bit of regret overcomes her as she silently prays for divine guidance. *Dear God, why has all this happened? What have we done to bring your anger upon us? It is over for me, but what of my children and grand babies? What will come of them? What will become of my country? Please let the punishment end!*

Her weary eyes return to the television screen. A somber reporter summarizes the current state of affairs. He is reporting from an upscale neighborhood in upstate New York that is in appalling condition. Video pictures of fallen wires, garbage strewn streets and fortress like residences attest to the plight of this once fashionable area.

A cameraman is slowly panning the neighborhood as the reporter begins his dialogue. "America is under siege! It is impossible to understand how all this happened. A quick look at this upscale area reveals the depth of our ongoing problem. Boarded and bricked windows and doors hide the elegance of these fine homes. Booby trapped devices have replaced flowers and trees in the once fashionable landscapes. Gangs of marauding thieves and gun totting vigilantes have driven out the children and families that once frolicked in the streets. The playful shouts of kids at play are lost to the ever present sounds of gunfire. And yet—all this is but a microcosm of what is happening throughout America today."

The cameraman now focuses on the reporter as he continues his assessment. "Its mind numbing to think just six months ago, our country was in great shape. The President and government officials were touting our resilient economy. We were told that the United States is the greatest country in the world and that our system is the finest in the history of mankind. No one seems to be able to explain how the dollar suddenly collapsed. Everyone thought such a thing was impossible—that the countries of the world were reliant upon us for their survival and that no country would ever move against us. But move against us they did, and with disastrous consequence for America. Our government quickly reacted by attempting to cover the federal debt with a flood of hastily produced dollars. This process normally worked to settle economic concerns, but this time the end result was hyper inflation. Wall Street joined the catastrophe in short order. Declines in the stock market were trailed by massive lay offs, bank failures and corporate bankruptcies. The economic problems spilled over into the streets as people vied for jobs, money, food and the other staples of survival. Finding no way out, the populace soon turned their rage on the government, the financial institutions and finally, one another! The army and the National Guard have been called out, but they are barely able to protect government buildings and politicians from the growing wrath."

The broadcaster becomes more passionate and he injects his personal feelings. "The country is in a state of absolute anarchy. Looters, murderers and vigilantes are the new rule of law. The government can not protect you! I repeat—the government can not protect you! Each of you must defend yourselves in any way you can! This is an ominous time for America."

A quizzical look appears on the reporters face as he questions the origin of the dilemma. "What I don't understand and what no one can explain is how something like this could have ever happened to our country. We had it all—homes, jobs, incomes, and a standard of living that was the envy of the world. We had the best system, the best technology, the best managers, the best companies and the best people. When America talked, the world listened. When America instructed, the world responded! Clearly, we are the undisputed best! How is it possible we have fallen so far, and so quickly? I don't understand!"

The voice from the television grows distant as the old woman begins to lose consciousness. Her final unspoken plea is for her children. *Spare them Lord so they may right whatever wrongs that have incited your fury. Please show them the way out of this inferno!* She draws her final breath oblivious to the origin of the debilitating cancer that has infected America.

She is among the hundreds of millions of Americans who will never comprehend the enormous crime that has been perpetrated on the American people. Complacency, arrogance and feelings of superiority had become the blinders of the bewildered masses. Generations will suffer the pangs of economic denial with their only hope being the fleeting memories of a once great country. Americans have just begun the painful process of daily survival, human degeneration and social injustice that accompanies any failed country. At a point, the fatal outcome was avoidable. Some knew of the specific problem and tried to avert the economic disaster. This is a story of the problem and those who gave their lives seeking to change the inevitable conclusion.

CHAPTER 2

▼

Chou Bing's face contorts as he absorbs still another blow from the group of vicious attackers. The latest strike caused a large gash to open on his cheek bone. Blood flows freely from the wound as he feverishly seeks to bury his head in his arms. Chou wraps his body in a fetal position even as he feels new pain coming from the continuing barrage of flying fists and flailing boots. In the background, he hears the drunken slurs of his assailants as they persist in the savage beating. "You god damned slanty eyed chinks should learn to keep your yellow asses out of this neighborhood. We're going to fuck you up real good! Maybe you people will learn to stay in Chinatown?"

The assault continues as his small frame is kicked around like a rag doll. Suddenly, they stop. Chou peeks from the safety of his folded arms to see four men dressed in black leather jackets swigging beer and laughing. They seem to be huffing in exhaustion from the violent thrashing they just delivered. He hears the voice of another goon. "These people never learn. We kick their asses, send them home and in no time they are back pushing their chink drugs in the zone. We need to deliver a message they will understand! We need to hurt him bad so——"

Another voice interrupts. "I got it!" He slowly unzips a side pocket of his jacket and pulls out a pearl handled object. He pushes a button on the device and a six inch stiletto hops out of the holder. "Maybe if I straighten out those eyes and peel off a little yellow, he won't be so obvious the next time he sneaks his ass into the zone?" He raises his beer bottle, and the four simultaneously clink their bottles in agreement.

Chou hears the words and fear envelopes him. A surge of adrenalin energizes his beaten body, and he jumps to his feet and begins to run towards a light at the end of the dark alley. In the distance, he could see the outline of a stream of by passers. He attempts to yell out for attention, but his vocal cords respond with a raspy whimper. Chou looks back to see the four black jackets in close pursuit. He turns back to the light and attempts to pick up his pace. He is running for his life and he knows it! Suddenly, he trips over the corner of one of the irregular cobblestones which pave the alley. He falls uncontrollably to the hard surface and immediately feels the pain of his old and now, new wounds. He quickly rolls over to resume his escape, but the brush of leather against his face followed by a blow to the back of his head calls a quick end to his flight.

"Stand him up boys and muzzle the son of a bitch. It's time to carve up a chink. I got to give him credit though—the yellow bastard can run!"

Immense horror overcomes Chou as he struggles in vain against the jacketed oppressors. He is held firmly by his hands, feet and head and feels powerless to resist. He hears the mechanical click as the pearl handled knife is again opened to reveal the long slim blade. He is trembling uncontrollably as he views the ornate patch behind the oncoming knife. *Skulls, crossbones, Pagans from Hell—Is this the way I am to die?* He looks into the face of the man with the knife and sees a bewildering image. The man is smiling hysterically and his lower lip spasms as he draws the knife closer to Chou's eye. Suddenly, the blade stops as the man admonishes himself. "Not so fast with the eyes. I want to peel you a little first!"

The man rips at Chou's shirt and exposes his chest. Slowly, the knife approaches Chou's heaving chest. The knife is turned sideways to thinly cut his chest. Chou feels a wave of agony as the knife begins its treacherous journey. Chou hears his attacker gleefully announce the surgical intrusion. "Slice and dice boys—slice and dice! Anyone like some yellow meat?" Chou struggles in vain as the knife continues to cut into his flesh. His fear has turned to hatred even as he seems resigned to his fate.

Chou looks into his attackers face just as a surprised grimace replaces the lusty grin. The eyes of his assailant roll back into his head and he falls in a lump onto the ground. There is shouting as he views a piece of metal coming in the direction of the men who are holding him. "Take this mother fucker—you're going to die!" Chou feels the grip on him loosen and he immediately unleashes a series of punches and kicks on one of the stunned aggressors. He hears the deadly thud of the steel and the accompanying screams of pain as it makes contact time and again. In a little less than 30 seconds of relentless attack, three of Chou's assailants are unconscious on the ground and one is hastily retreating into the darkness of the alley.

Chou looks up at his college friend, Todd Robbins, who is holding the bloodied piece of rebar in his hands. "They were going to kill me Todd. If you didn't come by when you did, I would be dead now!"

Todd is shaking as he replies. "What happened to you Charlie? The last time I saw you was in the bar talking with one of the girls. I started to look for you and the girl motioned to the alley. I went outside and heard the noise, and saw the four men holding you. I grabbed the bar and started swinging." Todd continues to ramble as he notices the slicing wound on Chou's chest. "Christ—Charlie—are you all right? It looks like they hurt you bad! What are you doing out here?"

Charlie is stumbling towards Todd. "I had to take a piss man. As soon as I walked out the back door, the four guys jumped me and started to beat me. I don't think they like Chinese people!" Charlie reaches out to embrace Todd. "Man—you saved my life! I owe you everything!"

Todd looks at Charlie whose eyes are glistening with emotion. Todd holds his friend up as he responds. "You would have done the same for me. You're bleeding badly. I need to get you to a hospital. How do you feel? Should I call for an ambulance?"

"Thanks to you, I am okay Todd. I think we can just drive to the hospital. The wounds look worse than they are. I'll be okay. In fact, I feel more alive than I have for a long time! I do have a serious dignity problem though. I think I pissed in my pants! Let's get out of here before they come back!" Todd supports Charlie as they slowly hobble to the end of the alley.

Todd Robbins and Chou Bing have been room mates since starting college at Harvard. It is now late spring of 1977 and they will complete their undergraduate work next week. Today had started rather ordinarily with Charlie visiting some relatives in Boston's Chinatown. He asked Todd to go along. After the visit, they decided to celebrate their impending graduation with a stop at Boston's famed Combat Zone for some special entertainment. They have been to the zone on many occasions and never had a problem. Tonight was different. They didn't get drunk and they didn't get laid, but they did develop a special bond that would last a lifetime.

Both men had decided to get their masters degrees at Harvard. Beyond that, both seem to have divergent paths. Todd planned to go into his father's real estate business, while Chou was to return to his native China to pursue the business and political interests of his political sponsors. Neither realized that the events of this day would cause them to eventually partner in the greatest social upheaval in the history of mankind. They were to become kindred spirits who would place their common objectives before all other considerations. They didn't know it then, but they were fated to become the scourge of modern day America.

CHAPTER 3

▼

On New Years Day, 1980, the seeds of economic destruction were sown in a contrasting scenario of hope and despair, life and death, naivety and perception. In the preceding decades, the killing fields of America have been fully prepared, cultivated and fertilized so as to insure the toxic seeds of 1980 would successfully germinate.

The last minutes of the last hour of the last day of ones life can sometimes be deceptively joyful. Joe Robbins opens the patio door and a beautiful sight comes into view. The first glimpse of light on a cloudless morning promised a spectacular sunrise. Joe steps through the opening onto the expansive granite patio and views the hundred yards of white silky sand that precedes the endless blue ocean. Joe is thinking of the festivities that had ended just one hour earlier. Normally, he would have retired immediately but his mind raced as he reviewed the preceding evening's activities. Joe Robbins had hosted the New Years party of the decade. 1979 had been a profitable year for many of his business associates and they found reason to celebrate with gusto. He had entertained many of the major business leaders in the country, and had done so with marvelous success. Not only was the party a smashing hit, but he had also managed to make the necessary contacts to salvage his faltering real estate empire. Although he is approaching 60, Joe feels a youthful surge now that his multi-billion dollar enterprises would be rescued from a pending bankruptcy.

Joe scans the beach and notices a grove of coconut palm trees being awakened by a gentle breeze. He inhales the early morning musty odor of the Atlantic Ocean. The ocean winds carried a salty residue which irritates his eyes and Joe vigorously rubs them to clear the initial blurriness. In the distance, he could see the outline of a man and woman holding hands as they enjoyed an early morning stroll along the beach. Joe glances beyond the beach to the Atlantic and then to the horizon. Suddenly a blinding flash of light pierces the horizon and races across the ocean, causing him to wince. It is the blazing first rays of sunlight. The emerging beam temporarily blinds him and he covers his eyes in a futile effort to stay the effects of this new day's sun. His pupils adjust as he lowers his hand, and he slowly squeezes open his eyes to once again reveal the picturesque scene. Joe thought to himself—*Another beautiful day in tropical Florida. The first l will totally enjoy in months.*

Joe walks the fifty feet to the end of the patio. He rests his hands on the ornate railing that protects the unwary from a sudden drop into a lavish tiered garden. Joe let his eyes roam the horizon squinting to avoid the full force of the now half exposed sunrise. He quickly focuses on the beach to avoid the raging beams of sunlight that had cut a shimmering path across the calm ocean. He marvels at the white sands and begins to take in the full beauty of his private paradise.

A flash of light from the right distracts Joe. He looks directly at this new light to evaluate its origin. As he strains to focus his eyes, he reaches into his jacket for his glasses and places them on his head. Joe adjusts his view to revisit the mysterious light. Immediately, he feels a sharp, piercing pain in his chest. He instinctively grabs at his chest to soothe the massive ache. As he looks down, he sees his white shirt bathed in red fluid. Instantaneously, he realizes he had been shot and gasps "Oh, my God". He steps backward slowly retreating, but is suddenly thrown sideward by a second throbbing pain in his lower rib area. Stumbling to remain on his feet, he weakly clutches the railing and senses his life rapidly flowing from him. Joe lifts his head in fatalistic resignation just as he feels a final dull and blunted pain enter his head near his ear. The bullet severs the side retainer of Joe's glasses as it finds its way into his brain. His head jerks violently sideward pulling his body off balance as he collapses. Joe's head hits the floor with a sickening thud. Blood flows freely from the fatal head wound and quickly forms a pool around his upper torso. His leg rapidly twitches in a series of death spasms just as his eyes assume the unseeing eternal stare of the dead. Joe Robbins draws his final breath just as the sun is fully exposed on the horizon.

Word of Joe Robbins death spreads rapidly through Boca Raton and the business community. His friends and associates could not imagine who would want to execute him. Joe had been extremely successful over the years and he shared his wealth with many of his colleagues. He had made millionaires out of 23 people who were lucky enough to have involved themselves in his life. He was a very methodical thinker who made money by shrewdly re-investing his profits in real estate and business acquisitions. A sixth sense for making money had proven him infallible and his fortunes had increased accordingly. Joe did not have enemies. His character did not permit him to maintain or develop adversarial relationships. Joe had a knack for ending potentially damaging relationships with an accord which left all parties content with the outcome. He was an intelligent, hard working man who lived with a strict code of ethical and moral rules. It is with this background that Detective Allen Merrill of the Boca Raton police department began his investigation into the death of Joe Robbins. The case would prove to be a puzzler, devoid of leads and full of dead ends. None the less, the death of such a powerful personality in the middle of an elitist town would call into play the considerable resources of the authorities.

However, the repercussions of Joe Robbins death would go far beyond the search for those who committed the murder. No one could have possibly guessed the long term and far ranging implications of the execution. Forces were set into motion that would ultimately change the economic structure of the world. Like the seemingly insignificant death of Archduke Francis Ferdinand led to World War 1, and the innocuous rise of Adolph Hitler resulted in World War II; so too the relatively obscure death of Joe Robbins would culminate in the destruction of the economy of the United States. Each of these underlying events seemed incapable of the cataclysmic results, but each would set into motion world altering events. It seems that the forces of injustice and inequality wait only for the right spark to ignite the explosive fuse of change. Joe Robbins death would prove to be one such spark. The beginning of the end is now at hand!

CHAPTER 4

▼

In October, 1979, Joe Robbins is in his New York office busily preparing the guest list for his annual New Years party. The gala event has been the season's social spectacular for the top echelon of American business. Some news commentators speculated that only those with assets in excess of 100 million dollars were invited. Indeed, the guest list was restricted to the industrial movers and shakers who had accumulated extensive fortunes.

Joe is putting the finishing touches on the distinctive list just as Todd Robbins steps into the office. Todd Joseph Robbins, the only child of Joe and Lisa Robbins, is at 22 years of age a picture of youthful vibrance. Todd has light brown hair with striking blue eyes. A strong chin and chiseled cheek bones accent his handsome face. His 180 pounds are physically proportioned to his 6 foot height. The playful glances of many of the secretaries of Robbins, Ltd. are a testament to his classical good looks.

Todd is a graduate of Harvard where he earned his Masters of Business Administration in June of 1979. He was a brilliant and motivated student who jumped a year ahead in college on a bet. His strong ambition drove him to immediately start his working career upon graduation. He was assigned to real estate acquisitions. Although a newcomer with Robbins Ltd., he had already put together a transaction that would net the company a $600,000 profit. Not bad for four months with the company.

Todd is dynamic, intelligent and extremely independent, yet he remains a diligent and devoted student of his father. He holds his father in high esteem and is in awe of the patriarch's prowess as a business man. The love, respect and admiration for his father becomes apparent to anyone who knows Todd. When Todd was 15 years old, his mother died in a tragic car accident. The loss of his mother almost psychologically broke him. Todd had loved her dearly, and the sudden loss wounded his fragile and compassionate personality. He had contemplated suicide to be with her but his father, always the rock, had recognized the problem and quickly came to the aid of his vulnerable son. Together they shared the common tragedy. In doing so, they became closer and the bond between them strengthened.

Todd greets his father with a smile. "Hi Dad, do you have the guest list finished?"

Joe looks up to acknowledge his son. Joe could not help but to admire the sharp image before him. Todd is an excellent dresser, and his six foot frame perfectly fills out the blue silk suit he wore. Joe responds. "Not quite son. I'm considering some new business acquaintances that I met last week, but I am just not sure that I should invite them. They're in the banking business and they are quite influential in Washington D.C., but something strikes me as being wrong. I just can't put my finger on it." Joe's concern stems from his initial meeting with Curt Davis and Bob Mellon.

Sitting down beside his father, Todd said "Your judgment has always been great. If it doesn't feel right, don't invite them."

Joe thought again, and decides that he may have been too hasty in drawing his first impressions. These men were introduced to him by his good friend, Paul Trump of Dallas. Joe has an office building in Dallas directly across from the headquarters building of Computer Services, Inc., the giant business services company founded by Paul Trump. Trump spoke highly of both men and personally vouched for their financial credentials. Besides, Joe knew that he had some pressing financial obligations that these men said they could help him with.

Reconsidering, Joe responds. "I think I am going to ask them to the party. It never hurts to know a few more bankers."

Todd leans over to look at the list of the business elite and approves. "I think you know what's best. Who else is new this year?"

Joe writes in the names of Curt Davis and Bob Mellon as he replies. "That's it, just these two new guys. All the rest you have seen or met before."

The list is replete with the names of many of the country's wealthiest and most powerful people. Included is Charles Mock, the Chairman of Eureka Oil, who had in 6 years made a fledgling oil company into the second largest oil producer in the world. Leo Baltroff, CEO of Pittsburgh Steel Company, the nation's leading steel producer, would be invited. The automobile industry would be represented by a few companies including Global Motor Corporation and its dynamic leader, Craig Evans. The name of H. Paul Trump of Computer Services, Inc, was listed as well as top executives from two other computer firms. The list is impressive. CEO's, Presidents, Chairmen and leading entrepreneurs representing a cross section of America's industrial and technological might are represented on the exclusive list. In attendance would be leaders from manufacturing, banking, finance, publishing, oil production, construction, media, electronics, computers and an assortment of less conspicuous industries.

Todd looks up and marvels at the ability of his father to attract such men. Todd muses "The guest list looks rich! When do you want to get the invitations in the mail?"

Joe stands up and walks over to the window. He looks down on the Hudson River and the bevy of activity on 43rd Street and replies. "Not for awhile. I'm going to use our Boca Raton estate for the party this year, and I'm still making travel and lodging arrangements for our guests. In any event, they'll have to be in the mail by November 10th. I'll let you know when all the arrangements are completed."

Todd acknowledges. "Okay. I'm going over to accounting for awhile. Need anything?"

"No thanks Todd, but speaking of accounting, I just received the final figures on your uptown real estate deal. You have netted the company a $618,000 profit. Not too shabby for your first time at bat."

Todd is a bit flabbergasted. He's been checking with accounting for the past week about the final figures, but as usual his father managed to stay a step in front of him. Todd beams at the compliment, but quickly retorted with youthful brashness. "Thanks Dad. You have not seen anything yet. Be ready to build a bigger building because I mean to grow this company! See you later for lunch."

CHAPTER 5

▼

During the third week of November, Joe is in his Dallas office making arrangements to refinance a regional mall he owns. The original financing is a balloon
mortgage which is payable this December. He is shopping for a new source of
funds. As was his experience with other refinancing he had completed this year,
he found interest rates considerably higher than what he has been paying. It was
these unusually high interest rates coupled with his future development commitments that had gotten him into a financial bind. Just this one transaction would
increase his annual interest expense by over seven million dollars, and the banks
were gouging on the origination fees. In his 36 years of real estate experience, he
has never seen interest rates escalate like this year. Moreover, he could not understand the logic that the economists were using to explain the phenomena. They
claim inflation was driving up the cost of money, but Joe thought the steep
increases were not justified by the current rate of inflation. For now, Joe had no
choice. The mall must be refinanced.

Joe completes the necessary paperwork on the new loan and is preparing to
review income statements on a California property when his intercom sounds.
Susan, his Dallas secretary, announces an incoming phone call from Curt Davis
of Associated Bank Holding Company. Joe agrees to take the call and his phone
immediately rings. He answers cheerfully. "Good morning Curt, it's great to hear
from you again."

"Hi Joe, I just received your invitation to the New Years party, and I wanted
to let you know that both Bob Mellon and myself will be attending."

Joe replies "Terrific! You're in for a great time."

"So I've heard. I am really looking forward to it. Listen Joe, I need to discuss some business with you. I understand that you're looking for financing on your Dallas mall."

"That's right. How did you know that?"

"Well, you're aware that Bob and I are principals in a bank holding company. We control three banks in Dallas—Dallas First National, First Federal of Texas and Rio Grande Trust and I believe you've been to every one of them on this deal."

Joe is caught off guard as he did not realize that this recent acquaintance had so much financial clout in Dallas. The banks Curt had referred to were among the three largest banks in town.

Joe replies just a little miffed. "Well, you're right. I have been to those three banks plus a half dozen more. The interest rates are terrible everywhere! In fact, I just signed a commitment with Rio Grande Trust. They have the best offer. Any chance you can do better before I return the paperwork to Rio Grande?"

Curt waits some time before answering. "Joe, I sure wish I could do better for you. Fact is I have to withdraw the Rio Grande offer. Normally Charlie White, President of Rio Grande, would be handling this, but when I learned you were involved, I wanted to give this my personal attention. Joe, I'm afraid the 13 percent you were quoted isn't good anymore. Our best offer is now 15 percent, and that's only if you do the deal today."

Joe is caught short of words and after clearing his throat angrily retorts. "That's ridiculous—those kinds of rates will not work on this property. This is bullshit! What's going on? The interest rates are going crazy! Why?"

"Joe, it's those guys over at the Federal Reserve. The FED has been increasing the rate because of the inflation problem, and well, you know banking. We exist on a marginal point spread over the FED rate. I wish I could do better."

Joe ponders how none of this makes financial sense. *Sure, inflation was up, but the problem had to do with those damned Arabs and the OPEC cartel that had been driving oil prices up by withholding supplies of oil. Still, that didn't justify these ungodly interest rate increases. Something was wrong!*

Regaining his composure, Joe responds. "I am really shocked. I need some time to think and shop the deal."

"I understand Joe. Keep in mind I can't promise the 15 percent offer will be good tomorrow. I'll make you one guarantee though. I'll beat anyone in the marketplace. I'm not talking any large percentage differences, but an eighth of a point on a 225 million dollar loan is significant. Let me know what you want to do as soon as possible so as I can lock you in on our best rate?"

"OK Curt, I'll probably call you tomorrow. I have to get the refinancing done. Let me know if anything changes. Good bye."

"Bye Joe. Sorry I had to deliver the bad news."

Joe clenches the phone after Curt disconnects. He places the receiver to his head in a subconscious effort to massage a developing headache. He knows the interest rate would put the mall in a bad financial position if he accepts Curt's offer. He recognizes his financial position is rapidly deteriorating, but it appears he may have to accept this deal. *If all else fails, I would have to call Curt.*

That evening, Joe Robbins is working late at the office. He is evaluating his current position. He has one more refinancing he must arrange for an office building in Los Angeles. His interest rate shopping efforts had confirmed what Curt told him. Interest rates are increasing just about every day. Joe is discouraged as he summarizes his real estate holdings. Eight properties that were profitable just nine months ago were now suffering large losses. Moreover, 1980 is scheduled to be a big development year for Robbins Ltd. Joe had already made sizable financial commitments on the new projects based on much lower interest rates. A sick feeling overcomes him as he speculates he would be bankrupt by July if interest rates did not decline.

CHAPTER 6

▼

During Christmas week, Joe is back in his New York office. He is edgy and extremely depressed. He had used Curt Davis for the financing on the Dallas mall. He now had nine big losers. He still needs to refinance his Los Angeles office building, and decides to call Curt Davis again. *After all, Curt did have the best rate for the mall even if it was a lousy one.* Joe looks up Curt's private business number and rapidly touches the keys setting off a series of short pulsing rings. In a moment, a near silent click precedes an acknowledgement.

"Good morning. This is Curt Davis."

"Hello Curt, this is Joe Robbins. How are you today?"

"Just fine Joe. And yourself?"

Joe replies rather tentatively "Let me answer that after we discuss another project. You'll recall the LA office building I discussed with you earlier. I need 34 million dollars for the refinancing of the building. The complex has a current appraisal of 102 million dollars and I own a 67 percent equity position. I need your very best rate on this one."

As Joe completes the details on this deal, he notes how every property he owns have substantial equity positions. His healthy financial statement includes over 3.4 billion dollars of real estate with loans of slightly more than one billion dollars.

Curt answers quickly. "I know I can help you. As always, you're as good as gold. I can get you the 34 million, but the interest rate is going to be higher than your Dallas mall."

Joe had anticipated a small increase but what happened next was as if a dagger had been stuck into his heart.

Curt continues "The best rate that I can get you is 19 percent and I will also need 4 origination points." Seeking to soften the traumatic news, Curt quickly adds "I already have all your financials so if you can get me a copy of the appraisal, I can have the documentation completed and the money can be in your hands in two days."

Absolute pandemonium breaks out as Joe hears the last of Curt's rapidly spoken words.

"What the fuck? Are you crazy? No businessman in his right mind is going to pay that rate. You God damned bankers think that you can get away with this kind of shit, but it won't happen. I'll find the money cheaper. You people are going to ruin me."

Joe's heart is beating rapidly as he pounds his fist on his desk.

Curt now spoke slowly and cautiously. "Joe, I know you are upset and I don't blame you. Let me assure you that this rate is being given to businessmen of your caliber all over the country today. The rate is high, but it is competitive. The really crazy thing is that even at 19 percent, the demand for the money is still very high. Deals are being made at 19 percent."

Knowing full well that Joe had to get the money, Curt attempts to placate him. "If I were you, I would hold up for awhile. These rates have got to drop sometime. I just don't see it happening in the near future."

Still lacking control, Joe quickly replies "Yeah Curt, more bullshit. If I don't get the building financed by the end of the month, I lose it next month. If I finance it at 19 percent, I lose it in 6 months because the damn thing will bleed me every month. You have me between a rock and a hard place, and you know it. I can't even sell it because no one in their right mind is going to pay your interest rate to buy it. Got any more bright ideas?"

Curt quickly realizes his blunder. "I'm sorry. That was awfully stupid of me. Joe, I want to assure you that I will get you the lowest competitive rate. I know it won't be low enough to suit you or for that matter any business person, but I will deliver the lowest rate."

Joe now speaks in a tone of righteous arrogance. "And just how is that going to help me? An eighth or a quarter point is not going to save my ass!"

Joe finds himself divulging his personal business situation. Over the years he made it a practice never to discuss the intimate secrets of success and failure. Now he was blurting out the details of his impending crisis. "You don't seem to understand. I will be bankrupt by July if I am forced to borrow money at these fucking rates. Do you know what that means? I don't know how everyone else does business, but I'd guess I won't be the only one broke in 6 months."

Curt senses an opportunity and interrupts Joe's tirade. "Hold on for a moment Joe. I think I may have a means to help you. It's different and unconventional, but perhaps it's a way out. I can't really give you any details until I discuss it with Bob Mellon. Do you think you can stop by my offices on December 26th, about 11:00 AM? I think it could be worth your time."

The sudden relief was almost too much for Joe. Breathing a sigh of relief, he responds. "If you know of a way I can get around the 19 percent, you're damn right I can meet you. 11:00 AM on the 26th will be fine."

Feeling embarrassed about his earlier outburst, Joe continues. "I hope you do not take offense at what I said. I've been under a lot of pressure recently."

Curt diplomatically replies. "Hell, if I took offense at every man who called me a son of a bitch because of high interest rates, I would be a manic depressive. No Joe, I really do understand and I do empathize. I'm a businessman myself and I know how situations I can't control affect me. Let's get this worked out together."

The conversation concludes with good wishes for a Merry Christmas and some small talk about the New Years party. Joe is delighted that he may be able to salvage his situation. He didn't know the details, but for now all he wanted to do was enjoy the upcoming holiday.

Upon hanging up, Curt immediately was on his telecom to Bob Mellon. "Bob, we have Joe Robbins where we want him. Set aside the morning of the 26th so we can discuss strategy, and meet with Joe."

CHAPTER 7

▼

Joe and Todd Robbins decided to go to Boca Raton for the Christmas holiday. They left on the 22nd to give them time to finalize arrangements for the New Years party, enjoy Christmas and make it back to New York for the meeting with Curt Davis on the 26th. Joe had not informed Todd of his crisis. He decided that he would take time on this holiday to review the problem with Todd and take him along to the meeting on the 26th.

As their private Lear jet taxied LaGuardia's runway in preparation for takeoff, Joe began to tell Todd about the financial dilemma. Joe goes into detail about the impending crisis including the possible collapse of Robbins, Ltd.

Todd is stunned by the depth of the problem. "You should have told me about this earlier. I thought we were business partners and we were going to share the good and bad together."

"I'm sorry Todd. I thought I had a handle on it, but it kept getting worse. At first, it seemed every time I was about to tell you something came up. Later, it got so bad I wanted to spare you the burden. Now, I need your help."

Todd is visibly upset. "Cut the crap, Dad! When I agreed to enter the business, you promised that this would not happen. You said you needed me and I believed you, but as always you want to be a one man show. You know how I am. I am far too independent and I need challenge. It's not my fault. It's the way you raised me! How do you expect that I would ever understand this business if you insist on insulating me from the problems? With that attitude, I may as well use my Harvard degrees to wipe my ass. If you feel you must treat me like a kid, then maybe we should go our separate ways."

Joe is not surprised by the ferocity of Todd's outburst. He had raised him to be honest, straightforward and independent. Joe feigned intimidation at the admonishment and warily replied. "I do need you in this business—now more than ever. Maybe, this time, you can forgive your old man. Call it poor judgment, pride, an overprotective father or whatever you like. Let me assure you once and for all that this will never happen again."

Sensing his father's vulnerability, Todd relents. "I hope you are sincere. I know I can help you if you let me. I'm with you through good times and bad, but if you ever do this again, I will leave. For now, tell me more about our problem so as we can work on it together."

At that moment, Joe was prouder of his son than at any other time in his life. He had matured into a man and he obviously would not accept any other status ever again. Little did Joe know how Todd's involvement in the business would so radically change his son's life! These revelations and the subsequent repercussions would prove to be the type of life altering force that would damn his son to a precarious and vindictive existence!

CHAPTER 8

▼

The balance of the holiday went well for Joe and Todd. Joe brought Todd completely up to speed on the business problems. Together they finalized all the details for the upcoming party. On Christmas Day, they went to church services together, and later exchanged gifts. Christmas Day was beautiful, lacking only the seasonal chill and a bit of the white stuff demanded by New York natives. Father and son were drawn closer together as they shared the business burden.

They boarded the Lear at 5:00 AM on the 26th. Joe and Todd were ecstatic, but somewhat apprehensive about their meeting later that morning in New York. A solution was promised, but there were no commitments. The devil is always in the details! The three day holiday complete with their disagreement, discussion and solution had once again bonded them. Together, they seemed an indestructible force. The plane, boosted by a favorable tail wind, arrived in New York at 7:02 AM leaving them adequate time to clean up and check in at the office.

They decided to take the company limo over to the offices of Associated Bank Holding Company which occupied six floors of the World Trade Center. The Lincoln stretch pulls up to the buildings, and Todd and Joe, impeccably dressed, emerge from the car. They are pleasantly surprised to be greeted immediately by an Associated Bank Holding executive at curbside, who acknowledges them and brings them directly to the executive suites on the 67th floor. The reception lobby is flamboyant. Thick plush carpets, antique early American furniture and the classical pictures on the wall left one with a feeling of ornate yet conservative grandeur. The chamber is literally fit for a king.

Immediately, a voluptuous corporate secretary escorts them into an adjoining conference room. Todd's hormones race as he views the perfectly proportioned beauty in front of him. Todd is temporarily without words as she offers refreshments while casting a seductive smile at the young executive. The conference room is tastily furnished in a motif similar to the entry vestibule. The major exception is a wall full of paintings by the old masters. Works by Rembrandt and DaVinci were the most prominent. Joe admired the originals and speculated their value to be in the neighborhood of 120 to 150 million dollars. *There's a fortune hanging on just that one wall. The banking business must be good.*

Curt Davis and Bob Mellon enter from a door on the far side of the room. The four exchange greetings and sit down at an immense mahogany table in the center of the room. Curt opens the discussion with some social information before addressing Joe. "I didn't realize that Todd was going to be here today."

Joe quickly replies "Todd joined the firm in July and I have been busy showing him the ropes. I figured there would be much to learn today. Todd is looking for a practical education."

Bob chimes in. "We're delighted to have him with us today." Without anymore small talk, Bob Mellon cuts quickly to the business at hand. "Joe, I have taken the liberty of reviewing your financial statement. Your major holdings include close to 4 billion in real estate and approximately another 1.8 billion in various operating businesses. Against those assets, you have loans payable amounting to about 1.7 billion dollars most of which you will have to refinance in the next two years. On top of that, I believe you have made monetary commitments in the amount of 950 million dollars for various projects scheduled to start in 1980. Does that sound about right?"

Joe acknowledges that Bob is correct in his analysis.

Bob went on. "Curt tells me that a number of your holdings are in a negative cash flow position, and that today's interest rate climate might just throw you into bankruptcy. Is that correct?"

It was only at this point that Joe realizes he had spoken too freely during his last conversation with Curt. He reacts quickly and defensively. "Sure, I am having a problem, but it is not of my making. All my properties were doing well subsequent to these damn rate increases. I have a lot of property with plenty of equity. I want to know how you fellows can help me weather the storm. Curt told me you would have some creative ideas!"

Bob replies. "We do, but you will have to make some sacrifices. We would propose to take care of all of your financial needs at a rate you can live with. All of your properties will be profitable again. Additionally, we will arrange to meet all of your 1980 development commitments at a rate that will keep those projects on their planned course. How does that sound to you?"

Joe was anticipating a solution on a property by property basis. He was astounded by the depth of the offer. *It would solve all of my financial problems, but perhaps it was another too good to be true story.* Intrigued Joe responds "You certainly have my attention. Do you realize that you're talking loan commitments in the neighborhood of 2.5 billion dollars? Do you have the muscle to pull it off?"

Curt is prepared for the question. He produces a corporate graph of Associated Bank Holding Company. The chart reveals a myriad of banks, savings and loans and finance companies all arranged in a series of lines under the parent company. Curt summarizes the graph. "In answer to your question, we have a lot more muscle than what you require. The chart lists a total of 162 institutions that control over 9,200 branches with combined assets of over two trillion dollars. We can get the money for you."

Joe is surprised that these two men controlled so much wealth. Joe thought he knew business, but he had somehow spent his entire career not knowing of this large bank conglomerate. Joe comments "Very impressive. If you don't mind, I would like to hold onto the chart for purposes of verification. I have another important question. What interest rate are you proposing?"

Bob Mellon answers. "We're flexible, but I calculate that an interest rate at 9 percent would make all your holdings viable again."

Joe is puzzled "I don't understand. The banking business exists on a profit margin above the FED rate. When you quoted 19 percent last week, I assumed the FED rate was about 17 percent."

Bob answers quickly. "You're correct. The FED rate this morning is 17 and one quarter percent. You can verify that at any bank."

Joe is incredulous. "Curt, forgive my ignorance, but how do you propose to lend me money at 9 percent when you have to pay over 17 percent to get the money?"

Bob is grinning as he responds." Joe, you're not ignorant. We have tens of thousands of passive investors who are satisfied with low rates of return. We can lend this money at whatever reasonable rate we please and still make money."

Joe pounces again. "Do you mean to tell me that there are people who are satisfied with 7 percent return when they could get a 15 percent return? That doesn't sound right!"

Curt Davis fields the question this time. "I know it sounds simplistic to a businessman like you. But there are, as Bob explained, literally tens of thousands of depositors who are complacent on these matters. Why not let Bob and I worry about getting the money for you at 8 to 9 percent? You do not need to be concerned about that."

Joe is taking all the precautions, but now the big question. "Let me suppose that you can loan me 2.5 billion dollars at 8 percent. Why would you do that? What's in it for you?

Bob Mellon replies. "Good question. I told you at the beginning to expect some sacrifices. As consideration for arranging this transaction, Associated Bank Holding would become a partner with you in your business. We would need controlling interest. That is a 51 percent interest, in the stock of Robbins Ltd. as well as a similar interest in every property or business interest you hold outside of Robbins, Ltd."

Todd, who had been silently observant up to this point, now enters the conversation in a fury. "No way is that possible! Do you realize that you are asking for better than 3 billion dollars to guarantee these loans. We have that much in equity. Why should we do that?"

Curt counters "Todd, you do have plenty of equity, and I am saying that we will loan money to you at 19 percent on your equity. But if you want 9 percent, we need a 51 percent ownership in all Robbins assets. It's that simple. You do the choosing."

Joe realizes that he is being legally squeezed by some very limited options. He used the tactic often in his career. Todd continues to fume as he looks upon the offer as blatant opportunism bridging on extortion. Both Joe and Todd realize that they had a ponderous decision to make. *Either lose the business in 6 months or give up a huge part of their equity to a controlling partner.*

All agreed there was much to think about and consider. The meeting adjourned. As Todd and Joe exited the World Trade Center, their faces were visibly worn and their shoulders were slumped in an outward display of impotence. The morning had been a roller coaster of emotion as the problem was batted back and forth across the wide mahogany table. The final result was that they needed to choose between two distasteful situations.

Todd spoke first after they entered the limo. "Dad, we can't go along with this. Those guys are raping us. Why can't we check with some of your business contacts to see if they can help financially? We have plenty of collateral, so their investment would be fully protected."

Joe was deep in thought. He considered that possibility earlier, but his pride would not permit him to solicit his wealthy friends. Joe responds with a renewed vigor. "I agree. It is time to check with some of our friends and associates. Someone will be able to help us through this. When we get back to the office, we will begin making phone calls."

Both men were silent for the trip to the office. They each labored to find a solution to a problem with a very short fuse. Todd had learned more about business today then he really wanted to know at his young age. But, they were lessons that would never be forgotten. Joe was distressed because he had let himself become so vulnerable. Soon, their lives would be totally changed by some new revelations. Joe's skepticism about Bob Mellon and Curt Davis would prove to be a testament to his business judgment!

CHAPTER 9

▼

Back at the 43rd Street office, Todd and Joe divided up a list of their closest business contacts. Jointly, they decided to seek financial assistance for the office building complex in Los Angeles. They thought a piecemeal solution to their problem would be best received. They briefly discussed their approach, and enthusiastically retired to their respective offices to make the phone calls.

Their fervor was not rewarded. Both Joe and Todd met with similar responses. "I would like to help, but money is really tight right now. Check with me in a couple months when things settle down."

The results of the first day of solicitations were disheartening. Many of their wealthy acquaintances are having financial problems of their own. Some were caught off guard by the rapid increase in interest rates and were busy trying to plug the leaking financial dike in their businesses. Others wanted to stay liquid because they were concerned that interest rates would increase even more leaving their personal interests in a precarious position. A few even intimated that they were about to call Joe for his help. And one confidentially confessed his business bankruptcy would be public knowledge by the end of the day. Some of the more self-concerned questioned whether the New Years party would be cancelled this year.

Over the next two days, 78 phone calls yielded the same results. There was no lack of sympathy from the dissenting chorus. "Sorry, I can't help you. Keep me posted." "Let me know if there is some other way I can help." "I sure hope things work out for you."

At the conclusion of the 3 days of phone calls, both Todd and Joe feel desperate. Todd is racking his brain for an answer while Joe is painfully realizing the inevitable. Joe may have to take in partners in the form of Associated Bank Holding. Before he did that, he wanted to call one final name on his list, Paul Trump. Joe would save the call for the morning when he was fresh.

CHAPTER 10

▼

On December 29th, Joe was in the office early. Around him, he saw many of the festive decorations put out by his staff for Christmas and New Years. Try as he might, he simply could not get motivated for the New Years party. He definitely was not going to cancel the party, but his spirit is definitely lacking. The annual event had become a tradition that he would spend his last dollar on if necessary. Conversely, he dreaded the thought that he may one day regret spending his money so freely on a lavish party when financial collapse is so imminent.

Joe curtly brushed aside the thought. He sat down at his desk and dialed the Dallas number of Paul Trump. As the phone rang, Joe considered briefly the very small shadow that Trump cast. He smiled as he thought of the contrasting visions of this self made man. *Trump might be small, but only in physical size. He is a recognized giant in the business world.* Joe frequently compared Paul Trump to a caricature out of the Sunday New York Times comic section. *The man had a giant mouth, a larger than life personality and the biggest heap of bullshit in the world. Add to that a Roman treatment of his thinning hair and his conceited demeanor, and you either had to love him or hate him. But, hell, the man could sell anything to anybody when he set his mind to it.*

Trump was born and raised in Texas. His ability to rattle off all the quaint country bumpkin sayings is proof of his heritage. Trump rose rapidly in the business world seizing on a fledgling market for computer services. He took on the giants in the computer business as he struggled to gain a toehold in the market place. His perseverance proved to be his strongest business trait as he proceeded to wear down potential clients with an unending list of reasons why they should do business with him. Starting from scratch, he formed Computer Services, Inc.

to service his newly found clients. In 10 years, Trump became a leading player in the computer business.

Joe smirked as he thought again of Trump's unyielding persistence. *Trump never knew no was part of the English language.* Trump also has a keen ability to perceive situations. Sometimes, he is uncanny as he scoops a big business deal on a hunch. Amazingly, he is right far more than wrong. It is with these tools that Trump rose from a country bumpkin to one of the most cunning and successful businessmen of the century. *I hope Trump can help me out!*

Paul Trump always answered his own phone when he was in town. Today was no exception. The nasal voice of Trump was apparent as he answered the phone. "Paul Trump here. Can I help you?"

"Hello Paul, this is Joe Robbins. How are you doing today?"

"I am doing fine Joe. The real question is how you are doing. I must have gotten calls from a half dozen people telling me you were in trouble. Quite frankly, I've been expecting your phone call."

Joe wondered at how Trump always seemed to have an inside track on information. Joe replies "I have a serious financial problem on my hands. The interest rate thing is killing my business. You probably won't believe this, but I had profitability on every project last year. Now, I have 9 developments that are losing big money every month because of the skyrocketing interest rates. I am calling for your help and advice."

Trump wanted to know more about the situation that was plaguing his friend. "Tell me Joe, how much trouble are you in?"

Joe responds "Pretty deep. I went through all the numbers and it looks like I may not be able to pay my bills by next July. I have an extremely large equity position, but I am afraid that doesn't mean much right now. In the short term, I need loans of approximately one billion dollars at not more than 11 percent interest in order to come through this thing."

Trump answers. "That is pretty serious. The interest rate is a little more than 19 percent today. Right off hand, I don't know where you will find 11 percent money. What even makes you think that 11 percent is a possibility?"

"Paul, you remember those two banker friends of yours that you introduced me to, Curt Davis and Bob Mellon. Well these two fellows claim they can get me two and one half billion dollars at 9 percent interest. The problem is they want a controlling interest in all my assets." Joe explains all the details of the recent meeting with Davis and Mellon. By the time Joe finished the story, he once again had worked himself to a fevered pitch. "There's no way I can justify giving up my company to those two. I know they are capitalizing on my problem, and I hate them for it, but I can't find another way out. Just how well do you know Davis and Mellon?"

Paul is deep in thought about the offer and surmised that the two bankers had correctly analyzed Joe's financial problem and were about to make a killing. Paul did not believe that there are enough lackadaisical investors who are willing to accept a 7 percent return on their money. *Something was wrong. Maybe the two were investing their own money in order to gain control over Robbins Ltd.* He made a mental note to check.

Paul responds to Joe's question. "I have known them for about three years. They grew very fast with the help of some of their Washington contacts—almost too fast. Rumor has it that they are connected to higher ups at the Treasury who were instrumental in their growth. Both of them are married with picture perfect families. In business, they are very accommodating but share a reputation as sharks. But hell, we are all called sharks at one time or another. That's business. They did do one deal for me awhile back. They treated me as they said they would, and I had no complaints. Your situation, however, is completely different than mine."

Joe sighs as Paul finished talking. He sure identified with the shark analogy. Right now, he was feeling like one of those bloody morsels placed on a hook whenever a fisherman wants to attract a shark. Joe tapped his pencil rather coyly as he prepared to ask him for assistance. "Any chance you might be able to financially help me through this crisis? You know, I have a lot of equity that I can secure a loan with. I simply need a reasonable source of funds."

Paul fully anticipated the question and without hesitation replies. "About six months ago, I liquidated all my real estate that had loans on them. At the time, interest rates had just started to edge up and damn if I could figure a reason for it. I saw it wasn't going to be a factor I could control and I got out. Sold everything and got a pile of cash. Point is, I am getting 18 percent in a money market fund, and I am not anxious to do real estate while the interest rates are going berserk. It turns out what is ruining you is making me richer, and all without a bit of risk! Joe, if you were to ask me for a million dollars for a personal loan, I will give it to you today, and I would not be concerned about the rate. But, for a business loan on your real estate, I'd be a fool to lend you a dime! Sorry, I can't help you!"

Joe knows Paul is right given his current cash position. Joe thought Paul is quite a work of art. Paul Trump, once again, manifested his astonishing ability to steer clear of problems when he elected to get out of real estate before the bottom dropped out. Joe wondered why he had permitted himself to be lulled into a continued acceptance of the illogical rate increases. *No matter now—what's done is done.* The most important issue now is to salvage whatever he could of his business empire. Joe was worn down from the continuous rejections he had received the last couple of days. He thanked Trump for his consideration and advice. Feeling urgently rushed, but with no place to go, he rapidly concludes the telephone conversation.

Before hanging up, Trump interrupts. "I'm going to make some calls tomorrow to try to get to the bottom of this interest rate fiasco. I will call you tomorrow afternoon. Good luck Joe."

Normally, Trump would not be concerned about the interest rate dilemma since he was on the profitable side of the rate crisis. Trump's curiosity was aroused by his friend's plight, but more so because he couldn't understand why investors would be satisfied with a 7 percent return when they could be making 17 or 18 percent like he was doing. He would be formidable and persistent until he understood what was happening.

As soon as Trump was off the phone with Joe Robbins, he called a few of his Washington D.C. correspondents. Trump knew the insiders and how the system worked. In the course of the conversation he casually mentioned he would be willing to pay $200,000 for the legitimate explanation for the interest rate hikes. True to form, the answers started to pour in. Unfortunately, all he received was the standard public explanations such as inflation, government loans and the money supply. Trump dismissed all of these reasons and he continued to pursue the illusive cause. The following day Trump's world would be shaken by the information he received.

CHAPTER 11

▼

The information came in the form of a revelation from Preston Orient, a former CIA agent and the consummate Washington insider. Orient's career path included a stint at the Treasury Department, until finally settling in with the Federal Reserve Bank. He is presently working for the Federal Reserve as a consulting analyst. Orient became close friends with Trump when they worked together to computerize data files at the CIA. They remained close associates thereafter because they found each others companionship very profitable. Orient would give Trump an inside track on proposed government computer projects. Trump, in turn, would give Orient a finder's fee for the referral. In addition, Orient received a generous commission if Trump landed the contract. With Orient on the inside with the CIA, the Treasury Department and now the Federal Reserve, Trump had landed quite a few lucrative government contracts. Orient's job as an administrator permits him to gain an unusual overview of the federal government. Orient understood that the government inevitably responded to wealthy individuals and special interest groups with deep pockets. The more money you had, the more attention you received from good old Uncle Sam.

Preston Orient called Trump in the morning on December 30th. Orient had flown into Dallas this morning to meet with Trump. Orient learned of Trump's $200,000 offer, and he knew he could help his old associate. Orient asked Trump if he could meet him personally as he did not want to discuss the matter over the phone. They agreed to meet at Giovanni's Restaurant, a small informal dining spot with an excellent culinary reputation. Giovanni's did not normally draw a large luncheon crowd and would make an ideal private environment for their meeting.

When Trump arrived at Giovanni's, Preston Orient is seated in an isolated corner of the room enjoying an appetizer plate of escargot. Trump joins him and together they place their orders for lunch. They enjoy some social small talk until the food orders arrived after which they quickly get to the purpose of the meeting.

Preston Orient spoke first. "Paul, what I am about to tell you, you may not believe. I know why the interest rates are increasing so rapidly, but before we talk, you need to know what you're getting into. Once I share this information with you, your life may be in danger. This is really dirty business involving some of the most powerful men in the country. Do you still want to hear the story?"

Paul is intrigued that his old friend is being so mysterious. None the less, the potential for danger simply wets his appetite. "Yes I do! But please, no more discussion about my life."

"OK, here it is. A business arrangement exists at the very highest levels of our government that is creating the interest rate increases. I have valid information that the Director of the CIA, the Secretary of the Treasury and the head of the Federal Reserve are partners in this venture. Ever since the rates have started their unusual jumps, these three have been making money hand over fist."

Trump is astounded by his friend's disclosure. His first reaction is his associate is under tremendous pressure that is causing him to be paranoid. Seeking to appease him, Trump questions Orient. "Come on Preston. Have you become another conspiracy nut? I have difficulty believing all this conspiracy nonsense. That's all I hear about anymore! Conspiracies of one sort or another are responsible for everything! Moreover, how can I expect to believe this knowing the elaborate checks and balances that exist to protect our money supply?"

"I know it sounds a bit far out, but think about a few of the great conspiracies of our time? For instance, the fixing of the 1919 World Series; or the military industrialists who propelled us into and capitalized on the Vietnam war; how about the rigged oil crisis that is going on right now; or Nixon and Watergate; or the manipulation of the world silver prices by the Hunt brothers. These were all bigger than life and no one suspected the schemes which duped business and the general public. It was only after months and years of tedious scrutiny that the scams were ultimately uncovered and revealed for what they were. And even then, the worse thing that happens to the perpetrators is a mild slap on the wrist. Most of us shake our heads in disbelief and clamor for more controls, but the crimes are soon forgotten as a new wave of problems grabs our attention. Confusion, greed, complicity and the ever present spin are the tools of those who conspire to cheat us. The people resent these situations and believe something is wrong, but, they are too busy trying to manage their own little lives. It seems that the larger the rip off, the more the public is inclined to believe that it just can't happen. As far as checks and balances, they can be compromised if you are in the right position. For instance, I doubt that one of your employees could seriously jeopardize your company without being exposed. You have a system of checks and balances which protects your business. But I would imagine that you could lead your company straight into hell if you wanted. You could do it and your employees would never suspect a thing, because you control the checks and balances. I suggest that this is what is happening to interest rates in the United States today. The guardians of our treasury have sold us out and very few even suspect such a thing is possible."

Trump replies still humoring Preston. "That's fascinating, but just how do these people profit by increasing the interest rates?"

"It's really rather simple Paul. First, the interest rate increases are a necessary distraction. The real problem is control of the money supply! How much does a counterfeiter profit when he manufactures hundred dollar bills and slips them into the money supply? The answer is obvious! The FED is doing the same thing as the counterfeiter, but the FED has the official printing presses and is manufacturing millions of hundred dollar bills. When the FED legally issues hundred dollar bills, the current interest rate to the banks is 15 percent. However a few institutions are able to get money from the FED at no cost. The few chosen banks profit handsomely from the illegal issuance of money. In fact, it appears that this scheme is netting over four billion dollars a month to the participants. Does that sound like sufficient motivation to you?"

Paul replies "Four billion dollars a month would certainly be enough motivation, but I still can't see how it could all come together?"

"Okay Paul, let's take it from the beginning. Three very powerful people in the federal government get together and have the power to change interest rates and create money. They legitimize the increases in interest rates explaining they are fighting inflation. In a relatively short period of time, they have driven the discount rate to 15 percent effectively increasing the cost of money for every man, woman and child in the country. Increased interest rates translate to increased costs of all goods and services. The very act of increasing the interest rate is inflationary—but keep in mind interest rates in this scam are just a distraction. The real action is in the hidden arrangement which permits a few privileged bankers to get money from the FED for free. These selected bankers are essentially laundering the free dollars by getting them into legal circulation at high interest rates. The end result is tens of billions of untraceable and untaxed dollars."

Paul's beady eyes flash back and forth signaling his increased curiosity. "So, even if the right people are involved in the cover up, how can the money be untraceable?"

"It happens in a way you will fully appreciate. The computers at the FED and the Treasury are programmed to hide the illegal transactions. The hundred dollar bills mysteriously disappear in a computer glitch which occurs in the time the bills are printed by the Mint and released to the FED for distribution. There are hundreds of controls that are meant to account for every bill issued by the FED, but they have been effectively compromised by a sophisticated programming anomaly. The computer slight of hand is a work of art. One other fine point of protection is built into the program. If anyone were to engage an inquiry of the money lost in cyberspace, the program self destructs and the entire data file is destroyed. It's built into the system and there's no way around it."

Trump is intrigued. "And just who are the whiz kids who designed the programs?"

"Not whiz kids, just one modest genius, and you know him. It is Jules Woodcock, the programmer, who worked with us on the CIA project. You're aware Jules died in a car accident recently on the Capital Expressway!"

Trump did indeed recall Jules Woodcock. He was highly principled with an absolutely brilliant intellect and a devoted family man as well. He always made short work of difficult problems. His genius in computer engineering was recognized throughout the industry. Trump tried to hire him, but he remained loyal to his government employer.

Trump inquires further." Wasn't Jules's death ruled an accidental homicide with the cause being alcoholic intoxication?"

"Yeah, they said he was drunk, but don't believe it. Jules came to visit me a few days before his death. He was a mess. He had been setup in a sexual liaison with a hooker. The videos and pictures he showed me were anything but flattering and they proved to be his undoing. Jules was blackmailed into doing the illegal programming at the FED and the Treasury. He was seeing first hand the lives and businesses being destroyed as a result of his handiwork. He wanted to make a clean slate of it and asked me to help him. Jules knew the key to unlocking the destruct mechanism in the computer. He also knew the main players at the FED and the Treasury. I agreed to help him, but before I could do anything he was found dead. Without anything but an intoxicated corpse as a witness, the case was closed by the local police."

During the past 15 minutes, Trump came full circle from questioning Preston Orients sanity to lending some credibility to the logical and believable scam being presented to him. Trump questions further. "Who are the players behind the money conspiracy?"

"At least 3 high government officials are involved. There is Ray Seasons, Assistant Director of the CIA, Ted O'Neil, the Under Secretary of the Treasury and John Vetter, head of the Federal Reserve. There may be more, but I am sure of these guys."

Trump is completely engrossed in the scenario "What about these banks that get the special treatment. Who are they?"

"I know of only 2 bankers. Their names are Bob Mellon and Curt Davis. Together, they run a large conglomerate known as Associated Bank Holding. They're all over the country!"

The bell goes off abruptly in Trump's head and he blurts out a comment. "Of course, it all adds up." Trump now fully comprehends the scam. His only reservation is that the conspirators had to be racking up considerably more than a couple billion dollars a month. *They were about to get about 3 billion just from his friend, Joe Robbins. How many other businessmen were in similar straights?* Trump would normally be skeptical and attempt to verify Orient's information, but his long covert history with Orient overrode his concerns. Trump is convinced that he has uncovered the reasons for the interest rate increases and finalizes his conversation with Orient. "Preston—another stellar performance. Thank you for sharing this information with me. As usual, everything seems to fit. I'll have the cash for you tomorrow. You sure have earned it!"

"Thanks Paul, but let me remind you I can't prove a thing. I know everything I've told you to be the truth, but it won't hold up anywhere."

Trump is thinking about Preston's warning. This truly is dangerous ground just as Preston had indicated at the beginning of the conversation. He wanted to get himself out of the middle while still keeping his promise of assistance to Joe Robbins.

"Listen Preston, would you like to make an additional hundred thousand. I would like you to make an anonymous call to Joe Robbins. I want you to share the entire scenario with Robbins. Spare no details, but under no circumstance can you let him know I am involved. I strongly suggest you do not divulge your identity."

"No problem, Paul. This thing has really been driving me crazy since Jules died. Give me Robbins's phone number, and I will contact him first thing in the morning."

"No, it's important you contact him today—before 5:30."

"What ever you say Paul! Consider it done!"

Paul Trump extended his arm for a parting handshake. "Thanks again for the information. I'll see you again soon."

The two made small talk as they departed Giovanni's, and went off in separate directions. Orient received a briefcase with $300,000 cash the following day. They would never physically meet again. Preston Orient would mysteriously disappear two days later leaving no trace of his existence. It would be 12 years before Trump and Orient would once again cross paths.

CHAPTER 12

▼

Later that evening at about 8:00 PM, Paul Trump called Joe Robbins. Paul is apologetic as he begins speaking. "I'm sorry Joe, but I don't have any new information about the interest rate thing."

Joe Robbins thanks Trump for his efforts. "I appreciate your efforts, but I think I may have stumbled on the answer. I want to tell you all about it, but I want to verify some information first. Besides that, I don't feel comfortable discussing this on the phone. I will have everything wrapped up by the time I see you at the party. For now, I feel confident our banker friends will negotiate a bit more."

Paul replies. "Glad to hear that Joe. It sounds like you solved your own problem!"

The conversation went on for another five minutes with talk of the upcoming party. Joe is clearly upbeat. He is sounding like a new man. He is cheerful and openly confident. Paul was happy to find Joe in such good spirits.

The call was almost complete when Joe posed a final question. "Have you had any dealings with Peter Benson?"

Paul Trump answers quickly and decisively. "I don't recognize the name. Why do you ask?"

"No reason. He just came to me with a business deal and I'm trying to verify his credentials."

"When I get back in the office, I'll check our files and let you know anything I have."

Joe thanks Paul for all his efforts and concludes the call. He sits back in his chair and ponders his recent dilemma. *I have them cornered, but I'll let them down easy.* Joe Robbins decides that he will call Curt Davis and invite him and Bob Mellon to a 5:00 PM dinner on New Years Eve at his Boca Raton estate before the party begins. He would let them know that it was important that their business be settled that evening. Joe would carefully word his dinner invitation so as to let Curt Davis assume he was going to accept their offer.

After Joe hung up, Paul knew that Preston Orient had done his job. He smiled as he realized that Peter Benson is really Preston Orient. He also knew that he would avoid any conversation with Joe about Bob Mellon, Curt Davis and Associated Bank Holding. He thought it imprudent to be in any way associated with the public disclosures that may come as a result of Joe Robbins. He would let others leak the information if they pleased. For now, Paul was content to be making a killing in the money market. If it came to an end, so be it. But in the meantime, he will continue to profit from the money supply conspiracy. Paul smiled the conniving grin of knowing capitalists. *Is there no end to our greed and the unscrupulous way we sometimes make money?* In a way, Paul was envious of the extremely lucrative financial position that Bob Mellon and Curt Davis were enjoying. He wondered for a moment if he might avail himself of a similar opportunity if it presented itself. Paul quickly dashed the thought before he could address the hypothetical question. In his heart, he already knew the answer.

It is one of those rare times when everyone seemed happy. Curt Davis and Bob Mellon were pleased with themselves over their pending 3 billion dollar windfall. Joe Robbins was exuberant knowing that his financial burdens were soon to end. And Paul Trump was enjoying the moment because of his friendship with Joe. He was happy Joe was off the hook. Of course Trump was happy with himself having second guessed a fabricated interest rate situation that could have badly damaged him. He is extremely pleased with his $300,000 investment in Preston Orient. *I got a lot of bang for the buck. The information will pay off in the future.*

Less than 48 hours later, these perceptions of joy would be replaced with deceit, disappointment and death as each of the participants find out how messy big business can be.

CHAPTER 13

▼

On December 31st at 7:30AM, Joe Robbins was flying south over the Shenandoah Valley heading to Miami to host his New Years Eve party. Joe is feeling exuberant as he takes in the view of the magnificent expanse of the scenic valley below. It is sunny and clear across the entire Eastern region of the country and the unimpeded visibility gave Joe some unusually breathtaking views.

He has been under a tremendous amount of stress, but is now feeling euphoric since learning about the money supply conspiracy from Peter Benson. At first, Joe questioned the authenticity of the information he received over the phone from an unidentified caller. Benson's detailed explanation of the plot did much to convince him that the story might have some merit. It was the most credible of the explanations so far offered for the rising interest rates. He considered inflation, increased labor costs and the other explanations advanced by economists to be pure bullshit meant for the naïve consumption of the masses. Experience taught him that there were greedy and ambitious people behind every major movement of money, and although this ploy would be the largest ever mounted against the American people, it is none the less very plausible.

Joe had convinced Benson to reveal his identity and to meet with him personally. He offered 50 thousand dollars for the meeting which Benson at first refused. Under Joe's relentless verbal pressure, the lure of 50 grand, and the promise of another beneficial long term contract, Peter Benson threw caution to the wind and agreed to meet with Joe. Benson emphasized the need for absolute confidentiality.

Joe is to meet Benson at 10:30 AM at the Atlantic Shores Motel on Collins Avenue in Miami. The location is convenient, yet enough out of the way to insure discretion. Joe reviewed his schedule for the balance of the day's activities.

He is going to meet Todd for lunch at the Boca estate at 1:00 PM. Joe recalled the recent abrasive encounter with Todd and is determined to share his findings about the money supply with him. *Todd is mature enough to handle the information. It is probably the best business lesson that I could ever give him.* The next meeting was the 5:00 PM dinner with Curt Davis and Bob Mellon. He was looking forward to it with vengeful relish. Briefly, he smiled as he whimsically drew a mental picture of them staring agape as they get caught in the act of swallowing the proverbial canary. It would be quite a meeting. As was his style, Joe had no intention of chastising the duo. His preference was for a solution that would alleviate his business problems with as little harm to the two bankers as possible.

The last item on the agenda was the party. In spite of his financial dilemma, he had made arrangements for the most extravagant party ever. He delighted in the accolades his business associates lavished on him after one of the parties. This year, his efforts surpassed those of every other year. He is certain that his guests would be impressed.

Joe also decided to treat himself to a week long vacation. His next business activity on the calendar was January 8, 1980—a new year, a new decade and a new prospective. *Life was good again!* Slowly, the Lear begins to lose altitude as the plane descends on Miami International Airport. Joe sees the sparkling blue Atlantic Ocean through the cloudless sky. The temperature is 84 degrees with low humidity, and a "0" chance of rain. Florida weather almost always complements his entertainment plans. The plane landed smoothly evidenced by an almost silent thump as the tires met the tarmac. It was the beginning of the last day of his life!

CHAPTER 14

▼

By the time Joe had rounded up luggage and rented a car, it was 9:35. He has sufficient time for a leisurely drive to south Miami. He is scheduled for a 10:30 meeting with Peter Benson at the Collins Avenue motel. Joe arrived at 10:20 in an inconspicuous Ford Tempo. He proceeds to the desk to pick up the key to his room. He registered under the name of Ken Dowd and quickly found room 210. Joe enters the room and notes the musty odor that typifies low cost motels. The room is clean and neat, but well worn. The RCA television is dated and the phone shows signs of built up grime. He sits on the bed and notices several discolored marks on the spread. Not quite his standard of living, but perfect for his clandestine meeting with Preston Orient.

Joe couldn't have been in the room for more than two minutes when he heard a soft knock on the door. Joe walked to the door and inquired. "Who is it?"

"Peter Benson."

Joe opens the door and is greeted by a stooped 6'4" slim man. He appears to be in his mid forties. He is casually dressed in summer shorts, golf jersey and Nike shoes. Beads of perspiration run down his forehead as he extends his sweaty arm for a handshake. He quickly withdraws realizing the heat pouring from him may be offensive.

Joe reaches out and clasps the retreating hand with a firm shake. "I am pleased to meet you Mister Benson."

Benson apologizes." Sorry I'm a mess. Got here early and decided to do some laps while I was waiting. Please feel free to call me Peter"

"No problem Peter. How did you know the room number?"

Peter replies "I spotted you coming across the lot and watched as you checked in. I knew you from some newspaper photos that appeared awhile back in USA Today. I hope you had a good flight."

Joe had done the USA Today story over a year ago. His picture appeared despite his protest and preference for privacy over publicity. It was a rare photo that Peter Benson located. Benson (Orient) refused identification details and physical description when the meeting was arranged, choosing to rely on his sleuthing guile and training to locate Joe Robbins.

Robbins replied, "You are a bit of a detective. Have a seat."

Joe and Peter continued to eye one another up in forming that lasting first impression. Each was trained to look for those physical traits and motions that signaled security and comfort. Together they walked to a small table in a corner of the cramped room. Joe waited until Peter was seated before seating himself.

Joe wastes no time in getting down to business.

"Peter, I must admit that I've been looking forward to meeting you. Your assertion of a money supply conspiracy left me with a lot of questions—especially about your credibility. How do I know you are who you say you are?"

Peter immediately produces an old CIA identification card, a current top secret clearance, and a current Federal Reserve employee card from a slim black wallet. He pushes the cards across the table to Joe. The cards were all bogus, but Joe Robbins is not capable of challenging the professionally prepared forgeries.

"Look at these for starters. I'm willing to answer any reasonable question about my legitimacy or to support the story I told you about the money supply. Where do you want me to begin?"

Joe examined the cards and felt that they were authentic. He had seen similar identification cards before. Joe had a number of questions to air.

"It's an incredible story you tell. How do I know it's true and not just Capital Hill bull shit?"

"Joe, I can assure you that you will not hear this explanation from any other source in Washington, or anywhere in the country for that matter. Forget your concerns about bull shit. This is as real as it gets! As to the truth of the matter, I can only say that I know everything I've told you to be the truth. Let me tell you a little more about my background. I have worked closely with the primary per-petrators. Ray Seasons was my supervisor at the CIA. Ted O'Neil originated the major projects I worked on at the Treasury. John Vetter used to be at the Treasury before he went to the Federal Reserve. I shared lunch and social situations with all of them. Often, in conversation, we solved the nation's problems. They are smart, ambitious, hard working and dedicated to government service. They make a lot of money, have excellent career prospects, and each has an impeccable reputation all of which makes them an unlikely team for fraud. I think that they realized that together they had the ability to control a big pot of gold. As I mentioned earlier, the scam is netting them billions of dollars monthly. But, I don't think it's just the money!"

Joe's interest is peaked. "What do you mean? If it's not the money, then what?"

"These guys have seen their share of dirty deals over the years. Some get caught and some don't, but all the dirt is forgotten in fairly short order. Personally, I feel that the three of them got pissed off over the oil price fixing scheme between the Arabs and our oil companies. The oil fix was not one of these little dirty deals that affected a few of us and then went away. Rather it continues to be one of the biggest rip offs of all time, and it looks like it may continue indefinitely. The Arabs and the American oil companies forged a deal that has become a way of life. Hell, when it all started in the early 70's, all we ever heard about was how supply and demand in a free economy would correct the high price levels. Man, were we dumb! It never corrected itself because the producing cartel and the oil companies determined that they could withhold supply and drive up the price of oil. They have absolute control over the oil market. It's not about competition, quality products, good people, or any of that bullshit. It's about greed and knowing that if you can control the supply of oil, then you can make more money by creating artificial shortages. Our government can stop it, but everyone who can do anything about it is either directly paid off or is the beneficiary of large PAC donations. So the three bureaucrats have front row seats to the fucking rip off of the century and witness its acceptability through the government's failure to react. More than once, I stumbled into a heated debate involving one or more of them over oil prices. They were logical, moral, righteous and full of passion. Then, all of a sudden about a year ago, they stopped complaining. I mean no discussion on oil at all! For awhile, I thought they were reprimanded and told to keep their mouths shut. But soon I realized that they became quiet just before interest rates started to edge up. They hatched the money supply scheme, not so much for money, but because this is the way the game is played in America today. Just as the oil companies found they could drive up the price of oil, so too Vetter, Seasons and O'Neil determine they could drive up interest rates, and the American people would pay because they had no choice. The rest is academic as they forged the operating relationship with Davis and Mellon at Associated Bank Holding.

Joe was fixated on every word from Peter's mouth. He stammers a response, "Uh, uh, unbelievable. Or at least that is what we are expected to believe."

Joe thought of the American work ethic as a wary combination of hard work, progress, and doing whatever you have to do to get ahead. He, like most Americans thought they were being screwed by the oil companies. *But this money supply thing is different—or is it?* Joe returned to a logical line of questioning. "Isn't what you are telling me just speculation based on your personal observations? How do we prove a conspiracy?"

"Please Joe, don't say we. I'm not interested in proving anything to anybody. However, let me answer your questions as best I can. You're right in saying that most everything is based on my personal observations. What you need to understand is that I have an overview of our government at work shared by very few individuals. Unfortunately, only those with that vantage point can appreciate what I've told you. I've speculated only on motivation. Everything else is factual. Unfortunately, it cannot be proven. Let me give you one further bit of information. At a point, I questioned the validity of my conclusions and sought out an old friend to help me. My friend is a Geneva financier whose life I saved when we were both attached to the CIA in the late 60's. He is in a unique position to identify so called nameless numbered bank accounts in Switzerland. He checked and found multi-billion dollar accounts under the names of the three bureaucrats and the two bankers. I can't and won't give you his name, and I ask that you do not divulge the Geneva link to anyone. This entire mess has all the makings of a perfect crime. The self destruct computer program, the dead programmer, the complicity of powerful government officials, and the anonymity of those who know even just parts of the scam all make the possibility of detection extremely remote. I don't think the case could be proven in a court of law."

Joe is now convinced that a money supply conspiracy does exist. The need to prove a conspiracy was not the issue. He had sufficient information to solve his personal financial crisis without the help of the courts. Joe did have one important question that needed to be answered. He presses on. "I think I can strategically use the information without proof. I believe what you've told me. Help me with one other thing. Why did you call me and tell me about all this? I don't know you! I never met you. Why would you ever volunteer this information?"

Peter is prepared for the obvious question. He had carefully prepared his reply so as not to compromise his friend, Paul Trump. "You made it known to quite a few people that you were in a financial bind. Let's just say that one of your associates who could not help financially elected to help you in another way. The feeling is that you will know how to use the information to neutralize your problem.

Don't ask for names of your friends who wanted to help. Suffice it to say you have some invaluable friendships. Quite frankly, I envy those relationships!"

Joe is now satisfied. He reaches down beside the table and produces a brown leather briefcase containing $50,000. He hands the case to Preston. "You will find what I promised you in the case. The information is worth far more than 50 thousand. I am deeply grateful."

Peter Benson reaches out for the case saying, "Glad I could help. I've told you a lot more than I should have. I trust you will forget you ever spoke to me on this matter. Be careful how you use the information. The people involved are powerful enough to do just about anything. They will kill to protect their asses."

"Believe me, I won't say a word, but I would like to meet with you again when you think the timing is right. I think we can be helpful to each other. You've helped me more than you can ever know. I'm in your debt."

Peter Benson (Orient) leaves the room and immediately paces himself into a comfortable jog, briefcase in hand. He ran 3 blocks to his rented car in a Wal-Mart parking lot. As he pulled out, he reviewed the net results of the past 24 hours. *$350,000 all cash—not bad for a days work!*

CHAPTER 15

▼

Joe drives directly to Boca Raton for his luncheon with Todd. He is fidgety with excitement, and catches himself singing along to the radio. Playing was John Lennon's 'Imagine'. He is happy with himself. He hasn't sung for a long time. By the time Joe arrives at the Boca house, Todd was there and gone. He left word that he went into town to pick up a few custom made suits from a Chinese tailor. Todd's message said that he'd be back in time for the 1:00PM luncheon.

Joe busied himself with a few last minute party preparations. He called the Pinkerton Detective Agency to verify the security arrangements for the day's activities. Joe normally had 3 security people on the property at all times. Additionally, he maintained a full coverage monitoring and alarm system at the main house and on the primary travel paths. The Palm Beach County Sheriff's Department also provided regular security checks at scheduled times around the clock. Many of Joe's wealthy friends frequently traveled with their own bodyguards which allayed some of Joe's concerns about security. He had a list of 28 private bodyguards who would accompany his guests. None the less, Joe provided a heightened level of security which could best be compared to secret service treatment afforded the U.S. President. He had never had a security breach at the estate and this year was to be no exception. In addition to the regular precautions, Joe had hired an additional 35 detectives to look after his guests at the estate and the Boca Raton Club. Wealth had its unique benefits and luxurious accompaniments, but Joe was cautiously aware of those who would try to take it by force from people of substance.

Satisfied that the security arrangements were adequate, Joe reviewed the entertainment and service agenda. The household staff at the estate included a fulltime maid, cook, butler and a gardener. They lived in separate quarters on the estate. Joe hosted many business functions throughout the year at the Boca house. He also made the estate available to vacationing friends who received unsurpassed service while they enjoyed the solitude and complete comfort of Joe's private paradise. This year, the four regular servants would be complimented by a contingent of 78 additional servants brought in to cater to the needs of the party goers.

There would also be a renowned 12 piece orchestra to provide musical entertainment in the ballroom. Two mimes, one juggler, two singers and three dancers were assigned to roam the estate looking for any un-entertained guest. Including security personnel, there would be nearly 2 servants for each of the 68 invited guests. The 7 permanent household staff shared responsibility for the temporary hires with the butler having overall control of all activity except security.

Joe reviewed the laser and firework tributes he arranged to honor his guests. This was to be a first at the party. Joe's idea was to have special displays that highlighted the business achievements of each of his associates. The displays were set up at the lower wall of the compound where they could be viewed from the tiered area with the Atlantic Ocean providing a colossal background.

Finally, Joe called the limousine company to verify the fleet had been gathered to pick up and deliver his guests. Each of the couples would enjoy a private, chauffeur driven ride in a stretch limousine. Although not unique to any of the affluent cadre, the sight of the 34 oversized luxury cars gathered at the Boca Club would prove to be an ostentatious display of wealth. Even the staff of the exclusive club, accustomed to lavish displays, would be in awe of the vehicular spectacular.

CHAPTER 16

▼

Todd bursts in the room just as Joe had hung up the phone. He is carrying a couple of suits in is left hand and furiously waving a greeting with his right hand. "Hey Dad, Happy New Years!"

"Hi Todd, did you have a good flight?"

Todd had some business to finish in New York and wasn't able to join Joe on their private jet. "Yeah smooth flight, decent grub and a really hot stewardess! You should fly commercial sometime! Who knows? You might meet someone to take home."

Joe could tell Todd was in a festive mood. He laughs as he responds. "I wouldn't know what to do with her after I got her home! It's been so long."

"That's exactly what I mean. You need to do something outrageous. You're always so serious, and always working. Give yourself a break. You've earned it."

Joe ignores the comments as he motions Todd towards the dining room. "Let's have something to eat while I fill you in on our banker friends."

Up until now, Todd effectively hid his concerns about the business, and particularly Davis and Mellon who had disturbed him so much in their last meeting. He visibly cringes when Joe brings up the subject. Todd looks at his father sympathetically as he replies. "I know I said I wanted to know everything, but this is New Year's Eve and I would like to enjoy the holiday. Why not save the business bad news until later."

Joe could plainly see the pressure his son was under. He was anxious to relieve the burden. "It's all good! I found a way out without giving the business to those two thieves.

Todd sits down across from Joe. A sparkle in Joe's eyes signals favorable news. "If its good news, then fire away. I could use some."

Joe explains in detail all the information he received from Peter Benson (Preston Orient), but he did not reveal his source. He is thorough in his review and includes the part about the Geneva financier he had pledged to keep secret.

After completing the conspiracy story, an incredulous Todd shakes his head in a negative manner. "Are you sure about this? Is it possible?" Nothing in Todd's background prepared him for this kind of business. In graduate school, he studied case histories of fraudulent business practices including the Hunt Brothers silver scandal. But, the magnitude of this hoax together with the collusion of high government officials left Todd feeling very disconcerted.

Joe replies, "I know it's difficult to handle when you first hear about it, but there is plenty of hard evidence. Unfortunately, as I mentioned, nothing can be proven. Think about everything I've told you. The pieces will fall into place."

Todd continues to have difficulty mentally dealing with the sheer massiveness of the fraud. Frustrated, he tries to be practical. "Dad, you said none of this could be proven in court. If so, how does this help you solve our financial problems?"

Joe answers, "I need to play a little dirty pool, but I'm in a dirty game and when in Rome—. In just a few hours, I'll be meeting with Bob Mellon and Curt Davis. I intend to tell them just about everything that I have learned. I anticipate they will deny the entire story. My hole card is Ted Thorndyke, the head of Continental News Network, who will be at the party tonight. I'm going to tell those two louses I'm going to Thorndyke with everything, and that I will convince him to do an initial expose and an investigative report. If I don't miss my bet, they'll fold like a house of cards. At that point, I'll settle with them if they agree to do all my loans at 9 percent with no strings attached. After all, 9 percent is probably the legitimate rate if the show were not rigged."

Todd is concerned as he replies. "No good! That would make you an accomplice to the actual crime. In essence you're doing the same thing as they are. I can't let you do that."

Joe sensed that Todd was torn with the morality of youthful innocence as well as a touch of concern for the welfare of his old man. Joe seeks to further convince Todd of his course of action. "This is all about survival. If I can't prove a conspiracy in a court of law, there is no crime and subsequently no law is broken. And if I can't get protection under the law, then I must provide my own protection in the best way I can. We have to survive and although you find what I must do objectionable, you need to realize there is no other way! It's very important you understand this."

Todd looks at his father intently. He is confused and hurt, but relieved at the same time. "I don't understand, but I'm behind you. Maybe some day I'll appreciate what you have to do. Right now, it's more than I can handle."

Joe questions his judgment in telling Todd about the conspiracy without giving him sufficient time to mentally digest it. He should have handled it differently. He speaks carefully in an effort to reduce Todd's anxiety. "In time, you'll understand. For now, maybe you can be satisfied to know we won't lose our asses to the bunch of maggots who thought up this scheme. I know its hardball, much harder than even I have ever played. But, we either play or we'll be thrown out of the game."

Todd feigns an acknowledging smile. "I know you're right and I'm with you all the way."

"That's all I can ask at this point. We'll beat them together."

Todd interprets Joe's last remark as an invitation to the meeting with the bankers. "So, do I get to go to the meeting with you?"

Joe quickly responds, "No, its best I handle this meeting myself." Joe has never lost sight of the fact he would be moving against some powerful people. He thought he was safe, but was unwilling to see Todd exposed to any potential danger. He would keep him off the firing line.

Todd did not second guess Joe's decision. He was still caught up in all the conflicting forces at work on him. Thoughts of business, morality, corruption, ethics, and survival were banging around aimlessly in his head. Todd feels he couldn't think clearly enough to help his father, and silently acquiesces with a nod of his head. Without further discussion, the issue is settled.

Joe continues, "Smile Todd, the outlook is 1000 percent better than just a few days ago. Are you up for the party tonight?"

"Sure am—got me a hot little date and now I don't have to worry about finding another job in six months. Hell, I have a lot to party about. I plan to really enjoy myself. I might even get totaled." Todd is rambling. It is obvious the news still weighed heavily on him.

Joe regretted being so open with Todd. "Do I know your lady friend?"

"Sure you do. You met her a few days ago at Associated Bank Holding. Remember, she brought us to the conference room and served us coffee."

"Do I remember? I recall thinking I would have to pick up your eyeballs off the carpet. She was quite a looker and I did notice a special smile flashed in your direction."

Todd loosens up a little. "Yeah, she's very attractive and she doesn't seem to be an airhead. She might even be a practical sort."

Joe senses the tension easing, but feels he must issue a few warnings. "It sounds like you're a little smitten with this young lady. I don't anticipate a problem, but be careful what you tell her about our finances. And just one other thing. Have a good time, but if you must get drunk, please do so in the privacy of your room."

Todd smiles, "I'm a step ahead of you. I was thinking about business implications when you told me Bob Mellon and Curt Davis were involved in the conspiracy. Don't worry. I'll be careful about what I say to her. As for getting drunk, I really don't want to do that. I was just talking bullshit. Sorry."

"To be honest, I didn't really think you would get drunk—so we were both talking bullshit. By the way, what is your new girlfriend's name?"

Todd wipes his mouth as he finishes lunch. "Donna Santora. And speaking of Donna, I have to pick her up at the airport at 3:15. I'm going to leave now. Traffic at the airport is a mess with all the holiday travelers."

"Ok, Todd, are you all right on the other thing?"

"I guess. Just let me know when and where you need me. Be careful yourself, I don't want to have to visit you in Danbury."

In a minute Todd was gone and Joe was off to his next project. He had to review the culinary arrangements with his staff and make a final check with the pyrotechnics company.

CHAPTER 17

▼

Joe's day has been exceptionally busy. After going over all the details of the party, he goes to his library to enjoy a little quiet relaxation. He glances over the shelves to locate a book that would be light and entertaining. Joe reads frequently whenever time is available. He peruses the shelves and spots an old photo album. He picks up the album and pages through the pictorial history. Its been years since he opened the book, and he was immediately caught up in feelings of intense nostalgia. In the front of the album were some of his earliest pictures as a baby, a growing lad, a gangly teenager and a confident young man. The friends of his youth were sprinkled throughout the chronological display.

Soon he is viewing the pictures of Lisa, his high school girlfriend. Then Lisa, his senior prom date and Lisa with his college fraternity pin. Then came Lisa, his party favorite and Lisa, his fiancé followed by Lisa, his newly wed wife. In quick order came Lisa and Joe nestling a new born Todd between them. Time races by as Joe flips through the pages of his life. Todd, the infant followed by Todd, the little leaguer and Todd, the perpetual honor roll attainee. Prominently displayed in the picture history is the ever watchful, proud and beautiful Lisa. She seemed to never age and was always radiating that special womanly glow that had captured and forever retained Joe's heart.

Suddenly, Lisa is absent from the photos never to be viewed in the album again. Joe sighs as he recalls her sudden and tragic death. He is overcome with emotion as he continues to page the album, mentally seeking an impossible glimpse of his lost love. A tear comes to his eye as intense feelings of remorse fills his mind. *I might have—could have—should have done more for Lisa while she was still alive. She was so good, so innocent and was always there in times of need. Why was she so suddenly taken from me in such a senseless way? I never had a chance to comfort her in her final moments on earth. I never had a chance to wish the love of my life a farewell on her final eternal journey.*

Joe's hand swipes his eye to remove a trace of moisture as he rests his head on the back of his chair. He stares blankly at the ornate, sculpted ceiling as he recalls fleeting moments of their lives together. He closes his eyes seeking an image of his life long friend and lover. Joe is tired and groggy. The pictorial trip has sapped him of his energy. He intensifies his mental effort to find his lost love. A picture of a soft white cloud accented by a hazy blue background appears. Around the edge of the cloud radiates a shimmering red glow as if the mass of whiteness had attempted to hide the sun. A feeling of peace and serenity pervades the surrealistic scene.

Abruptly, a familiar voice breaks the silence of the tranquil setting. "Joe, I've missed you so much. When are you coming to be with me?"

Joe's heart beats feverishly as he realizes that he is in the presence of Lisa. He reaches out blindly. "Lisa. Is that you Lisa?"

Suddenly, Lisa is in front of Joe. She is beautiful, alluring and timeless. Joe focuses on her face as her lips part again. "Joe, won't you please come to me? It's been so long. It's time for us to be together again."

Joe reaches out and embraces the lovely Lisa. Her body molds to his arms in the familiar embrace of yesteryear. He eagerly explores her body seeking those secret identifying contours that would authenticate her being. Lisa sighs as she returns the embrace holding Joe in an intimate manner that gave him complete assurance. Tears of joy stream from Joe's eyes as he seeks out her lips. He touches her lips briefly and then kisses her. Joe holds her tightly and kisses her deeply surrendering himself in complete ecstasy. He is completely at ease. Nothing else matters except Lisa. As his lips linger on her mouth, he is awash with euphoric happiness and drugged by the eternal charm of his long lost love. It is Lisa who pulls away and slowly loosens her gown. Joe is aroused as Lisa sensuously lies back in the billowing clouds.

"Joe, I need you so much. Please come to me."

Joe kneels down next to Lisa. His hand reaches out to touch Lisa's alluring body. "Lisa, I'm so happy. I've waited so long for this moment. We'll be together forever. Nothing will separate us again." Joe briefly brushes Lisa's cheek before she begins to drift into the mountainous cloud.

Lisa is slowly being engulfed by the milky layers and she desperately cries out. "Please come with me now. It's time we are together again. Hurry Joe."

Joe is desperately struggling and he reaches out to grasp her rapidly disappearing body. He begins to panic as she drifts further into the cloud. He screams out in frustration. "Lisa, don't go. I'm coming with you! Wait for me—wait for me." He grabs for her as her form disappears. Joe yells again as his arms and legs rapidly flail in a seemingly motionless effort to reach her. "Please don't go! I want to be with you. I love you. Wait for me! You must wait for me!" Unexpectedly, he is in the middle of a pitch black hole.

The elusive Lisa calls out. "You said you were coming with me. Where are you?"

Joe reaches out into the blackness, but all he could grasp were handfuls of nothingness. Lisa's voice is becoming more distant. Joe's movements become slower and more labored as he increases his efforts to find Lisa. He cries as a flood of built up anguish releases itself in tearful frustration. Joe reaches out again and again. Each time the movement becomes more difficult.

Lisa speaks once more, this time, in a clear and distinctive voice. "I need to go now. We'll be together soon. Good bye my love."

Joe becomes like an enraged caged animal. He is frantically clawing, pushing and banging against an invisible force that prevents him from reaching his beloved. Abruptly, Joe awakes in a startled frenzy. His face is sopping wet and he tastes the salty moisture of tears. His sweaty hands are clutching the armrest of his chair. As he opens his eyes, he is looking at the cherubs and angels which dot the gilded ceiling. He gropes at his body to test his realness. He immediately thinks of Lisa, who just moments ago, was in his arms. A tremendous wave of passion permeates his entire body. Momentarily, he remains immobile. Slowly, he inches his head downward stopping at the open photo album lying on his lap. He is looking at his vivacious princess in their last photo together. They were admirably smiling at one another as their fingers clasped in a tender embrace.

Joe glances at his watch and is quickly yanked out of his slumber. It is 4:45. Davis and Mellon will be arriving soon. He would have to rush to freshen up and change. He closes the album and places it in the center of his desk. He gets up from the chair, feeling lethargic and weak kneed. Everything had been so real. In spite of his drug like condition which seemingly regulates his movements to slow motion, Joe proceeds toward his bedroom. At the library door, he glances back at the album and thought how wonderful it was to be with his beloved Lisa. All else now seemed shallow and without purpose.

CHAPTER 18

▼

At 5:00 sharp, Curt Davis and Bob Mellon are announced. Joe asked the butler to show them into the formal dining room while he finished dressing. When Joe entered the dining room, both bankers rise to greet him. Joe is dressed in a formal black tuxedo. Davis and Mellon are in similar attire. After initial well wishes and holiday tidings, the three sit down to a sumptuous meal of pheasant under glass with accompaniments of shrimp, caviar and escargot.

As they finish eating, Bob Mellon comments on Todd's demeanor during the recent meeting at Associated Bank offices in the World Trade Center. "Todd sure is a feisty son of a gun. I thought for a moment we would have to fight our way out of our own offices. I'm glad you were handy. It seems age and experience brings the kind of temperament needed to solve difficult problems."

Joe effectively hides his feelings at the back handed remark. "You're right! It's just as important to be up for the settlement as it is to be up for the fight. I'm sure we are prepared to settle our business like gentlemen today."

The meeting starts with all the subtlety and finesse demanded of top level executives. Curt Davis produces a folder of legal papers which transfers 51 percent of Robbins Ltd. to Associated Bank Holding. Joe reviews the documents. He slowly gets up from his chair and casually strolls over to the large stone fireplace in the center of the room. He strikes a match for an after dinner cigar, inhales once on the premium Cuban stogie and speaks. "Gentlemen, we have much to discuss. It may seem we are starting all over, but we will get our business settled."

Davis and Mellon were weighing his words when Joe, still holding the lit match placed it under the packet of legal papers and deposited them into the fireplace. A flash of fire and a billow of smoke escaping into the chimney signaled the destruction of the documents.

Curt was the first to respond. "Just what the hell do you think you're doing? We had a deal."

Joe smugly replies. "I would like to renegotiate. I need a few changes made."

Bob Mellon retorts. "Don't you think it's a little late for changes?"

Joe responds. "It's only too late after the deal is signed. I want to introduce some very important considerations before we finalize our business."

Curt is annoyed. "Get to the point. What are you talking about?"

Joe joins Davis and Mellon at the dinner table. As he looks directly into their faces, he proceeds to tell the story of the money supply conspiracy. He includes the conspiratorial involvement of government officials with Mellon and Davis. No comment is made during his dialogue and the room is deathly silent as he finishes. Joe pauses for a few moments for effect before continuing. "Based on this information, don't you think we should renegotiate?"

Joe is carefully watching the two for the tell tale signs of complicity. Davis and Mellon sit poker faced as they listened to the assertions.

Mellon responds first. "I don't know what you're trying to pull, but let me assure you we know nothing about any interest rate conspiracy. You've been under a lot of pressure lately and I think you've been duped with some bad information. I'm willing to forget this Joe. I have a duplicate set of papers in my case. Let's get on with our business and forget this conspiracy nonsense."

Joe expected the feigned reception and the rehearsed response, and he continues with his assertions. "Bob, everyone in this room knows there is a money supply scheme and soon everyone in the world will know—if that's what it's going to take. We can continue to stonewall or we can settle. Please understand that your previous terms are unacceptable."

Mellon responds. "You're going to look like a fool. Not only is everything you said untrue, but it's so far fetched, it sounds like fabricated sour grapes to me. I'm still willing to work with you on our original two options. Either pay the going rate or take advantage of a substantially reduced rate in exchange for 51 percent of your business."

The game of cat and mouse continues as Joe snaps back. "I don't think you're listening to me. Your terms are unacceptable!" Joe's comments were blunt and forceful. The fact that the bankers did not leave at this point is a clear sign that he has them. He simply needs to convince them. Joe presses on. "Let me give you some more details." Joe proceeds to tell them about Jules Woodcock, the deceased programmer who had rigged the computers at the FED and the treasury. For added effect, he mentions the Swiss bank accounts controlled by the 5 co-conspirators. After he finished, he again inquires. "Gentlemen, do we have sufficient grounds to renegotiate yet?"

Bob Mellon calmly replies. "Joe, you are absolutely paranoid. If you were not as successful as you are, I would think you are a real nut."

Joe could now see the first signs of deterioration. Curt Davis was noticeably quiet—probably fuming. The more controlled Mellon had a slight twitch in his right eye. He decides to turn up the heat one more notch. "Gentlemen, I knew you would be real hard cases. That's why I scheduled a 6:30 meeting with Ted Thorndyke, the chairman of Continental News Network. I believe you both know him. If not, he will be arriving shortly and I would be pleased to make the introductions. Now, let's stop the bullshit! If you continue to deny this, I'm going to Thorndyke with this entire mess. He'll do a story that will put all of you out of business and into jail for a long time."

Mellon persists. "None of what you said can be proven. No responsible journalist would even consider doing that story, and if they did, our lawyers would have their asses! Why don't you settle down? You're only making things worse for yourself!"

Joe now knew that he had won. "You're right. I can't prove a conspiracy in a court of law. But Thorndyke will do the story if he could test run a rigged transaction and the Fed computer system crashes on queue. And he would do the story if I release the name of the Geneva businessman who knows you and your partners have multi-billion dollar numbered Swiss bank accounts. It's up to you. When Thorndyke arrives, I either give him a press release on tonight's party, or I give him the scoop of the century on the money supply conspiracy."

Once again total quiet descends on the room. Davis sits up straight. His face has a deep red flush and his hands are clasped tightly together.

Mellon breaks the silence. "Suppose what you say is true. How would you propose to negotiate a settlement?"

Joe is courteously reserved in his victory. He does not want enemies. "I need two and one-half billion dollars refinanced at 9 percent. If you can arrange that without any other contingencies, then I would agree to forget about the money supply manipulations."

Davis could handle no more. He rises from the table with fists clenched as he explodes in a verbal tirade. "Just who the fuck do you think you are? You came to us for money. We arranged it and now you want to screw us. We'll see who gets fucked, you son of a bitch."

He is walking menacingly towards Joe when he is sternly reprimanded by Mellon.

"Curt, sit down! We came to discuss business. There's nothing to be gained by flipping out."

Curt looks disapprovingly at Bob, but quickly retreats under his intimidating glare.

Bob then addresses Joe. "I apologize for Curt. I think you can relate to his dilemma. You were in a similar situation just a few days ago. If I were to accept your conditions on the loans, how can I be assured that this conspiracy talk will go no further? It will be of primary importance to my partners. In fact, one might think you were inserting yourself as a partner." Mellon is checking on Joe's future ambitions.

Joe replies, "I don't like what you guys did. You're screwing all of America with your scheme and I strongly disagree with your methods. I have no desire to be your partner. From a practical standpoint, I need to save my business. As for assurance, the only guarantee I can offer is my word and my hand. I will forget everything if you arrange the loans at 9 percent."

Bob Mellon is beat and he knows it. Mellon slowly gets up from the table. "I think we have a deal." He walks toward Joe extending his arm. "Your word and your handshake are good enough for me." Joe and Bob shake hands.

Bob turns to Curt Davis who is still visibly shaken. He directs his partner. "I think you owe Joe an apology!"

Curt looks away in disgust.

Bob reiterates his request. This time, his tone denotes a distinct command. "I will tell you once more. You owe Joe an apology!"

Curt gets up and walks hesitantly toward Joe. They shake hands as Curt whispers a barely audible apology.

Bob Mellon smiles. "Now we have a deal, let's celebrate."

Joe responds in kind. "Curt, Bob—have an enjoyable time at the estate tonight. Let me know if you need anything. We can finalize our business next week when I'm back in New York."

Mellon and Davis leave together. They take a walk outside in the direction of the gardens. They are standing at the rear terraces overlooking the Atlantic before either of them speaks a word. The tension is palpable.

Curt Davis speaks first. "I'm getting the fuck out of here. I can't stand this shit and you bought into it."

Mellon again rebukes Davis. "Listen Curt, it's important you stay the night. You must be on your best behavior the rest of the evening. Nobody must even suspect that you are the wee bit pissed. Nobody! Do you understand me?"

Bob's instructions are absolute and Curt knows it. Instantly, his attitude changes to full compliance. "I do understand Bob and you can count on me. You won't tell the others—will you?"

Bob is looking at the wide expanse of beach in front of him as he replies. "No damage done. Just do what I said. I think our business with Joe Robbins will be settled sooner than next week."

Bob pats Curt on the shoulder. "I need to go to town, pick up some things and make a few phone calls. I want you to circulate and cover for me. I'll be back in about an hour."

Curt feels relieved. This had been Curt's deal that went sour, and he needed a strong ally in order to save face with his other partners. Bob surveys the beach once more. He makes a mental note of the surroundings before leaving for town.

CHAPTER 19

▼

On schedule, a steady procession of white stretch limousines begins to arrive at the mansion at 7:30. The entrance to the property is secured by an exquisite scrolled iron gate bounded by a massive 10 foot stone wall that surrounded the estate. The gate is controlled by a full-time guard who also watched 12 security monitors. Each of the monitors randomly scanned 21 different locations every 10 minutes. Motion detectors tied into the cameras and monitors instantly pictured any physical movements. The elaborate guard house, which contained the various security devices, has 5 rooms and is restricted to security personnel. In addition, located close by, but out of sight, are the dog kennels. The kennels house 7 well trained German Shepherds who are on regular rounds at all times. When visitors are expected, the dogs were always accompanied by a handler. At any other time, the dogs have a free run of the property. A few years back late at night, a wealthy but inebriated neighbor had somehow gained access to the grounds. The drunken man was savagely retained by 2 of the dogs who held the hapless trespasser in a thorax death grip. The man lived but required 87 stitches to various parts of his body.

Once a visitor is passed through the security gate, they travel a winding road for about a quarter mile before the magnificent main house comes into view. The roadside is superbly landscaped and manicured. The main house contains 32 rooms with over 27,000 square feet of living space.

Tonight, each of the couples is provided a personal attendant who offers a tour of the house and grounds. Those who elect to take the tour are given a room by room walk through the house, followed by a golf cart preview of the 16 acre site. The grounds are 100 percent developed and accented by tropical displays of the exotic plants and trees of the world.

Inside the huge mansion, all fixtures are gold plated. Floors are either covered over by custom designed oriental carpets, Italian marble, or the simple elegance of teak wood. Old world craftsmanship is abundant throughout the structure. Artistically finished stained glass, sculpted stone and marble accents, satin wall coverings and hand-painted murals are used throughout the house to give each room an exclusive motif.

The exterior architecture is Spanish Mediterranean tastefully colored in white, pearl and pink. The mansion is set on four levels and gracefully follows the contours of the built-up earth. The terrain of South Florida is boringly flat and Joe Robbins had spent a small fortune to develop the rolling hills which cascaded away from the main house and gently flowed across the entire property.

Three tastefully decorated observation towers run to a height which offers an unimpeded view of the town on one side and the ocean on the opposite side. An immense man-made waterfall seems to naturally spring from the left side of the house forming a two acre pond of water which embraces three sides of the house. A wide bridge crosses the pond and winds behind the waterfall before ending in a secluded veranda. This area serves as one of three patios set to the sides and rear of the house. This patio contains an Olympic size swimming pool complete with a diving tank, and two spas. A number of cabanas are laid out over Bermuda grass, white sand or pink pavers giving sun bathers a selection of environments.

Suffice it to say, the list of comforts and amenities offered at the estate staggered even many of Joe's wealthy guests. A recent appraisal set the replacement cost of the extravagant mansion and grounds at 63.2 million dollars. Without question, the property is a premier residential location in South Florida.

By 8:30, all of Joe's guests had arrived. America's elite were decked out in a dazzling array of gold, jewelry, and original fashions. Saks Fifth Avenue and Cartier could have used the party for an exclusive product showroom. After a brief introductory session in the ballroom, Joe kicks off the festivities with a pyrotechnics display honoring American industry. The orchestra plays a moving rendition of The National Anthem to the synchronized fireworks and laser show. The spectacular is viewed from balconies which surrounded the ballroom and overlook the ocean. The grand finale begins when a 20 foot high businessman standing in front of Old Glory is lit up in a series of sparkling explosions. A caption sitting high above the colorful picture was detonated one letter at a time to reveal **'AMERICA'S INDUSTRIALISTS ARE THE REASON FOR HER GREATNESS'**. The finale is more than the inflated egos of the members of the eccentric group could absorb, and the crowd spontaneously bursts into a round of self-admiring applause. Following the exhibition, dinner is served in the main dining room. The meal is a veritable delight as course after course of culinary excellence is consumed by the select group. After dinner, the gathering disburses to pursue various entertainments.

CHAPTER 20

▼

Joe Robbins is anxious to speak with Paul Trump about the events of the last couple days. He spots Trump in the middle of a small crowd. From a distance, Trump appears to have developed an audience. The individuals seem mesmerized watching the charismatic Trump. Joe admirably drew an analogy about fantasy's Pied Piper and Trump. *He could lead a group wherever he wanted—and they would go willingly, smiling and appeased the whole time.* Joe motions to Trump, but the talkative Texan was so engrossed in his conversation that he did not notice.

Joe began to walk towards Trump when he is tapped on the shoulder. It was Leo Baltroff, the CEO of Pittsburgh Steel. Without a hint of what he was talking about, Baltroff queries Joe. "What do you think Joe?"

Joe smiled as he shook the hand of America's leading steel maker. "How are you Leo? What do you want me to think?"

Having added to his audience, Baltroff went to center stage. "We've been discussing unions, wages and profits. I'm being eaten alive by the damn unions. All they ever want is to work less and get paid more! Every time I concede an issue, they come at me for something else. They're never satisfied. Profitability is slipping, the shareholders are getting edgy, and my performance bonus is getting smaller. I'm seriously thinking about eliminating some plants in Pittsburgh and Gary, and replacing them with some southern mills. Some of the fellows have already moved their operations, and they're getting considerable relief in wages and benefits. There's a different work ethic down South. People are more willing to work for reasonable wages. Not only that, but they are more independent. They want to do more on their own and do not like unions. I think the people we employ in many of our old plants like Pittsburgh, Youngstown and Gary have forgotten where their bread is buttered."

Baltroff is interrupted by his wife Lucy. "Leo is right. He works hard every day so these people have jobs, and it seems they just do not appreciate it. They are the best paid workers in the country and they still want more. I think Leo should open plants in areas where the people are a bit more grateful." *Huh!*

Joe is listening half heartily. Whenever these captains of industry gather, there are always conversations about business problems. They never seemed reluctant to express their opinions and frequently even reveal their future plans. To a person, they share a righteous contention that they could do no wrong as long as it was profitable.

In the interest of social conversation, Joe decides to play devil's advocate. "Let's just say the unions permit you to shut down the Gary plant and go to Georgia, you would lose the skilled workers who are the backbone of your business. Your costs may well increase, even with lower wages, because of labor inefficiency."

Leo knows he is being baited, but he is always up for a verbal joust. "The entire steel industry was built on the backs of immigrant Irish, Italian, Polish and every other ethnic group for that matter. If it were possible to teach a mob of unskilled wetbacks how to make steel over 100 years ago, I'm certain we can show Americans in the South how to make our products. At least they understand English!"

The small gathering chuckle as they acknowledge Leo's remarks.

Joe continues to question Leo. "Don't you think you have an obligation to the people who have spent their lives building your company?"

Leo eyes Joe suspiciously. "I'm not heartless. There is an obligation that gets met every payday. And then there is an obligation that gets met every time a steel worker takes his kid to a doctor. And there is an obligation met every month when we mail pension checks to retired workers. Just who do you think is responsible for all these obligations? The buck stops here. I either meet these commitments or I am out of a job. Realize that I have one obligation that supersedes all others. The long term profitability and financial health of this business is all that matters because without that I could not meet all the other obligations. So if it means I need to furlough a few thousand steel workers to insure profitability, I would do it in a heartbeat. Everything and everybody including disenchanted workers take a back seat to the shareholders."

Joe knows he had sufficiently riled the patriarch of steel and decides to retreat. "You make all the sense in the world. If we don't provide the proper leadership, the whole system will collapse. It sounds as if you're convinced that you may have to move some plants!"

Leo replies. "I hope moving a few plants is the answer. As soon as I can make the right deals with the union bosses, I will be testing the idea. Problem is that we're also against some unconventional business practices. The Germans and the Japs are hitting the market with steel products that are high quality and a lot less expensive than ours. I'm not sure that lower wage rates will be sufficient to keep us competitive."

Out of nowhere, the high pitched voice of Paul Trump enters the conversation. The spunky Trump twangs out his take on the problem. "If you need to clean out the barn, make sure you do it right the first time. Never did like unions. They thrive on weak people who want to suck the vitality out of hard working people. If I were you, I would develop a plan to get rid of the lot of them. It's simply a matter of time before those Southern boys get greedy, form a union and place you in the same position you are today. They're just like weeds in a cornfield. Guarantee they'll be back if you don't give them a stiff shot of poison. You need to eliminate the weeds if you're going to get a decent crop. Right!"

The group hushes while a few members subconsciously nod the affirmative. Trump continued to lay on his country boy analogy. "If you're plowing a field and your only concern is straight furrows, chances are about 50-50 you set up an erosion problem that may wash your field out. Point is, if all you do is close the plants and move to the South, maybe you might wash yourself out of business in a river you create."

Baltroff is paying close attention, but is a bit stymied. "I'm not following you Paul. Be more specific."

Trump was now in his glory. He had the undivided attention of the assembly and now he was asked to perform. His eagle eyes raked through his audience for any sign of disapproval. His quick mind set his sharp tongue into motion. The high pitched banter continues. "OK. Let's make it simple. We need to address the entire problem. You said the union was a part of the problem, and foreign competition was another part of the problem. Unless you deal with both of them, you're only doing half the job. Right?" Without waiting for approval, he goes on." You said you're making a deal with the union bosses. That's good! But, what are you doing about the foreign competition? If you build new plants in Georgia and you still have the same problems with the Japs, then for all practical purposes you will have destroyed your business. You have to address the competition before you make any big moves."

Leo is a little miffed as he responds. "It's not like we haven't tried! I have lobbyists in Washington every day of the year complaining about foreign competition, but nobody is listening. The politicians are turning a deaf ear, even when we wave our PAC purse at them. They say foreign competition is good for the economy, and then lower tariffs in support of free trade. Every time they lower the tariffs, our competitive position gets worse. And to beat all, it's damn near impossible to get any public support because the American consumers are getting their products at lower prices. They're happy, the governments happy, and business is getting its ass kicked! So what do you do with a mess like that?"

Trump raises his arms as if to start preaching. "First of all, forget about the American public. Maybe 1 in 10,000 realizes that free trade is a double edge sword. The first edge swipes through established prices and rains inexpensive products on the public. Meanwhile, the other edge is poised to chop out their jobs because they're not supporting the companies that are employing them. All they understand is the great deal they got when they bought jeans, televisions or that new Honda parked in the garage. Oh, they may bitch because Uncle Harry in Pittsburgh lost his job, but damn if they can connect the two. The American public is as useless as tits on a bull. In addition, the DC propaganda machine is pumping out all the bullshit about how great free trade is and the public reacts like lambs to the slaughter. Hell, they're so damned brainwashed, it would take unemployment lines from here to Hiroshima to make them realize they're being had. The public's really naive. Don't look to them for support until they get hurt pretty bad. And even then, you better have a bigger and better propaganda machine."

Joe Robbins has been quite attentive and he poses a question close to his own situation. "You're right about the public. They just don't understand business. But, how do you figure the governments position on lowering tariffs in support of free trade? Surely, the bureaucrats can see American industry is being beat up."

Trump shrugs his shoulders as he replies. "That's anybody's guess. The only thing I know for sure about our capitalistic system is that nothing happens in government until some money changes hands. Once the way is cleared with greenbacks, I think they must have a logic machine that spews out reasons to justify any course of action. The only thing certain is someone is benefiting big time. Otherwise, it wouldn't be happening. But, that's beside the point. We all play games not to our liking because we have to. Our first choice is to control the game to maximize profit and our second choice is to adapt to the game for the same reason. The dilemma for all of us is determining how to use the system which has been created for someone else's benefit. Right!"

Baltroff confirms. "I agree. I think we frequently have to find a way to profit in spite of the government. It's nice to have them in your pocket, but too often it's impossible because someone else already has them in their pocket."

Trump was on a roll. He thrives on giving advice to the big shots of industry. Trump elaborates. "Yes, but to be more specific. We must profit in spite of the government; in spite of each other; and in spite of ourselves. The best way I can describe it is by example. A few years ago, there was an average tariff of 23 percent on foreign goods moving into the United States. Today, the rate is down to 9 percent and falling. What does that tell you? If you're paying attention, two things are happening. First, someone—maybe someone here tonight, or some foreign government, or some special interest has influenced our government to lower tariffs. It really doesn't matter who benefits or how much. Just be aware that when the tariff went from 25 percent to 9 percent, somebody made a lot of money. Now, we can sit around and bitch about it while we get clobbered with cheap foreign goods, or we can look at alternatives. This is the second thing happening in our little example. American companies are reacting. They're moving plants to foreign countries, or they're making manufacturing and distributing deals with their foreign counterparts. Either way, they're positioning themselves to benefit from the low foreign wages and the falling tariff rates. The companies that choose to maintain just American based operations don't have a snowball's chance in hell."

Baltroff is troubled as he replies. "I understand what you're saying-establish new operations in the most profitable area-even if it's out of the country. I've looked into that and I have some concerns. Today, I pay an average of $19.00 an hour plus benefits to my employees in Pittsburgh. If I go to Georgia or the Carolinas, I will pay an average of $8.00 an hour and I can reduce the benefit package. If I go to Mexico, I can pay 38 cents an hour and I don't have to worry about the benefits. Trouble is I don't know weather I can control a Mexican operation like I can control an operation in Georgia. Trying to work with our government is difficult enough. I'm afraid working with the Mexican Government might be impossible."

Trump is well acquainted with the international business situation and replies confidently. "I would be concerned too if I were the first out of the gate. The road to Mexico and just about any other country has already been traveled. Let's talk Mexico, but keep in mind we could be talking about any number of foreign countries. Let's use the television manufacturing industry as an example. There is hardly a company left in the United States producing TV's. A lot of Americans lost their jobs. But, all you have to do is travel the Mexican side of the United

States border, and you will find just about every major American electronics producer with big factory complexes. Those that you don't find in Mexico, you'll find in Korea, Hong Kong, Singapore, etcetera, etcetera, etcetera. You get the point. And if you don't find American names, it's because a profitable arrangement has been made with a foreign counterpart. Most people think the American television industry is dead, but American businessmen are controlling much of the industry through their foreign operations. The beauty of it all is that profitability is skyrocketing because of the reduced costs of foreign labor. Throw the lower tariffs in and you literally have a goldmine. As far as control, there is too much American investment in Mexico for that government to get cute. Your investment is as safe there as it is in Chicago!"

Joe speaks next. "What about the long term for America? How many jobs do we export until we begin to erode the standard of living? And what about the social consequences? The country is experiencing dramatic increases in divorces, murders, and other violent crimes. We're losing our central cities to gangs. Both you and I know that the crux of the social problem is economic. At the rate we're going today, in 15 years Mexico City will probably be a safe haven compared to Chicago! Can we afford to ignore all these warnings?"

Trump answers. "Joe, as I mentioned, most of us don't get to make the rules. Rather, we must adapt to the rules in order to survive. I agree with you. The way business is being done today is hurting America. Unfortunately, the American people are not complaining because they think they're getting a good deal with cheap foreign goods. Now if the government chooses to do business this way, and the people passively condone it, then, by God, we had better accept it or we're in big trouble. Understand we are talking business survival. Sooner or later, someone with influence will recognize that the present course of action is hurting America. When that happens, the rules will change. All of it won't mean a damn if we don't survive! The best advice I can give any of you is to go with the flow even if you have to fire every American worker. If and when we wake up as a country, we will at least be around to offer jobs and to help with the social problems."

Joe backs up as Trump continues to elaborate on corporate strategy for his spellbound audience. It is an incredible experience to watch Trump in action. One gets the feeling he believes and practices the advice he so freely passed onto others.

Joe feels a hand on his upper arm. He turns to look at Mary Trump, the charming wife of Paul. Mary stroked Joe's hand as she spoke. "Wonderful party

Joe. With so much to do, I'm surprised to see so many of you gathered around Paul!"

Joe replies. "You look beautiful tonight—just like always. Paul was giving us some of his business advice spiced up with a lot of his home spun verbiage."

Mary smiles. "He sure knows how to throw out those always appropriate Americana expressions."

"Tell me about it. He must have a library of those quaint sayings stored in his head. Is he ever at a loss for words?"

Mary shakes her head. "No, I don't think I've ever seen Paul without something to say. He is laying it on a little thick tonight, but he always does that when he has an audience."

A sudden revelation hits Joe. Mary is right. Paul Trump spoke differently when addressing a group of people. Joe quickly reviewed some of his private conversations with Trump. He could not recall one where Trump had resorted to his back country slang in order to make a point. Joe laughed out loud as he realized the complex personality of Trump. *Paul Trump had a switch which he turned on and off at will.* A mental picture of a scurrying chameleon changing colors to meet conditions ran through Joe's mind. A tug on his arm brought Joe back.

Mary muses. "Will you buy me a drink?"

"I'd be honored. I know the bartender so just name your pleasure."

Arm in arm the two walk off just as Paul Trump ends his lesson. "Change is frequently necessary. If you don't rotate your crops from time to time, pretty soon the soil's shot and your farm is not worth a damn! Right?"

CHAPTER 21

▼

The evening rushes by as couples dance, cavort and are well entertained. During the evening, Joe's special tribute to each of the business magnates is well received. The special pyrotechnic displays lasted only two minutes each, but the attention to individual detail thrilled each of the honored guests. Baltroff is pleased with a steel skyscraper reaching high into the Florida sky. Trump is depicted in bursts of light which culminated in a picture of a crown prince sitting on top of a world captioned **'the computer empire'**. Craig Evans, Chairman of the colossal Global Motor Company is treated to a rocket salute ending with a stunning aerial view of his prototype sports car. Everyone is amazed with the precision of the rocket firings which seemingly hung in the air until the sports car was formed from the remnants of spent rockets.

At 11:40, Joe calls his guests together to honor the businessman of the year. The award was typically given to the executive who had the greatest profit margin. This year, the winner is Charles Mock, President and CEO of Eureka Oil Company. In fact, 1979 was a banner year for all the oil companies and with good reason. Oil prices increased as a result of the oil cartels who were withholding oil supplies to drive up prices. America's oil companies were supposedly victimized along with American consumers. But the signs of windfall profits at Eureka Oil were apparent as 1979 came to a close. It became general knowledge that the oil companies had to increase expenses in order to diminish the profits. An unprecedented spending spree took place as sharply revised budgets were given to purchasing agents with instructions to spend it all before the end of the year. Special one time bonuses were awarded to all management personnel. Top level managers were granted the largest across the board bonuses ever given in the history of the industry. Everyone at Eureka Oil, from the janitor to Charles Mock, was wearing big smiles. A bountiful dividend was paid to the stockholders who dismissed the spending binge as good fiscal management. Of course, all allegations of profiteering were denied by the oil companies, but the loose purse strings spoke volumes about the true status of the oil industry. A deal had been struck with the oil cartel, and the American consumer was the sucker who paid the bills.

So it was that Charles Mock of Eureka Oil gained the recognition of his peers as **'most profitable businessman'**. The fireworks accolade is fantastic. A 15 minute flaming commendation to Mock and Eureka Oil fills the skies. The show could best be seen from the roof of the mansion where one could turn a full 360 degrees and view the aerial spectacular on all sides. The finale is an unforgettable experience. At exactly midnight, effervescent explosions set off in rapid sequence presented a 100 foot oil well with sparkling gushes of multi-colored lights spewing from its pinnacle. The big one had come in for Charles Mock of Eureka just as the New Year arrived. He knew it, his peers knew it and everyone that mattered knew it.

CHAPTER 22

▼

Todd Robbins is noticeably quiet during the evening. He is pensive and remote contrary to his gregarious personality. Normally he was a social tiger who inevitably brought smiles to even the most reluctant guest. Shortly after midnight, before the orchestra had finished Auld Lang Syne, Joe searched the crowd for his son. He spots Todd with his date dancing in the corner of the ballroom. He hurries across the room past the couples, friends and associates who were riotously hugging and kissing as they wished each other future success. Todd is kissing Donna Santora as he approaches. Todd pulls away from Donna to greet his father. He is misty eyed and embraces his father before any words could be exchanged. The moment is emotionally charged.

Joe whispers "Happy New Year son."

Todd returns the greeting and began to apologize for his behavior earlier in the day when Joe raised a finger to his lips in a gesture for silence.

"Todd, I love you. Everything is OK! The meeting went well. I'll tell you all about it tomorrow. Please enjoy the rest of the evening."

Todd looks affectionately at his father. While the sentimental music played, the joyous passion of the moment briefly overcame Todd as a lone tear slowly inched down his cheeks, cascaded over his lips, briefly stopping at his poised chin and falling to the floor. Todd gulps out a few words. "I know you were right. I want you to...."

Joe hushes Todd mid-sentence as he again embraces his son. Joe extends an arm to Donna who joins with Todd and Joe in their special moment together.

CHAPTER 23

▼

The festivities continue into the night and the usually reserved tycoons displayed their social stamina. When they worked, they labored long, hard and persistently. And when they played, each demonstrated how human they really were. But for the luxurious surroundings, this could have been the neighborhood New Years romp at Charlie's tavern in the Bronx. The big boys of business had let their hair down.

Approximately half the guests had left by 2:30 AM. Trump is at it again this time capturing the attention of Craig Evans of Global Motor Company and Ted Thorndyke of Continental News Network. Trump, the consummate business-man led a group of people into a discussion of the problems in the auto industry. He was in his favorite position at the center of attention and is obviously relishing another command performance. The situation in the auto industry is similar to the steel industry where foreign competition was beginning to take sizable chunks of the market at the expense of Global Motors and the other American car companies.

Craig Evans is speaking. "We have sizable clout in Washington, but we're still having a hella'va time convincing Congress to protect our industry. I know we're going to get relief, but God only knows when!"

Trump chimes in. "So what are you doing in the meanwhile? If you're doing the same thing as yesterday, you're obviously on the wrong path. If you're waiting for the government, you may well be waiting until hell freezes over."

Evans fires back defensively. "Paul, change at Global Motors is not as simple as you might think. There is a multitude of consultants who have to get the approval of a mess of committees, who in turn need approval from thousands of technical personnel before we can change a light bulb. I know it sounds ridiculous, but we have got a bureaucratic nightmare on our hands. I doubt that there is any solution that we haven't discussed. We know the problems and we know the solutions. Implementing solutions is our biggest headache. Failure to develop a consensus with our own people has stopped many a beneficial project before it got off the drawing board."

Trump's face flushes with excitement. "Just who the hell is in charge at Global Motors. Sounds like too many chiefs and not enough Indians. You need to take the bull by the horns and show them who is the boss. I agree it's nice to be amiable and hear people out, but in the final analysis, who the hell cares what they say if they don't agree with you. You have way too many consultants and I can show you a deep dark cave where you can shove every committee that ever existed. Committees are a waste of time, energy and ideas. I've seen too many times where they have a tendency to overstep their bounds. I often compare a committee to the infamous rattle snake that infests Texas. You just never know when the slithering conniving beast will strike."

Evans thought the analogy was cute yet very close to the point. He mounts a defense. "You're half right. It would be more effective to simply issue marching orders, but in a large company like ours, it's important that everyone is hearing the same message. Paul, you have the advantage of being the undisputed head of a relatively young company. Your style is dictatorial and you're able to get away with it. I don't think that you can compare the management methods you use at your company with what happens at Global Motors."

The red flush that started at Trump's neck has slowly risen past his chin and consumed his cheeks. He replies in folksy fashion. "They claim you can't teach an old dog new tricks. I disagree. The only dog I can't teach is a dead dog. Ten years ago I was a salesman with the largest computer company in the world. I quit because the biggest and the best couldn't adapt to new ideas. So I started my own business using those same ideas to generate business for myself. Point is, while my former employer was thinking about it, I was doing it! That's what's made the computer industry such easy pickings. It was dominated by a few large companies that because of their bureaucratic structure became slow to react in the marketplace. I'm gaining market share and they're losing it. If they continue to resist change, then they may well become that dead dog who can't learn the new tricks. You have an obligation to make sure that Global Motors doesn't become a dead dog. Right!"

Evans acquiesces with a head nod before replying. "You may have something there. Our sales continue to slip while our costs continue to increase. You're probably right! We have to do something."

Ted Thorndyke who had been silent joins in. "A lot of what Paul says makes sense. Business never was and never will be democratic. Strong business leaders are relentless dictators first and capable negotiators second. I think many of our older corporations have put away their dictators and let the negotiators run the show. And the only thing I know for sure about negotiators is that they have more talk than action."

Trump beams. "You hit the nail on the head. It's like the difference between the dreamer and the doer. One's always thinking about it while the other is always doing it. You can only paddle your canoe upstream for so long, and then you realize you're not going anyplace. If you don't change, it's just a matter of time before your best efforts are taking you backwards."

Evans looks at his watch as he replies. "Gentlemen, time for this old man to hit the sack. Paul, I appreciate your comments on change. You simplify some very difficult issues. Perhaps, we can discuss it further over lunch?"

Trump responds with uncharacteristic humility. "I appreciate your kind comments. This old seed salesman comes up with a decent idea now and then. I'll call you for lunch soon."

CHAPTER 24

▼

The group is breaking up just as Curt Davis and Bob Mellon stop by to announce they were leaving. Both of them had made the rounds of the remaining guests wishing them farewell. Trump and Thorndyke are finishing their conversation when they were approached by Mellon. Bob Mellon made it a point to let them know he and Davis are leaving the party and will be returning directly to New York.

Mellon shakes Trump's hand and then Thorndyke's while he briefly reviewed the evening. "Old Joe sure throws a hell of a party. I can't recall when I've had a better time. The food was incomparable, the entertainment sensational and his guests—well let's just say I'm honored to be among such a select group."

Trump is incredulous as he feigns a smile. The memory of Mellon's involvement in the money supply scandal is still fresh in his mind. He chose to remain anonymous as the damning information passed from his close associate, Preston Orient, directly to Joe Robbins. There was nothing to be gained by involving himself and he elected to remain in the background. Still, it was everything he could do to restrain himself in the presence of two of the key conspirators. Trump responds tongue in cheek. "I believe this is your first time at Joe's shindig. Let me assure you that the parties get better every year. Hopefully, we will all get to see another of Joe's extravaganzas, and that he can solve those financial difficulties that he talked with everyone about."

Trump's comments were innocent enough, and they got the desired response from Mellon. "We met this afternoon and I am sure that Joe Robbins will be in business for a long time. All the documents have been drawn up and we will be signing them next week when Joe returns to New York."

Trump weighs the comments. "I'm sure glad to hear that. If anybody deserves a break, Joe does. Nothing like good news to cap off a great time!"

Thorndyke had not heard of Joe's financial problems and his news-nose was aroused. "This is the first I've heard about Joe having financial problems. You say it's all taken care of?"

Trump answers. "Yeah Ted. Twenty four hours ago, it was a newsworthy event. Right now, it sounds like just another loan. So call off your journalistic dogs and enjoy the rest of the evening."

Mellon laughs as he joins in. "If a loan was big news, I would get free advertising 365 days a year." Mellon eyed the large grandfather clock and continues. "Gentlemen, Curt and I need to get out of here. We have to be back in New York for a meeting tomorrow morning of all things. Our jet is waiting at the airport now."

With that, Mellon and Davis leave immediately having effectively announced their departure from Florida. It was a subtle touch that would place them beyond suspicion in the disaster that would strike in just a few hours. They would be arriving LaGuardia just as Joe Robbins was meeting his fate in Boca Raton.

CHAPTER 25

▼

By 4:00 AM, all the guests had left with the exception of Trump. Trump jumped from one conversation to another until there was nobody left to talk with. His wife, Mary, left with the Baltroffs and returned to the Boca Club. This in itself wasn't unusual. Mary accepted the fact that her husband had an obsession with solving the world's problems especially when they involved business.

Todd retired earlier to his upstairs bedroom in the company of the alluring Donna Santoro. The security staff had largely dispersed with the guests. The wait staff was busy doing a late night superficial cleanup. The party was down to Joe Robbins and Paul Trump. Together, they walk through the mansion discussing the night's events. Soon, they found themselves in the library where they each took seats in the lavish oversized leather chairs surrounding Joe's desk.

Trump queries Joe about his financial situation. "I was speaking to Bob Mellon. He indicated that he was able to help you with your re-financing. I assume everything worked out OK."

Joe answers. "Yes, I'm out of the woods. I really feel good about the way things worked out. Sorry if I burdened you, but I just didn't know what to do and I value your advice."

"No problem Joe. I really wasn't much help. It appears you worked out the problem yourself."

Trump thought that Joe would bring up the details of the hard negotiations with Mellon and Davis. He is relieved that Joe did not bring up the conspiracy or the negotiations that had taken place earlier in the day. Joe has no idea that Trump knew anything about the conspiracy. Having settled his business with Mellon and Davis, it is Joe's intent to maintain complete secrecy.

Trump wishes to change the subject and began to ask Joe's opinions about some of the business situations they discussed earlier at the party. "There sure is a lot of concern about the way our government is being run. Can you believe that just about all of the business people here tonight thought their government was working against them? Some believe that America is being sold out by the politicians. All of them agree that government policy is largely detrimental to business. Most blame unemployment and the accompanying problems of poverty and crime on government actions that are stymieing free enterprise."

Joe is listening, but he is distracted by the photo album he left on the desk earlier that day. Joe replies. "I agree with that analysis. We need to get government off our backs. Every area they get into is ultimately either corrupted or made inefficient. The end result is they become totally ineffective at best, or a parasitic leach at worse. But, I think we all recognize these things. The real problem has always been finding someone who is willing to fight the damn system."

Trump is scratching his chin. "You know, I view government to be much like some of our large corporations that have gotten out of control. Both government and wayward corporations seem to exist on momentum. Their sheer size permits them to continue in spite of their obvious shortcomings. In business, I delight when I compete against one of the corporate dinosaurs. I know I will make a lot of money. Unfortunately, government doesn't have a competitor, so it has a tendency to perpetuate inefficiency."

Joe is in agreement. "You seem to have a firm grasp on governmental problems. Why don't you get involved? Politicians need to have balls of steel, and that just happens to be one of your primary attributes."

Trump laughs. "Problem is none of our politicians have balls at all. If they did, they would stand up for their beliefs and not their wallets, and we wouldn't be in the mess we're in today."

Joe repeats his question. "You're avoiding the question. You're the best businessman I know, and you have a firm grasp on how government should work. Why don't you get involved?"

Trump responds. "To be honest, I've considered it. Worst part of the job would be to be called a politician. I don't think I would have a problem running the country. Not much different than running a profitable company. First thing you need to do is get rid of the undesirables. Second—the rules need to be changed. Third—only one person can run the show. Fourth—align policy to benefit business. The more business prospers, the more everyone benefits. Fifth—clean up the streets so people can feel safe again. Sixth—fix the education system. There's more, but you get the idea. Good government is as much a one man show as an effective business. The appearance of democracy is important. But, all that matters is people feel they are part of the process. The people realize they don't know how to run the government and so they place their trust into the hands of the politician. The problem is that most politicians are self-serving. People would eagerly follow someone who will fix the system if they think he's sincere."

Joe shows some concern as he replies. "I think people are anxious to find leadership. And they probably would let the right person have a lot of power. But the public is so skeptical that I think Jesus Christ would have a hard time convincing them of his intentions. The citizens in this country have been burned too many times. It would take a tremendous sales job to win them over."

The conversation went on for the next hour. Both agreed in principal that strong independent leadership was the key ingredient for righting America's social and economic difficulties.

It was 4:45 when Trump glances at his watch. "I think I have overstayed my welcome. I want to thank you for a most enjoyable evening."

Robbins walks Trump to the limousine. Trump was one of the few corporate powers who traveled without his own personal bodyguard, and it reminded Joe of how strong the man always seemed to be. Joe ponders how Trump always radiated self-confidence. *Trump is a man who was genuinely comfortable with himself and it always seems to show.* Joe shakes Paul's hand as he says his farewells.

He prompts Trump once more on his latent political ambitions. "Paul, give serious consideration to some political work. The county needs someone like you."

Trump smiles as he easily slides his small frame into the huge limousine. "Who knows what the future holds. It's a possibility. Thanks again for an unforgettable evening."

Trump sits back in the limo for the 20 minute ride to the Boca Club. He reviews the evening's highlights with much satisfaction. He knows he impacted the thinking of some of America's leading businessmen. He prides himself on his ability to lend direction in an honest straight-forward manner. He considered many of his peers to be intellectual giants who frequently let themselves be sidetracked by unimportant events. They would lose their objectivity and then wonder why they didn't get results. He thought they were brilliant, but asinine. In his relentless striving, he loved them as competitors and despised them as contemporaries. That's why his advice was always so valuable. He was able to sort out seemingly complex issues and present simple, logical solutions. His whole career focused on persistently pursuing simple solutions until he got what he wanted.

He rests his head peering through the moon roof into the clear star-studded sky. A shooting star came out of the eastern skies racing toward a preordained destination. Trump momentarily thought himself to be that fleeting star. *I too am a powerful, elite and resolute force racing towards a new mission.*

His righteous convictions make him a candidate for life's most exciting adventures. After all, God did bestow upon him the unique talents that had made him so successful. He recognized an obligation to use those talents to achieve his fate. As the star disappeared on the horizon, Trump knew he had his next task from the Almighty. He whispered to himself. *I will be the president that will solve America's problems and restore her greatness.* Having mentally committed himself to the task, he rested his eyes contemplating the strategy that would take him to his self proclaimed prophecy.

Joe Robbins is pleasantly tired. He walks back to his library drawn by the memory of the open album on his desk. Standing over his desk, he recalls the startling reality of his dream earlier that day. He flipped through the album hoping to recreate those precious moments he had subliminally shared with Lisa. Realizing the futility of his actions, he closes the album and places it back in position on the shelves.

He walks toward the French doors which open onto the rear patio. Joe wants to view the morning sunset which would rise in just a few minutes. He is pleased with himself having solved the most critical business problem of his life. The party had been everything he could have wanted. He is completely at peace with himself as he strolls the last few steps to the doorway. As he clasps the knob, his bliss is interrupted by the longing he had for Lisa. *It would all be perfect if only Lisa could be with me!* Joe opens the door and steps onto the patio. His final moments of life are filled with haughty euphoria as he walks toward the eastern sky in his date with destiny.

CHAPTER 26

▼

Todd gets up from bed glancing briefly at the naked figure of Donna Santoro. She is sleeping soundly even as Todd attempts to wake her with a series of purposeful jarring noises. It's been quite a night with the ravenous woman and he hoped to wake her for still another romp. Realizing that his contrived attempts to wake Donna were in vain, he walks over to the French doors. He opens the doors and is treated to a cool morning breeze as he steps onto the balcony. He looks down the side of the mansion and sees the eastern sun fully exposed on the horizon. He guesses that it is about 7:00AM. Todd has been in bed for less than 5 hours, but he is not tired. Most of the time had been consumed in love-making with Donna, needing only an occasional shut eye interlude to recharge his youthful passions. Too energized to lie in bed, he decides to go for an early morning jog on the beach. He returns to the bedroom, closing the doors firmly with a slight bang in a final attempt to awaken Donna, but to no avail. Todd is somewhat frustrated by his futile efforts, but remains respectful of the tired beauty. He gathers his running attire, silently dresses, and makes his way downstairs.

Todd descends to the first floor using the ornate railing of the elaborate staircase for a series of stretching motions. He makes his way to the kitchen where he grabs a protein bar before scurrying out the side door. He opens the breakfast snack, and hastily devours it while simultaneously beginning a slow paced run. He proceeds around the lake heading in the general direction of the beach. He begins to pick up the pace as he hits the sand. The increased resistance of the loosely packed soil would ensure a vigorous workout.

Soon, his mind is full of the activities of the last 24 hours. *What a day!!* The revelation from his father that the company was no longer in jeopardy along with the attendant explanation had left Todd relieved, but confused. *How are such high crimes possible? I can't believe Dad was able to pull it off! Is it really over?*

Mentally, he jumps to the pleasant memories of the day, beginning with greeting Donna at the airport. She was radiant, standing curbside, waving feverishly to attract Todd's attention. Jumping into the Corvette convertible, she leaned over and gently kissed Todd, while speaking hurriedly about an uneventful flight. Her piercing blue eyes entranced Todd as she continued to chatter about the upcoming New Year celebration. Soon, they were pulling into the estate and Todd was showing her around the house and grounds. The brief tour of the luxurious mansion had its desired effect. The young woman is swooning with ecstasy as she realizes how fortunate she was to have met the young executive. Todd was in continued admiration of every move of the well proportioned Donna. He frequently stumbled for the suitable words which would further impress her. It was a good beginning for them, and they both sought to further their new relationship with whatever favorable impressions they could muster. Todd is relishing these recent memories as he jogs his way down the beach.

Todd is now running at a fairly rapid pace and sweat from his forehead begins to bead into streams of salty water attempting an attack on his eyes. He brushes away the intrusion as he continues to recall the prior day's events. *The party was unreal. You had to be there to appreciate it! Donna was hot—dressed to kill in an evening gown that accented her youthful body. Everyone noticed her and they should!* She was vivacious and full of youthful banter among a group of older, sophisticated rich people. They greeted Donna graciously, and left leaving Todd with a knowing wink or speculative grin. The people, the dinner, the fireworks, the orchestra and the surroundings had left Donna filled with anticipation, and vulnerable to the ever attendant Todd.

Todd ran about three miles before turning back towards the mansion. He again brushes the accumulated sweat from his face. His mind was still engaged with his pursuit of Donna. *The evening had worked its magic.* He recalls how Donna had subtlety grabbed his hand, looked into his eyes and proclaimed she was tired. *Would he walk her to her room?* The passions of this endearing couple were fully aroused, and they would play out over the course of the night. *What a night!!*

Todd decreased his speed to a slow trot, and then to a rapid walk as he began the cool down process. He is aroused as he approaches the mansion still entertaining the blissful thoughts of the glamorous Donna. He rapidly ascends the granite stairs leading to the rear patio. He hastily takes two steps at a time, playfully thinking that Donna might be awake by now. His body glistens with the excess body water, and now gives off a faint odor. *I have to shower. Wow! Donna and I in the shower!* The thought is pervasive and his passion was again stoked with the pleasant visualization of bathing with the just awakened vixen.

He is immersed in this mental picture as he approaches the top step, and is grinning excitedly as his toe catches on the end of the final step. Instantly, his body goes out of control as he spins haphazardly toward the unforgiving stone surface. His knee hits the hard surface first, instantly opening a wide gash. He is still falling and turning uncontrollably as his elbow clips the rough surface. In a second, the spin ends with a hard sounding thud as the back of his head absorbs the final shock from the accidental fall. Todd lies on the ground and momentarily observes the quirky stars that accompany head trauma in comic book depictions. Temporarily, he loses consciousness.

In less than a minute, he awakes to an escalating pain. He reconstructs the event that placed him in this position. *Donna, shower, trip, fall, head—stars! I feel pain!* With his eyes partially opened, he begins to search his body for evidence of any damage. He raises his right elbow, which is throbbing intensely, but did not detect any discernable damage. Agonizing, he bends and raises his right leg while slightly lifting his head, to reveal the opened wound on his knee. The direct hit on his knee cap hurt a lot, but the two inch gash appeared superficial. Feeling woozy, he gradually lowers his leg and his head to regain composure. *Stars—I took a pretty good shot!*

The back of his head pulsates with pain, and he explores the source of the incessant throbbing. Instinctively, he raises his right arm, but the pain from that area is still intense. He lowers the arm to relieve the hurt. He then raises his left hand and reaches behind his head to inspect the source of the ache. He raises his head slightly, and feels a large knot and the presence of sticky moisture. He mentally acknowledges that he must be bleeding and wipes his hand over the ground to remove the clammy residue. Instantly, he panics as he feels his hand moving through a seemingly endless pond of wetness. *What have I done?*

He jerks his head up to access the situation, but becomes dizzy and nauseous with the sudden movement. Todd then gradually rolls his entire body to the left side squeezing his eyes shut to alleviate the rush of fresh agony that engulfs him. As he rises, he opens his eyes to reveal a sea of dark red liquid. Amidst so much blood, he is surprised he could still lift himself. *I must be dead!* The final horror struck Todd in his next movement when he raises the left side of his body to a prone 45 degree position. His face contorts with feelings of fear and intense anguish as he gasps "*Oh no—God no!*" He is looking directly into the death stare of his father. Todd loses conscience and collapses on top of the corpse of his father.

▼

Detective Allen Merrill of the Boca Raton police department was at home when his beeper flashed the message. It was approximately 8:15 AM, January 1, 1980, and he thought he would have a relatively uneventful day. He volunteered to be on call this New Years Day as he had done in the past. In the past, it had proven to be a good day to get rid of the rotating holiday obligation. *Quiet with little or no disturbances.* Today would prove to be the exception.

Merrill calls into the station and is immediately informed of the homicides at the Robbins estate. The information is incomplete, but the relayed 911 emergency message indicates that two men are dead at the estate, and that street patrols had already been dispatched. Merrill immediately jumps into his vehicle and proceeds to the Robbins home.

The wealthy of Boca Raton gave freely to support the needs of the Boca Raton police, and the most aggressive of budgets was never an issue for the elite of this prosperous city. In exchange, the affluent residents insisted on the very best personnel, equipment, technological resource, protection and service. Merrill thought of the implications of the deaths of two residents as he raced to the estate. *No stone would go unturned!* Soon, the occasional sound of a police siren turned into a continuous blare as the response level increased. Speeding through lights, stop signs and around various obstacles, the sound of his siren is soon lost in the high pitched crescendo. Police were erecting road blocks at every intersection. Some of the officers are half dressed indicating their rapid response to a general call. *This is a big deal!* thinks

Merrill is close to the mansion when he thought of the personal insecurity of these fabulously rich people. He recalls a conversation with one of the magnates when discussing a security issue. *If I have two and the other guy has one, he will try to find a way to take one of mine so he has two.* This simplified statement spoke volumes of the need of the rich and accomplished to protect their holdings. Merrill had seen the needs of these affluent few supersede the needs of the less privileged majority. He often privately notated that our country claims to be a democracy where the interest of the majority are given the greatest priority, but nothing could be further from the truth. His experience has shown that we are a republic which is a nation of laws, and the people who make the laws generally do so in a manner which gives the minority the greatest priority. *Money talks and bullshit walks!*

His conclusion was simple. People acquiesce to the system because they benefit from the system. Merrill is proof of the statement. *In five more years, I get a great retirement, equal to 90% of my full salary. In the meanwhile, I have great job security, good pay and lucrative cash side jobs. And best of all, nobody bothers me. I got mine!* Merrill pulls into the driveway and turns off his siren. There are two squad cars at the gate and five more in the driveway. *It's going to be a long day.*

Merrill speaks to an officer who directs him to the rear patio. Merrill goes through the house, into the library and out the doors to the patio. Lying before him, two feet from the railing is the body of Joe Robbins surrounded by a puddle of blood. Allen Merrill knew Robbins from previous security jobs he had done at the mansion. The first officer at the scene was standing by waiting for Merrill to take charge.

Merrill approaches the officer "Where's the second victim?"

The officer replies. "There's just one homicide, sir. There is another person, who we initially thought was dead, but he has injuries to his head, arm and leg."

Merrill looks around and sees a man and a woman sitting on the patio steps watched over by another officer. Observing the blood soaked shirt of the man, he asks "Is that the injured person?"

"Yes sir. When I arrived, he was lying, unconscious, beside the dead man. The woman was screaming beside him. He came to a few minutes later and I asked him to sit there until you arrived."

Merrill approaches the man on the steps and recognized him as Todd Robbins. In the most comforting manner he could muster, he questions Todd. "What happened?"

Todd looks up briefly. His eyes are inflamed and red, his face is partially covered in blood, and his lips are quivering. He grips his head without responding and quickly buries it in the lap of the woman. A low moan emanates from the man, and then a deep guttural mourning sound. A loud tortured scream precedes his verbal response. "God why? Why God—Why?"

The attending officer speaks. "He's been that way since he awoke, Sir. He is not responding to anyone, including the woman."

Merrill decides to wait to question Todd. He motions to the woman to come to him, but as she attempts to get up, Todd firmly grabs her and would not let her go. Merrill waves the woman off, and requests a doctor for Todd.

Merrill knew the house, grounds and security system well. He was also aware of the grand New Years party, the guest list and the extensive security precautions. His first thought was that the case should be easy to solve given the advanced security measures that were in place. Nothing would be further from the truth.

Merrill returned to the first officer on the scene and queried. "Who called this in?"

"The woman said she phoned it in"

"Do we know who she is?

The officer replies. "Donna Santoro. She said she is a friend of Todd Robbins. She said she found them lying together on the ground, and called 911. At first, she thought they were both dead, but claimed the young man stirred briefly before we arrived. After the man revived, I ask that they sit down on the steps until you arrive. That's everything we have to date."

Merrill notes the comments and asks. "Where is the house security detail?"

"I have not seen any private security people."

Merrill continues. "Where are the house service personnel?"

"Sir, I have not seen anyone other than these three since I arrived."

Merrill knows there are always a security and a help staff on the grounds. "Gather a detail, search the grounds and bring anyone you find to me, immediately! Do not disturb any physical evidence on your search. I will check the guard house."

Merrill immediately goes to the familiar guard house where he had spent many days and nights doing special details for Joe Robbins. Entering the house, he calls out for anyone. There is no response. He next went to the monitoring room where every monitor is shut down. Finally, he went to the camera tape storage area, and all the current tapes are missing from the video decks. There is a secured power supply room complete with a power back up system in a separate area. Both of these systems had been compromised. Merrill is convinced that professional assassins had done this job.

The grounds search detail came up with nothing. Merrill was drawing a complete blank. He put out a call to bring in the house security staff and the house help staff. He ordered them all back to the estate immediately. He needed to speak with Todd Robbins and Donna Santoro as soon as they were able. Reporters had begun to assemble at the front entry gate. The incessant wailing of sirens together with the police road blocks had created a frenzy which would peak in 24 hours with the arrival of news crews from around the world. A knot in Merrill's stomach tightened knowing he had nothing to say to them.

CHAPTER 28

▼

Curt Davis and Bob Mellon were to enjoy their wildly profitable scam for a brief period of time. After the death of Joe Robbins, they found themselves in a bit of a quandary. They realized they had been badly compromised in the money supply scheme. They tried to discover the sources that led Joe Robbins to so adeptly describe their illicit business, but ran into a series of brick walls. Even after invoking their considerable financial and regulatory influence, they were unable to discover the source of the leak.

Davis, Mellon and their associates at the United State Treasury, the CIA and the Federal Reserve decided it was time to shut down the swindle. Jointly, they devised a computer crash which safely and forever buried any indication of the irregularities. The crash made major headlines in March of 1980, but the arranged journalistic spin revolved around gaping holes in national security systems, and ignored the financial implications.

Gradually, interest rates fell to the traditional 8 to 10 percent, and the return of a robust economy effectively hid the siphoning of hundreds of billions of dollars by the gang of five. After carefully reshuffling the hidden profits with a series of money transfers through select Swiss banks, the ill-gotten billions disappeared in the cosmic black hole of finance.

The cause of the computer crash was ultimately blamed on a computer hacker who gained access to government files, and created havoc with the data bases. Although thoroughly investigated, the trail ended abruptly and without any suspects in a sophisticated computer room in an abandoned Pittsburgh warehouse. The genius behind the digital slight of hand had disappeared!

But, the culture of greed which manifests itself in unbridled capitalistic pursuits will create the environment for still larger raids on business, government and the economy. Greed would be condoned as a necessary prerequisite for success, and gradually more and more Americans would adopt the philosophy of profits at any cost. Ones greed will be tempered only by one's imagination. Small thinkers would be drawn to petty larcenies while those with grand ideas would up the ante as they raid our paychecks, our pensions, our corporations and our government in thousands of clever schemes. If you can dream it, you can do it! The only caveat is to not get caught before you have accumulated sufficient wealth to buy yourself out of any crime you may have committed! The future would present opportunities for larceny on a grander and more prevalent scale for those willing to sell their souls for tomorrow's earnings! This is the wind song that will infect the American dream in the decades going into the 21st Century. It is this slowly growing cancer which will ultimately consume us and lead to our demise. It will be left to a modern day avenging angel in the form of a distraught Todd Robbins to devise the plot which will cause these excesses of capitalism to destroy the world's greatest country!

CHAPTER 29

▼

The early 1980's were chaotic times for the economy. The roller coaster changes in the interest rates were just one part of a seesawing economy which saw large industries literally disintegrate in a climate of competitive turmoil. Such was the case for the steel industry in Pittsburgh, Pennsylvania. Steel production represented the foundation of a vibrant economy. For more than 100 years, generations of Pittsburghers earned good pay, great benefits and lifetime job security in the steel mills which lined the Allegheny, Monongahela and Ohio rivers. The mills and the related support and fabricating industries went on for tens of miles at a time. They appeared like a giant octopus with 3 huge tentacles emanating in downtown Pittsburgh and winding themselves along the three rivers in an endless scene of large industrial buildings, noxious smokestacks and giant blast furnaces. Pittsburgh had obtained an absolute dominance in the steel business, and was internationally recognized as a major world supplier of the industrial metal. This mammoth industry, with the immense investment in land, buildings, and infrastructure seemed invulnerable. Add to this the highly skilled workmen with proven abilities developed from their years in the business, and it appeared that it would be near impossible for anyone to compete with this well established industry.

Over the years, small towns had been established along the rivers which provided homes and shopping for the largely working class laborers who were the backbone of the steel industry. In many neighborhoods, a man could walk to his job in the mills, and after his shift, he could pick up groceries for the family on the walk home. The work was hot, hard and dirty, but over time as wages and benefits increased, the workers acclimated to the working conditions. Many Pittsburghers lived, worked and played in clear view of the steel mill facilities. Quiet living was frequently interrupted by the sound of sirens announcing the change of a work shift, or some loud explosion emanating from the mills. Daily, but without schedule, a large cloud of dust accompanied by the venomous smell of sulfur filled the air as one of the smokestacks spewed forth the residue of the continuous steel production. The dust settled in a thin veneer over cars, trucks, buildings and ground painting the towns in the reddish, gray sooty remains of the steel making process. Industrial noises and air pollution were an integral part of the steel business. It was in this environment that Pittsburgh became one of the leading producers of steel for the nation and the world.

Opportunity and adversity were the opposing forces that lead to the birth, growth and death of the steel business in Pittsburgh. The opportunity was in the form of thousands of jobs which became available to the surge of immigrants who came to the United States in the 19th century. Culturally different, poorly educated, but none the less strongly motivated, these new Americans invested their energies in the emerging steel business. Their hope was they become part of the growth and prosperity of the enterprise. For awhile, the paltry pay and the regular job offered by the steel companies was adequate to meet the meager needs of the fledgling immigrants. Slowly, they began to want for more. Whispered sounds of individual discontent gave way to blatant shouts of worker demands, and the spirit of unified adversity was born. The rebellion culminated in Homestead, a suburb of Pittsburgh, where a clash between workers and company hired police resulted in the deaths of hundreds of workers. The company won the battle of Homestead, but the awakening of a national social conscience paved the way for a new beginning for the steel worker.

Adversity gave way to opportunity as the workers organized unions who gained increased pay, new benefits and job security. The business grew as the economy grew, and the union made certain that the workers enjoyed an equitable part of the prosperity. Pittsburgh seemed to have hit the magic formula and new buildings were added to the ever expanding steel complex.

But then adversity struck again as the industry hit a decade long impasse in the 1930's as the effects of the Great Depression wreaked havoc on the economy. The industry and the working man both suffered during this oppressive period.

Opportunity came, as it frequently does, in the form of a war. But, this was just not any war. This was World War II. In 1941, America was jolted awake by an attack on Pearl Harbor, and was pulled into a raging conflict that had already consumed much of the world. American workers wiped the sleep of the depression from their eyes, brushed the cobwebs of inactivity from the machinery, and proceeded to develop an industrial mechanism that became the envy of the earth. The steel industry led the charge, as their products were needed for tanks, trucks, canons, ships and the other necessities of war. The steel mills operated 24-7 in an effort to supply the tools for the conflict. A shortage of labor forced the available workers into mandatory overtime, and Rosie the riveter was called upon to make up for the labor deficiency. World War II was a great time for American industry. The war abruptly ended the decade long depression and began a period of renewed growth and prosperity. Industry and workers both benefited from the 4 year long encounter, and shared in the affluence of the period. America was a winner!

The war did have a cost. The cost in blood for the engaged countries was on a scale not witnessed by mankind. Fifty-two countries actively participated in the encounter and the cost was over 62 million lives. The United States contributed 418,500 lives to the conflagration, which paled in proportion to the 23.2 million casualties incurred by Russia, the 5.6 million Polish dead, and the 10 million Chinese victims. Germany lost 7.5 million lives and Japan lost 2.6 million lives.

The post war years represented an unparalleled period of opportunity for the United States. Yes, America paid with the lives of their soldiers, but the country was otherwise untouched. The only material signs of war, beside the soldier's cemeteries, were the immense industries and highly efficient factory complexes that had rapidly developed in support of the war effort. The pent up consumer demand that started during the depression years and continued through the war years was about to explode. American citizens had pockets full of cash they were unable to use during the war years. The spending spree began as soon as the returning troop ships entered the harbors. Americans wanted cars, houses, appliances and a full range of consumer goods they were unable to get during the war. Businesses shifted gears into peacetime production and the economy boomed as it sought to satisfy the pent up demand of the past 15 years. The victorious Americans were jubilant.

To the victors go the spoils, and Americans would enjoy the spoils for a very long time. With the exception of the United States, many of the countries of the world were obliterated by the war. Homes, businesses, factories, industries, roads, bridges, utilities, and complete infrastructures had to be rebuilt throughout the world. America stood in the enviable position of being the primary provider of goods and services to the planet during the post World War II years. Faced with little or no competition, The United States would become an economic super power in the ensuing years and decades. Business was, in fact, so good that there was plenty for everyone. Labor and management shared in the windfall, and the county prospered. A large and secure middle class formed along with a growing and profitable business community. This period represents the high times for capitalism in the United States.

The steel industry fully participated in the robust times following World War II. Steel was necessary for just about any part of the rebuilding process. From basic transportation to building construction and renewed infrastructures, steel was a basic ingredient of the recovery. The steel mills multiplied to supply the demands of American consumers and the world reconstruction. The economic windfall continued through the 1950's and the 1960's carried on largely by the momentum of the war years.

But, cracks slowly started to develop in the industrial boom during the 1970's. Steel workers, represented by powerful unions, pressed their demands for more pay, more benefits, fewer hours and a torrent of impractical work rules. Steel industry management had grown content with prosperity. They agreed to the unreasonable worker demands in order to continue production. Management, having grown fat and lazy, failed to implement the technological advances and work practices that would have countered the unrealistic worker demands. Greedy workmen, usurping unions, outdated production facilities and complacent management comprised the formula for failure that would ultimately destroy the steel industry in the United States.

These inefficiencies were witnessed by the growing economies of Europe and Asia. Steel imports from these sectors became competitive with steel produced in the United States. Slowly, a trickle of imports began to entice American consumers. The dribble turned into a torrent as Americans recognized increased value from the lower priced and higher quality imports. The 1980's would witness the demise of the steel industry in Pittsburgh. Giant complexes were, at first, scaled back and then closed. Tens of thousands of steel workers were fired and the miles of factories that lined the three rivers of Pittsburgh turned to rust as the steel industry went through its death throes. By the 1990's, only a smattering of survivors could be found in the ominous City of Steel. By the turn of the century, the steel industry was a minor part of the Pittsburgh economy. Pittsburgh now seeks its future in the ambiguous arena of information technology. Many of the river front mills have been replaced with parks, shopping centers, restaurants and other service businesses. The single greatest reminder of the lost industry is the Pittsburgh Steelers, and chances are the origin of this name is lost on many of the younger fans.

So-What happened to this seemingly invulnerable and gigantic enterprise? The workers blamed the companies, and the companies blamed the unions, while the government promised an economic rebirth in something called the information economy. The steel industry has relocated to a climate of lower wages and reduced worker benefits. Pieces of the business can be found in the non-union south, but largely the business has migrated to foreign lands where cheap labor is abundant, and ready workers compete for the opportunity to earn the meager pay.

The steel industry has followed the lead of other manufacturing businesses in the United States. Increasingly, the business of making things has been exported to other countries. These countries offer masses of laborers willing and able to work for much less than their American counterparts. Chances are your clothing, televisions, electronics, dishes, pots, pans, toys, watches, appliances, building materials, telephones, cell phones and computers are substantially made in a foreign country.

The automobile industry in the United States is now going through a fight for survival as it seeks to compete with a host of lower priced and higher quality imports. As is in all the other failed American industries, consumers are choosing the higher valued imports over their own products.

By 2000, the United States produced very few goods for the world, but offered the world an immense marketplace of some 300 million consumers eager to spend their money for imports. By 2005, the American consumer was basically tapped out as our economy recorded the first negative savings rate since the Great Depression. Effectively, we lost our ability to consume.

But do not fear because we still produce one item that is the envy of the world. Peoples and countries gladly surrender their goods and services for this all important, uniquely American resource. This exclusive product is sought after throughout the world, and the world continues to accumulate it in immense quantities. No, it is not the information based business that the politicians and economists promised was the economic wave of the future. It is something that costs only a fraction of a penny to produce, but the world craves it none the less. This wondrous creation is none other than the American Dollar!

CHAPTER 30

▼

It was March of 1984 when David Paine entered the State Unemployment office in Braddock, Pennsylvania. The office was crowded, as usual, with 10 organized lines each equally holding about 35 individuals. He paused briefly, glanced at his watch, and guessed it would take about 2 hours to be waited on.

David was 41 years old and in good health. He was of Italian and German descent. His blue eyes and light brown hair favored the German lineage, and few people suspected he was 50 percent Italian. He weighed 180 pounds, and was about 5'9" tall. All in all, his appearance was quite average. He had graduated high school and went on to college for 1 year. David was a quick learner, but a poor student. In high school, he was a border line "C" average student who became bored and sometimes disruptive in the mundane class atmosphere. David considered education a waste of time, and when the opportunity came up to work in the steel mills, he quickly abandoned any thoughts of higher education.

David worked hard at his job, and received a rapid series of promotions that permitted him to provide quite well for his wife and four children. Promotions in the strong union mills were a difficult task, but David was able to advance. He had an ability to get along with both his peers and supervisors.

David had another problem. He always felt he should be doing something else. His work earned him a good living, but he was always searching in his mind for some purpose to his life. Being busy, earning good money and providing for a growing family was enough to stifle the haunting desire. And so, he drifted through two decades of work in the steel mill. As time went by, the frustration grew. David continued to seek out the answers in his mind, but was never able to find the meaningful purpose he sought. When his lay off notice arrived, he was full of mixed emotion. He was concerned about how he would be able to provide a similar income, but he was happy that he might be able to pursue another dream. He simply needed to find that meaningful purpose that had been so evasive for so long!

David was always on edge when he had to visit the unemployment office. The State of Pennsylvania had a procedure of causing all applicants for unemployment benefits to appear ever 2 weeks to prove their eligibility, and to update the record of their search for other employment. He pulled the Pittsburgh Sun Telegraph from his jacket pocket and reluctantly joined one of the lines. The headlines proclaimed **'Pittsburgh Steel Closing Homestead Operation'**. The article read Leo Baltroff, CEO of Pittsburgh Steel was closing the plant and moving operations to Mexico. Baltroff said the operation was not profitable and that the move to Mexico would place the ailing steel maker in more competitive position with other foreign steel companies. Twenty thousand local jobs would be lost in the next year.

David motions to a man in the adjacent line and comments. "Looks like the rats are deserting the ship. We lose again!"

The big black man in the adjoining line replies. "Yeah. What else did you expect? We gave them our lives in those stinking mills, and this is the way they repay us! I should have left them 9 years ago when my brother asked me to join his business, but I couldn't leave. My wife just had our fifth kid, and I was concerned about the future. So, here I am living in the future, collecting unemployment checks, looking for a decent job and hoping I can make the mortgage payment."

David responds. "I know the feeling. I got 23 years in the mills. I started right out of high school. I don't know any other line of work. I can't find any work that pays even close to what we were getting in the mill. I keep looking, but not too much out there."

"Tell me about it. My wife throws me out the door every morning, and tells me to find something. She's a good woman, but she's afraid. I only have 2 months of checks coming from the State, and then I will have nothing. Hell, I'm already behind on my bills, and the damn credit people keep calling about money. My wife says we are going to lose our home. The bank started proceedings. I don't know what's going to happen? To tell you the truth, I'm scared!"

The big man pauses to retrieve a handkerchief from his rear pocket. He wipes the sweat from his eyes. David looks at the large hands that are scarred and calloused from the years of work in the mills. He was over six foot tall, with broad shoulders which tapered to a much smaller waist. A protruding stomach pouch evidences the inactivity of the past year since he had been laid off. All in all, the black man had an over powering physical presence. David's mind briefly drifted. *I would hate to run into him in a dark alley late at night! But, then again, the man is in the same quicksand as I am. No job, no prospects, nothing to do, bills piling up, and a constant fear of the future always tugging at your mind.* None the less, David feels sorry for this giant of a man who appeared to be so fragile in this climate of uncertainty.

The line continued to inch forward as man after man went through the indoctrination, and signed the form which entitled him to a few more checks. The person in front of him finally approached the enclosed cage, and quietly discussed his situation with the young clerk. The man was apparently having some difficulty. He was pointing erratically at his card, and poking the card in frustrating gestures obviously attempting to make some point with the clerk. The clerk was responding underlining information with a pen. The whispered conversation continued for some time.

And then the clerk suddenly broke the hushed conversation. "Why can't you people understand the way this works?" The clerk grabbed his head and visibly ridiculed the man with rolling eyes and a contemptuous glare. He then ordered the man away from the cage in a loud voice." Please move away! There's nothing more I can do to help you! You are out of benefits!"

The retort was loud enough to capture the attention of the large group in the office. The applicant was temporarily frozen in disbelief. He stammered "You don't understand1 I have to feed my family. I don't have any money. I need help."

The youthful clerk was relatively new at the unemployment office. The state hired a number of new employees to process the final payments of the dying industry. The large lines of unemployed workers were a daily occurrence at the Braddock office. These lines were due to the massive shut down that had occurred in the giant steel works in Rankin and Braddock. The local economy, which had been totally dependent on the steel business, was in a shambles. In an ironic twist, the State Unemployment office was the one of the few employment opportunities available in the area.

The clerk, in a state of youthful petulance, then made a big mistake as he loudly proclaimed. "Buddy, you need to get a job. The State can't support you forever!"

The applicant briefly stared at the clerk. He clenched his fist and his face turned a brilliant red as his blood boiled with resentment. He screamed out. "You're an asshole!"

The enraged man jumped onto the counter and hurdled over the caged barrier. Within seconds, he was swinging at the clerk with wild punches. One of the blows found its mark, and the clerk's nose spewed a torrent of blood. He continued the assault on the dazed clerk who had fallen to the ground and huddled in a protective fetal position. Another clerk jumped on the assailant in an attempt to subdue him. Simultaneously, a security guard appeared with a club and hit the aggressor on the head, instantly opening a gash on the man's forehead. The guard continued to swing at the semi-conscious man with the bloodied club.

The other men in the hall were clearly agitated. They shouted and screamed obscenities as they moved forward in mass. It was the big, black man who made the next move. In a frenzied attempt to assist his fellow worker, he grabbed at the bars on the caged divider and pulled at it in an attempt to tear it down. The crowd joined the effort, and the barrier tumbled and the mob descended upon the security guard. It was not a pretty site as the horde then proceeded to tear the office apart.

In the midst of this mayhem, David found a side door and left the office. The frustration and futility that engulfed the jobless workers had vented itself on a few clerks, a security guard and an office building. It did not seem to make sense, but it raged out of control, none the less.

David got into his car, and proceeded to leave the area. Police cars whizzed past him heading to the besieged unemployment office. As he rode down Braddock Avenue, he noted the deterioration of the many retail stores, banks, movie house and service businesses which had once served a prosperous town. He recalled a time, not long ago, when workers and families came from surrounding towns to shop and entertain themselves in a well maintained business district. The regular pay days brought the habitual customers, and everyone benefited from the area's affluence. And now, broken windows, empty buildings and garbage strewn sidewalks evidenced the precipitous decline that had transformed the area. David wondered how and why something so good for so many turned into something so bad. Although he did not realize it at the time, David had found the basis for his life's work. The economic and social calamities that accompanied the shattered steel industry would provide the meaningful pursuit he frantically sought for so many years.

CHAPTER 31

▼

In the years that followed his aborted career in the steel business, David Paine was to become involved in numerous social, political and economic issues. He did many different things to earn a living, but by and large, his true vocation lied in the quandaries posed by American business failures. The many reasons advanced for the failure of the large and prevalent steel industry never satisfied his searching and inquisitive mind. No doubt greedy workers, usurping unions, mindless management and unconcerned government all played some part in the breakdown. He was searching for the underlying force which at first unifies and directs the components of success which are necessary to build a business, but later corrupts these same components and sets into motion the adversarial conflicts which result in the inevitable collapse of the enterprise. David thought *how is it that so many can work for so long just to fail?*

The latter part of the 20th century was a time when many industries failed in the United States. The steel industry was just one of many enterprises that would not succeed. It was accompanied by television, textiles, electronics and a host of other manufacturers. Large and successful companies furloughed American workers, deserted American plants and elected to start over again in a foreign environment. David thought that there is a great boldness and arrogance in the decisions made by these fleeing companies. The boldness comes in the act of firing the very Americans who had built the businesses. The arrogance comes in the anticipation the absconding companies can still sell their goods and services to the very Americans they forsook. The lingering question remained the same in David's mind. *How is it that so many can work for so long just to fail?*

As time passed, David came to recognize the inherent desire of all people to advance their interests in their pursuits. Self interest is and will always be an integral part of the human being. For the majority of people, work is but a chore necessary to increase one's self interest. Indeed in a materialistic world, work is a mandatory if one is to survive. Self interest in the form of work becomes the building block of human endeavor. Companies develop, build and become successful based on the work associated with self interest. None the less, the recurring question remained the same. *How is it that so many can work for so long just to fail?*

Part of the answer to this pervasive question lies in another human trait. What happens when people no longer wish to work to increase their self interest? In a materialistic world, less work or no work results in decreased self interest. Quit your job tomorrow and your material self interest will be immediately diminished by the amount of your paycheck.

The greater problem is more insidious. Slow down on your job and ultimately your self interest is diminished. When the union insists on inefficient job rules, the self interest of the worker and the company is ultimately diminished. When the company makes unfair demands upon the workers, both the worker and company self interest is diminished. When a company fails to give the workers the proper tools to accomplish the work, both the company and the worker self interest is diminished. When management condones and accepts inefficient practices, both company and worker self interest is diminished.

The idea of enhanced materialistic self interest based on work is not an exclusive American concept. It applies to all human beings who seek materialistic gain. When an industry moves from the United States to South America with the same flawed concepts of work, then it becomes simply a matter of time before that industry fails in its new environment.

David reached these conclusions in the early 1990's. He felt that moving industries to other countries resulted in substantial long term damage to America and Americans while giving relatively short term benefits to the companies who moved their plants to foreign countries. Given these conclusions, David was left with the same question. *How is it that so many can work for so long just to fail?* He now added a second question. *Why are American companies permitted to destroy American jobs by exporting our industries to foreign countries?*

CHAPTER 32

▼

David Paine moved his family to Fort Myers, Florida in 1988. Initially, he worked in a retail store as a sales and service consultant. He lasted 2 years before moving on to another job in a similar capacity. David never found much satisfaction in working these jobs and found himself frequently changing positions. He earned enough money to get by, and found himself always seeking answers to economic, political and social problems. In his spare time, he involved himself with different organizations and causes which he thought could make some difference.

His quest for meaningful involvements followed a meandering path. He found himself supporting groups sponsoring lower taxes, political term limits, representative government, government waste, accountability and foreign trade policies. Some efforts were successful and resulted in legislative changes. Unfortunately, many of the changes were soon subverted by the politicians who found new ways to raise taxes, spend frivolously, and waste tax payer's money. It seemed that genuine representative government was elusive, and perhaps not possible. David thought political party affiliation was incidental. He believed both Democratic and Republican platforms and candidates were unresponsive to American needs. So he abandoned his traditional Democratic affiliation and became an Independent. Most causes proved to be exercises in futility, and David became disgusted with his inability to create meaningful change. *Perhaps, you really can't fight city hall!*

In April of 1992, David Paine made a decision to become involved in supporting the presidential aspirations of Paul Trump. The decision did not come easily for David. He had involved himself in so many fruitless issues that he thought this could be a waste of time.

The phone call came in from Nancy Phillips, an activist that he had worked with on a term limitations for politicians.

"David. There is a meeting at the Breeze restaurant next Tuesday concerning Paul Trump. I think you would be interested in helping this man."

David replies. "I do not know Paul Trump. What makes you think I would be interested?

Nancy answers. "I have heard of him, and I have done some research. He is an independent business man from Texas, and he is taking serious opposition to both the Democrats and Republicans. He lumps them together as Republicrats. He is opposed to the North American Free Trade Agreement and claims the American people do not have representative government. He feels America is losing its industrial and manufacturing base to foreigners, and that it needs to stop now!"

Nancy continued with the background information for another five minutes. Her excitement resonated in her presentation and she sold David with her enthusiasm. Nancy had said enough to interest David in the meeting.

"Okay Nancy. What time is the meeting?"

"Ten o'clock next Tuesday morning."

"All right! I'll be there."

The conversation concluded with some comments on local politics. After hanging up the phone, David briefly reflected on Nancy's comments about Trump. He had heard of the man's business accomplishments, but had not followed his political aspirations. He marked his calendar for the meeting.

CHAPTER 33

▼

David Paine is now working as a real estate agent and he enjoyed a flexible schedule. On Tuesday morning, he set aside two hours to attend the meeting. As he traveled north on Cleveland Avenue, he thought of the many issues he had worked on in the last 3 years. He bounced from one issue to the next seeking an illusive satisfaction for his work. He had thought of completely abandoning political work because of the continued frustrations, but seemed to be drawn to matters he thought needed work. He pulled into the parking lot at the Breeze restaurant, and quickly noted the meeting would not be crowded. He entered the restaurant and spotted Nancy with a group of about 10 people in a one corner. He approached the group and recognized six of the people from his past political efforts.

Nancy was moderator for the gathering. She made the appropriate introductions before proceeding to discuss the agenda. David immediately picked up on the energy coming from the meeting. They were genuinely thrilled with Paul Trump. Everyone but David seemed to know of the credentials of this presidential candidate. The Trump Petition Committee was formed out of this meeting. The committee's purpose was to get the voter signatures necessary to get Trump's name on the presidential ballot in the State of Florida. There was a political uniqueness to this gathering. They were all local people and the small group was quite diverse. There were Democrats, Republicans and independents, old people and young people, women and men. The common denominator was change, and every person seemed to seek change as if they sought after some long lost parent. David decided to stay involved with the group strictly because of the latent power of so much energy. He would check out Paul Trump later!

Weeks and months went by and the small group grew exponentially. The 10 people turned into hundreds and the hundreds turned into thousands. The primary appeal of the movement was the promise of change. It was not the man, his reputation, his credentials, his background or his character. Although most of his supporters talked as if they knew the man, it became apparent they simply thought the man to be different. They liked his outspoken criticisms, twangy wit and folksy humor. But mostly, they liked Trump for what he was not. He was not a professional politician. He was not a Washington insider. He was not a Republican or a Democrat. The masses that supported Trump simply wanted change! The committee was successful in gathering the petitions and Trump's name would be on the Florida ballot. Similar efforts in other states ended equally successful, and Paul Trump would appear as a presidential candidate on all ballots in the United States. It was quite an accomplishment for a largely populist and unaffiliated movement. What was even more remarkable about the success was that it started and gained momentum solely on the promises of one man who said he would make a difference. The movement spoke volumes of the political futility that consumed so many Americans. They all seemed so willing to give so much for the changes Trump had pledged. David was somewhat skeptical. Too many people were pinning their hopes and dreams on a distant promise!

But, all was not fun, roses and good cheer for the members. Controlling the loosely organized, headstrong movement proved to be a challenge. The rallies frequently turned into mob melees as some of the zealous participants made frivolous and offensive remarks. The ill timed remarks and insensitive comments closed many of the meetings prematurely. Everyone was a volunteer and no one was paid, but there was always a passionate undercurrent critical of anyone who attempted to control the effort. David thrived on the unbridled energy, grew with the movement and soon became Chairman of the Committee. David Paine effectively channeled the diverse forces and developed a more harmonious group. He became a local spokesperson for the group, and involved himself in debates with Democrats and Republicans. By late September, 1992, it appeared the political unknown, Paul Trump, had a reasonable shot at being elected president.

Then, something happened. David Paine, who had worked so hard at developing the movement suddenly started to feel uncomfortable. For no apparent reason, he resigned his position with the committee, and stopped all work for Paul Trump. He had no explanation for his withdrawal. He quit as rapidly as he had begun. He had no explanation other than his sense that something was wrong. He had always thought the populist movement was bigger than Trump.

Without any fuss, fanfare or explanation David left the group just before a Trump rally was to begin one evening in early October.

One week later, Paul Trump, announced that he would not run for office because of family reasons. Trump did not go into detail, and this left many of his supporters feeling betrayed. There was talk of political conspiracy, sell outs, and threats on Trump's family. But, no one knew why Trump withdrew! Paul Trump again changed his mind within 10 days and attempted to restart his campaign, but it was too late. The bubble had burst. The disenchanted electorate that had propelled this obscure man into national prominence would desert the cause. They were confused and beaten. Many went out to vote on Election Day, but Trump only received a poor third place showing. The energy turned to apathy, and the down trodden masses became skeptical. This incident would become the kiss of death for political change in America for many years to come. What happened?

CHAPTER 34

▼

Paul Trump had a dream. His early morning discussions with Joe Robbins just prior to Robbins death in 1980, had occupied his mind since that fateful day. The self image of himself as the shooting star that could make a historical difference for America had consumed him for many years. Paul Trump had decided to run for president.

The day after Robbins tragic death, he was visited by Detective Merrill of the Boca Raton police department. Merrill knew that Trump was the last person to see Joe Robbins before his death. Merrill was extremely thorough as he questions Trump.

"Why would anyone want to kill Robbins?"

Trump replied. "I have no idea. Everyone I know liked Joe. He was a good man, treated people fairly, and made a lot of money for his associates and partners. I do not know anyone who would want to kill Joe!"

Merrill continued. "Robbins had some financial problems that he spoke to you about. Could his money problems be a possible motive for his murder?"

"Could be, but I don't think so. Joe had massive financial problems due to the unusually high interest rates, but my understanding is that he was able to successfully refinance his projects and everything had been worked out. In fact, Joe told me that Bob Mellon and Curt Davis of Associated Bank Holding had personally worked out a comprehensive financial package that solved the issue. To my knowledge, Joe solved his financial problems!"

The interview continued for some time as Merrill attempted to gain some insight into Robbins death. He questioned about the party, potential family problems, business associates, possible sexual troubles and a host of other exploratory issues. But, there was to be no revelations coming from the interrogation. Trump had nothing new to add, and Merrill had no reason to be suspicious of Trump.

Trump had successfully hid his intimate knowledge of the details concerning the money supply conspiracy. When he first heard of Robbins murder, he immediately knew why Robbins was killed and who would have been responsible for the slaying. His conversations with Preston Orient had clearly detailed the roles of Ray Seasons, Ted O'Neil, John Vetter and the principals of Associated Bank Holding in the elaborate money scam. The complicity of these high government officials with one of the nation's largest banks in the scheme was mind boggling. He had attempted to reach Preston Orient in the days and months following Robbins death, but the man was gone. He had disappeared without a trace.

Trump had decided that he would not offer any information to anyone about the plot. He surmised that his own life may be in danger. His feelings were reinforced as his repeated attempts to locate Orient drew blanks. *Perhaps, Orient was also killed!* For awhile, he felt paranoid and fearful for his own life. *Had Orient divulged his relationship with him? If so, I could be next!* Trump continued to be obsessed with the situation. Ultimately, he took control and hired armed body guards to insure his protection. In his heart he knew that a few guards could not stop the gang of five if they found out about him. None the less, the guards gave him sufficient assurance so he could resume his normal business and personal activity. As time passed, Trump became more comfortable with the incriminating knowledge. *It just might be helpful in my future political pursuits!*

CHAPTER 35

▼

In 1989, Paul Trump decided to run for president. His business interests had expanded beyond computers and he ventured into other industries. His street savvy, strong business acumen and folksy wit continued to be his trademark characteristics. Financial success followed him on every venture. Trump considered himself infallible. He had been around the government halls of power for many years. His computer business had largely been established and grown with lucrative government contracts. He knew politicians and what made them tick. He became expert at greasing the palms that would loosen the purse strings at any level of government. Paul Trump is the ultimate businessman and the crown prince of capitalism. His sole goal in business was making money anyway he could.

Over time, he had developed a strategy for his presidential run. He would use his successful business model to promote his concept of efficient government. Although his personal fortune was established by taking advantage of the many cracks in government foundations, he would be quick to criticize the large holes of incompetence and corruption that permeated the government. Trump decided to form another political party because the Democrats and Republicans had developed strong negative feelings with many people. Because he knew government catered and responded to big business, he would run as a populist promising to return representative government to the people. He portrayed himself as an outsider knowing there was a disdain for Washington insiders. He understood, through profitable experience, that the government was corrupt and decided he would run his campaign as a reformer. This is the essence of the Trump presidential platform. He would direct a manipulative campaign of heretical personal behavior designed to rally popular support.

Trump is a man of contradictions who is astute in judging peoples reactions. He will tell you what you want to hear, while doing what is profitable. He is critical of government inefficiency, except when it is profitable to him. He sees a third political party as a new venture which needs to be made profitable. He views most politicians as company insiders, who knowing the next move, can profit from their exclusive knowledge. And, he sees the presidency as the consummate inside trader. The president, who is instrumental in formulating policies and laws, profits both before and after any changes occur. *Why else would a person agree to run the world's biggest enterprise for a mere $200,000 a year salary? There are billions of dollars to be made. Just shape your presidency towards your goal, and your insider knowledge will take care of the rest! The President of the United States is the consummate capitalist!* It is not the lofty ideals of equal representation, government reformation or democracy that guide Trump's efforts. Rather, it is money and power that drives Trump in his quest for the presidency.

CHAPTER 36

▼

It is August of 1992 and Trump is in his Houston headquarters reviewing the progress of his campaign. Trump is in a jubilant mood as he has just received notification that his supporters have qualified him as a presidential candidate in every state. He has just reviewed recent polling numbers, and his candidacy continues to enjoy increased acceptance from the voters.

There are camera crews and journalists from around the world awaiting him in the lobby. He gets up from his desk and makes his way down the hall to the media room. An assembly of reporters and cameramen await him in the room. Trump grins as members of the group push and shove as they jockey for position. A single question is soon joined by a chorus of screamed inquiries. The group has evolved into a frantic mob as they all simultaneously vie for the attention of Paul Trump. Trump grins and enjoys the moment, allowing the verbal chaos to continue, while he bathes in this moment of victorious delirium.

Trump throws up his arms and signals the swarm for their attention.

"Ladies, gentlemen. Your attention, please. I will get to all your questions!"

Gradually, after several requests, the gathering responds and order is restored. Trump points to and identifies a reporter, before acknowledging a question. A young female journalist responds. "Your run for president is unprecedented in the political world. We are all astonished that you were able to become a viable candidate! What makes you think you can win against the Democrats and Republicans?"

Trump pushes back from the podium as he acknowledges the question. "You're right. No one has ever run for president as an independent, who has had to rely on the people to get his name on the ballots in all 50 states. Just that accomplishment speaks volumes of the peoples cry for someone who can make a difference. The Democrats and Republicans are not worthy representatives of the people, and the citizens know it! For years, they have been in the service of big business and the wealthy Americans. There is no way I could ever beat the organized power of the two established parties if they properly represented the people. The simple fact is they don't, and because they don't, I will be elected the next President of the United States!"

In classic Trump style, he was beginning to feed off the energy of the group. He pointed to a reporter from CBS who inquired. "Paul, you are a very wealthy man who runs a big business. Do you mean to tell us that you are different from the other big businesses, and do not get special benefits from the two parties you are criticizing?"

Trump had rehearsed the question hundreds of times. His comfortable reply was complete with his county wit and Texan dialect." If I were getting special benefits, why would I go through all the money, time and trouble to change the system? You don't bite the hand that feeds you! Yes, I do a lot of government work, and I saved the government a lot of money on every contract I was awarded. I earned my business with hard work. The point is the Republicrats have made the government corrupt, sloppy and inefficient. I intend to change that. The old dog will have to learn new tricks if I am elected president!"

Trump acknowledged the frantic waving of another reporter. "What's so wrong with America? Companies are growing. People are working. More people than ever own homes and are enjoying a good standard of living. We are free and our economy is the envy of the world. Why mess with success?"

Trump stepped around the podium, approached the reporter and replies. "To hear you talk, I should have stayed in bed today. Point is the rosy picture you just painted is what Washington tells us everyday. If you believe that nonsense, I have a bridge in Brooklyn to sell you. Yes, the companies are growing, but their American employees are not! In the last 10 years, America has lost good paying jobs and industries to foreigners because of dirt cheap labor. The lost jobs are replaced with jobs paying lower wages, fewer benefits and less opportunity for growth. The standard of living is declining. Now days, all household members are forced to work in order to have what their parents had. More work and less pay does not sound like good economic growth to me! What you call success, I call a recipe for disaster."

The questioning continued for another 35 minutes. Trump made his case for change in government as he continued to hit on the haunting issues that had driven so many people into political apathy. He said all the things that people wanted to hear, and he looked and sounded credible. People flocked to Trump with fervor and passion, and accepted him unconditionally. It seemed as if America's hope for the future had finally arrived.

Unfortunately, Trump believes in himself and his money more than any perceived need of the people. America's great hope for tomorrow would soon change into an immense disappointment.

CHAPTER 37

▼

Paul Trump was at home reviewing his presidential campaign. It was late September of 1992 and all has gone as he had planned. His national exposure over the last three months had made him a well known political celebrity in households throughout America. He was viewed as a legitimate contender and his support base has continued to expand. Even the Democrats and Republicans have been forced to recognize his rogue campaign when he was, belatedly and begrudgingly, invited to participate in the national presidential debates. During the debates, he made political mince meat of his opponents as he attacked the failed policies of 40 years of political mismanagement. His opponents stumbled through their standard political rhetoric, while Trump, in his own folksy style, introduced the proposed changes Americans have sought.

Trump smiled as he thought of the utter simplicity of his plan. *Tell the people what they want to hear, but do it in a sincere way.* Trump had correctly estimated the timing and impact of his populist themed campaign. *People were biting at the bit, and they need to be fed.* Trump continued to think of how well his approach has worked when a ringing phone interrupted his mental review. The call was coming in on a private line known only by his executive campaign staff.

Paul picked up the phone. "Hello."

There was a pause before the caller responded. "Hello Paul. This is Preston Orient."

Paul Trump easily recognized Preston's voice, but was astonished to hear from him after a 12 year absence. Following the death of Joe Robbins, Trump hoped Orient was either dead, or permanently undercover. Paul was temporarily speechless as his mind raced over the details of their last business encounter which had exposed the money supply scam. Trump regained his composure and asked. "Jesus, Preston—where have you been? I tried to find you for years, but I couldn't locate you anywhere?"

"Sorry Paul. I disappeared out of necessity. We were involved in some pretty messy business, and I took a long vacation. But that's not important. What is important is that you were never in any jeopardy. Your successful business career and long life is proof of that, isn't it?"

Paul was still staggered by the sudden sound of this voice out of the past. "I suppose so Preston." Overwhelmed with curiosity, Paul quickly added. "Why are you calling me now?"

Preston responded. "I need a special favor and only you can help me?"

Trump grew suspicious and feared something might be said on the phone which may be incriminating. "I don't know what you have in mind, but I can meet you to discuss it in privacy."

"No need to meet you Paul. We can discuss the matter on the phone. I already know your phone is not tapped and that you are alone." Preston paused and presented his special favor. "Paul, I need you to withdraw from the presidential elections!"

Dead silence followed as Trump absorbed the remarks. He was partially perturbed and partially intimidated when he responded. "Preston, I can't withdraw. There are too many people counting on me! Moreover, why should I quit?

Preston now responded in a measured but forceful manner. "Paul, I need to be brutally honest with you. I know it will not be easy, but you can and will withdraw. We both know you have been protected for years after Robbins died. All the protection will go away if you deny me this favor."

Trump was now angered. "Listen Preston, I was never involved with the money supply swindle. You are the one who had all the information, shared it with me and then shared it with Joe Robbins. For all I know, you killed Joe, took all the money and then disappeared!"

"I agree with you. For all you know, you just might be right. But, that's not important. What is important is that I know where you are. I can prove you had knowledge of the scheme and did nothing about it. Finally, your name is just a phone call away from people who will kill you because of what you know about the money conspiracy. I don't know if you will die a slow death politically, or if you will be mortally dead in the next half hour. Either way, your life is over! Do me this favor, and withdraw!"

In just five minutes of phone conversation, Paul Trump's life was completely changed. In his mind, he went from President of the United States to a groveling pawn. *There must be some middle ground!* "Preston, if I agree to this, what's in it for me?"

"You don't know how happy I am to hear that. I was hoping you were still a good businessman. How does 100 million dollars sound? Additionally, we can arrange it so you save face on the presidential withdrawal."

Paul Trump was first, last and always a money man. Even his run for the presidency was all about money. Although Trump thought he had a shot at the presidency, it was far from a sure thing. Trump inquired further. "What do you want me to do?"

"In two weeks, announce your withdrawal. Explain that the lives of your family have been threatened, and that you can not continue. Offer no other explanations to either the police or the public. After another two weeks, announce that you intend to confront the threat and will run for the presidency. You will save some face, but your political career will be over. As for the 100 million dollars, next Monday you will receive a federal bid form for computer parts. The bid will be closed. Bid 325 million for the contract and that number will be approved. Check the numbers and you will see that you will make a net profit of between 100 and 125 million dollars."

Trump was concerned about being coerced in the future because of his intimate knowledge of the money supply scheme. "Preston, how can I be assured that you will not come at me again?"

"There is no guarantee that I can offer you that would make you comfortable. Look at it this way. Rather than calling you, I could have given your name to certain government officials who would have killed you because of your knowledge of their affairs. That would have been messy because of your presidential run, but they would have killed you to protect themselves. I have no interest in hurting you. We were friends and made money together in the past. I would like to think we can continue to work together if the need arises in the future. After all, we are both cut from the same piece of cloth!"

"You're right Preston! Money and power is our common link. One more thing before you vanish again. Who sent you?"

"If I told you, I would have to kill you! Let me just say you were getting too close for comfort. The present and future course of this country is better left to the existing two political parties. I need to go now. Good bye and good luck!"

The phone went dead before Trump could say his farewells. Trump leaned(s) back in his chair and strokes his chin. His dreams of billions are gone, but he will be around to fight another day. Mentally, he justifies what he must do. *I did it to make money and I will! Besides that, I am tired of cow tailing to the sniveling masses who think they can ride my coattails to a better tomorrow. They need to fend for themselves! Ultimately, I would have shown my true colors. Better to bust their balloon today!*

CHAPTER 38

▼

Chou Bing awakes at 4:30AM as has been his habit for years. It is New Years Day, 2006. He stretches from side to side briefly, and rubs his closed eyes vigorously as he gets up from his bed. He walks over to the dresser mirror and brushes back his raven black hair. Regular exercise has resulted in a tight, hardened body. His 135 pounds is in Herculean proportion to his 5'3" frame. His Asian complexion, physical conditioning and boyish good looks effectively mask his age. Although he is 49 years old, most people thought him to be in his late thirties. Chou is an extremely successful businessman born and raised in Shanghai. Like many of his peers, he came to the United States when he was 18 to pursue his college education. He had sufficient mental and financial resource to gain entrance into Harvard where he majored in business and accounting. Later, he obtained his masters degree in economics and banking. Chou proved to be brilliant as he pursued his career in a variety of businesses. His status in the international community is indicative of the success he enjoys.

Chou walks to the balcony where he views the expanse of Manhattan Island from his 3 million dollar apartment. The morning air was comfortably chilly with a stirring breeze. A fresh covering of undisturbed snow made for a picturesque scene in this city of giant buildings. Chou closed the balcony slider and went to the entry door to secure his morning paper. He gathers the paper and heads to his favorite recliner in the living room. Comfortably reposed, he begins to read the paper.

The large bold headlines scream—**HAPPY NEW YEAR—2006.** He especially enjoys the first edition of the New Year because it typically had extensive

reviews of the previous year. Chou quickly pages to the various articles highlight-
ing the major news items of 2005.

An article on presidential leadership indicated the president is continuing to
lose public support, but remains persistent in his efforts to spread freedom and
democracy throughout the world. Chou Bing is bothered by the swaggering,
arrogant American President. His thoughts are intuitive. *The world knows when
America speaks of democracy, it is a diversion. America is not even a democracy. She is
a republic, a nation of laws, where the elite make the laws to their advantage.* Chou
frequently references the recent presidential election where the winner did not
have a majority of the popular vote. In this particular election, the people were
denied twice. Political institutions in the form of the Electoral College and the
Supreme Court set aside the will of the majority in favor of the rule of law.
Chou's thoughts consume him as he continues to read. *The entire election process
is flawed. From candidate selection through the popular vote, the people are led to
believe they have a voice. Americans only get to chose from the chosen! Can the American people be that stupid?*

An item on the war in Iraq claims an inevitable victory, but recognizes a stub-
born resistance from insurgents and concludes that the United States is unable to
set a date for troop withdrawal. Chou has his own analysis. *The capitalists have
bitten off more than they can chew. They will face the same disastrous conclusions as
the Russians experienced in their invasion of Afghanistan.* Chou believes the Americans only objective is to control the price and distribution of Iraqi oil, and mentally notes his feelings. *They will not leave Iraq until they had brother fighting
brother with the United States in control of the oil. Divide, conquer, and buy the Iraqis who will do the bidding of America capitalists. There will be no peace in this
country for a long time.* Chou believes the war on terrorism is a distraction meant
to channel the American people into the acceptance of wider military actions on
behalf of the capitalists. His thoughts are conclusive. *It is all about money and the
control of resources by a handful of uncontrolled capitalists.*

The next article summarizes an ongoing problem with corporate corruption.
Bookkeeping irregularities and accounting manipulations are being used to
deceive corporate shareholders and employees. Profits are either invented or hidden depending on the objective of the perpetrators. The article highlights a large
energy company whose fraudulent actions resulted in the loss of tens of thousands of jobs and billions of dollars. The money simply evaporated in a series of
questionable transactions. Chou briefly recalls his feelings. *There appears to be no
end to the greed of American businessmen. Ah—these capitalists—when there is no*

one or nothing else to exploit, they deceive one another, their employees and their families!

Another vignette assesses the decline of the American middle class due to the loss of manufacturing and high tech jobs. The article states that many major companies have moved their operations overseas because it is more profitable. Chou casts a knowing smile. Many of the manufacturing jobs have gone to his native country, China. Again, he acknowledges his personal beliefs. *The greedy American elite are truly predictable. American style capitalism has no concern for the welfare of its citizens or its own national interest. Truly, the American merchant has no country. I have counted on this inherent trait!*

Another commentary attests to a booming housing market. The industry had a fabulous year owing to lower interest rates offered by the Federal Reserve. The FED Chairman is receiving accolades as a result of his interest rate policies. Unfortunately, the article hints at a potential problem due to the rapid increase in housing prices, and the adjustments of interest rates. It indicates many home owners and investors in a rush to get into the housing boom may have overpaid for the homes. Now that interest rates are rising, they may find they may lose their home or investment. Chou nods his approval knowing that banks own the Federal Reserve, and the banks are, in turn, owned by a few wealthy capitalists. His thoughts are vindictive. *In the final analysis, a few elitists will be the real benefactors of both the housing boom and the ultimate bust. Was anyone paying attention when the bankruptcy laws for individuals were toughened in the middle of the housing boom? The business people who run the government mean to make economic slaves out of the American citizens. Once again, this dilemma has played into our plan, and not by chance!*

Chou reads another summary on the American trade deficit. During 2005, America incurred a 720 billion dollar trade deficit bringing the total trade deficit to close to 5 trillion dollars. Chou continues to read as he mentally notes his conclusion. *It appears the Americans have nothing to trade except their printed dollars! Most Americans can not comprehend what 5 trillion dollars is or what it can buy. We are counting on this deluge of dollars to buy out the greatest economic power in the world—the United States of America. Thank God for the greedy Americans. They will have destroyed their own greatness—not with a cold war, not with a military encounter, but with their own mismanaged and uncontrolled system!*

As he closes the newspaper, he recalls the words of an economist, John Maynard Keynes. *"The best way to destroy the capitalist system is to debauch the currency."*

Chou rises from the recliner, briefly stretches and walks over to the telephone. He needs to call a good friend. New Years is always a difficult day for his associate of many years. Chou will do whatever it takes to comfort his cohort, and get him through a difficult day.

CHAPTER 39

▼

A recurring tragedy plays out day after day, night after night, with no relief in sight. It is as if you are in prison for life with no chance of ever being released. Picture the seemingly endless portrayal of a religious person who dies in sin, and has been condemned to the everlasting fires of hell. It is a story of constant mental and physical torture. There is no respite except for the occasional fantasy that one may conjure to escape the bounds of hopelessness, only to be awakened to the reality of a desperate situation.

Todd wrestles with his demons as he is fitfully jolted from his restless slumber. He immediately goes into his daily litany of despair. *There is no faith. There is no hope. There is no escape. There is no drug. There is no life and there is no reason to live, and yet I continue to exist. Thoughts of suicide are my closest ally in the quest to end the endless struggle, but even suicide is an enemy. To quit would be to abandon the crusade of hate which is my only reason for living. Hate consumes me, but it remains my only respite. It is the only relief from the constant anguish which strains to reduce me to a mumbling idiot. Hate is the nourishment which gets me through the tortured days, nights, months and years of a miserable existence. Hate inspires me to go on. I will be free when the hate is satisfied. Until then, I will bear the intolerable and continue to exist.*

Such are the thoughts that consume Todd Robbins as he awakes on January 1, 2006. Today is the 26th anniversary of the death of his father, and it is as if Joe Robbins had died just 5 minutes ago. The mental picture of the bloody corpse is as vivid as the next thing to come into view. Time has not diminished the fatal scene, but has acted much as recorded video on constant loop, playing and replaying the tragic sight. The sameness and futility of the continuous reminder had tested Todd's sanity in the early days and months following his father's death. Gradually, he was able to cope by analyzing his problem, and designing a plan that would exact the vengeance that would relieve him of his burdens. In his mind, he has clearly identified the true killers. He has been on a patient, yet persistent crusade to fully implement his plan of destruction. Twenty six years of planning, organizing, changing, modifying and implementing has set the stage for his final retribution. Soon, he will release the carefully prepared forces, and the murderers of his father will reap the whirlpool of hate that has consumed him.

The phone rings startling Todd out of his comatose ramblings. He is comforted as he looks at the monitor and identifies the caller. It is Charlie. Todd answers the phone. "Hello Charlie. How are you?"

Chou Bing responds. "I am doing fine, but I am concerned about you. How are you feeling today?"

"I'm alive, and the plan is another day closer to realization. That's all that really matters!"

Sensing the hurt, Charlie suggests a social outing. "Listen Todd, I have a few young ladies available. Would you like to get out for a few drinks, some lunch, and whatever?"

"No thank you Charlie. I'm not in the mood. I will be working on the project today."

Charlie persists. "Why not give yourself a break? You are always working. Today would be a great day just to kick back and enjoy yourself?"

"Sorry Charlie, I have to work on the project!"

The finality of Todd's words was all too familiar, and Charlie senses that Todd needs space today. "OK Todd, if that's what you want. Call me if there is something I can do. I want to help if I can!"

"Thanks for offering, but I must work today. I will get with you sometime next week to discuss some changes. I'll call you when I am ready."

"All right Todd. Call me as soon as I can do something!"

As the call terminates, Charlie laments how much their relationship has changed. *We used to be so close going through college—and I can never forget how he saved my life in the Combat Zone.* Charlie and Todd had been room mates at Harvard for the better part of 6 years. They did everything together from debating to dating. Steadfast in their mutual respect, they never failed to watch each others back as they resolutely pledged their youthful allegiance to each other. They were the ultimate team of individualists as they plodded their way through the exacting trials of undergraduate and then graduate work at Harvard University. They both graduated at the top of their class, and both had brilliant prospects for the future. Todd joined his father in the family business, while Charlie returned to China to work with his official government mentors.

After college, they fell out of contact while they each pursued their ambitions. Charlie did not hear from Todd for 8 years. Charlie read about the death of Joe Robbins and had unsuccessfully attempted to contact Todd. Then one day, Todd was on the phone calling China searching for Chou Bing. The ensuing reunion was pleasant for both Charlie and Todd. Charlie recalls that the new relationship, although trusted and mutually advantageous, was largely devoid of the plutonic binds that formed the basis of their college relationship. Charlie missed the antics, frivolities and gregarious sentiments that characterized Todd during the college years.

The present day Todd is driven with an intense desire to avenge his father's death. He is without social purpose unless the event furthers the project. In fact, his whole life is the plan, and only those events that contribute to the project are entertained.

Charlie, none the less, fosters the pragmatic relationship, partially because of the college years, but mostly because Todd had saved his life. More important, Charlie has successfully analyzed the underlying cause of Todd's pain and fully concurs with the end objective. He knows that hate is the defining force pushing Todd, and agrees it is a necessary ingredient to reach their shared objective. Together, they will avenge Joe Robbins and in the process will also radically change the world.

CHAPTER 40

‎ ▼ ‎

Todd hangs up the phone and briefly laments his inability to be more cordial to his long time friend. *Charlie has been much more than a friend. I should have treated him differently.* Todd moves toward his desk in the study and picks up an analytical document dealing with the dollar money supply. He reviews the document, makes notes and inserts figures into a spread sheet on his computer. Todd works intently for the next 3 hours until he tires and finds himself unable to concentrate on the detailed information. He gets up from his desk and goes into the bedroom. Approaching the mirror, he is stunned by the self image in front of him. Todd is now 48 years old, and time has not been a friend. His pudgy face is etched with the wrinkles of continued anguish and worry. His hair is thin and graying, and he weighs in at an unhealthy 245 pounds. He grabs his protruding stomach, and shakes it violently watching as the gut recoils and rolls from side to side. He is unhappy with his physical appearance, but he decided years ago that it was not important. He quickly looks away from the mirror disdainful of the grotesque picture in front of him.

Todd walks over to the bed and lies down. It is only 11:30 AM, but his mind is weary and he feels physically tired. *Perhaps a little nap will permit me to get on with my work.* He closes his eyes, and is immediately engaged by the horrific image of his dead father. He is quite accomplished at dismissing the eerie sight and goes into a fidgety nap. As he sleeps, a progression of unpleasant nightmares race through his mind. Soon, he is face to face with Detective Merrill of the Boca Raton police.

Merrill questions "Do you know who would want to kill your father?"

Todd speaks lucidly "No sir. My father was known and respected by all his associates. He made a lot of money for people who were fortunate enough to be around him, and he made it a point to never hurt anyone. My father was a pariah in that respect."

Merrill quizzed "What do mean he was a pariah?"

"My father was in big business. It is near impossible to deal in millions of dollars daily and not hurt people either financially or physically. But he prided himself on his ability to be fair, and he would walk away from deals which would hurt people. In a way, he did not belong in business!"

Todd immediately regrets his last statement, and the astute Merrill picked up on the discrepancy and asked. "In what way did your father not belong in business?"

"I don't know! All the things you hear about, or read about where business people cheat one another, their customers, the government, or whoever just to make a buck. It's the system of self service which demands one do whatever is necessary to be successful. My father wasn't that way."

Todd continued to ramble, and Merrill grew more suspicious of Todd. Todd knows something! He is not telling me everything. Detective Merrill continues the questioning. "Was your father involved in anything which would motivate someone to kill him? Was he having financial problems?"

Merrill already knew from many of Joe Robbins friends about the pending money problems that were plaguing the Robbins real estate empire, but had carefully worded the succinct question to get Todd's reaction.

Todd had regained his composure and curtly replied. "Dad was very concerned about his current financial situation. He did have some serious financial difficulties. We worked on resolving them together. In fact, dad made a tentative arrangement with the owners of Associated Bank Holding Company. We agreed in principal to accept their offer to fund our businesses." Todd concluded the interview and would say no more.

Merrill confirmed the arrangements with Curt Davis and Bob Mellon who echoed Todd's statements. In the months that followed, Todd would sign the documents which saved the ailing Robbins Ltd. None the less, Merrill instinctively knew that Todd was not sharing all he knew!

For his part, Todd Robbins was fearful of additional reprisals. He was emotionally raw, confused and hurt. He felt he knew, but was not certain, who had killed his father. Additionally, he anticipated his father's reputation may be jeopardized if he should expose everything he knew of the money supply conspiracy. After all, his information was vague, and essentially flowed from a 15 minute conversation he had with his father. It was this logic, mostly based in fear for his personal safety, which determined his course of action. He would gather more information, and then expose the killers on his terms. Little did he realize the line he had crossed?

Todd wakes up from his brief slumber. He immediately returns to his desk to work on the details of his elaborate plan. He will work late into the night to perfect his revenge and to avoid the unpleasant thoughts that always consumes him on every anniversary of his father's death.

CHAPTER 41

▼

"America is truly a great country. Is it any wonder why so many seek out the American dream? You supplied much of the world with your goods and services. Your economy and your standard of living was the envy of the world. Your workers had access to good jobs that paid great wages. They received comprehensive health benefits and were promised an adequate pension upon retirement. It seemed anyone who wanted to work could find one of these good jobs. The pay was sufficient to get married, buy a home, own a good car, and raise a family. America's companies grew as a result of product innovation, increased productivity and a devoted work force. As the companies grew and profited, the workers also matured and prospered. There were few child day care centers as most families were financially able to live comfortably on one income. A mother was able to stay home and raise the family. Adequate health care seemed to be available for all who needed it. There were far fewer prisons, and hardly any of us knew a convict."

David Paine went on for another 9 minutes extolling the greatness that was America. He was speaking to a group of 129 people that gathered at a local library. David had started these community meetings just three months earlier in March of 2006. He felt a need to speak out about current social and economic conditions. He was still refining his presentation, and occasionally verbally fumbled as he sought to make a point. He knew what he wanted to say, but was constantly searching for the right words to excite and energize the audience. He advertised his meetings under the banner of Wake Up America.

The meeting format consisted of a 10 minute review of the things that made America great, followed by 10 minute appraisal of the factors that were eroding

America. After Paine's presentation, there was an open question and answer period. The question and answer period occasionally wound up in near fights as people exercised their right to violently disagree. None the less, the size of the audience progressively increased in size. Recently, the demographic make up of the group included a growing number of young adults in their twenties and thirties.

David continues into the second part of the presentation. "America, what went wrong? What happened to the American Dream? You are no longer the great provider of goods and services to the world. Rather, you are the largest importer of goods and services from countries around the world. In 2005, America had a trade deficit of over 723 billion dollars. This means that Americans went into debt to foreigners by 723 billion dollars. This translates to one dollar going to a foreign country for every 4 dollars each of us spends on consumer goods. We are buying cars, trucks, clothes, televisions, radios, computers, cell phones, underwear and tooth brushes made in China, India, Japan and a host of other countries. These are products we used to make in America, but we now buy from foreigners. We buy them from abroad because they are either cheaper or of higher quality than American made products. American companies have for many years recognized the increased profitability that occurs when Americans are fired and production is shifted to low wage foreign countries. It started as a trickle, about 40 years ago, when a few companies shifted their production facilities to foreign countries. Over the years, the trickle turned into a torrent as thousands of American companies moved to foreign shores in their quest for lower wages and higher profits. Today, the exodus includes not only manufacturing concerns, but a large variety of service jobs. The age of computerization has enabled American companies to export office jobs, engineering work, accounting jobs, legal positions and a myriad of other professional occupations to foreign countries. It seems there is a ready foreign work force willing to do the work at a fraction of the cost of American labor. The jobs flight is now so prevalent that chances are good when you call an 800 number, you might be greeted with a foreign accent. I know some of you think it presumptuous of American companies to produce goods abroad which are then imported to the United States for consumption. It doesn't make economic sense! But, it gets worse! Our own federal, state and local governments have gotten into the act, and recently began shifting some of their functions to other countries. How do you feel about paying taxes to our government so a foreign worker can enjoy a higher standard of living while your standard of living slowly deteriorates? This perhaps is the final slap in the face for Americans! Our Revolution of 1776 had a popular slogan. Taxation without representation is tyranny. Today, we may easily proclaim paying taxes for foreign wages at the expense of American jobs is stupidity! Earlier, I questioned what happened to the American dream, and now I answer the question. We have sold it to the lowest bidder!"

The presentation continued with references to the emergence of the two person working family, the proliferation of day care centers, the gradual disappearance of health care benefits, the fraudulent manipulation of promised pension benefits, the abundance of low paying fast food and retail jobs, the decline in the standard of living, the manipulation of the stock markets and the housing markets, and the governments naive perception of these conditions as indicators of positive economic growth.

David Paine concluded this segment once again proclaiming. "Earlier, I questioned what happened to the American dream and now I answer the question. We have sold it to the lowest bidder!"

David could see that he had aroused some members of the attentive group. The discernable mumblings coming from the assemblage were largely in agreement with the presentation. He felt pleased with his speech, and wanted to evoke a more passionate response from the audience.

"Before I answer your questions, I would like to ask each of you a few questions. By a show of hands, how many men and women in the audience have lost a job because of foreign competition? This would include anybody who worked for a company that closed its doors in the United States; or it would include anybody who lost their job because of foreign competition; or it would include anyone who lost their job because of an illegal foreign immigrant. Could I please have a show of hands?"

The results astounded David as close to 70 percent of the audience raised their hands. He paused briefly allowing the individuals in the audience time to look around and view the number of raised hands.

David continues. "I will refer to all of you as the contributors to globalism. This is a good thing according to our government and big corporations who view globalism as an economic miracle. It supposedly is the hope for the future of the world! But, has globalism been good for you?"

"This next question is for only those who I have identified as global contributors. How many of you global contributors have gotten a better paying job after your job was taken from you?"

A small minority, perhaps 10 percent raised their hands.

"Let me refer to each of you as the benefactors of globalism. You, along with a number of foreigners and illegal immigrants have benefited financially from the change. The rest of you have lost and will continue to lose financially. And even those of you who have been identified as global benefactors will eventually lose also! Understand this! The process of globalism is ongoing and will continue to drive down our wages and our standard of living as cheaper labor is located throughout the world. You lose, your family loses and America loses. In the final analysis, the only winners are the multi national corporations who continue to profit from our misery!"

David continued to question the audience on issues from pensions and health care to inflation and housing costs. Each question engaged more members of the audience, and soon, the entire group was thoroughly aroused.

"Let me ask you a final question frequently posed by politicians. A simple yes or no, please! Are you better off today than you were 10 years ago?"

Confusion reigned as the shouted no's far out numbered the few yes's. David let the gathering settle down for a few minutes. David then repeatedly shouted to regain their attention. Finally, after four attempts, order was restored.

"Can I answer any questions for you?"

An older lady sitting in front was first to respond. "Most of us are aware of the problems and have been frustrated for some time. Quite frankly, you have opened old wounds for many of us. Did you come out to stir us up, or do you have an answer?"

David smiled compassionately at the woman and replied. "I have the answer!"

CHAPTER 42

▼

It was November of 2006 when Chou Bing met Todd Robbins in Orlando, Florida. The two associates had agreed to meet at the emergency meeting of the National Real Estate Coalition. The meeting was called because of the rapidly declining real estate market and the speculation of a total collapse.

Prices on residential and commercial real estate increased close to 100 percent over the past 3 years. The period had been one of immense profitability for those who saw the price trend and invested in real estate. The insightful investors were purchasing homes and reselling them 6 to 9 months later, making clear profits of 100 to 150 thousand dollars on transactions where their exposure was 30 to 50 thousand dollars. This translated to annual cash on cash returns of anywhere from 150 percent to over 1000 percent. The investors were delirious with the obscene profits and reinvested in still more properties. The cost of new homes and existing homes soon increased in value driven primarily by the huge speculative spending binge.

Soon, more investors and home buyers entered the market enticed by the tremendous appreciation and low interest rates. As more people entered the market, home inventories dried up. The market responded with an incredible increase in new construction, accompanied by an influx of existing home sales. This process continued for a period of 5 years when suddenly the market met resistance in October of 2005. It was not a gradual stop. It was as if the green traffic light suddenly turned red as you were approaching it at 90 miles per hour. The market screeched to an abrupt halt!

By November of 2005, the sentiment towards real estate changed from unbridled enthusiasm to diminished expectations. Most experts predicted a soft landing where prices would adjust before resuming the upward trend. Some predicted a hard landing with declining prices continuing for some time. The hard landing would bring about severe price cuts and increased interest rates. A very few predicted a market bust where prices would free fall. In this period, home owners and investors who had overpaid for the properties would either lose the homes or a lot of money. The downward spiral would feed on foreclosures and bankruptcies until equilibrium was restored. Either way, the bust seemed to foretell a long term crisis with the potential to severely impair the American economy.

In the twelve months of decline from November 2005 to October, 2006, the picture had taken on a decidedly grim nature. The proponents of a soft landing had disappeared in the wake of declining sales and price decreases. More of the experts were drawn to the hard landing, while continuing to preach the gospel of market resurgence. A few were sure a real estate bust was on the horizon and had positioned their businesses to profit from a real estate market collapse. It was this continued ambiguity that caused the National Real Estate Coalition to call the emergency meeting.

Both Todd Robbins and Chou Bing had extensive real estate holdings, but neither of these astute businessmen had been harmed by the downturn! They had both participated in the upswing timely purchasing developments and selling them, piecemeal, to home buyers and investors. They made ungodly profits as they catered to the growing hoard of greedy investors. With a seemingly infallible sixth sense, they purposely exited the booming market in August of 2005. They sold the last of their speculative inventories in October of 2005, and did not purchase any other real estate. The properties they kept were primarily commercial holdings, purchased well before the boom. In December of 2005, they shut down an extremely profitable country wide mortgage business after packaging and selling off their entire loan portfolio. The mortgage company specialized in an array of exotic adjustable rate mortgages. They were safely positioned from the declines that would shortly hit the market. Their associates described them as business geniuses with impeccable timing. However, this sixth sense and supposed genius was simply part of an elaborate plan. The plan was based around reliable inside information as to the direction of future interest rates. They pocketed tens of billions of dollars at the expense of unwary home buyers and investors. More important, the financial ramifications of the housing and mortgage debacle were a planned part of an intricate arrangement to bring down the economy of the United States!

CHAPTER 43

▼

Chou Bing rushed over to greet Todd Robbins at the Orlando airport. Todd had just flown in from New York. Chou had arrived a few days earlier flying in from Shanghai, China. Chou hugged Todd briefly before enthusiastically shaking his hand.

"Good to see you again! Did you have a good flight?"

Todd looked over his friend and replied. "Yes. The flight was comfortable. You look great Charlie."

Charlie always looked the picture of health. His small, yet well proportioned physique seemed timeless. He always exuded a contagious enthusiasm. Todd always felt comfortable in his presence and enjoyed his infectious spirit. It had been seven months since the two comrades last met in New York City. Chou noted that Todd had gained weight and seemed tired.

Todd glared at Chou briefly with an intense stare. It was a visual statement of the many restless nights and his unrelenting dedication to the sole purpose of his life. Todd seemed distant, but Chou knew that he was a driven man. Todd was a man on a mission, and he never failed to show his complete resolve.

Todd queried. "What news do you bring from China?"

Charlie knew Todd was always anxious to get to the point. "I have great news for you. But first, let's get to the hotel where we can speak freely."

Charlie and Todd went outside where a limousine was waiting to take them to the hotel in downtown Orlando. The hotel was in walking distance to the convention center where the real estate meeting was being held. They had planned to stay for two days. The first day would be at the real estate meeting. The second day would entail an extensive review of their special project.

On arrival at the hotel, Todd and Charlie checked in. They were shown to separate penthouse suites. While the elevator was ascending to the top floor, Charlie tapped Todd's hand for attention. "Todd, I am going to stop at my room. I will meet you in ten minutes at your suite."

"OK, but please hurry. I really need to talk with you about the project!"

Urgency was a constant demand from Todd. Some may have been offended by his single mindedness, but Charlie understood the relentless Todd and accepted him on that basis. "Try to relax Todd. The project is on schedule and you will be extremely happy with my update. We have new partners. We will talk later."

Todd shook his head affirmatively. He knew he was demanding, but could not help himself. This project has been his life's work for decades. He would be on edge until he received the update.

CHAPTER 44

▼

The following morning Todd and Charlie leave the hotel. They decided to walk to the convention center. The meeting of the National Real Estate Coalition was scheduled to begin at 9:30 AM, and they had plenty of time to enjoy a leisurely stroll. The air was crisp with autumn air and the cloudless sky exposed the shimmering sun. A slight breeze added to a near perfect Florida morning. The two walked together at a relaxed pace towards the convention center. The contrast between the short, lean Charlie and the taller, semi-obese Todd was almost comic. Mutt and Jeff, renowned business leaders, walking through the canyon of tall buildings while discussing their common mission.

Todd opens the conversation. "Charlie, are you sure the other countries are with us?

"Absolutely sure. They are eager to participate. Their leaders are committed to the project."

"What about security? Can they be trusted?"

"Todd, I know you are concerned. As I explained to you last evening, everything is in order. They know only what they have been told, and they have been told only what they are supposed to know. Trust is a two edged sword, so there is always a possibility of betrayal. But, they will find their swords dull if they decide to compromise the project. My contact in China personally engaged them on the project. They have much to gain if they are true to the project, and will lose all if they should abandon us. Place your trust in me. I will not fail!"

As the two approach the convention center, Todd takes comfort in the reassuring words. Charlie has always been true. His dedication to the project has always been beyond question. It has been close to 20 years since Todd and Chou discussed the basic concept of the project. *Chou has never vacillated from the objectives. He is a true believer!*

The center is packed with over 300 business leaders. Todd and Charlie greet some of the participants as they enter the hall. They look around and see many familiar faces. Todd notes he has not seen this many of the business elite gathered together since the collapse of the stock market in 2000. *The vultures have gathered to feast on the carcasses.* In attendance are 4 US senators and 7 US congressmen. He did not expect to see politicians at the event. Tomorrow is November 7th, Election Day, and a lot of seats will be voted on. It seems that the politicians would do better at this late stage campaigning in their home districts. But then again, they are probably here to hedge their bets in the event they lose. *How often do you get to grovel before Americas 300 business leaders on the eve of an election?*

The six hour session begins with a review of the real estate market. Five years of double digit appreciation in housing prices were caused by a few documented factors. The dot.com collapse of 2000 drove herds of investors out of the stock market who were actively seeking other investment venues. The Federal Reserve, beginning in May, 2000 had begun to lower the federal funds rate. The rate would ultimately fall to 1 percent by June of 2003. The inexpensive money lured tens of thousands of investors into the heavily leveraged real estate business. Lending institutions eager to loan the cheap money encouraged the investors with mortgage products requiring little, if any, personal capital. The rush began and soon millions of people jumped into real estate for either a quick buck, or an opportunity for home ownership. Prices escalated as investors and home buyers bid up prices for property. New home builders jumped into the fray. The builders increased prices and profits in response to the low interest rates and the higher demand. Building suppliers and sub contractors joined the party increasing their prices and profits. Everyone wanted a piece of the action and they all prospered. And then it ended without much fanfare in late 2005.

The moderator explained the conditions which caused the abrupt end to the red hot real estate market. "Beginning in June, 2003, the Federal Reserve began to slowly inch up interest rates from the record one percent low. In the history of the Federal Reserve, the rate had only been at one percent during one other period, and that was during World War II. How does one equate the financial needs of World War II with 2003? The interest rate increased to over five percent by November of 2005. The real estate market responded to the increased rates and the down turn began. Demand slackened as higher home prices and higher mortgage rates made home ownership less affordable. Home inventories started to increase as the end users were unable to buy. The market decline started in the form of increasing home inventories, lower sales levels, waning home prices, increased home foreclosure and rising real estate taxes. The market has now been in decline for over one year, and there is no sign of relief. Job losses in construction, real estate, mortgage lending and related businesses threaten to further dampen the market. There is considerable speculation that the problem could spread to the general economy and bring on a severe recession."

The meeting continued with dire predictions for the future. Solutions were offered in the form of subsidized housing, lower tax initiatives and government grants. It soon became apparent to the audience there were no good short term answers.

Todd and Charlie left the meeting early. It was amazing how easily so many intelligent people could be deceived. They both understood the moderators of the meeting had no clue as to what had happened to real estate, or why it happened. Because the moderators did not understand the origin of the problem, they could not possibly understand the solutions. Todd and Charlie began the short walk back to the hotel.

Charlie spoke first. "It is just as you said. The people do not understand. They truly believe that market forces created the run up in housing prices. I find it hard to understand how so many successful people can be so easily manipulated."

"Charlie, you should not be so condescending of successful people! We would be equally ignorant if we did not have inside information as to why and when these events would happen. What's the saying? It's not what you know—it's who you know! We just happened to know the people who caused the housing market to behave as it has, and they were willing to share that information with us."

"I can't disagree with you. We made over 160 billion dollars in the last 5 years, after the special tax." Charlie was referring to the 20 percent kickback money they paid the Washington DC marketing firm for consulting fees. The consultations consisted of secretive bits of information. The information was paid for in 64 monthly invoices totaling close to 40 billion dollars. But the 40 billion dollars was well worth the information. There was no risk. No doubt. No speculation. It was a sure thing that could not fail. A slam dunk!

Charlie advances another question. "Speaking of who you know, how's our man at the FED doing?"

Todd was huffing as he responded. He is overweight and out of shape. The extra weight, short walk and the warm afternoon sun left him slightly short of breath. "I think he's doing fine. No need to talk to him much. I presume he will continue to be happy as long as the company receives the monthly checks."

Charlie smiles at his companion. "You have done an excellent job in dealing with your enemy. It is good that you will be free of this burden shortly. I could not do what you had to do for so many years."

Todd stops walking to catch his breath, grasps Charlie's hand and responds. "I am so tired. I have been so consumed with the project for so many years and I can not rest. Unfortunately, hate has been my driving force. Doing business with my enemy has been difficult, but it was necessary. Charlie, you know my health is deteriorating. Promise me if something happens that you will finish what we have started."

"You have my word Todd. The project will be completed! We are well prepared. Your efforts have been truly instrumental in exposing the delicate underbelly of the snake. Take heart! You will live to see the death of your enemy and the completion of the project. It is my ardent wish that your victories over these monsters will ignite the healing forces that will return good health to you."

CHAPTER 45

▼
———————————— ▼ ————————————

Todd is back at the hotel. He has ventured out to the balcony where is able to view many of the Orlando high rise buildings. *Not much different than New York City, Atlanta or Dallas when viewed from a mid town pent house suite.* His mind soon wanders to his last conversation with Charlie as they walked from the convention center. *Keep your friends close, but keep your enemies closer! It is easy enough to say, but very difficult to do.* He recalls his last business arrangement with the enemy.

In the years following his fathers' death, Todd had built an international real estate company with properties, contacts and resources throughout the world. It had taken Todd 9 years to pay off the debt to Associated Bank Holding, and to buy back the stock of Robbins, Ltd. He owned his sprawling real estate empire free and clear. His ability to turn questionable ventures into successful enterprises was heralded throughout the business world. His financial capability was a rare combination of sophisticated financial knowledge and street sense. In 1989, he bought back the stock of Robbins in an all cash transaction valued at over 5 billion dollars. No one was sure of how Todd pulled it off. Rumor had it that Todd was involved in a junk bond scheme, but no one really cared. Associated Bank Holding had a windfall profit and Todd Robbins had regained control of his company. Best of all—there were no complaints from the investors who supposedly financed the deal with junk bonds. Everyone was happy!

It was in September of 2000 when he had received a phone call from Bob Mellon. Bob Mellon had, 11 years back, won an appointment to the Federal Reserve Board. He served as the FED governor for the New York District. Within a few years, he was appointed to Chairman of the Federal Reserve. He was now the most powerful financial person in the world. His partner at Associated Bank Holding, Curt Davis, continued to run the large banking conglomerate while Bob Mellon attended to the financial needs of the United States and the world.

"Hello Todd, this is Bob Mellon. How are you today?"

Todd was taken back momentarily. It had been a long time since he had spoken with Mellon. "I am fine Bob. What can I do for you today?"

"You never were much for small talk. I've admired that in you. I would like to meet with you about some business. I think you will find the time well spent and very profitable."

Todd knew instantly not to quiz the Chairman of the Federal Reserve Board about the specifics of the business transaction over the phone. Intuitively, his street sense kicked in.

"Bob, where would you like to meet?"

"I will be in Washington next week to update a Congressional committee on the economy. Could you meet me at the FED offices at two o'clock next Tuesday?"

"Yes. I will be there next Tuesday."

Todd hangs up the telephone and questions his decision to meet with Mellon. He knows it will be difficult to hide his feelings, but he has done it many times in the past. A long time ago, he decided to temper himself when in the company of Mellon and Davis. *I will see what Mellon wants. My time for revenge will come. I must keep my enemies close!*

Todd did make the meeting with the FED Chairman on Tuesday. He was shown into Bob Mellon's office by an aged secretary as soon as he arrived. Mellon sat in a large leather chair besides an oversized oak desk in a huge ornate office. Everything was large and lavish as is appropriate for the big daddy war bucks of the free world. The secretary asked if she could get any refreshments for Todd. Todd nodded a no, and the secretary left the room closing the door behind her.

Todd's instincts warned him the meeting would be in the grey, if not black area, of business. Subsequently, he was well prepared for the illicit proposal from the FED Chairman.

Bob Mellon utters a few pleasantries before presenting his proposal. "Todd, I know you like to get straight to business, so I will forgo the formalities, and get right to it! I have a unique opportunity for you that will involve no risk on your part and will make you a lot of money. Are you interested?"

"Of course I am interested. I need more details."

"I need to hedge a little, but I can speak in generalities. Many people in the country lost a lot of money when the stock market crashed recently. People called it a dot-com bubble, and when the bubble burst, a lot of money was lost. Most of the losers were investing in cyber potential, and lost sight of the basics of income, profits and dividends. At its peak, the dot-com investors were delirious with the paper gains that resulted from a run up in stock prices. But, as we know, paper gains turn into cash losses when raw emotions overtake sound financial analysis. That's pretty much what happened when a few of the big traders sold their dot-com stocks, took their profits and exited the market. They pricked the bubble, and the balloon was leaking air. Soon, others joined in the sell off, and prices began to decline. The rest is history as a selling frenzy ensued and the unsustainable stock prices plummeted."

Bob Mellon went into further detail about the debacle. He noted the substantial loss of national confidence that had occurred at the same time. The dot-com stocks with all their precarious promises of technological supremacy were our hope for the future. Even as our manufacturing and industrial base was being exported to foreign shores, the government had touted the new information economy as America's future. A substantial part of that future was vaporized along with the paper profits of the ailing dot-com companies.

Todd looked incredulously at Bob Mellon. "Thank you for the history lesson, but all that has nothing to do with me. I never invested a dime in the techno dream, and I am not interested in it today!"

"I'm sorry Todd. Permit me to get to the point. In your real estate business, what has been the single most important financial factor that you can not control?"

Todd knew the answer, but feigned confusion. "I'm losing you Bob. Dot-com. Real estate. Financing. Just where are you going with all this?"

The Chairman leaned back in his over stuffed chair, retrieved a large Cuban cigar from his humidor, and lit it. He looked Todd in the eye as he inhaled the cigar, and then exhaled a perfect ring of smoke.

"Todd, we first came together in 1980 because your father had lost control of his finances. Your Dad was concerned he would lose the business. The business was saved because I was able to negotiate an interest rate with him that enabled you to continue in business. I'm saying, and I know you agree that the uncontrollable factor in the real estate business is the interest rates. If you knew with certainty where the interest rates would be in the future, do you agree that you could make an immense amount of money?"

Todd acknowledged. "Yes Bob. I agree that if I knew the future price of money, I could make money in a number of ways. What are you proposing?"

Another ring of smoke preceded the answer. "I know with certainty where the interest rates will be for the next 5 years. If I share that information with you, would you be willing to sign a consulting contract with a well known marketing firm. The consulting fees would be 20 percent of your net profit. The fees will be payable monthly, and will continue for as long as I furnish you with the future rate information. We both know the profits will be in the billions!"

"I agree the potential profits are extremely large. Why have you selected me for this enterprise?"

Mellon responds promptly. "From 1980 to 1989, I was your controlling business partner, owning 51 percent of your business. In those years, you paid off your mortgages, while paying an 8 percent dividend to me. I made a lot of money with you, and to be perfectly frank, I had no idea as to how you made it all happen. At first, I thought you might be manipulating us. But, the company kept growing and the dividends kept coming. And then, one day, you came in with 5 billion dollars, all cash, and bought back my stock in Robbins. Hell. You made me a lot of money. I don't know how you did it, and frankly, I don't care. I do know that you are the right man for this job for a lot of reasons. Your record of success and your positioning in the real estate industry are the main criteria. A man of your caliber will be expected to make money in the business climate I propose. Subsequently, you will be beyond any suspicion when you do make a lot of money. People eagerly follow visionaries, and they will follow you because of your track record. You're a natural for this situation!"

Todd had been listening intently. "I appreciate your kind comments Bob. I know we would make a lot of money. This whole thing sounds too easy. What happens if we get caught?"

"It sounds easy because it is easy. The only way we would get caught is if either you or I make the issue. Insider trading is a common crime in the corporate boardrooms of America, but it is rarely prosecuted because it is rarely disclosed. Confidential information has made just about every billionaire that I know. We will not get caught because you and I will not disclose the special information we will share."

"Are you saying that I would be the only person with this special knowledge?"

"No Todd. I am not saying that at all. I will have a few other people similarly involved. The potential and market in the United States and the world is far too great for any one person or company. I can assure you that only you and I will know of our specific arrangement."

Todd Robbins and Bob Mellon talked for another 45 minutes discussing the arrangement and firming up the details. When they were both comfortable, they agree to proceed. Bob lifts himself from his chair and walks around the desk toward Todd. He extends his hand to Todd.

"Congratulations, we are partners again. I'm looking forward to a long and profitable arrangement."

"Thank you for the opportunity. When do we get started?"

"Right now. Here is everything you need to know. The Federal Funds rate is currently six and one half percent. Beginning in January and continuing through December of next year, the FED will drop the rate to at least two percent, perhaps lower. The rate will drop in increments of one quarter to one half percent during each month of the year. Presently, the plan is for the rate to be at one to two percent for the next couple years. Here are the current projections. I will advise you if there are changes. There will be no need for us to meet again on this matter. Barring some unforeseen event, I will contact you next December for another update."

Todd was flabbergasted. "Incredible. You're saying the interest rate will be in the range of one to two percent by next December and will remain in that range through 2003."

"That's correct Todd. Make your business arrangements accordingly!"

"Bob, I hope you don't take offense at this, but why will the FED be dropping the interest rate so aggressively."

"No offense taken Todd. In fact, I would have been disappointed if you didn't ask. The government is in quite a mess with this dot-com mess. Trillions of dollars were lost in the bust and the stock market is continuing to lose ground. Due to the suddenness and severity of the dot-com crisis, consumers are not buying. Businesses have large inventories of products, and are beginning to scale back production. This means lower prices, lost jobs, and no profits. It's bad. We are in a downward spiral with no relief in site. It appears we have a liquidity crisis, which could lead the country into a deflationary period. Unless the FED injects enormous amounts of money into the economy, the entire system could collapse! I anticipate that you will lead the investing charge into the real estate sector and open new areas for economic expansion."

Todd understood the scenario. His company had gone through a similar problem when his father died. The only difference was in 1980, the high interest rates were supposedly used to fight inflation. Now, the low interest rates were being used to counter a potential deflationary period.

Todd responded. "If I am hearing you right, I will be instrumental in saving the economy from disaster. Forget the talk about insider trading. We are statesmen doing our patriotic duty to save our country."

Bob laughed. "I couldn't have said it better. It's a patriotic event. And what could be more American than making a few bucks in the process? Lets save America!"

Todd is suddenly interrupted from his reminisces of 2000 by a loud thunder clap. He winces as he instinctively jumps back. The sky was an ominous grayish black and he could see the dark circle of rain that was rapidly approaching. Todd steps into his suite and closes the double doors behind him. His devious grin betrays his inner most thoughts. *Nothing is as it appears to be! Keep your friends close, but keep your enemies closer!*

CHAPTER 46

▼

Todd Robbins is preparing to meet with Charlie Bing to make additional plans for the project. The prior days meeting of the National Real Estate Coalition had been rather uneventful. It did provide valuable insight into the state of the economy as viewed by many of Americas leading businessmen. Todd noted he never saw so many prominent men so uncertain of the future. He reflected that he might share their ambiguity if not for his special arrangement with Bob Mellon. His only quandary with the Mellon windfall was choosing from the many money making opportunities that were presented to him. He made billions of dollars every year, but making money had long ago become irrelevant. His sole objective was the project!

At 9:30 AM, a door chime announced the arrival of Charlie Bing. Todd opened the door and greeted his ally. "Did you sleep well Charlie?"

"Yes, quite well. Thank you. Did you watch the early news today? Today is Election Day. There is much discussion about the Democrats possibly taking back both houses of Congress. Who do you think will win?"

Todd knew Charlie was baiting him, but replied anyway.

"I have no idea who will win. I know the losers, and they are the American people. The Democrats and the Republicans are cut from the same cloth. Philosophically, they agree to differ for the purpose of the election. But, their agenda is the same. It is of no consequence if either a Democrat or a Republican wins. They both answer to the same master, and that master is not the American people!"

Charlie acknowledges. "America is truly a strange place. It is comprised of similar yet contradictory ideologies. She lectures the world about democracy, but abhors the concept in practice. She is comfortable in permitting people to vote, but only if the decision is already known. She openly declares economic opportunity for her people, but then places the advantage with a privileged few. What chance do the ordinary people have in such a system?"

"Your question is rhetorical. Ordinary people have no chance other than to continue to be ordinary. The answer is the same as always. The people are fed an evasive concept referred to as the American dream. They get to work, plan and save for an ambiguous future which constantly changes at the whim of the political forces that rig the outcome. Yes, they get to vote. But, choosing from the chosen is more an exercise in futility than it is an opportunity for change. Most Americans recognize the uselessness of voting and subsequently do not vote. The order of things to come is decided before the vote by the very few who hold the reins of government firmly in check with their wealth and money. This is America. This is the way she has always been. The only way to bring about change is to be recognized. The only way to become recognized in America is to make money—a lot of money. It is only then that you can participate in America. For all the others, they get to pursue that wispy, elusive cloud called the American dream. The dream is really a political concept called hope which—"

Charlie interrupts. "I should know better than to get you going. But, I enjoy your passion, and it excites me to hear you speak. Let's get on with the project. I have much to share with you, and I know you have new information for me."

Todd shifts his train of thought and begins to discuss the project. "We need to continue to shift our dollar resources into short term oil and gas futures. We will have to stay with a strict schedule of investment so as we do not disrupt the current market. We want to increase our participation, but it is critical that our partners are not perceived as major players. I want us to continue to be subject to the volatility that is currently driving the market. I know we stand to earn or lose dollars depending on the major players, but that is OK. Just have each of our partners slowly increase their holdings. They must be viewed as autonomous at all times. We must also continue to increase our stocks of gold, silver, platinum and palladium. Again, this must be done in a subtle manner so as not to arouse suspicion in the markets. I have a schedule of investments for oil, gas and precious metals for each of our partners. They must strictly follow the timetables and guidelines. Bear in mind that we must all remain above scrutiny in making these purchases."

Charlie marvels at Todd's thorough analysis of the markets and the purchase timetables. For the last five years, each of the partners has slowly increased their holdings. Charlie notes the purchase quotas for precious metals has increased significantly.

"It will all be done according to your instructions. I am told our Asian partners have allocated the necessary dollar reserves to make the purchases. Our newest partners in the Mid East are concerned because we will not share the project details with them, but they have committed to staying with the plan. When do you think we can give them further details?"

"We can not release any details of the project to any other partners. We are too close to implementing the project to have it compromised. If they wish to continue to participate, they should purchase their assigned allocations, without question!"

"I understand Todd, but my Chinese coordinator is having a difficult time asking our new partners to stay involved. They claim they are frequently losing profit opportunities in order to build portfolios of precious metals. Is there anything we can tell them?"

Todd is disturbed as he replies. "Charlie, you of all people, should know better. No. We will not share any information on the project. They will know when the time is right. In the meanwhile, consider everyone an agent of the FBI or the CIA, including our new partners. We have come too far to jeopardize the project!"

"I'm sorry Todd. I'm coming under a lot of pressure from numerous people. Many of our old partners want us to move now, and are growing impatient. They know the details and fully understand the project. But they are tired of waiting. The old partners are pushing to get going and the new partners are pushing for more detail. I guess I am equally anxious. It does appear that our enemy is extremely vulnerable. Will we implement the project soon?"

"I wish I had an answer for you. True, America is vulnerable. Perhaps, she is more exposed than anytime in her history. We must be certain that once we start the project that the collapse will be inevitable. I can't afford to gamble at this point. Please. Have our partners exercise more patience. They will not be disappointed with the results once we have implemented the project."

Charlie knows Todd as a man of immense patience. He has tolerated the close presence of the men who killed his father for over 25 years. For close to 20 years, he has carefully orchestrated an elaborate plan to bring about the demise of a corrupted system. *He above all others has complete control of the project. He can not and should not be rushed!*

"Your instructions together with your assurances will be passed along to our partners. We shall all exercise more patience. All our partners are behind you and will respect your timetable."

"Thank you Charlie for your continued support and encouragement. The project would not be possible without you. You are the liaison to our partners. You have convinced them of the worthiness of the project. You have persuaded them to invest their fortunes and futures into the outcome of the endeavor. I often marvel at your ability to control our diverse group of partners. Without you, the project would be just a dream. I appreciate all you do. Now, what news do you bring me from our partners?"

The discussion continues for some time as the two associates continue to refine their plans. Todd will gather more information that will affect the project. He has chosen to remain the anonymous brain child of the project. Charlie has become the voice of the movement. He has been steadfast in implementing the elaborate plans, controlling the old partners, and bringing in the new contacts who add further substance to the project. His international business connections and close ties to Chinese government officials permit him to organize and control the elaborate scheme. Soon, these two old college pals who cavorted together in their youth will lead a world class fraternity in a unique mission of change.

CHAPTER 47

▼

David Paine is on an early morning walk. The weather is perfect. The cloudless skies and moderate temperatures were accented by a cool tropical breeze. The lush green landscapes and the palm trees were highlighted by a variety of colored flowers and shrubs. Florida is a beautiful place in the fall. There is a special peace that David enjoys on these solitary walks. The quiet serenity of the pre dawn morning permits David a special opportunity to explore his deepest thoughts.

For several days, he has been absorbed with an incident that occurred during a recent meeting of Wake Up America. During the question and answer segment, one lady complained about the rising interest rate on her home mortgage. She is middle aged with large glasses that substantially consume her face. She was joined by two other people who had a similar issue. All three had purchased their homes in the last two years, and they were concerned that they might lose their homes in the near future. It was the kind of concern that was becoming increasingly common at the meetings. The loss of industries and good paying jobs inevitably translates to individual financial difficulties. At first glance, this was that type of affordability issue. David Paine worked in the real estate and mortgage businesses and he was able to quickly diagnose the problem.

"What kind of mortgage do you have? Is it a fixed or adjustable rate?"

The lady with the big eye glasses responded first. "My mortgage has an adjustable rate. I couldn't afford a fixed rate when I bought my home two years ago. I was told I could refinance to a fixed rate in the future if the adjustable rate got too high. Well, the rates have increased and I am forced to pay an additional $375 a month for the additional interest. I checked and the fixed rate is still more than the adjustable rate. There was also some concern as to the value of my home. The lender I checked with said home values were falling, and that I might have to come up with $40,000 to $50,000 in order to get a fixed rate mortgage for the same amount as my present mortgage. I don't have the additional money for my present mortgage, so converting to a fixed rate is out of the question. What can I do?" The other two people also had similar mortgages.

David knew the answer to the question and it was not good. He is hesitant to answer quickly because there is not a good solution. Prior to November, 2005, real estate had experienced rapid growth. Double digit increases in prices and appreciation were the rule and not the exception. In South Florida, during 2004 and much of 2005, price increases ranged from 30% to over 100%. The real estate boom traced its origins to a few factors. Investors had entered the market in droves. These investors had taken a severe financial hit when the dot-com bubble burst in 2000. They were on the prowl for other investment venues. The opportunity in real estate became apparent as the Federal Reserve began to drop the short term interest rate in 2001. In a 30 month period starting in January 2001 and ending in June of 2003, the FED lowered the short term interest rate by more than five percent. Investments in real estate increased proportionately to the decline in the interest rate. The seeds for the real estate boom were planted.

Mortgage companies anxious to profit from the infusion of cheap money created a number of financial products which catered to the needs of the investors. Real estate is heavily leveraged and one can control large real estate investments with relatively small amounts of personal capital. The mortgage companies lowered the personal cash exposure and potential risk exposure with a number of programs largely built around adjustable rate mortgages. It was a no brainer for tens of thousands of investors. Most determined that new construction would provide the best venue for future profits. New construction required six to twelve months of building time before an investor needed to take possession. Cash requirements to control the property during the construction time were minimal. The investor had the ultimate advantage of time to earn appreciation on a home that is not built. When the home was completed, most investors had either already resold the home, or had it listed at a price which netted substantial profits. The formula worked and every investor made windfall profits. Cash on cash returns ranged from 100% to well in excess of 1000%. Appreciation, prices and profits continued to increase as more people invested in real estate.

People wishing to own homes soon found the low interest adjustable rate mortgages as their ticket to the American dream. The low interest rates and creative mortgage programs made it possible for many marginally qualified people to buy homes they normally could not afford. Friends and neighbors bragged about the increased value of their homes inducing others to join the home ownership rush. At a point, everyone felt like a financial genius as they continued to reap the benefits of price appreciation.

Home builders were quick to jump on the band wagon. The builders rapidly increased prices on new homes as demand increased. Again, the low interest rates made the higher priced homes appear to be affordable. Builder profits soared as new developments were sold out in a pre-construction phase. Soon, the developers introduced a construction reservation system designed to maximize their profits. Thousands of buyers jumped at the dubious opportunity. They agreed to purchase reservation agreements for properties not yet started, at a price not yet determined, which would be completed at some ambiguous date in the future. Prices were increasing so rapidly that some builders refused to honor construction agreements when a home was completed. These builders elected to renounce the agreements, and then sold the homes at a higher price.

It seemed everyone was happy with the rapidly appreciating market. Investors, builders and new home owners rejoiced as their wealth increased. Even existing home owners cashed in portions of their growing home equity, compliments of the low FED interest rate policy and the adjustable rate mortgage. Profits, appreciation and dollars flowed to whoever might venture into the real estate frenzy.

And, then suddenly it all ended in late 2005. The multitude of buyers who stood by and promptly bought up just about any property at any price suddenly disappeared. It was like a wisp of smoke on a windy day vanishing before your eyes. Unbridled enthusiasm turned to cautious optimism as the real estate boom threatened to turn into a real estate bust. Talk of a real estate bubble became more prevalent.

During 2006, real estate prices declined, but not at a precipitous rate. Investors had deserted the real estate market. Those investors who got caught in the down turn offered the biggest price concessions. They hope to exit the market before prices decline further. Home sellers are still enamored by the heady days of appreciation and are reluctant to make price reductions. Home builders are hesitant to retreat from their exhilarating price levels. Instead, they offer free upgrades and other subsidies, in lieu of price reductions. Home buyers are looking at a growing inventory of available homes, but are extremely reluctant to make purchase decisions. The market seems to be in a stalemate as sellers and buyers wait for the other side to blink.

David Paine felt sorry for the people caught in the financial dilemma, but knew there were few good alternatives. He looked at the lady with the big glasses and responded. "You might try to refinance with a mortgage with a longer amortization period. Recently, 40 year mortgages have been introduced by a number of lenders. There may soon be some 50 year mortgages available soon. The rates will not be lower, but the longer amortization period may bring your monthly payment into an affordable range."

David knew that many people would be caught up in a financial emergency as more of the adjustable rate mortgages came due for an adjustment. It was difficult to determine how many home owners would be adversely affected. The subsequent problems with credit blemishes and impending bankruptcies would create still more instability. He anticipated that the current calamity is just the beginning of a much larger crisis.

David sympathized with the lady with the big glasses as well as the thousands of others who would soon be immersed in similar difficulties. *Why had the FED permitted the rates to go so low? Why had the mortgage lenders and banks permitted so many people to get involved with mortgages they could not afford?* A large segment of the real estate and mortgage industry appeared as a house of cards. The slightest shift will collapse the house as well as the hopes and dreams of hundreds of thousands of Americans.

CHAPTER 48

▼

An article in the Fort Myers News Press tells of a few local activists who gathered about a 1000 signatures from people who supported local government control over illegal immigrants. The advocates of the movement requested that city and county government institute laws that would penalize employers who hire illegal immigrants. They also sought penalties for landlords who would rent to the immigrants. The petitions were presented to the local government officials for action. The immigration issue is a hot potato for federal and state government officials. Most politicians side-stepped the problem because of the upcoming elections. The local officials quickly stated the problem was a federal issue and refused to further acknowledge the petition. No one in the country is seriously interested in addressing the problem at this time.

David Paine is having lunch with George Reefer, a real estate associate. George read the article and felt compelled to comment. "Talk about people with nothing to do with their lives but to attack those trying to build a life! The illegal immigrants are performing an important service in the economy. They are doing jobs that most Americans do not want to do; and they are doing it for less money. What harm can come from that?"

Paine responds. "George. Supposedly, the number of illegal immigrants in the country ranges from 12 to 20 million. No one knows for sure how many illegals are in the country because no one is counting. The numbers are evasive and somewhat scary. Since the destruction of World Trade Center, politicians have spent hundreds of billions of dollars to enhance our internal security. In addition, they have curtailed some of our freedoms with legislation they claim is essential to security. But for some reason, the illegal immigration issue is largely ignored. Let me answer your question. A great concern for many is internal security. If so many people can illegally infiltrate the country, how comfortable can we feel with our security?"

George interrupts. "I understand the security concerns, but you have to admit the immigrants are great for our economy. South Florida is a tourist driven service economy, and we would virtually grind to a halt if we did not have the immigrant labor to support our growth! I was on the construction site of a national builder just last week. I met with the superintendent, and he acknowledged that over 80% of the work force was Spanish speaking immigrants. Most could not speak English. He explained there was always one man on a crew that understood English, and he was able to communicate his needs through that individual. Later, I spoke with a property manager at a golf course community. Again, the subject of immigration came up. The largest recurring task in the community is grounds maintenance. The property manager said that 90 to 95 percent of the work force is immigrants. He said these percentages were the same in all the communities he managed. At lunch, I stopped for a hamburger at McDonalds. When I entered the restaurant, it looked like every employee was Hispanic. A little later I attended a real estate marketing seminar. The presentation evolved around the importance of Spanish speaking representatives to be able to sell to an emerging group of Hispanics seeking homes. That evening, my wife and I went shopping. She had to pick up some groceries before stopping at a department store for a clothing sale. The super market and the department store were both clearly staffed with a majority of Latinos. I could go on, but you get the point. All these businesses could not operate without the immigrants!"

"George, I see the same thing you do, and I agree with you. Our economy could not sustain itself at the current level without the immigrants. I am just not certain how much real benefit we get by employing so many illegal immigrants."

George is very opinionated and again interrupts. "We benefit with more construction, more products and more services at lower prices. Hell. Everyone knows that the illegals get paid less, work harder and don't complain! Business benefits with lower costs and the consumer benefits with lower prices. Americans have a real economic win—win situation using these foreign workers."

David has heard the same argument before, and is fully prepared to respond. "All that glitters is not gold. The appearance of these benefits is deceptive. Let me explain with a quick overview of the construction industry. You said, and I agree that much of the home building industry is manned by immigrants. You also said a national builder has a work force that is over 80% Hispanic at a local development. How much have new home prices declined as a result of the lower cost employees in the past 3 years? We both know that prices on new homes have increased substantially over this period. Construction is labor intensive, and it seems that new housing prices should have reflected the cheaper cost of immigrant workers, but it has not. So, where did the money go? My guess is that the higher priced homes and the lower cost labor are reflected in the financial records of the home builders. Check the profits, dividends and retained earnings of the builders, and you will find who reaped the benefit of cheap illegal labor. I know this approach is simplistic. There are many other influencing factors. Supply, demand, the cost of materials and the cost of land should all be considered. However, the point is still made. Cheaper labor did not translate to lower priced homes!"

George has been listening intently as he gobbled his luncheon salad. "Maybe you're right! The builders made a ton of money at the expense of cheap immigrant labor. That's the way the system works. Find a better and cheaper way to do something, and you become entitled to the increased profits that result. Isn't that capitalism? It's as American as you can get. We built our country that way! Besides, these guys were mostly illegal. They deserved to be taken advantage of!"

David counters. "Again, I must disagree. I am not sure who is taking advantage of who. Twenty years ago, I was associated with quite a few people who worked in the construction industry. They were all hard workers and they all made more money in construction than is made today. The industry was just as labor intensive, but workers made more money and new houses cost a lot less. There were very few immigrant workers, but even those few were paid on the existing scale. Construction work was considered a real job where a worker could get married, raise a family and buy a home. The workers made a living wage, the builders made a fair profit and the consumer paid a fair price for the end product. But then, things gradually changed. Immigrant labor increasingly replaced American workers because the builders came under a lot of pressure to reduce costs. Construction wages were continually lowered as more immigrants became available to work for lower wages. American construction workers left the industry because it no longer provided a living wage. Contrary to what you eluded to earlier, I do not think immigrants work harder than Americans. I think most Americans had the advantage of working smarter, and left the industry to seek other opportunities that would provide for their financial needs. The real question becomes this. You said it was OK to take advantage of the illegal worker. Is it OK to take advantage of the American worker who is displaced by an illegal immigrant?"

"David, you must be one of those liberals that I hear about constantly. I suppose you would favor taking care of the displaced American, and guaranteeing his living wage. Things change and people should change accordingly, or they deserve to be left behind! The American worker expects too much, while the immigrant is willing to accept less. Our system has proven that our economy works best when we constantly strive to be more efficient. This means increasing productivity, reducing costs, or innovating a completely different way. Those that can't adapt should be left behind, or they will become a burden to all of us in the future."

David is starting to get disturbed. "I don't think I said we have an obligation to care for every displaced worker. Our obligation is to the welfare of our country. I am favorable to anything that truly benefits America and its citizens. Immigration is one of those gray areas which appears to benefit America in the short run, but is problematic in the long term. Short term, low wages for illegal workers brings more immigrants to work for low wages. The inference is the lower wages will bring lower prices, but it is not happening. The only benefactors of low wages are business owners. Big business loves immigrant workers because they keep the general wage level from increasing. Just the potential threat of an immigrant invasion into an industry keeps the general wage level in check. Immigrant workers are the modern day equivalent of the company police. It is a subtle form of intimidation. The federal and state government refuses to address the problem of immigration because of pressure from business. Illegal immigration is big money for business, and the government acquiesces to the demands of the business community. Short term, millions of low paid illegals have displaced American workers, and act as a brake on the general wage level. Long term, the consequences are potentially disastrous. More American workers will be displaced into lower paying jobs, and they will find their purchasing power diminished. The American standard of living will deteriorate, and people will not be able to afford many of the things they now enjoy. A good case in point is the home building industry. The invasion of illegal immigrants in this industry has resulted in higher home prices. Prices have reached a level where the average worker can no longer afford a home. I used to sell homes to construction workers, but today, a new home is out of their reach. Similarly, wage stagnation has priced many other professionals out of the housing market. You know what's going on! Teachers, fire fighters, police and many other essential community support people can not afford a home. Lower wages and reduced purchasing power are the apparent consequences of the mass illegal immigration. There are many other hidden costs!"

George replies. "I guess I never thought of the negative implications. I just assumed that lower wages in these jobs were beneficial to the economy. You may have a point! What are the other hidden costs?"

"They are not so hidden George. Have you noticed how many new schools are being built in the county? Or how much your property taxes have increased? Did you know that school officials are mandated by state and federal law to provide an education to all that apply? A wave of immigrant children is putting immense financial pressure on the school system. It costs about $15,000 a year to provide a student with an education. Who do you think is paying? And, there is the issue of medical care. Our public hospitals are under a government mandate to care for anyone who walks through the doors. How much do you suppose the illegal aliens contribute to the rapidly escalating health care costs? The latest statistics indicate that some 50 million American citizens can not afford health insurance. Now add 12 to 20 million illegal immigrants to the mix, and you wind up with spiraling insurance costs to the Americans who are fortunate enough to afford health insurance. Every year, the incremental property tax and health insurance increases needed to pay for the unfunded mandates force more Americans into an affordability crisis. Unless something changes, the system will collapse!"

George quickly responds. "Whoa. Now you're saying the immigrants are responsible for a potential collapse in education and health care. If that is the case, we should ship them all out today! You're right! My taxes and hospitalization costs are always increasing. I don't want to pay more than my fair share. Now that you got me all in a lather, what is the solution?"

"George, these problems have been around for a long time. The influx of illegal aliens has magnified the problems, and has served to hasten the possibilities of a collapse. At the crux of the problem is the business employer who continues to reduce wages so he can make a bigger profit. The concept of a fair living wage was under fire long before the immigration predicament. For years, government and business have fought increases in the wage levels. Even modest increases in the minimum wage are frequently opposed. They claim these increases are inflationary, and subsequently bad for the economy. The solution lies in government demanding that businesses pay a living wage to all American citizens. A living wage should be sufficient for a worker to raise, feed and house his family in a respectable manner. A living wage for all American workers means they could pay taxes and buy health insurance to protect their families. With everyone paying their fair share, the financial problems in housing, taxes, health care and education would be solved. Everyone would pay a fair and equitable amount."

George skeptically nods his head. "You are much worse than a liberal. You are a utopian dreamer and probably a socialist! Where do you think all the money would come from to pay everyone a living wage?"

"Money is not an issue. There is plenty of money available. The equitable distribution of the money is a big part of the solution. The massive flow of profits and wealth to the few must be redistributed in order to provide a living wage for all American citizens."

George laughs. "I changed my mind. You are not a socialist. You are a frigging communist! I guess you are in favor of taking the money, property and wealth from the rich and giving it to the poor!"

David hesitates briefly before answering. "I do not consider myself a socialist or a communist. However, I do have an admiration for Henry Ford. I believe he was a capitalist of sorts. I think he concluded many years ago that it was beneficial to the economy to pay workers a living wage. To the astonishment of his industrial peers, he doubled the wage of his factory workers without pressure from unions or government. His motivations were purely capitalist. He reckoned that he could sell more cars if his workers were better able to afford them. He also contended that the higher pay would assist in developing a stable and more efficient work force. His thinking proved to be correct and Ford became the leading producer of automobiles in the world for many years. I share Henry Ford's capitalistic sentiments. Paying American workers a living wage is good business!"

"OK David. Let me assume you are correct. What does all this have to do with the illegal alien problem?"

David checks his watch. He has an appointment in 15 minutes and needs to wrap up the lunch meeting. "I am thinking a little like Henry Ford. Perhaps American workers will become a little more loyal and efficient if they worked at jobs that paid a living wage. Businesses would reap the rewards of lower turnover and a more experienced work force. This would do much to cut into the 20 million illegal immigrants. Once the word got out American workers would be paid a living wage, my guess is that a sufficient number of citizens would come forward and fill the needs of the economy. The illegals would no longer be needed in the work force. We simply enforce immigration laws and the exodus will begin. We develop a time table to discontinue free health care, free education and the other subsidies to the illegals, and the balance of the illicit aliens will leave the country of their own accord. Our country can then develop a guest worker program that works to fill the labor needs not met by American citizens. The primary obligation of our government and our economy should be to the American citizen."

David and George shake hands as they leave the restaurant. George offers a parting comment. "I really enjoyed lunch today. You make a lot of sense on the immigration and economic problems. I will probably attend your next meeting!"

David gets into his car and is on his way to his real estate appointment. It was an interesting lunch which served to reinforce his thinking on the future course of America. *America and her businesses must serve the interest of Americans at all times. There can be no compromising on that issue. How do we convince government and business of their obligations to American citizens?* He smiles as he recalls his reply to some of George's comments. *No. I am not a liberal, a socialist or a communist! I am an American who believes in capitalism as long it works to the benefit of our country and its citizens!*

CHAPTER 49

▼

Chou Bing is in China. It is mid November, 2006 and he is meeting with his Chinese government liaison on the American project. Chou has come under increased pressure from the government to implement the project. Chou has remained adamant that all involved parties must comply with the time tables dictated by Todd Robbins. "The project is not yet ready to proceed. Our partners must continue in the program to purchase quantities of precious metals. It is important to stay within the purchase guidelines or we will arouse the suspicion of the Americans."

Chou Bing was speaking to Liu Yin at his home in Beijing. Chou and Liu meet each month to review the project. Liu is his contact with the Chinese government. Liu coordinates project demands with high Chinese officials. The names of the Chinese chain of command have remained secretive since the early days of the project. Chou has only spoken with Liu about the scope and status of the project.

Liu Yin responds. "I am under severe pressure to implement the project. Our government is under demands from officials in Russia, Korea, India, the Mid East and South America. Everyone wants to know when we will start. Perhaps, we can buy the metals on an advanced schedule. We have plenty of dollars. Our own central bank currently has over 950 billion dollars in reserves. We can buy 100 times the requested amounts through various sources which the Americans will not detect. Just say the word and it will be done."

Chou is emphatic in his response. "No. We must stay with the plan, and the plan permits us to purchase no more than the allocated amount. If you recall, one of our partners in the Mid East exceeded his quota and caused the price of gold to spike to $750. You forced him to resell the excess gold and the price level fell to $600. I know we have many dollars, but if we are forced to buy the metals at inflated prices, we may not be able to reach the long term goal."

Yin replies. "I only want to help! We have much resource to place with the project. Do you know how much of the precious metals we will have to buy in total?"

"I do not know. Our American contact gives me a schedule of purchases each month. His instructions are firm, and I am instructed not to deviate. I am sorry. There is nothing else I can do!"

The two comrades review the metals purchase allocation. Then they review the oil and gas purchase allocations. Yin frequently analyzes the purchase requirements in an attempt to detect the strategy. He has been unable to breach the secretive plan. It has become a source of constant frustration for Liu Yin. Yin gives Chou the reassurances he requires. "Everything will be done per the plan. The allocations will be met!"

"Thank you Liu. There is comfort in your words."

Liu then seeks an update on American political affairs. "I understand that November 7th was a day of great victory for the American Democrats. Perhaps, they might do something about their arrogant President!"

"You should not complain Liu. The American president has caused the project to advance significantly since he was elected in 2000. His egotistical manner has driven away many allies, and has created potential adversaries fearful of his agenda. He has made many enemies for his country. His greatest enemies are in league with the project, and will continue to follow our instructions on the project. Even America's allies are uncertain of the president, and have remained at arms length of his unpredictable policies. They criticize his agenda and are unsure of his motives. They are suspicious of American objectives and offer only token support for his wars. The president refers to his side in the war as coalition forces. But one need only count the few troops contributed by American allies to know their interest is only conciliatory."

Liu is always interested in Chou's views. Chou has years of experience with American society and offers valuable insight into their culture, policies and objectives.

"I'm sorry. I was not complaining about the president. President Plant is a man hopelessly lost in his own agenda. He seems to relish war with weak countries with abundant resources, and so he is very dangerous. I can understand how many of his allies would distance themselves from this man. My comments on the Democratic victory were more pragmatic. Will the Democrats be able to rein in the president? If so, and the president moderates his demands, perhaps the resolve of our partners on the project might soften?"

Chou responds. "I sense your concern, but take heart. Changing President Plant's demeanor would be akin to removing the stripes from a zebra. His leadership style is self-centered and largely dictatorial. I think he has mannered himself after another American president, Teddy Roosevelt. They are similar in many ways. Roosevelt was proud, arrogant, and demanding. Roosevelt's philosophy was to speak softly, but carry a big stick! Under that mantra, Roosevelt invaded small countries that did not acquiesce to his demands. He was the American cowboy at the beginning of the 20th century. Roosevelt was successful in extending American influence through something called battleship diplomacy. The inherent objective during the Roosevelt years was the extension of the imperialist ideology. Plant could well be a Teddy Roosevelt clone. He is confrontational and self righteous in his approach to political problems. He courts religious fundamentalists as he openly proclaims his Christian heritage. He launched a preemptive invasion of Iraq because he claimed the country was a threat to the United States. When the threat could not be substantiated, he rallied his forces in the name of democracy. As I examine his words and actions, I find Plant to be a man of extreme contradiction. I do not think he truly believes in Christianity or democracy. I think he is in the mold of his idol, Teddy Roosevelt, the imperialist. But, he is an imperialist of a different sort. I think his objective is the expansion of business interests for himself and his supporters, and then incidentally for the United States. Christian values, democracy, good, evil, life and terrorism are the words he freely uses to incite the masses. These terms all have strong meaning and he speaks them with great deliberation, but his actions and his body language reveal the inherent lies. Plant believes only in himself, and those who pledge their unqualified loyalty to him. I would describe him as the ultimate capitalist. Make money at any cost! Have no fear. The democrats will not change Plant. They are in league with Plant."

Liu is intrigued by Chou's analysis of President Plant, but was concerned about his conclusions. "Many men, small or powerful, are of the same self centered nature. They exist in America, in our country and throughout the world. I have seen many people change when it was practical for them. Why would Plant not change if he were pressured to do so?"

"I have not been specific. Plant would change if people of substance demanded change. In the process, he would sacrifice his principals and his supporters. For example, within hours of the Democratic election victory, he fired his loyal Secretary of Defense. He will do all that is required to advance his personal agenda, but he would secretly harbor the same objectives. The zebra can not change his stripes!"

Liu persists. "But, just the appearance of change as a result of pressure from the Democrats may be enough to diminish the tenacity of our partners. It might endanger the project!"

Chou answers. "In the past, such a change may well have weakened our resolution. Those days are past. China has long been aware of the insatiable appetite of the Americans to control more of the world's resources. They are constantly demanding more land, oil, money, financial control and military power. What they do not take by political manipulation, they steal with their International Monetary Fund or World Bank. When those docile means fail, they are quick to resort to their CIA or military forces to take what they want. All of our partners have been victimized in some way by America. Our comrades can no longer be fooled or manipulated with the peaceful gestures of the Americans. Their attitude to the world community has become more transparent since the decline of the Russians. It is bad for the world to have just one super power."

Liu Yin has been listening carefully. "You are right. The United States is much more aggressive in their actions since the fall of Russia. Their attack on Iraq and their veiled threats to Korea and Iran have greatly unsettled the world. I think my greatest concern is that America will once again be successful in changing their image with their deceitful tactics. They have a way of using democratic principals to confuse the people while enslaving them with dictatorial edicts. If they are not successful in seducing the people with the anticipation of democracy, then they pour their dollars into a country to buy off the leadership. If they can not buy the leadership, they start a campaign to tarnish the leaders. If that fails, they engage the CIA to start an insurrection, arrange a coup or assassinate key officials. They inevitably find a way to obtain their objectives."

"I wish I could comfort you Liu. America is like all other great civilizations of the past. She uses her might, money and influence to keep the rest of the world in check. It is important to the United States that alternatives do not exist which can contest her supremacy. Iran and Korea are presently testing America's dominance by attempting to develop nuclear capabilities. America has enlisted the assistance of the United Nations to sanction the Iranians and Koreans. They are in contact with our officials and the Russians in an attempt to stop the nuclear ambitions of these countries. America is determined to protect her position of dominance, at any cost. I fear America might invade Iran or Korea if necessary!"

Yin is aggravated with the explanation. "America has much to learn about diplomacy. How can she expect Iran and Korea to forsake their nuclear programs when President Plant has proclaimed the countries are part of an axis of evil? Iraq was invaded without provocation when Plant said that country was also a part of an axis of evil. Any country so indicted would be foolish not to prepare for an invasion from the Americans. Iran and Korea should not be dissuaded from their nuclear programs. China may well pay lip service to the Americans, but I would hope we will not take any firm action to impede the nuclear programs."

Chou Bing nods in the affirmative. "China has for some years paid considerable lip service to the wants and desires of the American behemoth. We were compensated well for our servility. The United States permitted the infusion of large amounts of money to build factories and industries. She then provided us with access to her markets so we could sell our products. Our country has prospered under this arrangement. In a short period of time, we were able to build immense industries and create jobs for millions of our countrymen. America benefited with a flood of inexpensive products, and so she injected more money into China to build more factories in our country. The economy of China has grown immensely due to this arrangement. But, the end is near. America wishes us to change our currency values so she can get further benefit. This has become a common American trick with countries that have made economic gains in dealing with the Americans. If we were to agree, our products would earn fewer dollars. Moreover, the dollars we have already earned would be devalued. Fortunately, our leaders are not that stupid. Once again, we are forced to pay lip service in order to delay any decision that would hamper the project. It is not in our interest to devalue our currency, and so we will delay our decision. We have learned it is best to avoid saying no to the Americans. The same is true as respects the nuclear ambitions of Iran and Korea. We will placate the Americans with our participation in the talks, while protecting the interests of our partners with our procrastination."

Lin views Chou with admiration. "You have a great deal of insight into the way America thinks. I know you were educated and spent many years in the United States. Your thought process is clear, and you have been able to explain many things to me very concisely. One thing is bothersome and I do not understand! Perhaps you can explain. Why did the American Government permit China to become an economic power? I understand that many Americans lost jobs in the factories and industries that were moved to China. Why have the American people been so submissive while losing their jobs?"

Chou Bing responds. "The American people have been fooled by their government into believing that they will benefit from lower cost goods and services as a result of something they refer to as globalization. But the government has lied to her people. True. We supply lower priced goods than Americans can produce. But what good does it serve if Americans can not afford the cheaper goods because they have had to take an inferior job? The people remain gullible and they continue to accept the false reasoning of their leaders. Occasionally, they vent their anger by voting out the prevailing Democrat or Republican Party. But it is of no consequence and no true change ever occurs because both parties serve the same master——business! Understand this! In America, big companies run the government, and the government does the bidding of her large corporations. Big business instructs and the American government obeys by permitting the exportation of jobs and factories to China. Big corporations prefer this because they are able to make greater profits by firing Americans and hiring lower paid Chinese workers. The businesses do not care about American workers or for that matter, America herself! They certainly do not care about China or the welfare of our citizens. These businesses are driven by profits, and only profits! It is a philosophy that proclaims the greater good is served as long as there is money to be made. At the heart of all this greed is the capitalist system. I do not fault a system. I fault the mentality of those who believe in the system without qualification. Even China has accepted certain capitalistic traits. But our country and our culture hold our national interests in high regard. Because of this distinction, China and her partners will beat the Americans with their own system. It is the basis of the project. America will have sewn the seeds of her own destruction with her unregulated acceptance of capitalism!"

Chou Bing and Liu Yin conclude their meeting. Yin will report to his supervisors on the progress of the project. Chou Bing will catch a plane to Hong Kong where he will meet with another influential participant on the project. Hong Kong will be his final stop before returning to the United States. In Hong Kong, he will meet with Larry Yang. Yang is the personification of the pitfalls of both democracy and capitalism. Yang is rich, personable and influential. His special vocation exposes the soft underbelly of the American political system.

CHAPTER 50

▼

Chou Bing is having breakfast in his suite at the InterContinental Hotel of Hong Kong. He is mentally preparing himself for his meeting with Larry Yang. Yang was born and raised in Hong Kong. He has made a fortune in transportation over the years. His wealth was built around his ability to service the needs of a diverse portfolio of clients. His special talent is working with adversaries to their mutual benefit. He has strong family ties to Chinese officials on the mainland and vast business interests in Hong Kong. His ability to balance these frequently conflicting interests is legendary. Yang has further fortified his businesses over the years by growing and cultivating his relationships with British and American corporations. He has developed a world wide directory of influential contacts that he is able to access to solve just about any problem. He is sought after to arbitrate many issues because of his reputation for finding solutions which work to the benefit of all involved parties.

He could have easily become Secretary of State for any country in the world if he had chosen a political career. Instead, he uses his considerable credentials in a field that is frequently considered sleazy. Larry Yang is an international lobbyist. The majority of his work is in Washington, DC. He uses his power and money to buy favor from political contenders seeking high office and incumbents desiring to extend their influence. He carefully hedges his support, contributing to candidates from both parties, so he will always wind up with a winner. Chou inherently dislikes what Larry Yang does for a living!

Chou finishes his breakfast and walks over to the balcony. His suite is on the 16th floor of the lavish hotel. From his perch, he has an unobstructed view of Victoria Harbor and Hong Kong Island. He is always amazed with the tranquility of the Harbor as it is set against the myriad of skyscrapers that envelope Hong Kong. *China is growing rapidly, but Hong Kong is the crown jewel.* He can envision the Chinese mainland and all the Chinese people enjoying the growth and prosperity that is now Hong Kong. Chou checks his watch. *Larry Yang will be here in one hour. I must prepare.*

At 11:30, a telephone call from the concierge announces the arrival of Larry Yang and three companions. Chou approves their entry and proceeds to the front door to personally greet his guest. Chou meets his guest at the elevator entrance. "It is good to see you again old friend. You look well."

Larry Yang has the small body structure characteristic of many Chinese. He does show a protruding gut and husky face, no doubt symptomatic of his prosperity and Western indulgences. Larry extends his hand and embraces Chou as he responds. "Thank you Chou. As always, I am delighted to be with you again. I have important information to share with you. We will have an enjoyable meeting!"

Larry points to his companions as he acknowledges their presence. Chou has met the other men on many previous occasions. They are the body guards for Larry Yang. They have been Larry's constant shadow since he first met him over 15 years ago. They are not big men, but they appear physically capable. Although they take pains to keep their suit coats buttoned, he saw one of them in the past with an open jacket. Secreted and almost molded to his body frame was an automatic pistol. Chou acknowledged their presence and leads the cadre into the living room. Larry Yang and Chou Bing take seats as the guards take positions at the door, elevator and balcony.

Chou inquires. "I have never met anyone dissatisfied with you in any way, yet you never travel without your three associates. Do you fear for your life?"

Larry has not been questioned about his companions for many years. Most simply acknowledge their presence in a matter of fact manner. Larry responds. "It is odd that you ask that question after so many years. It is true that most appear to be happy with my services, and I have never known of anyone who would want to harm me. In the past, I have kept the guards because my business exposes me to the confidential secrets of many powerful men. I have never divulged any of the privileged information. However, out of caution, I protect myself from those who would like those secrets buried. My body guards are a relatively minor security gesture considering the importance of the private information I have dealt with over the years. My death would be a comforting convenience to many men. Why do you ask after all these years?"

Chou answers. "I guess it is because of the project. The closer we come to executing the project, the more I become concerned with our lives. There are many men who would kill us if they learned of the project. The ramifications of the project will be felt world wide, and will destroy many powerful people and complete countries. Sometimes I tremble for the bleak futures of the Americans and their allies. And other times, I am exalted and euphoric with our pending victory over the oppressors. There are powerful people who would pay dearly for information about the project. Partially out of fear and partially out of personal security, I find myself questioning the motives and means of people around me."

Larry Yang smiles pensively at Chou. "You are a clever man Chou. It is proper that you question my allegiance. My work as a lobbyist causes me to be on all sides of an issue. I do that well and you fear I will be on both sides of the project. I can only assure you verbally of my intentions. I am one with the project and I shall not waver. I know you don't approve of what I do, but it has been a great source of new information for the project. I have pledged my loyalty to the project, and I hope I can overcome your suspicions! I sincerely hope that you do not feel for the dismal fate of the Americans."

Chou approves. "You are a perceptive man. Thank you for alleviating my concerns. You and I have been such an integral part of the American system that I grow concerned we might hesitate to destroy it. Every day we witness the traitorous acts of Americans who sell out their fellow men and their country for a profit. I know you witness this situation much more than I do. Your work creates the environment for their greedy and self serving decisions. Your dollars makes slaves out of leaders. I have become cautious because so many are so willing to sell their souls for the American dollar. But, enough of this! What news do you bring?"

Larry appreciates Chou's approach to a very difficult situation. Deceit is a common aspect of his work, and it is understandable that one should question his integrity. Larry feels more secure in knowing his partner is alert enough to recognize the potential for treachery. "Yes. Let's move on. As you are aware, our partners on the project have accumulated 525 million dollars to be used in the American elections of 2006 and 2008. The results of the current elections are as we predicted. Fewer than 50 percent of the eligible voters actually voted. Most Americans feel betrayed by the political system and refuse to vote. It is an important factor which will contribute to the success of the project. The Democrats have taken control of both the House and Senate. In total, we spent over 150 million dollars in contributions to the Republicans and Democrats on the recent campaigns. As always, the eventual winners were incidental to our cause. Because we give to both sides, we curry favor and gain influence with both the victors and the defeated. I am solidly positioned to request whatever favors we may require."

Chou replies. "I know the 150 million dollars were well spent. In the past, we have been able to recover our contributions with special requests that favor our businesses. My instructions are to stay clear of any requests of that nature. We do not wish to do anything that might benefit us temporarily, but might serve to endanger the success of the project. A decision has been made to create some friction on some of the divisive issues. We are not interested in supporting any one side of an issue. We want to create more separation among the American people, and would like to use passionate issues to further divide the populace. Immigration is an issue we wish to pursue. You are authorized to contribute 30 million dollars to groups supporting both sides of the immigration problem. Another volatile area we wish to further inflame is religion. We wish to contribute 30 million dollars equally to evangelicals and those who favor separation of church and state. Another area we would like to further divide is the pro life and pro choice movements. You are authorized to contribute 30 million dollars to the opposing groups on this issue. Finally, there is the gun matter. We wish to contribute 40 million dollars to opposing groups on the gun control issue. Can you arrange for these things to be done?"

Larry Yang is well aware of the politics of divide and conquer. The process of separating the people with an issue, and then further dividing the populace with other issues is a favored tool of mayhem. The public become confused, and the confusion leads to disenchantment. A democracy obsessed with people voting for issues in lieu of candidate qualifications soon is devoid of capable leaders. The American people already suffer from the lack of representation due to the money and influence of lobbyists. The end result of a leaderless mob lacking representation is either melancholy or anarchy. Either conclusion is disastrous. Yang acknowledges his instructions. "You can be certain that everything will be done as you have instructed. Can you share any other details of the project with me?"

"No! It is impossible Larry. Many of us are proceeding with a limited knowledge of the workings of the project. It is necessary to protect the interests and identities of our partners. Everyone is aware of the objective. Together, we will bring about the collapse of the United States. In time, I will be able to share more information with you. For now, you must keep faith with the objective and continue to implement the instructions you are given."

Yang persists. "I could do more to help you with the project if I had more details! Why won't you trust me?

"I'm sorry Larry, but I am under strict instructions. You now know everything you need to know in order to assist on the project. Please don't ask me for more. It could be dangerous for both of us!"

The meeting continues for another hour. At the conclusion, both men will leave Hong Kong for separate destinations. Larry Yang will go to Washington, DC where he will cavort with congressmen while secretly disbursing the monies to the various special interest groups. Yang is silently upset that Chou would not grant him additional information on the project. Yang is accustomed to controlling people. He does not like it when he is controlled. *Did Chou Bing just threaten me???*

In three weeks, Chou Bing will go to New York to meet with Todd Robbins for another update on the project. For now, he will remain in China tending to other business. Chou is elated with the progress of the project, but he is growing increasingly impatient. The desire to strike is strong!

CHAPTER 51

▼

David Paine scheduled a meeting of the Wake Up America group. It would be the final meeting of the year. The upcoming holidays makes it difficult for people to attend the meetings. Additionally, the negative tone of the meetings is generally not well received during the holiday season. Dealing with the problems of society is not pleasant work. People always rely on the holidays to bury their problems in the fantasy world of cheery Christmas music, continuous shopping, and feigned happiness. It is best the people get to enjoy this special time of hope for the future. After the New Year holiday, most people will return to the real world. As always, they will be frustrated that nothing has changed except they are deeper in debt.

The meeting is scheduled to begin at 7:00PM and will be held at a vacated building on Metro Parkway. Attendance at the meetings has continued to grow, and it was necessary to find a larger facility. One of the members volunteered the use of the facility for the meetings. The building was perfect. It was air conditioned and could safely hold up to 700 people.

David pulled into the parking lot at 5:00PM. He is scheduled to meet the owner to gain access to the building. The evening was unusually brisk owing to a cold weather front that had come through Fort Myers earlier in the day. The entry doors to the building were open. David sees Brad Peters, the owner of the building, at the entrance. Brad Peters invests in commercial real estate, but his primary occupation is farming. His company, United Quality Produce, grows tomatoes and peppers on fields in Immokalee. David had heard that Brad is now in another business. Brad Peters is a vocal supporter of the small farmer. His constant concern at the meetings is the continued deterioration of the agriculture business in Florida.

David approaches the building and greets Peters. "Hello Brad. I want to thank you again for letting us use your building for the meetings."

Brad extends his hand and replies. "No problem. The building is empty and I like what you're doing. You're welcome to use it as long as it is vacant. I've hustled up the folding chairs, a microphone and a few tables for the meeting. Here are the keys. Again, feel free to use the building as long as you need it."

David grasped the hand of the aging farmer shaking it firmly. Brad is a big man. He had to be over 6 foot, and looked to weigh about 250 pounds. His hands were huge and heavily calloused largely attesting to his years in the tomato fields. His face is leathery and etched with deep wrinkles. As they finish their greeting, David looks up at the hulking man. "I really am quite grateful. It sounds as if you have everything prepared for the meeting. I would like to pay you, but___."

Brad interrupts. "No need to pay. I know there's no money involved in your presentations. I'm glad I could help! The things you discuss at the meetings need to be said. Too bad the politicians won't address some of the issues. Most people who attend the meetings are quick to understand the problems. I think many of them like the meetings because they get to vent their feelings in the company of people who will listen and acknowledge their needs. It's been a long time since a lot of us have felt we are not alone in recognizing that America is in trouble. All we hear from the politicians is that the economy is growing with more jobs and more production. Meanwhile, most of us are making less money working at the left over service jobs. Your meetings lend substance to our true feelings. Just maybe, some of us will wake up and begin doing something constructive. You're doing a good job. Keep up the good work! The man is as big as a mountain, but speaks softly. His words and actions reveal a deep personal conviction.

"Thank you for the encouragement Brad. We have not had the opportunity to speak at length in the past. I sense you have been hurt in some way in business. Can you share the difficulty with me?"

Brad stiffens as he begins to answer. "I have worked the fields for 38 years now. I'm not well educated so I had to work hard every day of my life. I lived through a time in America when hard work and persistence were the primary ingredients of success. I started out growing tomatoes on 1 acre in my back yard while working as an auto mechanic to make ends meet. Over time, I got to know what I was doing. Soon, my tomatoes were bigger and tastier than my competition. I went from 1 acre to 5 acres and then 100 acres. I sold every tomato I could grow. Things went well and by 1995, I controlled over 1000 acres of prime Florida produce farms. I was doing well in a tough and competitive business, and was able to buy some buildings in Fort Myers with my profits. This property is one of my investments. At any rate, 1995 was my high water mark. After that year, the business began to fall apart. Do you have any idea why it happened?"

David was listening to the story and was unprepared for the question. He stammered his answer. "No, no. I don't think so!"

Brad quickly rejoined his story." It was NAFTA—NAFTA! You know the North American Free Trade Agreement. The politicians said agreements such as NAFTA would open up new markets for my products. I was always suspect of NAFTA because the Republicans had initially sponsored and supported the trade arrangement. I can recall 5 or 6 years of heavy resistance to the NAFTA proposals before it was suddenly passed into law. I did not think or learn much about NAFTA beyond the high acclaim given to it by the politicians. They promised hundreds of thousands of new, high wage jobs which would increase the standards of the citizens of the United States, Mexico and Canada. At the time, I went along. I was doing well, and the promise was I would do better! I was further placated by the fact that NAFTA was approved by a Democratic President. It was President Clinton that signed NAFTA into law. My family, as far back as I can remember were all members of the Democratic Party. I remain a Democrat, although I sometimes used to think I was wealthy enough to be a Republican! The traditional view used to be the Democrats were the party of the working man, while the Republicans favored the interest of the wealthy. Man. I was really off base on that one!"

David comments. "Don't feel alone! You and millions of Americans were convinced of that stereotyping. Even today, Americans choose a political party based on the self proclaimed principal of the party. The Republicans claim affiliation with independence, conservatism, family values and Christian beliefs. The Democrats still chant the credo of the working man promising higher wages, increased benefits and greater economic opportunity. Both parties consistently fail to deliver for the American people. Their true priority is to a different principal, or should I say a different master! Both parties are obligated to the lobbyists who give millions of dollars in campaign contributions in order to gain favorable treatment. Americans get the scraps which fall conveniently from the gourmet table served up to the special interest lobbyist. I tired of the leftovers in 1985 when I switched my party affiliation to Independent. I know registering as an Independent carries no benefit. It is solely a symbolic protest. It pleases me to inform the

Democrats and Republicans I am no longer their fool. Sorry for the interruption. Please continue with your NAFTA experience."

Brad continues. "As it turns out, your comments on political representation sum up the NAFTA debacle. I mentioned earlier that 1995 was my best year. After that, a downward cycle in prices and profits started. Year after year, the prices paid by the tomato buyers were reduced. The buyers claimed there was an excess supply of tomatoes that was driving down the price. The next growing season, I cut my tomato production to respond to the excess supply. The buyers, once again, cut the price due to an excess supply. The buyers blamed the excess supply and lower prices on Mexican tomatoes that were flooding the market. After a few years of cutting production and prices, I developed a true hatred for the Mexican farmers who were flooding the market with low priced tomatoes. Everyone knows that tomato growing and harvesting is labor intensive, and that the chief advantage was cheap Mexican labor. I could not compete. The local growers association contacted our congressman who claimed he was against NAFTA, and would check on the problem. That congressman and every other politician we contacted proclaimed their outrage, but all failed to do anything about it. By 2004, the national industry association claimed that over 38,000 farmers were driven out of business since the advent of NAFTA. Those farmers that survived saw their income continue to decline. I was upset with everyone. NAFTA, the politicians and the Mexicans were all sons of bitches! My personal situation continued to erode, and I sold off some farm acreage and a few of my commercial properties in order to pay my bills. I was quickly losing my life savings, and had frequent nightmares about being 75 years old and growing tomatoes in my back yard."

David Paine joined in. "I can understand the hatred, the nightmares and the frustration you must have experienced. The whole thing sounds unreal and traumatic. I have a few questions for you. First. If the price you received for your tomato crop has continuously decreased, why has the price of tomatoes in the super market steadily increased? And second. Why do you suppose NAFTA was legislated into law, and why was it not rescinded when the results proved so negative for the American farmer?"

Brad has started to light a cigar and coughed abruptly when he replied. "Let me finish the story and I think your questions will be answered. This will really get to you! About 4 years ago, I got out of tomato growing completely. The 10 year struggle had forced me to sell off all but 150 acres of farm land. At the time, I ran into a friend in Fort Myers who grew landscape plants and trees. There was a large demand for landscape material and my friend urged me to get into the business. My buddy took me under his wing and in about 9 months, I had my remaining land full with plants and trees. In the process, I hired on a lot of new help who knew how to grow plants. They were mainly Mexican workers, and at first, I had some mixed emotions. I blamed them for the collapse of my tomato business, but needed them for my new business. As it turned out, they were not so bad. They were hard workers and helped me get my new operation up and running in a relatively short time. I came to rely quite a bit on a lead foreman who spoke reasonable English. In the course of conversation, I asked him about tomato growing in Mexico. I was astonished with his reply. He said tomato growing in Mexico used to be done by a large number of small farmers, but that all changed in the late 1990's. He said prices for the crops continued to fall over the years, and many of the small Mexican farmers lost their land and their livelihood. These farmers were told that large supplies of tomatoes were coming in from the United States causing local prices to fall. He said many of the displaced farmers were part of the illegal immigration wave that swept across the United States in recent years. As you can imagine, my curiosity was aroused. The price of tomatoes was increasing while both the American and Mexican tomato farmers were losing money! Where the hell did all the money go?"

David was somewhat astonished with the revelation. "I am intrigued. If what you say is true, it goes a long way in explaining the huge number of illegal immigrants during the last 10 years. Did you find out who makes the money in the produce business?"

Brad sucks deeply on his cigar as he explains. "Yes. I found out. There are three leading companies in the agricultural business today, US Agra, MDA and Garcill. They, along with the big corporate farmers and food processors exploited small farmers in the United States, Mexico and Canada through a cycle of over production and dumping. NAFTA eliminated import quotas, reduced growing subsidies, and phased out price supports. The small farmers in all three countries were played off against each other by the big food brokers who took advantage of the NAFTA provisions. In the grain business, it worked like this. The big brokers would buy the production of a country and then move the products to another country prior to a harvest to create an over supply condition. These manipulations served to depress prices for the harvest which the brokers bought up. They used the products to either continue the cycle in another NAFTA country, or sold off the excess production to a non-aligned country at considerable profit. Under a special provision of NAFTA, the large farmers continue to receive government subsidies. They were able to continue producing the high volumes which kept prices down. The results were predictable. A handful of large agribusiness corporations controlled the market for farm products. They drove down the prices they paid, while increasing the prices to the end users. They made immense profits, while thousands of small farmers in Mexico, Canada and the United States were driven out of business. And the hurt went well beyond tomato growers. This same strategy was used for grains, chickens, pigs, cattle and just about any other farm product. In the end, small farmers were eliminated, while the big corporate concerns prospered, and the consuming public paid the increased price demanded by the few companies that manipulated the market place. We owe it all to NAFTA, and the politicians who permitted it to happen. I think that answers your questions!"

David is troubled as he responds. "It seems so many of our economic troubles are caused by our own government. I never thought much about NAFTA after it was enacted into law. It sounds as if NAFTA created the conditions for the destruction of a lot of hard working farmers. No doubt NAFTA was created by its primary beneficiaries, the big business interests. Where does it all stop! I have spoken with many people who have lost their jobs and livelihoods in similar situations. At the root of all these tragedies is our government in collusion with large businesses. It's a vicious cycle that continues to erode our pay checks, our job base, and our self respect while corporate businesses prosper. Why doesn't our government see that they are gradually destroying the very thing that made America great? America was built by hard working Americans, and it seems the politicians are content to see it destroyed by greedy self serving corporations. Somehow, we must convince our leaders it is in our national interest to promote the welfare of the American people! We must place the American people ahead of profits, or America will continue to decline."

Brad responds. "I agree with you in some respects. America was built by people who were free to make money however they could. We exist in a capitalistic society that encourages individual initiative, innovation and profits. I think that is important, and we must walk a fine line so as not to destroy these essential elements of economic freedom and success. Let's face it. Our system is not perfect, but it is the best system in the world!"

Don't get me wrong Brad. My concern is not capitalism. It is the way capitalism is used to create profits. There is something inherently wrong with selling off our manufacturing industries to foreigners in order to make a profit; or, permitting the sale of critical American technology to foreigners in order to make a profit; or, outsourcing American jobs to foreign countries in order to make a profit; or, creating a NAFTA which gives an unfair advantage to corporate sponsors in order to make a profit; or endorsing the nebulous concept of globalism in order to make a profit; or cooking the corporate books in order to make a profit. I could go on, but you get the point. Capitalism needs to be regulated. It must be modified to reflect the needs of American people, and it must always be conditioned on the best interest of our country. I guess I am a proponent of old fashioned American nationalism. Our politicians must be made to understand that American national interest must come first. The common interests of Americans must prevail before the lobbyist dollars, ahead of foreign influences and in front of corporate profits. All the other major nations of the world have prioritized their national interests. China does! Japan does! India does! And the rest of the developing world does! It is time that America recognizes the urgent need to look after herself. If we do not, I am quite certain that the other countries of the world will not rush to our aid when we have lost our advantage!"

Brad extinguishes the now spent cigar as he replies. "It certainly is an interesting thought. National interests should be a primary concern in all our decisions, but it obviously has not been for quite a long time. In fact, nationalism is almost a dirty word in America today. I don't know why, but the concept is not discussed! You will definitely have an up hill battle promoting that idea!"

David Paine looks toward the parking lot. A few cars have pulled in. He must prepare for the meeting. He politely excuses himself, and thanks Brad for the use of the building. As he enters the building, he is struck with his latest eye-opener. Nationalism, as an objective has never occurred to him before. It came out in his discussion with Brad as a second thought. Yet, the idea of national self interest seems to be an answer to the torrent of conflicting economic policies affecting America today. All of the other problems are simply symptoms of a system gone haywire. He would prepare himself to advance the politically unpopular theory of American nationalism.

CHAPTER 52

▼

It is Friday morning, and David Paine was on his way to meet with a supporter who lived on Captiva Island. He stopped briefly at the toll booth and paid the six dollars to cross the bridges that connect Fort Myers to Sanibel and Captiva. The brief trip over the causeway was filled with scenic views of the approaching island. Once on the island, he is reminded of the hurricane season of 2005 which had wreaked considerable damage to the homes and horticulture on the islands. Most apparent was the dramatic change in the main road. The road which was previously covered by the canopies of mature shade trees was now fully exposed. The replanting of young trees and shrubs seemed totally inadequate when compared to the majesty of the lush pre-hurricane environment. The bland scene bore witness of the destructive forces of nature.

Fifteen minutes later, David pulled into the private driveway of Amy Younger. A neat, yet natural, serpentine road was bordered on both sides by an array of tropical palms and foliage. Soon, he approached the two story stilt house. The house was also surrounded with plants, trees and flowers. The open area under the stilt house revealed the crystal blue waters of the Gulf of Mexico. The picturesque scene was uniquely breath taking.

David was greeted by two men who were raking up light debris in front of the house. The man closest to his vehicle approached and asked. "Can I help you sir?"

David was still absorbing the beauty of the surroundings as he replied. "Yes. My name is David Paine. I have an appointment with Mrs. Younger."

The young worker acknowledged. "Mrs. Younger is expecting you. Please park to the right, and follow the path to the rear patio."

David parked his car, and hesitated as he stepped out of the vehicle. The sand was neatly arranged and revealed the etch marks of the freshly raked area. He humored himself as he left his foot prints in the sandy soil of the manicured drive. *Ah. The lives of the rich and famous!* He approached the patio, and spotted Amy Younger sitting in a shaded area beside the pool. He opened the door to the screened lanai as he spoke. "Hello Amy. It's good to see you again."

Amy Younger waved her walking cane as a salutation. "Welcome to my home David. I'm glad you could make it." Amy was a young 84 year old who retained her vigor by staying involved with community matters. She is principled with a strong sense of social values. She could be pleasant as pie when the mood was right. But, she could be feisty and rambunctious when someone dared to accost her resolute ideals. More than once, David witnessed her walking cane used as a club to silence an adversary.

David pointed to the waving cane, and smiled. "I hope that is not for me!"

Without flinching, Amy throws the cane at a television she had been watching. "No. But, I am saving a few good licks for some of the politicians who are ruining this country. It seems their only function in life is to display their appetite for corruption and their utter incompetence! They are a bunch of stupid asses! I am sick and tired of all of them!"

Amy was clearly shaken as David sat next to her. Something has obviously disturbed the spirited matriarch. David pointed to the television and queried. "What's wrong Amy? Is it something they said?"

Her sunken blue eyes revealed the trace of a tear as she responded. "The news just summarized Thanksgiving Day in Bagdad. Over 200 Iraqis and two American soldiers were killed in a series of bomb blasts. The news showed all this violence and misery in a 15 second sound bite, and then immediately cut over to our countries big problem of the day. Care to know what afflicts America today? It seems that a national electronics chain just released a video game system, and the stores are being mobbed by some passionate game enthusiasts. A few people were injured in the resulting scuffle. The police were called out in some stores to contain the unruly shoppers."

Amy was emotionally caught up in the sad irony of these conflicting stories. She continued her tirade. "I guess serious problems come in all sizes. A lot of people in Iraq got killed today for leaving their homes, while a few Americans got hurt trying to buy video games. How's that for a fair and balanced world?"

David clutched Amy's hand in an effort to soothe her. "There is no fairness. There never has been. The poor and subservient of the world have always done the bidding of those in power. And those in power have always done whatever is necessary to protect their power. Today, the people of Iraq die because they seek a better life, while Americans folly in seeking temporary pleasures out of boredom and naivety. Today is Black Friday in America. For America, this means a return to profitability for many companies. In Iraq, Black Friday is a procession of endless wooden caskets. There is no comfort or justice in these situations. It is a sad day for Iraq, America and the world."

Amy clenches her fist and strikes her arm chair in protest. "Yes. It is unfair! It is unfair that we have created so much death and torment when we invaded Iraq! It is unfair that our own politicians lied to us to promote the invasion! It is unfair that we now hold the Iraqi government accountable for cleaning up the mess we made! I fear our country has lost its way. I am afraid that unless someone steps forward to alert the complacent American public of the excesses of America's leaders, that one day Black Friday in America will also become an endless parade of caskets. We must do something to wake up the American people! That is the reason I ask you here today."

David responds. "Amy. I feel strongly about these matters and will do everything I can. I will continue to run the meetings, and hopefully, others in our country will step forward with similar efforts. I can—."

Amy interrupts. "I have attended your meetings, and saw evidence of your conviction. I agree with your approach and I feel you can address a larger audience. I am sure there are others who are capable and will ultimately speak out. But, I also sense we are running out of time. In the past 6 years, America has lost much of the prestige and respect that our allies depended upon when they decided to support our war efforts. They are slowly easing away from their commitments to our country. And as our allies vacillate, our enemies have grown stronger. It is a recipe for an American disaster. I don't know how our enemies will come. I just feel they will! Many times I attempt to place myself in the situation of an enemy. I have concluded that if I were an enemy, I would be preparing the venue to destroy America. We must move quickly!"

David was not expecting the urgent needs that Amy was presenting. "Yes. But what can I do? I am limited. I don't think more meetings will make a big difference."

Amy looks directly in David's eyes as she answers. "I know you are limited, but I have some resources I want to contribute to the effort. My late husband made a fortune in radio and television. I own stations across the country. I would like to get you on a local radio station for a talk show. I will give you one month to refine your presentation. After that, I would like to begin to nationally syndicate the show. I will complete the syndication inside of six months. By that time, the show will be aired on both radio and television, 7 days a week. I will be sure you have the necessary advertising and support staff. Can you handle the job?"

David is stunned. "I'm not sure. But, I am willing to do everything I can to support the effort. Seven days a week is a lot, and I still need to work to support my family."

Amy interrupts again. "Your family will be taken care of. Can you handle the job?"

David smiles as he replies. "Amy. This would not be a job for me—it would be a joy. You have no idea how much I will take pleasure in doing this. I have been trying to stimulate people for years in the hope we can build a better America. I hope I can live up to your expectations!"

Amy offers a handshake to seal the accord. "I, too, have been looking for many years to find the right person to lead this effort. There is no question in my mind that you are the man for the job. God speed you on your mission. You have my unwavering support!"

David Paine and Amy Younger briefly go over some of the start up details before parting company. Amy instructs David to meet with Paul Phillips, the CEO of America Live Network, on Friday at the local studio. David returns to his car still unsettled by his new prospects.

After David departs, Amy slowly rises from her chair. She shuffles to the television to retrieve her cane. She is looking forward to the groundswell that will soon be created. A lot of people will disagree with her support of David Paine. Some may disagree violently. She will make the necessary arrangements to provide security for herself and David. Still, it may not be sufficient. David will create a lot of antagonism towards many influential people. And, powerful people can get malicious when they feel threatened! She decided not to brief David on the security concerns so as he can freely concentrate on the work at hand. *I will arrange security for David.*

CHAPTER 53

▼

On Friday, David Paine is driving south on Route 41 in Fort Myers en route to a meeting with Paul Phillips. His mind has been churning with various ideas since his meeting with Amy Younger. *What a fantastic opportunity to make a difference!* It has been a hectic time as he sought to prioritize his ideas into a coherent presentation. He was ecstatic with the potential, but nervous with his ability to adequately promote his agenda through the new venue. Just when he believed he was ready, a new idea emerged causing him to reevaluate the presentation. David Paine was consumed with these thoughts as he traveled the busy highway searching for his destination. He did not bother to get directions to the radio studio because he thought he knew where the building was. His eyes were darting back and forth as he sought out the telltale signal tower on the horizon. He had now traveled further south than he thought, and began to have second thoughts as to the location of the studio. A temporary panic sets in as he checks his watch. *I did not want to be late for this meeting.* David was preparing to turn around when he spotted the steel and cabled structure ahead. He breathed a sigh of relief, and turned on to the dusty road which leads to the signal tower. One final curve in the road, and suddenly an unpretentious building is in front of him. A small sign announces WFFM, AMERICA LIVE NETWORK.

David Paine enters the building and is greeted by the receptionist. "Hello. Welcome to WFFM. How can I help you?"

"Hello. My name is David Paine. I have an appointment with Paul Phillips."

The young secretary jumps to her feet. "Yes Mister Paine. Mister Phillips is expecting you. Please follow me to our conference room."

David Paine follows the secretary past a labyrinth of small offices and studio doors. He stops briefly and looks into a windowed room. The room is full of buttoned consoles, a few microphones and two people who are immersed in conversation. A red light above the door signals the room is in use. The secretary glances back and announces. "This is one of our studio rooms. There is a live sports talk show in progress at this time. David acknowledges and follows the woman into a conservative conference room.

"Mister Paine. Please have a seat. Mister Phillips will be in shortly. He is expecting you. Can I get you anything—coffee, soda, water?"

David Paine is investigating the room. "No. Thank you. I'm good for now!"

David notes a large picture of Amy Younger on the wall at the head of the conference table. He walks over to the picture and reads the inscription, '**Anthony and Amy Younger—Founders of America Live Network**'. The photo was obviously dated some 30 to 40 years ago. Amy appeared youthful, but she still had that mischievous glint in her eyes. *She must have been a handful!*

A tap on David's shoulder interrupts his musings. "Hello David. I am Paul Phillips. I am pleased to meet the man that made such a strong impression on Amy Younger." Paul Phillips points to the picture as he continues. "Amy does not give herself freely to casual acquaintances. I don't know what you said or did, but I have specific instructions to personally assist you with your program. How may I help you?"

David Paine was incredulous. Here was the chief executive officer of a national media network company offering his services. David looked into Paul Phillips's eyes as he shook his hand. "Mister Phillips. I am as flabbergasted as you. This whole situation came out of a visit to Amy's house last week. She was insistent that I start the radio program immediately, and said that I would be supported. I met Amy a few times at activist meetings that I conduct, but I had no idea she could be so influential!"

"Please call me Paul. It appears we will be working together for some time to get Amy's plan established. Amy is a lady who always knew what she wanted, and aggressively pursued anything or anyone who could contribute to her objectives. In this particular case, Amy feels America needs a severe adjustment. And, it is up to you and me to see that the adjustment takes place. I suggest we get comfortable with each other. It's going to be a bumpy ride, and we may have only each other to hold onto!"

David Paine and Paul Phillips then proceed to introduce themselves to each other with some background information. David proclaimed his humble background as a steel worker, his current occupation as a real estate agent, and his zeal for activist causes.

Paul Phillips cut a completely different portrait. His background since receiving his masters degree included stints with some of Americas leading corporations. He had been the problem solving genius who salvaged troubled corporations from the brink of financial disaster. He developed an uncanny skill to turn giant companies who were bleeding red ink into profitable entities. He amassed a personal fortune correcting the missteps of corrupt or incompetent corporate executives. Phillips made many enemies in the process as he stealthily unveiled the illegal manipulations of some of America's leading business leaders. As time went by, he observed an ever increasing number of illegal corporate activities. He found it stressful to continuously fight the surge of corporate exploitation that became almost common place. At a point, he tired of the process. He had concluded that corporate corruption is the rule and not the exception. He decided to go with a good, fair and reliable company to get away from the stench that had permeated American business. He knew Anthony Younger well and served on the board of directors of America Live Network. When Anthony Younger died suddenly in 1998, his widow, Amy approached him to run the media conglomerate. He accepted the position and was happy in his new pursuits. Although, he removed himself from the pig pen, the stink of the shady corporate culture continued to manifest itself. He knew that the continued cycle of corruption was not good for America. He vowed he would fight the corporate self-indulgence and dishonesty whenever he had the opportunity.

David was astonished with the distinguished background. He was anxious to pick the mind of this seasoned business leader. "Why do you suppose that our corporations and executives find a need to cheat and steal? Most of them are well paid with generous benefit packages! I don't understand why they resort to fraud, conspiracy and manipulation?"

Paul answers. "I have found that the common thread that links the fraudulent actions is greed. The upper level executives have the key to the money box, and there are never enough safeguards to prevent them from finding a way to loot the treasury. Enron ruined the livelihood and pensions of thousands of workers while a handful of executives were made to account for a small part of the losses. The cheaters are usually quite creative in their methods. I have uncovered elaborate schemes such as exotic accounting techniques, creative stock options and inter corporate conspiracy plots. Some of these methods were so sophisticated that I often thought the offenders could have exerted far less energy in running their companies legally. But, they would have made a lot less money. Greed is always the common denominator. On the other hand, the financial manipulations can be quite ordinary. Cooked books, two sets of books, insider trading and fraudulent expense accounts are as old as business. In every situation, the perpetrators commit the crimes because they can. They are the guardians of the company, the keepers of the treasury and the final word on policy. Having no checks on their actions and in a corporate culture that encourages profit at any costs, they become morally free to enrich themselves at the expense of the workers and stockholders."

David is intrigued with the analysis. "All right, I agree. All these things have been happening and have been increasing in frequency. But, how do you stop it?"

"I'm afraid the answer to that question is complex. The old system of checks and balances that controlled the excesses was reliant on the independent accounting firms and the government. We have recently found out that some of these independent accounting firms were part of the problem. Major accounting firms were caught in fraudulent conspiracies with major corporations. Together, they duped thousands of stockholders and employees out of hundreds of millions of dollars. And, I can assure you what we know is just the tip of the iceberg. Many of the illegal dealings still have not surfaced. We will see more of this type of scheme in the future! The controls failed because of the continued deterioration of ethical and moral standards that eventually fouled the accounting firms. These firms were once above reproach. Now, they are a part of the corporate corruption problem. And, then there is the government. Many years ago, they surrendered their oversight responsibilities over the conduct of business. Politicians are prone to turn their heads to dishonest business practices. In fact, government regulated entities have become the most incompetent of organizations. The Federal Reserve System is the best example of unbridled avarice and corruption. They make trillions of dollars out of thin air until they over produce dollars. This leads to inflation which causes slow erosion in the welfare of all Americans. The only benefactors are the few wealthy individuals and corporations who conspire with our legislators and political leaders. Together, they create the business schemes which swallow the easy to produce dollars. The rich get richer and the middle class and the poor foot the bill! Our government is charged with the responsibility of regulating the supply of money, but they freely sell that responsibility to the lobbyists who represent the financial elite. Examples of the sellout are copious. The failure of the government regulated Savings and Loans in 1989 was supposedly rescued by the Resolution Trust Corporation. It should have been called the Dissolution Trust Corporation because all they did was liquidate the assets of the Savings and Loans in a planned process which cost the tax payers billions of dollars! All this money disappeared into the pockets of the financial manipulators who created the crisis. ERISA is another government sponsored financial plot. ERISA is the pension protection program which the government instituted to protect the pensions of covered workers. It has lost billions of dollars since its inception, and has the potential for trillion dollar losses. More and more corporations are abandoning their retirement obligations to their employees in order to take advantage of this government bail out program! Again, the dollars have simply vanished without explanation. But ERISA pales in comparison to the financial trickery going on with the Social Security System. The story is that the trust funds have been raided for so many years and by so many politicians that there is a possibility of a future bankruptcy. Trillions of dollars of promised benefits are at risk. The political spin doctors are hard at work creating a wedge between young workers and the older workers closer to retirement. Politicians hope they are able to create a new retirement system which will effectively hide the looting that has taken place for over 30 years in the existing Social Security System. The number and frequency of these transgressions sometimes reveal a lack of creativity on the part of the government sponsored thieves. A repeat of the Savings and Loan debacle is in the making in the form of the fraudulent activities on the part of Fannie Mae and Freddie Mac. These two institutions are the primary brokerage houses for real estate mortgages in the United States. It seems that some corporate insiders cooked the books in order to show non-existent profits which would earn them giant bonuses. The reported discrepancy is in the vicinity of 11 billion dollars, but who's counting? I could go on, but the whole scenario sickens me!"

David was enthralled by the insight of this man. His input simply adds to the need for immediate action. David continues his questioning. "OK, the fox is guarding the hen house. But, what do we do? If the government has sold out to whoever can pay the price of collusion, what is the answer?"

Paul answers quickly. "I think Amy has decided that you and I are part of the solution. Amy has given me a blank check to advertise and promote your new radio show. In six months, you will be as well known as Bill O'Reilly and Rush Limbaugh. You will have more television and radio air time than both of these guys, and you will have a wider national and international syndication. The name, David Paine, will be as well known as President Plant. And hopefully, you will have a lot more positive impact on the people. Amy Younger has bet the farm on your ability to sway and energize the American people. She thinks you can do it and has instructed me to pave the way for you. My primary duty at America Live Network is to assist you."

David was clearly overwhelmed. "I can't express how much I appreciate this opportunity. About 8 months ago, I started Wake Up America at the local library. And now, Amy is arranging national exposure. I feel beleaguered! I want to do everything that I can to live up to Amy's expectations. I've been consumed with countless details since meeting with Amy. I will need good research people to help me formulate timely topics. I want to develop a point-counterpoint type of presentation. You know. Present a topic from one perspective, and then present an opposing viewpoint as a kind of devils advocate. I think this type of approach will generate more reaction and participation from a radio and television audience."

Paul thinks briefly on David's idea before responding. "We already have the research team. As for the point-counterpoint proposal, you will need another personality on the program to pull it off properly. Do you have someone in mind that you would like to partner with?"

David responds immediately. "Yes. I do! I was hoping you would consider doing the presentations with me? You have an ideal background for this work, and obviously you feel a need to get involved. I would be honored to work with you. Will you do it?"

Paul is smiling as he answers. "I would be pleased to work with you. You hit the nail on the head. I, too, have been waiting for the right opportunity to bring about some critically needed change. I think we will make a good team! I will need to begin some preliminary advertising for the radio talk show. Have you decided on a name yet? Bear in mind the name should be adequate for the local show, and be able to fit properly into a national forum."

David responds. "I was thinking that I would use the name of my activist group for the show. Would Wake Up America be a fitting name?"

"I think that would be a great name David. The first show is scheduled in a couple days. Do you have a topic for the initial show?"

David had been thinking of the first show since meeting with Amy.

"I would like to do the show on the minimum wage verses a living wage. It is a topic of significant local interest. Wages have been traditionally low in Florida. I think we can stimulate some very serious discussion. I would like to take the protagonists position, and perhaps you could present the opposing point of view."

David Paine and Paul Phillips discuss the talking points for the show and agree that there will be no rehearsal of specific details. Both would be spontaneous in their viewpoints, and would enter the debate format with just the topic and the talking points as their only guides. It would make for an interesting and provoking presentation.

Paul walks David to the front door of the studio where they part company. Paul watches as David drives down the road. Paul is excited with the upcoming event. He is a seasoned corporate executive who normally would be quite reserved in just about any business environment. And yet, he feels as giddy as a kid who is going on his first date. He and David Paine will be like spirits in this new pursuit. Both are anxious to jolt Americans from a state of melancholy.

In the upcoming days and months, they will slowly awaken the dormant feelings of a country long contained by the culture of corporate and government corruption. The people will respond strongly as melancholy is gradually replaced by the recognition of the misdeeds. The acknowledgment of the injustices will soon ignite the flames of activism as the people demand accountability on the part of their government officials.

Unfortunately, David Paine and Paul Phillips will also take on the bitter antagonism of the institutions they seek to reform. Paul Phillips was expecting the adverse reaction. David Paine did not care about the reaction. It would set the stage for a fatal encounter!

CHAPTER 54

▼

Amy Younger is in a discussion with Paul Phillips following the initial airing of Wake Up America. "Great program Paul! The two of you had fantastic synergy with the perfect amount of disagreement. I was caught up in your discussion of wage levels in the economy. Clearly, David made his point on the need for workers to make a living wage. He logically followed the financial implications of a broad base of low paid workers and their effects on the total economy. He concluded that America will be left with a dysfunctional economy which will either collapse in a social revolution or slowly degenerate into a third world economy because the people are financially unable to participate. And Paul, you did a fine job in presenting the classical corporate and government defense of rising wages. Your discussion of inflation concerns and the ability to remain globally competitive adequately countered David's arguments. However, when the telephones were opened to the listeners' comments, David was the clear winner of the debate. Given the nature of the topic, I feel the results were predictable. The tally of respondents on the hot line indicated a 92 percent approval of David's position. What was not predictable was the number of respondents. You and David were able to speak to 14 callers in the open line segment, but over 400 people registered and left comments on the hot line. Wake Up America has lived up to its name on the first show. Congratulations!"

"Thank you Amy. I think the advance promotions worked to get the audience in place, but David sure did his part to clearly depict the financial problems facing low and middle class workers. And, he did it with a passion that is infectious. You listened to him on the radio while I watched him in the studio. He totally believes in what he is saying. His eyes, his expressions and his body language reinforce his rhetoric. His enthusiasm is genuine and he has the ability to build hope and confidence in people who have given up. You found a winner in David. I hope we can control him before he gets himself hurt!"

Amy ponders for a moment. "Paul. I watched David quite a few times at his library meetings. From the first time I saw him, I was struck with many of the same impressions. He is charismatic, passionate and believable. Worse than that, he is a radical who is willing to do whatever it takes to advance the things he believes in. Subsequently, we can not and should not attempt to control him. What he believes in needs to be shared and said to those who have lost faith and hope in America. It is what attracted me to David. I believe he is the genuine type of person who can make a difference for America. I will support him in every way that I can!"

Paul responds. "I didn't mean we should control David. I meant we should protect him from himself. We both know and understand the vehement nature of the wealthy and powerful when they are under attack. David goes for the jugular as he verbally assails those in power. It needs to be done, but the implications of his actions will probably result in some severe repercussions."

"Paul. I have arranged for the best security for you, David and myself. There are absolutely no guarantees in the security arrangements. The job we have chosen to do is dangerous and those who would seek to harm us can find a way through any security plan. I have supported this cause because I must. I believe America must change for the sake of her future! But then again, I am 83 years old and have lived a full and prosperous life. Perhaps, I do not value life as much as you do. I would understand if you decided that this venture is too risky for you."

Paul is resolute. "You may have mistaken my concern. I want to be certain you and David understand the potential adverse actions. I have been through similar risky endeavors in my corporate dealings, and recognize the dangers. In the past, it was simply a job that paid well. I've agreed to work with this program because I, like you, feel it must be done for the future of my children and grand children."

Amy speaks. "We are of accord then. Lets us not talk any more on the potential dangers. There is too much positive work to do! By the way, there was another interesting development coming out of the first show. Our largest local advertiser, Clem Billings of Florida Development Industries, just happened to tune into the broadcast. This blowhard happens to be a neighbor on Captiva, and he called me personally. He threatened to cancel his contract if I continued to permit our station to air programs on wages and benefits. He said David Paine sounded like a communist and that you essentially were the only lucent voice on the program. I stroked him with a promise to look into the matter, and he hung up mumbling obscenities about bleeding heart liberals. I thought you might enjoy his comments!"

Paul laughs. "Thanks for the information Amy. He will probably be the first of a long list of companies that will cancel their advertising contracts in the near future. If David Paine is as good as we think you will be losing a lot of business real soon. But, you're not in this for the money! Are you?"

CHAPTER 55

▼

Larry Yang is in Washington, DC. He has been busy making visits to some of his favored Congressmen. Larry is a well known personality with government officials. He is always warmly welcomed when he shows up at a Congressional office for a visit. Larry has a gregarious and bubbly personality. He is quick witted and seemed to always have an appropriate joke for any occasion. He has been a regular on Capital Hill for a little more than 6 years, but it may well have been one hundred years. Everyone on the Hill either knows him or wants to meet him. And Larry makes it a point to know everyone. From the receptionist to the chief of staff, Larry knows the first name and hot buttons of every congressional aide. He has the perfect combination of allure and charisma necessary to open doors. More than that, his reputation as a wealthy Asian businessman with very loose purse strings enamors him to the always needy politicians. He can always be counted on to make a sizable donation for a reasonable cause. Because of this trait, Larry could show up at a congressional office and get an immediate audience with most representatives from the House and Senate. Larry owes his success to what he believes is an old American proverb. *Money talks and bullshit walks!*

Today, he is visiting Senator Eric Nagy. Nagy is an aged fixture who has had the same office for over 30 years. His recent political victory insures he will enjoy another six years of political power. Larry Yang has stopped by to develop a twofer. Larry has chosen to distribute part of 100 million dollars to causes that Senator Nagy will endorse. Nagy will subsequently obtain some benefit via a laureate, prestige or a kickback for his endorsement. This is a classic political twofer. Yang accomplishes his objective while endearing the Senator to him. He already knows the Senator is a pro life, gun advocate who would prefer the immigration issue remain in limbo. Larry straightens his tie and pushes back his hair as he enters the offices of Senator Nagy.

Yang bellows. "Hello Lucille. You look wonderful. What have you done to your hair? I like it!"

Lucille springs to her feet with a broad grin on her face. "Mister Yang. It is so good to see you again. I just had my hair done. You are the first to notice."

Yang is embracing the 60 year receptionist as he responds. "Well! Everyone must be blind around here. You look good enough to eat Lucille!"

A deep red blush covers the receptionists face as she responds. "Thank you Mister Yang. How can I help you today?"

"Any chance I can get a few minutes with the old man. I wanted to congratulate him for staying off the unemployment rolls."

Lucille smiles sheepishly as she reaches for her phone. "Let me see what I can do Mister Yang. Please have a seat."

Lucille dials the number for the chief of staff and announces Mister Yang. Before Lucille could place the phone in the cradle, three people rush in unison from the back offices. At the head of the pack was the youthful chief of staff followed by 2 senior aides. "Welcome Mister Yang. The Senator will see you immediately."

Yang smiles as he joins the trio. He approaches Brenda, the chief of staff, and comments. "Brenda, it is so good to see you again. You look younger every time I visit."

He turns to the other greeters and acknowledges each of the staffers by name. Brenda locks arms with Yang and leads the contingent to Senator Nagy's office. As they enter the office, the elderly Nagy painfully rises from his desk. Brenda announces the guest. "Look who I found in the hall flirting with a secretary!"

Yang responds as he approaches Senator Nagy. "Brenda, I would not be flirting in the hall if I thought I had a chance with you in the cloak room!"

Yang is vigorously shaking the Senators hand as he continues speaking.

"Senator, you are absolutely the most enduring person I know. I would like to congratulate you on another personal victory. And, I know the American people are grateful for another six years of your wise leadership."

The Senator signals Brenda and the other staffers to leave the room. "Thank you Larry. Your generous contributions were most helpful in a hard fought campaign. You know. I just barely made the cut. This war in Iraq and President Plant has made it real tough to be a Republican. For awhile, I thought I would wind up in the Smokey Mountains writing my memoirs!"

Yang responds. "That would have been a terrible waste of a great talent. You have too much to give to your country."

The Senator is tired of the small talk. "Enough of the flattery! What can I do for you today?"

Senator, I have a problem and I think you can help. I represent an anonymous man who would like to contribute 20 million dollars to responsible organizations. My client wishes to give 5 million dollars to a pro-life group, 5 million to a pro immigration movement and 10 million to an organization that fosters gun rights. Can you point me in the right direction?"

The craggy face of the elderly senator beams as he responds. "Will wonders never stop? I was sure you would be asking for a political favor, but instead you are giving away 20 million dollars. You never cease to amaze me! I will be certain the money is channeled into the appropriate support groups. Get with Brenda and she will arrange for the distribution of the funds in keeping with your request. Are you sure your client would not like to receive credit for these donations?"

"My client admires you and thought you would be the right person to distribute these gifts. He requests that you take complete credit for the donations. He is grateful for your many years of public service."

The old senator has been around for many years and senses an ulterior motive. He quickly dismisses the dubious thoughts. *There are no strings attached. I would just owe Larry Yang some favor in the future.*

"OK Larry. I will make sure your requests are honored. Thank your client on my behalf for the trust and confidence he has placed in me."

"I will do that Senator. Maybe there is something you can help me with. I have another 20 million dollars to contribute to these causes. My client wishes the money go to different groups for the most impact. I was wondering if you could get me a meeting with the Vice President. I am hopeful he may know of some good organizations that can effectively use the money."

Nagy wears the crafty smile of a knowing politician as he responds. "You want to spread the money around. I don't blame you. Get as much bang for your buck as you can. I am reasonably sure the Vice President will meet with you for 20 million dollars. I will get back with you with the time and place."

"Thank you Senator. I knew I could count on you."

Senator Nagy and Larry Yang have lunch together in the Senator's office. A discussion on the Republican losses in the House and Senate quickly consumes the lunch period. Again, the Senator blames the Iraqi war and an arrogant President Plant for the political defeats, but is quick to deny any personal culpability. The two men shake hands and embrace as they part company.

Larry Yang is pleased with the success of his twofer. He has almost completed the 100 million dollar distribution that Chou Bing had requested at their meeting in Hong Kong. He is satisfied that he has helped advance the project. However, his compromising nature demands he seek an alternative in the event the project fails. *After all, Chou Bing did refuse to share details on the project. I have too much to lose. I will hedge my bets with the Vice President when I meet him.* As he exits the Senate office building, he is quickly joined by his three waiting body guards. They will soon earn their pay!

CHAPTER 56

▼

"Hello Todd. It is good to see you again, old friend."

Todd Robbins and Charlie Bing shake hands and warmly embrace as they meet at the Westin Hotel in Pittsburgh. They had decided to meet here in order to attend the economic symposium held at the David Lawrence Convention Center. Business leaders and government officials combined their efforts to present their viewpoints on the global economy.

Together, Todd and Charlie make their way into the convention center. For the next 4 hours, they listen attentively to the economists, bankers, international businessmen and government officials who paint a rosy picture of economic health. They reinforce each others presentations with statistics showing substantial economic growth in the United States. They point to low unemployment and increased productivity as precursors to continued success in the future. They attribute globalism with the countries ability to grow in the face of the decline of two substantial market sectors. The real estate and automobile industries have been severely impacted by negative growth during the past year, and the trends indicate they will continue to be plagued by market conditions in the near future. None the less, America is enjoying economic growth as the United States continues to benefit from the effects of globalism. The presentations are in lockstep as everyone agrees the future of America is solidly based around the development of the global economy.

Todd and Charlie leave the meeting early to escape the repetitious banter. Todd is first to voice his opinion. "I can't believe so many accomplished professionals can be in agreement on the health of the economy. Why can't they see how much trouble the economy is in? Everything is so fragile today. And yet, there is not a single voice of dissension."

Charlie responds. "You must keep in mind that from their perspective, America is doing great! The people at the symposium are all business leaders. They represent the upper ten percent of Americans whose wealth has continued to grow under globalism. In their minds and in their wallets, the economy is booming. They are right in their personal assessment of the economy."

Todd shakes his head in agreement. "I suppose so, Charlie. I was thinking about the economic health of America when I spoke. I guess I can't help but to think about the big picture. Americans are turning into a society of hamburger flippers, retail clerks and service workers. This country is under a two prong attack. The better paying manufacturing jobs have left America for cheaper sources of labor throughout the world. The lower paid service jobs are up for grabs as American citizens are forced to compete with a hoard of illegal immigrants. The end result is a decline in the standard of living. Why can't the American workers see what is happening to them?"

Charlie and Todd are once again discussing a moot issue. Both know the questions, answers and implications of the adverse economic factors facing America. They run through the exercise regularly to find holes in their logic, and to reaffirm the timing and progression of the project.

Charlie responds. "Some Americans are shielded from the decline by the low prices for goods and services. Mass merchandisers like WalMart depend on a flood of imports to keep prices low. Service and retail businesses depend on low wage immigrants. Many Americans of the 'I got mine generation' think they benefit from the low cost environment. This generation is comprised of the retired or close to retired individuals. Now add in the corporate executives and small business owners that benefit from both the lower cost of wages and the lower prices of goods and services. These groups of people are in favor of low prices. They fail to see the inherent economic problems brought on by the onslaught of imported goods and illegal immigrants. And then there is another group of Americans who recognize the decline in the standard of living, but feel incapable to do anything about it. Some of this group may have lost a good paying job due to foreign competition, and are unable to replace the lost income. Other Americans may have been displaced by an illegal immigrant. Many of these Americans are part of the disappearing middle class. For them, globalization is a dirty word that has robbed them of their livelihood. They want to do something about the problem, but don't know what to do. Daily, they are bombarded by messages from the government, Wall Street and large corporations about the excellent health of the economy. They feel somewhat out of step with the real world. They are desperate for change. It is this group of displaced Americans that would be the solid base of any initiative that would challenge the concept of globalism."

Todd responds. "Suppose a white knight should come along who could energize this group of disenfranchised workers? Would they have any chance against the wealthy ten percent and their beholdened followers, the 'I got mine generation'? Or has the hill become too steep to climb?"

Charlie replies. "Change will not come easily or peacefully. Bear in mind that those who hold the advantage never easily part with their power. Those in control will fight with all the means at their disposal to stop any potential challenger. They will use the government, the police and the army if need be to retain their position. They will hire bullies to beat you, and if you still persist, they will pay assassins to kill you. In this situation, the white knight must be as his adversary. He must be capable of mayhem, violence and murder. He must be willing to die for the cause. The road is never too steep, but finding those willing to make the treacherous climb will be difficult. Americans are still too soft for this type of encounter. It would take a widespread disaster to harden off enough Americans to make a difference. In this case, disaster must precede change. Americans will continue to genuflect to the powers that be until a disaster awakens them. And then, change will come slowly. Only after they have wiped the sleep from their eyes and cleared their senses will they experience the rage necessary to make a difference."

Todd replies. "I agree with you. America is incapable of change. Her leaders have exploited the world with their lies of free enterprise and democracy. Now, they exploit the American worker through devices such as unregulated imports and illegal workers. They travel to China, India, the Mid East and Europe to take advantage of any situation which may enhance their wealth. They are without scruples and morality as they take their profits in the name of capitalism. America's government officials and business leaders are truly a formidable force. It is understandable how difficult it would be for America to change herself. Her leaders are too righteous, too arrogant and too greedy. Change must be forced upon America by an outside influence. We are prepared to bring about that change with the project. The project will destroy America's economy! Unfortunately, Americans will have to suffer with their leaders. In the final analysis, Americans will have to account for the misdeeds of their leaders. They have elected to sacrifice their future with their apathy. Apathy is the silent killer of many great nations."

The exercise ritual is now complete. It has been played out many times by Todd and Charlie to reinforce the project. Each time, more detail is added or refined as they perfect their objective. Todd and Charlie agree that conditions to launch the project are favorable, but Todd continues to hold the implementation date in abeyance.

Todd Robbins and Charlie Bing complete their meeting in the hotel room. Todd has prepared the next schedule for the purchase of precious metal. Each of the participating partners in the project is assigned a purchase quota for the precious metals and energy acquisitions. These quotas are a critical component of the project. The work is completed by late afternoon, and they prepare to leave to tend to their designated responsibilities.

Todd is saying his farewells when Charlie interrupts him. "I have some unpleasant news to share with you. I fear a partner may compromise the project. I feel it best to eliminate him from further participation. His name is——."

Todd abruptly interrupts. "I do not need to know who or why you need to do this. Just do what must be done to protect the project! I trust your judgment and have full confidence in your decision."

"Thank you Todd. I just wanted to keep you informed. I will not be seeing you for awhile. I am planning another trip to China."

"I appreciate your concerns. Have a good trip and be safe in your pursuits."

Todd and Charlie part company in the lobby. Chou is overcome with empathy for Todd. Todd looks physically worse on each visit. *I hope he will soon return to good health!*

Todd reflects briefly on Charlie's recent revelation. *It must be a serious problem for Charlie to eliminate a partner. Is elimination a death sentence? Have I just condoned a murder? I'm happy I do not know any details! I've been through this before. The project must be protected at all costs!* Todd has become a hardened man.

CHAPTER 57

Charlie Bing is in his New York apartment. It is late night and he is fast asleep. A ringing sound awakes Charlie, and he reaches for his bedside telephone. He wipes the sleep from his eyes and vigorously rubs his face and head as he attempts to become more alert. He lets the phone ring 2 more times before picking up the phone. He coughs to clear his throat as he answers. "Hello."

A coarse whispered voice slowly announces. "The work has been completed."

Charlie answers. "What work? Who is this?"

A sudden click followed by continuous beeping tones indicates the mysterious caller has hung up. Charlie looks over at an alarm clock. It is 2:48AM. He gets up from the bed and goes to the bathroom where he relieves himself and washes his hands. He returns to the bed and lies down. The night is very cold so he pulls the covers tight around his body before assuming a fetal position. He closes his eyes and he is reminded of the phone call. *It is good that the unfortunate business is concluded. It had to be done! I will verify in the morning.* Charlie slowly drifts into a deep sleep.

At 4:30AM, the alarm sounds a wake up call. Charlie opens his eyes and briskly jumps out of bed. He walks to the window and views the array of street lights visible for as far as the eyes can see. The clear night is only interrupted by the steamy fog which covers wide areas around the underground sewer openings. The cool air next to the windows sends a chill through Charlie. He wraps his arms around his torso as he walks to his study. He flips on the lights and fingers his television remote to the on position. As the blank screen comes to life, he is already involved in a series of body stretching motions.

Charlie looks up to the screen and laughs as a boisterous Ralph Kramden raises his fist in a threatening gesture. "You're going to the moon Alice—to the moon."

He always enjoyed the slap stick comedy of Jackie Gleason. He finished his warm up routine and stepped over to his running machine. He set his pace while reaching for the television remote. He touched in the numbers for a national news network. It is 5:00AM.

The commentator rapidly summarizes the important news of the day. "President Plant is weighing input for his new direction in Iraq. The dollar has fallen once again against the Pound, the Euro and the Yen. Bagdad is hit by 6 bombs killing over 200 Iraqis and 3 American soldiers. A natural gas explosion has killed 6 people in an affluent suburb of Washington, DC. Details of the days events will follow this message."

Charlie increases the pace of the machine to 2 miles per hour as his mind began to assimilate the news of the gas explosion in Washington, DC. *Why 6 people? It should have been 4 people at the most! Who are the other 2 people? What about Larry Yang?* Charlie continues to keep up with the revolving belt as he anxiously awaits details from the news caster.

After returning from what seemed like an endless number of commercials, the commentator starts to report on the details of the major events. Charlie kicks up the pace on the machine to 3 miles per hour as a small bead of sweat trickles down from his forehead.

It is another ten minutes before the broadcaster finally gets to the details on the gas explosion. "A natural gas explosion in Washington, DC has rocked the Capital City. Six lives were lost and a ten million dollar mansion was totally destroyed in the overnight disaster. The blast shook the exclusive Forest Hills subdivision shattering windows up to a mile away. Larry Yang, a prominent lobbyist and international business man, was killed. Three men who were identified as close associates of Yang were also killed. Two women killed in the explosion have not been identified. Apparently, an undetected gas leak in the basement was the cause of the tragedy. In other news,——

Charlie tunes out the television as his thoughts went to the deceased Larry Yang. Charlie had been uncomfortable with Larry Yang since he has known him. His superiors ordered him to use Yang because of his political connections in Washington. None the less, Charlie was uneasy when he met with Yang. Yang was always trying to get more information on the project, and he seemed distraught when he was denied. Ultimately, Yang's repeated requests for more information set the stage for his demise.

After the last meeting with Yang, Charlie reported on Yang's persistence. Charlie fully vented his feelings about Yang in a meeting with Liu Yin in Beijing. Charlie explained the job of an American lobbyist is to compromise principals for dollars. He opined that too much time in this type of environment can corrupt the soul of any man, including a Chinese nationalist like Yang. He thought it was highly probable that Yang would betray the project when he had the opportunity. Charlie had no strong evidence of betrayal to present. None the less, he convinced Liu Yin that Yang posed a strong potential danger to the project. Liu Yen said that Larry Yang would be dealt with soon.

Charlie has set the conveyor speed to four miles per hour. He is vigorously racing against the inclined belt. His heart is rapidly beating and a profusion of wetness has covered his entire body. His thoughts return to the meeting with Liu Yen. Liu Yen in his normal cautious mode had instructed Charlie as to how he would be notified that the problem had been taken care of. *He will say "The work has been completed, and you will reply what work? Who is this?" In this way, you will be protected if someone is listening in on your phone.*

Charlie is breathing rapidly as he wipes the streams of sweat from his eyes. He sets the machine to 2 miles per hour for the cool down. *It's too bad Yang had to die, but I guess there was no other way to handle the potential problem. I will have to make similar arrangements on behalf of Todd when he is ready to avenge his father. He has lived for over 27 years with the knowledge of his fathers killers. His vengeance is tempered by the needs of the project. I wish I had his patience!*

Charlie stops the machine and wipes his body down with a towel. He walks toward the bathroom for a shower. He is somewhat repentant as he thinks of the charismatic Yang with the friendly and engaging personality. *I hope I did not have an innocent man killed!*

CHAPTER 58

▼

Senator Eric Nagy is at his local congressional office in Charleston, West Virginia. It is about 1:00PM. It has been a rather hectic morning owing to the reports he received on the untimely death of Larry Yang. He is drinking coffee at his desk when Brenda, his chief of staff, comes into his office.

Brenda is saddened by the news of Larry Yang's death. None the less, she has skillfully assisted the Senator in handling a flood of phone inquiries about the tragic event. She could not help but note the number of calls from congressmen and high government officials. *An important man has died!*

Brenda approaches the Senator. "Here are the documents you requested Senator. Is there anything else I can do for you?"

The Senator has been admiring the tight skirt and revealing blouse of his young assistant. It's somewhat ironic how tragic events can sometimes kindle some very latent desires. "I think that will do for now. Thank you Brenda."

Brenda turns to exit the office. The 80 year old Senator is fixated on Brenda's ample rump as she gaits toward the door. *I may be old but I'm not dead!*

Suddenly, an intercom message from an outer office announces an incoming call. "Brenda, there is a call for the senator from Vice President Chimney. Shall I put the call through?"

Brenda quickly reels catching the Senator still gazing at her lower torso. Brenda forces a knowing smile at the Senator as she reaches for the phone. Brenda acknowledges that the call is from the Vice President, and then hands the phone over to the Senator. "It is the Vice President for you sir."

"Mister Vice President. It's an unexpected pleasure to hear from you. What can I do for you?"

"Eric, I trust you have heard about the explosion in Washington, and death of Larry Yang."

Eric Nagy quickly answers. "I must have received at least 7 calls from other congressmen, and many more from high ranking agency people. They were all looking for verification of the death and some further details. I don't have to tell you Yang was a very influential person. Unfortunately, I wasn't able to provide them with any more information. I found out myself from a morning news program."

Oscar Chimney responds. "Let me help you set some of the record straight. Larry Yang died in a natural gas explosion about 1:00AM last night. His home is totally destroyed and three bodyguards were also killed. The source of the gas leak has been traced to a corroded gas line in his basement. Apparently, the gas built up over time because the basement was tightly sealed. It seems that Yang used the secured basement as a vault to hold records he deemed confidential. Subsequently, the basement was rarely visited and the gas leak went undetected. The actual source of the ignition is unknown. Speculation is someone may have turned a basement light on, or someone with a lit cigarette may have entered the basement. At any rate, the explosion and deaths have been ruled accidental. This will be the official position on this incident."

The Senator is listening intently. "The news said that there were two women also killed. Do you have any information on that?"

"Yes, I do. Yang was entertaining two young women from a local escort service. Apparently, they were in the wrong place at the wrong time." Chimney continues to seek information from Nagy. "I have some questions for you! You called me last week to arrange some private time for Yang. At the time, you said that he had some money to distribute for some causes, and that he wanted me to recommend a few appropriate associations. I believe you told me he had 20 million dollars. Did he say anything about the source of the funds, or why he wanted me to help him distribute the funds?"

The Senator intuitively knew the nature of the inquiry. "No he didn't! I did ask him if his client wanted recognition for the donations, but he said no. I just assumed he or his client wanted to distribute the money through his political connections for some future recognition. You know how Larry operated! He was always quick with a dollar or a favor and never had strings attached. He gave me twenty million and mentioned he still had twenty million to distribute. He specifically requested that I try to arrange a meeting with you. That's all I know!"

The Vice President replies. "I scheduled some time with Yang next week. If there was more to this, I guess we will never know now. Keep your eyes and ears open Eric, and let me know immediately of any new developments. I expect the press and the Chinese consulate will be busy trying to dig up more detail. Stay on your toes until this dies down. It appears there is nothing wrong, but one never knows for sure!"

"You can count on me. I will let you know if anything new develops. I have one more question Mister Vice President. What of the confidential documents that were stored in the basement?"

"You can rest easy Eric. The FBI has secured the site and will be accumulating all the personal effects of Larry Yang! I will talk with you when you return to Washington."

Senator Nagy hangs up the phone and sips the coffee. It has grown cool and stale during the conversation. None the less, he feels comforted by the reassuring words of the Vice President. It seemed that all the favors, all the money and all the potential problems have died and will be buried with Larry Yang. He will pass along the soothing assurances to the many concerned politicians who called him earlier. The senator knew that their concern with Larry Yang's death was secondary to their fear of Larry Yang's legacy. He will be busy making political points for the rest of the day.

Oscar Chimney strokes his jowls as he mentally reviews the call. *Everything seems OK. The FBI has control of the site. There doesn't appear to be any loose strings. It should be done!* But the old pro of politics quickly decides that an abundance of caution is less costly than an overlooked detail. He will look deeper into the life and sudden death of Larry Yang. He reaches into his wallet and retrieves a coded phone number. Chimney picks up the secured phone and begins to dial the coded number. *I'm going to have Preston Orient check this out. Orient can always get to the answers!*

CHAPTER 59

▼

Sometimes, time just flies by! David Paine is busy at his desk preparing for the Wake Up America television show. David has been mentally reviewing the rapid sequence of events that propelled the talk show to a nationally syndicated program carried by over 200 television stations and close to 500 radio stations. The program was an instant and continued success as the carefully crafted format continued to address issues of deep concern to Americans. *I was speaking to a small group of fewer than 20 people when I started about a year ago at the local library. This evening over eleven million viewers and listeners will tune into the show.* Sometimes, he feels inadequate to the task and the accompanying fanfare. *Who could have ever guessed—from a steel worker to a national celebrity? Incredible!*

"Hello David. What do you have planned for today?"

The booming voice of Paul Phillips awakens David from his temporary stupor. Paul Phillips is the co-anchor for Wake Up America. He is the sounding board for the controversial subjects that David Paine so passionately introduces. Phillips frequently plays the perfect devil's advocate skillfully countering the populist viewpoints of David Paine. Together, they surgically expose the pros and cons of seemingly complex subjects laying bare the facts for their audience to absorb. In the end, the viewers and listeners have proclaimed their acceptance of the format with their ever increasing numbers. The show is hugely successful!

"Hello Paul. It's been a couple months since we did anything on illegal immigration. I thought the timing might be good to run this issue through the mill again!"

Paul responds. "The subject is hot! The politicians are ignoring the issue hoping it will fade away. The fence along the border has turned into a standing joke and Americans are pissed off with the whole situation. What a façade! The politi-cians are willing to spend hundreds of millions for a fence that can't work, but not a penny for law enforcement to deport the illegals! Let's go for it!"

"Ok Paul. That's the theme for the show today."

David and Paul sit together for the next hour discussing the talking points for the immigration presentation. It has been their practice to loosely discuss the per-tinent points for direction, but to avoid any prolonged rehearsal that might present the appearance of a scripted dialogue. It makes for an informal yet infor-mative presentation of some difficult issues. As they conclude the review, Paul notices that David has grown somewhat remote and fidgety.

"David. Is there something wrong? You have not been yourself lately! Is there something I can do?

David is somber as he replies. "I'm sorry. I did not realize that it shows. There is nothing wrong. It's just that sometimes I get the feeling the issues we present are not relevant. You know what I mean. We discuss minimum wages, health insurance, interest rates, home affordability, taxes, foreign imports, the decline of American industry, the loss of good paying jobs, social security, illegal immigra-tion, corporate corruption, cooked books, rich lobbyists, unresponsive politi-cians, rigged elections, blah, blah, blah. Do you ever get the feeling we are missing the big picture? That perhaps, all these things are simply diversions? That all these issues, although important, are symptomatic of a larger problem? Maybe, we should be talking about the real problem while there is still time!"

Paul is taken back by the sudden tirade, and is somewhat pensive as he responds. "I'm not sure what you mean! I thought we were addressing the prob-lems. You seem to be saying there is some mother of all problems and that we are running out of time. Help me out David! You've lost me on this one!"

David continues. "I know this is going to sound crazy, but hear me out. I think we are on a time clock. Sooner or later, the public will tire of our rhetoric. We are not saying anything new. We are just saying what our listeners already know. We have the advantage of two personalities dissecting an issue, and laying bare the good and bad. We offer a frank, back room evaluation in an entertaining manner. The public loves our methods and enjoys the coarse open discussion, but ultimately it translates to more of the same."

Paul is astonished. "I've been around this business for a lot of years and I know there is a shelf life for any broadcast show. But, you seem to think that the end is sooner rather than later. Hell David. We have only been nationally syndicated for less than three months, and we still are enjoying double digit increases in our audiences. Our ratings are off the charts! What's your hurry? And again, what is this real message?"

David is quizzical. "I can not explain the urgency. I just feel we are running out of time, and that we must finish the job. I wish I could explain. Everything seems so imminent! Please bear with me. As to the real message——for some time, I've believed there is an inherent problem in America from which these other issues flow. As individuals, as a people, and as a country, we have long accepted the basic principals of the very system I believe is the root cause of much of the conflict. I truly believe that unless we address this root problem, then all the other issues and problems will continue to increase in numbers and severity until they completely destroy America! The root problem is capitalism! Let me explain! Capitalism is a great system up to the point where it transcends the needs, objectives and well being of America. Unchecked capitalism results in the dismantling of the American empire in a number of ways. We have sold our manufacturing base, our industrial supremacy, and jobs to the highest foreign bidder. We import cars, clothing, electronics, oil and an array of everyday essentials from countries throughout the world. These countries largely offer cheaper goods, and their chief resource is an abundance of low cost labor. We are losing our prowess as innovators to foreigners who are producing more doctors, engineers and managers. Our government officials have in large part sold out our country to foreigners by permitting the flood of imports and the wave of illegal immigrants. In the name of globalization and free trade, our government has effectively masked a lower standard of living that is gradually infecting an unsuspecting American public. The American middle class is rapidly disappearing as professional jobs are replaced by an abundance of menial service jobs. Don't get me wrong! Menial jobs are good because we all have to start somewhere. But the greater danger is lack of upward mobility which thwarts personal growth. America suffered its first negative savings rate since the Great Depression in 2005 thanks in large part to the proliferation of lower paid service jobs. Our government is in such dire straits that it is forced to finance its day to day operations with foreign money. It seems foreigners have more dollars to invest than their American counterparts. American corporate leaders lie, cheat and steal from their employees and stockholders in order to invent the profits that insure their quarterly bonuses. And all the while, lobbyists from around the world visit our elected representatives in Washington DC for the sole purpose of buying favor and influence for their company, country or favorite cause. This is the true nature of American capitalism. It is remarkably efficient as a means to exploit the resources of the world. Unfortunately, nobody is watching the company store and it is America that is being exploited in the name of capitalism! America is running out of time! It seems we may be rather easy prey for the very system we so eagerly embrace!"

Paul is incredulous as he stammers a reply. "You want to launch an attack on capitalism? I really need time to think this through! Have you cleared this with Amy? Do you realize the implications of what you're proposing? Amy will be out of business within one week of your broadcast if——.

David interrupts. "Slow down Paul! I would not attack all capitalism. The attack is against unchecked capitalism that places money, profits and initiatives ahead of the best interest of America. We need to support a capitalistic system that is tempered by our national interests. Most countries of the world recognize the need to provide for their own best interests when dealing with other nations. Unfortunately, we have grown rather arrogant in supposing we can control the world regardless of our policies. We have forgotten the fundamentals of survival. Charity begins at home. If we do not take care of ourselves first, do we really expect another country will do the job for us?"

Paul is still visibly stunned. "I have to talk with Amy before I can support this effort any longer. Thank God! I can't authorize this type of presentation!"

"I understand Paul. When you speak with Amy, please tell her I would like two weeks of advanced promotion for this show. I would like to build the greatest possible audience. I think we will have only one shot at this issue and I would like for all of us to be well prepared. If Amy approves, I would like to present this problem on a Sunday morning show in about one month."

David is so passionate on this issue that he has already transcended any potential disagreements. In his mind, the special show is a done deal. David continues. "What do you think about titling the show '**The Detrimental Spirit of American Capitalism**'? I would present the flaws in the system and perhaps you might protect the capitalist mindset!"

Paul pulls up a chair and sat next to David. Intuitively, he suspected that this day was coming. David has become more aggressive in his topic selection, and he had harbored the thought that David might one day over reach conventional bounds. He takes some final notes as the meeting came to a close. He was flummoxed by the turn of events, even as his mind was beginning to rapidly assimilate David's theory on unrestrained capitalism. *Is national capitalism a legitimate form of capitalism—or is it an oxymoron?* Paul leaves the office still confused by the sudden turn of events.

David Paine sits back in his chair happy with the thought he would shortly cut to the chase on the American problem. He genuinely believes that unrestrained capitalism is at the heart of many American financial and cultural issues. He feels that the anti capital crusade would signal the end of his brief broadcasting career. Amy Younger and the America Live Network are already under intense scrutiny from the FCC and the IRS as a result of her support for the Wake Up America program. In spite of the strong negatives, he wants badly to proceed. He continues to reinforce his thoughts on capitalism as he recalls the words of Thomas Jefferson who said 'the merchant hath no country'. *I am on the right track!*

David begins a preliminary draft of some of the talking points for the show on capitalism. His thoughts are interrupted by a ringing phone. He reaches for the phone and cheerfully acknowledges the caller. Within five seconds, his face turns a vivid red while his body trembles uncontrollably. He is listening somberly without saying a word. His knuckles have grown white as his fist tightens around the receiver. Suddenly, he goes into a rage. "You son of a bitch. Do what you need to do. I'll see you in hell!"

He is clearly agitated as he violently slams the phone repeatedly on the cradle. The molded phone receiver breaks off in his hand as a jagged plastic edge slices into his still ratcheting hand. Blood is flowing freely from an open gash as he struggles to regain his composure. He wraps a handkerchief around his hand. His labored breathing and pounding heart testify to the ferocity of his heated response. He settles back into his chair sweating profusely, but now in firmer control of his faculties. This is the third threatening phone call he has received since going national with Wake Up America. For reasons that he has not shared with Paul Phillips or Amy Younger, David feels he is running out of time.

CHAPTER 60

▼

Charlie Bing and Todd Robbins are embracing and shaking hands furiously as they meet together at Bing's Manhattan apartment. It is 10:30 AM and the two have met to again review the status of the project. Bing is in great spirits as he greets his old college friend. Todd is enthusiastic, but somewhat reserved as he enters the meticulous apartment.

"Todd. It is so good to see you again. I have missed you since our last meeting. Please come in and have a seat. Can I get you anything?"

Todd smiles briefly as he moves to the library of the 3500 square foot apartment. "I'm good for now. Thank you. You are always in a great mood Charlie. How do you manage to stay so upbeat all the time?"

Charlie responds. "Believe me I don't carry this grin on my face all the time. I like seeing you and I enjoy our time together. For a brief time, I get to escape to a different time with an old friend. How have you been?"

Todd's heavy breathing as he walks through the apartment answers the question. Todd is panting as he lowers his corpulent torso into a large upholstered chair. He lets out an uncontrolled gasp as he settles into the seat.

"I've put on another 13 pounds in the last three months, and I feel very uncomfortable. Every physical effort is a task and it seems that all I do any more is sweat, huff and puff! Sorry to be so depressing, but I'm a mess! But, enough about me. How have you been?"

Charlie and Todd continue their friendly chatter for the next 45 minutes. Briefly, they escape to their college exploits of years past as they reminisce the carefree days at Harvard. As the conversation continues, they both come to realize the futility of the past when compared to the urgency of their present endeavors.

None the less, they always resort to the long gone pleasantries before addressing the pressing matters that brings them together.

Todd is the first to bring up the current business. "Here are the purchase requirements for precious metals and oil for the next three months. You will note that I have outlined a more aggressive purchase schedule for gold and oil while staying on course for the other metals. I've also included a list of gold mining companies that have strong potential and are located outside of the United States. The market has absorbed all our past orders without suspicion. I think we can up the purchase volume at this time. I would also like to see our partners hold at least 1 trillion dollars of American currency in reserve, while purchasing as many US treasuries as are available. Finally, please have our partners sell off their holdings in the following American companies."

Charlie reviews the schedules as he thinks. *It is the most aggressive activity schedule to date. Perhaps the project implementation date is imminent?* "As always, I am certain our partners will honor this schedule. They have sufficient dollars to do everything you've requested. As they sell off the American holdings, what should they do with the excess dollars?"

Todd replies. "Please have them convert the dollars to Euros for the time being. I will have a new set of potential acquisitions shortly that will require Euros. I need to gage market reaction from the current acquisitions before I can go any further!"

"I understand Todd. Our partners will await your future instructions. I hate to bring this up, but I am constantly asked when will the project be implemented? My country and our partners are most anxious. I need to be able to give them some information!"

Todd smiles as he replies. "I know you are under pressure, and I know you understand that what I am planning is not an exact science. If we move too soon, the United States may surmise our plan and figure a way out of the abyss. Time is our greatest weapon. The Americans continue to deluge us with the resources to destroy them. Just last month, they ran a trade deficit of over 90 billion dollars of which our partners received over fifty percent of the dollars. They continue to export substantial industries and jobs to China and our other partners. They continue to dig the hole for their own grave. I am inclined to let them dig the hole deeper!"

Charlie continues to press Todd. "There are two sides to that coin. Time may make for a more successful conclusion, but too much time may weaken the resolve of some of our partners. Sometimes, it is necessary to strike while the iron is hot! We have been successful to date in secreting the project, but time is the enemy of secrecy. I fear some little detail might leak out which may potentially jeopardize the project!"

Todd quickly rebuts. "Is that what happened to Larry Yang? Was he eliminated because he compromised the project? If so, how much information did we lose?"

Chou Bing is clearly astonished as he replies. *How could Todd have known that Larry Yang was involved in the project? He did not know of Yang's association! I can't lie to Todd!* "I continue to be amazed by your insight. Yes. Larry Yang was involved, but no information on the project was compromised. He was considered a potential threat and was eliminated. It emphasizes my point on too much time being a detriment to secrecy!"

Todd is stroking his rooster like chin as he responds. "OK Charlie. You've convinced me. Perhaps time may work against us. You may inform our partners that the project will be initiated very soon. I can't give a specific date now. But bear with me; I will set the date shortly. These quotas must be met over the next three months before we can evaluate a firm date. In the interim period, perhaps you can make the arrangements to take care of Bob Mellon and Curt Davis. I have no further use for either of them, and I want to do away with them at any convenient time in the next three months. The sudden demise of these two will do much to temporarily disrupt the American financial markets. They should both die the same time of the same day by similar causes. It will inject a taste of American style conspiracy which will serve to depress the financial markets while we finalize the project."

Charlie is incredulous. "Our partners will rejoice with the news. Final arrangements will be made for Mellon and Davis per your instructions. Let me say that it is genius on your part to have waited for such a perfect time for their deaths. No doubt it will have a substantial impact on the financial markets. I will leave for China tomorrow to make all the arrangements. Thank you for permitting me to save face with my countrymen and our partners."

Todd is apologetic. "No. Thank you, Charlie. Your persistence on this matter has brought it to a conclusion. I fear I may have procrastinated out of an abundance of caution. We are of accord."

Todd and Charlie complete their discussions and congratulate each other on their impending victory. A final wine toast to the success of the project caps off the jubilant mood. Todd struggles to remove himself from the overstuffed chair. When he finally completes the task, he waddles toward the door.

Todd is whispering his farewells when he questions. "Charlie. Have you watched the Wake Up America show recently?"

Charlie replies. "No. I haven't. I do not know the show at all. Why do you ask?

Todd is reaching for the door. "No reason Charlie. I was just thinking that we may not have had to do the project if people like the show moderators had addressed the issues some years back. It's not important. I thought you may have known of the program. It's probably too little too late anyway! Have a good trip to China. Call me when you get back."

Todd shuffles down the hall to the private elevator. He turns and waves a final goodbye before entering the elevator. Bing is contemplating Todd's final comment about the Wake Up America program as the elevator door closes. He is somewhat mystified by the off the cuff remark. His curiosity is aroused and he will make it a point to watch the next edition of Wake Up America. *What did he mean about not having to do the project?*

CHAPTER 61

▼

"I have good news for you comrade. We will be able to implement the project in the near future. Final plans are being made and then we shall make our move!"

Chou Bing is in the home of Liu Yin in Beijing, China. The two associates are reviewing the acquisition plans for the project.

Liu Yin quickly responds. "Is there a precise date for the implementation?

Chou Bing lays out a schedule and spreadsheet for the purchase of precious metals, US government securities, oil securities and other gold resources.

"No. The date is not yet set. We must make certain these purchase quotas are met over the next three months. After that, the start date will be announced. We are almost at the end!"

Liu studies the papers and points to the large quantities of gold. "Should we not be concerned that we will arouse suspicion with the purchase of so much gold? In the past, our purchases over the same period have been a fraction of these numbers."

Chou replies. "The market for all precious metals has become quite volatile. Many people and countries are growing concerned with the weakness of the dollar and are purchasing gold to hedge their positions on their dollar holdings. I think if our country and our partners follow the schedule, the action will be consistent with much of the world. The United States is painfully aware that it has overproduced dollars and, subsequently, they know they have flooded the world with excess currency. America is taking action to alleviate the crisis, but finds it difficult to further increase interest rates to cut the flow of dollars. I think American officials are finally beginning to recognize the dilemma their Federal Reserve has created, but are hard pressed to rectify the problem. For all these reasons, I do not think we will arouse suspicion if everyone follows the purchase schedule!"

Liu nods his head in agreement. "I think you are correct in your analysis. The position of the dollar is quite precarious. American officials are regularly insisting that we revalue the Yuan to soften the impact of the dollar decline. China has been dodging the demand for some time. We will only hurt our own financial position if we were to agree. I think that Americans think we are stupid. This idea of forcing lower currency values has been done many times by the Americans. In every case where it has happened, the Americans have benefited at the expense of foreign countries. The timing appears to be good for the project. I will notify our partners of their purchase allocations. I am certain they will comply. The United States continues to infuriate them with their insistent demands. America has forgotten how to ask for a favor. They seem only to know how to push and demand! Our friends in Russia, the Mid East, India, Asia and South America are anxious to see the American giant fall."

Chou is seeking to update his information. "Have the Americans made any new demands on our country recently?"

Liu answers. "Not through the American government. However, our officials are receiving strong objections from many American companies who are opposing changes in the Chinese labor laws. The Americans are concerned that Chinese products may become more expensive if we were to enact new wage laws for our people. There is even a veiled threat that some companies may move their production facilities out of China. Other than that, we continue to be bombarded by requests from American businesses to supply them with more products. As you are aware, our government monitors these requests on a daily basis. The number of business proposals is so great, I often wonder if America still has the capability to produce anything for themselves! In the past, during military conflicts, I often heard the United States referred to as a paper tiger. Today, I think the United States is more like a barren whore. She is very capable of receiving pleasure, but unable to produce the child!"

Chou laughs at the crude analogy, but is visibly disturbed by Liu's comments about the interfering Americans. "So the Americans are seeking to dictate Chinese law. Most of our people just barely survive on their present pay, and yet the Americans complain because we seek to pay them more! They are so greedy. I grow more disgusted with American business every day. But, then again, American companies treat their own countrymen the same way. Can we expect anything different? What has been our response?"

Liu replies. "You should not get so upset. You know how these Americans are. Our country has procrastinated on any decision while paying lip service to the demands and threats. Our officials have decided to bide their time so as to not disturb the calm waters."

Chou is still irritated as he replies. "I am concerned about Americans seeking to enter partnerships with us? Do we have adequate controls on these alliances?"

Liu responds. "Very few of theses requests for partnership are granted. They have only been approved where American business men have made large investments in plants and equipment in China. These alliances were arranged out of necessity. Generally speaking, the American businesses would not have agreed to make the investments if we did not give them a partnership interest. These arrangements have been to our advantage. The Americans gave us the money to build the factories and then provided the product orders to keep the factories in continuous production. This situation has worked out well for China. Does that alleviate your unease?"

Chou is still apprehensive. "Somewhat! I am pleased that the partnerships are financially successful. My greater concern is that the Americans will influence Chinese businessmen with their dollars and profits. America is capitalistic and China is mostly communistic, and I fear that these relationships might corrupt our ideological principals. America is deep in the process of destroying herself with her greed. Have we insured that we will not set China on a similar path?"

"Chou. I understand your discomfort. I discuss this same issue with my superiors. We are of the same mind that the potential corruption of our system by greedy Chinese is a possibility. Our countrymen are exposed to the enormous wealth and privilege of many American business men, and can easily be infected with their greed. We monitor the individual situations in an attempt to control the environment, but it is a moot exercise. We have come to realize that some will succumb to the evil, and when they do, their actions will betray them. Those of us that are weak will be retrained in our ideals. We feel that the traitors are the exception, and we are prepared to deal with them. Take heart Chou. You are a fine example of one who has been deeply immersed in American capitalism, but remain loyal to China and its ideals. You have spent the better part of your life in America, and have developed great wealth. But as a chief coordinator of the project, you are steadfast in bringing about the collapse of the erroneous American system. China will prevail!"

Chou is reassured by Liu's words. "I am happy that our leaders have given this matter so much thought. It is critical that we do not tolerate any actions that replicate American capitalism, less we give birth to a similar monster. China will be given a clean slate and a fresh perspective with her style of capitalism. Ours will be capitalism devoid of greed and dedicated to the improvement of all of our countrymen. Our biggest ongoing task will be the detection and elimination of those influences that may contaminate our country with greed and unjust enrichment. If nothing else, America has instructed us with her failure!"

Liu grins as he replies. "Your words are well said. China will have a fresh perspective on the capitalist ideology thanks to America. Communism and capitalism will be blended into a system worthy of leading the continued progress of all mankind. Our country has warred for years against the United States in an attempt to develop a superior economic and political system. It's ironic that America will defeat herself without a single shot being fired. Greed and unbridled capitalism are the only weapons we need to win, and America has provided us with these weapons of mass destruction."

Chou acknowledges the comments. "It is as you say. America will have defeated herself! There is one other item that requires your attention. It is time to eliminate the American bankers, Curt Davis and Bob Mellon. It is of importance that they be killed on the same day at the same time, and in a similar manner. Our American friend says they are of no further use alive, and that there will be considerable benefit in their deaths. Could you arrange this to happen in the next three months?"

Liu is scribbling notes on a pad. "I was wondering when this would be accomplished. Your friend has decided to take his revenge. It will be done as you request. It is a good sign the project start time is close."

Chou Bing and Liu Yin continue their self congratulatory conversation as they seek to further reinforce their final preparations. It appears the forces that forecast significant world changes are in place, and that the final days of fastidious planning will insure the success of the project. America's days as a financial world power are numbered. Chou will return to New York to monitor the final months. Liu Yin will report the progress of the project to his superiors.

CHAPTER 62

---▼---

"America is running out of time. We have been on a path of self destruction since the end of World War II. What started as a gradual, almost invisible, erosion of American values has turned into a rout of the things we hold near and dear! Our national resolve has been fragmented by a deluge of non-essential issues which has the effect of dividing and subdividing our attentions. In this manner, the powers that be have factionalized the American people to the point of absolute confusion. The American people are viewed by their representatives as an impotent mob. America is no longer a government of the people, by the people and for the people. Rather America is a government of big business, by their lobbyists, and for their capitalists."

David Paine pauses briefly for effect before reemphasizing. "You heard me right! America is a government of big business, by their lobbyists and for their capitalists. The American people are irrelevant."

Paine has opened a special edition of the Wake Up America show with an attack on capitalism. His opening remarks were carefully planned to incite a reaction from the millions of listeners and viewers. He has laid bare the faltering economy of the United States and placed the blame at the altar of capitalism.

Paul Phillips jumps in on queue. "Whoa! Just wait a minute David. Do I hear you correctly when you say that concerns such as abortion, gay rights, gun rights, woman's rights, civil rights and other critical issues are not important? I think you referred to them as non-essential issues. If these things are not important, then what is?"

David responds. "They are important, but what good does it serve any American if in the process of debating these issues, they ignore the larger issues of political and financial freedom. Let me put my comments into perspective. Our governments' only responsibility is the safety, health and welfare of the American people. We elect representatives with the intent they follow this rather simple mandate. However, the clear waters of this objective have been muddied with a vast array of choices. Are you a liberal or a conservative? Are you pro life or pro choice? Are you for gun control or the right to bear arms? The list of issues is large and growing. It seems that every issue garners about 50 percent proponents and 50 percent opponents. The continuing process of choice effectively turns one American against another until organized chaos exists. This is the dilemma all Americans have today. This tyranny of choice has been carefully crafted to divert Americans from their common objective, namely the safety, health and welfare of America and Americans. In the process of defending our stand on all these issues, we have effectively lost sight of what government can and should do for us. Abraham Lincoln said it best. 'A house divided against itself can not stand.' We have effectively lost control of our government by dividing our resolve with concerns that our government can not and will not deal with! Meanwhile, our government officials have chosen to respond to a different voice. This voice is much clearer than the confused and divided ranting of the American mob. It is the voice of the lobbyist, with his bottomless treasure chest of dollars that commands the attention and respect of our government officials."

Paul Phillips interrupts. "I understand the potential for division, but these concerns are important to millions of Americans. The government must respond to the people!"

David Paine is cautionary. "The government will not help because it can not help! If the government should choose a side on an issue, it would alienate approximately half of America. Government can't legislate on these difficult issues. War, rebellion and internal strife have been the only solutions to similar concerns in the past. The issue of slavery was solved by the Civil War. The issue of Civil Rights was solved by the riots of the 1960's. It is only after bloodshed and rebellion that the government finally takes a position on an issue. And these positions are frequently watered down in a spirit of compromise designed to temper the opponents. None the less, the American people insist their legislators take a stand on an issue. At election time, a candidate is made to reveal his preferences on a diverse number of subjects. It is all a moot exercise, because in the final analysis an elected representative will do what he feels best. Again, I think it is imperative the American electorate concern themselves with candidates and representatives who will dedicate themselves to the safety, health and welfare of

America and the American people! Forget the issues! Government can not help you!"

Phillips jumps in. "Okay. Let's presume you are right and government should not be involved in abortion, gun control, gay rights, etc. You continue to return to the safety, health and welfare of America. What do you mean?"

"I mean Americans need to start caring about America. America is under siege! We are slowly, but steadily, losing jobs, factories and industries to foreigners. Our middle class is disappearing, the general wage level is declining and our standard of living is deteriorating. While our people are busy defending some side of an issue, America is being sold out factory by factory to foreigners. I would like to call them competitors in the spirit of globalism, but I can't. The primary advantages foreigners bring are an abundance of cheap labor and very little government regulation. Over many decades, Americans have worked long and hard to develop the factories and industries that have produced the good jobs, great benefits and substantial profits that floated America to a position of preeminence in the world. Almost overnight, the good jobs have been exported, the benefits have been eliminated and the corporate profits have been used to finance the development of foreign industry."

Paul Phillips retorts. "David, I've been in the corporate world for over 30 years. American management and workers have gotten lazy, sloppy and inefficient. Industries such as television, electronics, steel, textiles, shoes and now automobiles have been relocated because they were no longer competitive. Americans have brought the decline on themselves because of their unrealistic demands, poor quality and lax work ethic. The changes are sort of an attitude adjustment for the ailing workers and industries in the United States!"

The dialogue is heating up as David responds. "I understand your point and I agree there is a tendency to become complacent when things are going well. There is also a tendency on the part of most people to improve themselves and to want a bigger piece of the pie. These are human traits which should not be used as an excuse to take their jobs. After all, these are the same people who worked diligently to build the business! The workers essentially cultivated small businesses into corporate giants, and produced the profits which turned them into multi-national corporations. And now, the multi-national corporations have used the profits to shut down American factories and to build new facilities on foreign lands. One can find some justification if the foreigners were more efficient, but they are not more efficient. Cheap wages can only translate into increased efficiency and productivity through a convoluted system called capitalism. And capitalism relies on exploitation when making calculations on efficiency and productivity. There is a sad irony in capitalism. Workers produce the profits which are ultimately used to eliminate them once they are successful!"

Phillips responds. "The United States was built on the precepts of capitalism. For the better part of a century, our country has been locked into ideological battles with communism, socialism, fascism and nazism. There have been military wars, cold wars and economic wars, but the results have been the same. Capitalism has been the clear winner. Why do you want to attack capitalism? It is the preferred economic and social system of modern times!"

David recants. "I should have been more specific. Not all capitalism is bad! It does deliver the goods and satisfies mans need to feel accomplished far better than any other system. The problem with American capitalism is that it has been corrupted by the power, money and influence of a relatively few. Capitalism has developed much as Karl Marx had predicted. Companies continued to be merged, consolidated or bought throughout the 20th century resulting in the mega multi-national corporations of today. These consolidations have resulted in the precarious environment we exist in today. As we speak, a relatively few elitist control the majority of wealth, money and capital resource in the world. America has produced a substantial number of these elitists. These people are so powerful they can move their assets around the world and take advantage of any promising situation. They have no regard for their own country other than it has the ability to produce or consume their products. Their only concern is the continued accumulation of money and power. There is no other objective besides profits. Herein lies the problem. Capitalism will modify or destroy any entity that interferes with its ability to produce greater profits. This type of unrestrained and unregulated capitalism can not and does not work for the safety, health and welfare of Americans. Our government officials must modify capitalism so it will always work to the benefit of America. The unregulated movement of jobs and industries to foreign countries for the sake of increased profits is clearly un-American. It must be changed so as all Americans benefit from the system. It is acceptable that the rich get richer, providing it is not at the expense and prosperity of the rest of Americans!"

Paul Phillips responds quickly. "I sense strong nationalistic leanings in your statement. America is going global in order that our country can reap the benefits of our advanced technology, the information age and our superior innovation abilities. These skills are what our highly developed economy is all about. In the end, America will win the economic battles and globalization will serve the needs of all America far better than nationalism. Thank God nationalism is dead! You should take comfort in the words of Albert Einstein! Einstein said 'nationalism is an infantile disease. It is the measles of mankind'. America is an advanced economy that will benefit from globalization!"

David is irritated as he responds. "Your words echo the statements of our government, our multi-national corporations and the financial press. You, like so many Americans are as ignorant as lambs going to slaughter. You have been successfully indoctrinated by the propaganda machines of the capitalist system. Do you realize that professional jobs such as engineers, accountants, computer technicians, scientists and lawyers have been moved to foreign countries? These professions are the backbone of research and development which is the precursor to innovation. The collegiate production of many of these professions has withered in tune with the loss of job opportunity in America. Our so called superior technology will dissolve as new discoveries are made by foreigners. The American advantages you speak of are as fleeting as yesterday's news. Our government officials have permitted this rape of America out of a sense of arrogance reinforced by the contributions of their ever present constituents—the lobbyists of the rich and powerful! Globalization is simply a tool of the capitalist designed to make them richer while slowly pulling the bread off the table of the common people. Nationalism is the only answer to reining in the usurping capitalist mentality. We need to place the needs of Americans in front of the cry for increased profits. America can compete with any country in the world providing the playing field is level. Wages, working conditions, environmental concerns and government regulation must be equalized if the concept of free and fair trade is to be realized. Other countries are protecting their people, products and industries from unfair competition. Is America so arrogant and so naive as to suppose we can ignore this basic protection, and still survive as a world power? Nationalism is our effective check on the capitalist system. As to Einstein and his take on nationalism——if nationalism is an infantile disease, then capitalism is the malady of the mature. If nationalism is the measles of mankind, then unchecked capitalism is the cancer of the masses."

The special presentation of the Wake Up America show continued through an hour of debate before the phones were opened to the comments of the viewing and listening audience. The control panel lit up like a Christmas tree when the phones were opened. The audience count was off the charts as over 21 million people tuned into the special two hour presentation. Amy Younger had done a fantastic job of advertising the event.

David Paine and Paul Phillips were euphoric. They congratulated each other before departing the studio. David Paine was feeling quite pleased with himself as he left the parking lot. *We did it! We finally woke up America. I need to keep them awake now!*

David was contemplating his future strategy while driving down the interstate. He would definitely stay involved in keeping the movement alive. But it would come at a cost and in a manner he had never planned! David would soon find out it is impossible to go against the interests of the powerful financial elite without suffering severe repercussions!

CHAPTER 63

▼

"David. You and Paul did a fantastic job today. The studio has been receiving calls all day about the show. I can't remember a time when I have witnessed so much enthusiasm from the American people. However, we have turned a critical corner. Everyone is looking for less talk and more action. Over 95 percent of the callers are looking for more direction. They want to know what can be done about the concerns you brought up about capitalism. Our goal was to educate the people, but it is time to set our sights higher. We need to develop a plan to channel all this energy towards a solution. Do you have any ideas as to how we can move forward?"

It is 7:15 PM. David and Amy Younger have been on the phone speaking with each other. Prior to taking Amy's call, David had been watching the evening news. As he channel surfed the various major broadcasting stations, the primary story was the same everywhere—'**the Wake Up America show has launched a campaign against capitalism**'. Most commentators assessed the program as a blatant assault with consequences reaching into the highest level of government. All of the stations had attempted to get reactions from congressmen throughout the country. Every representative and senator that appeared had the same story. They had not watched the Wake Up America show and were unclear about the content. To a person, they refused to issue a statement. David smiled discerningly as he watched the evasive officials. *Same old Washington DC side step. I bet they are burning up the telephone wires across the country seeking counsel with their cronies!* David sensed the ultimate government reaction would be denial with a spin. He knew he must be ready to counter the nebulous government statements that would soon be flooding the media.

David pulls the wireless phone closer and replies. "Amy. I am overwhelmed by the reaction to the show. I never anticipated the huge public response, and I totally agree we must move on to the next step. I have been brainstorming ever since leaving the studio. My thought is we start a group where we can direct the efforts necessary to bring about change. We can use the Wake Up America show to co-ordinate our activities, and our web sites can detail the specific goals. Our first order of business would be to establish local chapters and appoint local organizers. We will need to start immediately with an aggressive time table of activities and goals. To be very honest, I feel we will come under severe counter attack within the next week. We must act quickly to stay ahead of those who will oppose us. Before I go into further detail, I have to warn you of the consequences. Your business interests are going to be the primary target of our opponents, and you will come under severe personal scrutiny. Before all is said and done, you will probably lose everything. Do you want to risk it all?"

Amy is listening attentively. A caring sigh precedes her reply. "David. You are a sweet and honest man. I thank you for your concerns. When my husband was alive, we would talk often about the American dilemma. In our later years together, the need to do something constructive became more urgent. We always considered ourselves blessed with opportunity, and wished that we could somehow help our country. Being the simple people we were, we just did not know how to go about it! When Tony passed, I regretted we never did anything. For a while, I bumped from cause to cause hoping that I might find someone or something where I could make a difference. I funded quite a few efforts, but too often the organizers lacked the fortitude and persistence and they soon fell apart. It got to be quite discouraging and then one day, a neighbor told me about a meeting at a library. From the time I first heard you speak, I knew you were a passionate and sincere individual. After attending a few meetings, I was hooked. This little old lady would make a difference with the help of David Paine. You have never disappointed me and now that we are flush with success, I will not let you down! Tell me what you need, and I will make the arrangements. Let's finish what we started!"

David is emotional and his voice cracks slightly as he responds. "Thank— thank you for the vote of confidence. I can truly say I have never met a woman like you! You are far too young at heart to be as old as you are! Most women have passed the baton at your age, but you have chosen to run the entire race. I shall forever admire you. Please be aware of your personal safety."

Amy snaps back. "I'm sorry I don't meet your image of the aging matriarch in a rocking chair playing knit-pearl on an oversized sweater. And, by the way Mister Paine, I can take care of myself! Enough of the crap! What do you need from me?"

David is amused and relieved by the harsh comments of the feisty and independent old woman. He goes on to explain the ultimate goal of having a minimum of 1000 people go to each member of congress for the remainder of the current session, or until congress takes action to limit capitalistic pursuits to those that benefit the American people. At 100 senators and 435 representatives, there is a need for a minimum of 535,000 volunteers to visit their Washington DC offices every day. Paine would also like to have an additional 100,000 volunteers to visit the corporate offices of America's top 100 multi-national corporations. The 1,000 person contingents would stay in place until the corporations agreed to prioritize the interest of America and the American people in their business dealings. The progress of the 635,000 person volunteer army would be reported daily on the nationally syndicated Wake Up America show. Amy would do the preliminary promotion of the organization through her company, America Live Network. David and Paul Phillips would work together to establish the state chapters. They both agree time is of the essence!

David and Amy conclude their phone call with an agreement to meet at the studio office on Monday morning. At that time, Amy, David and Paul will finalize the plan and immediately begin the implementation.

Amy sets the phone down and briefly shutters as she begins to comprehend exactly what she has started. She has already received cancellations from close to 50 percent of her corporate advertisers. Moreover, she is under intense inspection from the Internal Revenue Service, the Securities Exchange Commission and the Federal Communications Commission. She has plenty of cash in the bank, but knows she can be shut down by one of the government regulatory agencies for some contrived infraction. She knows quite well that timing is critical. Within the next month, she expects an army of government officials to be pushing at the doors. Amy muses momentarily. *Maybe I should have learned knitting and the comfort of a slow rocking chair.* She quickly dashes the thought and picks up the phone to call her company lawyer. *It's time to batten down the hatches. A storm is coming!*

David is busy making notes for the new organization. The plan is simple, but the logistics are immense. He knows that getting together an army of 635,000 volunteers will be difficult. *People are quick to protest, but very slow in making the necessary personal commitments. I must continue to stoke the fire!*

He claps his hands together in an excited display of his resolve, and immediately feels the pain from his unhealed wound of a few weeks ago. The threatening call is a vivid reminder of the dire pearls of his pursuit. Amy has arranged security, but he realizes the power and influence of his opponents can easily compromise the safety net. He briefly takes comfort in the memory of his early youth in the steel mills in Braddock, Pennsylvania. *Good job, great pay, fantastic security and a growing family.* And then the reality of modern day America sets in. *The decline of the steel mills was a precursor to the decline of America. I am doing what I was meant to do! Anything that happens to me is of no consequence!* David returns to his note taking content that he is doing the right thing.

CHAPTER 64

▼

Todd Robbins is at his home in Boca Raton. He decided to spend a month at his Florida home to escape the constant rush of activity that always engulfs him when he is in New York. The rest has done him good. His skin radiates a recent tan and he has been successful in losing a few pounds.

He has spent the early morning hours casually walking the beach. Along the way, he was greeted by a small school of dolphins who have escorted him as he walked through the surf. He stops momentarily and the dolphins seem to circle almost like they were waiting for him to continue. When he again proceeds, he is delighted when the dolphins again join him. A rare smile glances across his face as he admires his playful companions. He approaches his mansion home and trudges through the sand towards the tiered steps of the rear patio. He is halfway to the steps when he pauses to take one last look at his marine companions. As he turns his head to the ocean, two of the dolphins in a synchronized move leap out of the water, twirl and fall into the pounding waves. Immediately after the display, the school of dolphins resumes their southern trek. He briefly follows their journey until he is blinded by the mid-morning sun. Turning, he continues towards his home.

He reaches the steps and slowly ascends. He stumbles slightly as he climbs the granite steps, and is instantly reminded of his trip and fall over 25 years ago. The flashback temporarily consumes his senses. He feels the pain as his knee tears against the patio stones and he hears the blunt thud of his head bouncing off the hard surface. His mind briefly drifts into an unconscious state before he is abruptly awakened by the vision of his father bathed in his own blood. The torment and helplessness consume him as he gazes at the spot where his father died so many years ago. He shakes his head and vigorously rubs his face effectively easing the tragic stupor.

Todd enters the house and makes his way to the library. He retrieves the television remote and softly touches a button. A large flat screen positioned above the fireplace springs to life. He fingers the remote a few more times and watches as the images on the screen change at his command. He sits down in a giant leather recliner just as the screen settles into a national news program. He adjusts the chair raising his feet comfortably and prepares to listen to the latest news.

The announcer runs through the national weather before summarizing some of the upcoming news stories. "Overnight, twelve soldiers were killed in Baghdad in a series of explosions that rocked the city. In Afghanistan, the Taliban has launched an offensive against two towns which border Pakistan. In Washington, President Plant is reeling from the unrelenting demands of Congress to modify his position on the war. Also in Washington, congressional offices are under siege by hundreds of thousands of protesters from a group named Wake Up America. Details of these stories will follow shortly."

Todd Robbins is pondering the news items as the station cuts to a commercial break. He quickly summarizes the first three items. *President Plant has screwed up the wars so badly that he deserves whatever congress can bring to bear. Plant should have concentrated on the war against terrorism, but he got greedy! He thought Iraq would be easy pickings for the military and a financial windfall to his oil friends. The whole thing has backfired and America is bogged down in a war we can't win. Moreover, Plant has destroyed the credibility of the United States with our friends, allies and our enemies. He is a political liability to America and needs to be severely disciplined. This man should be impeached. He is the essence of ineptness!*

Todd then summarizes his thoughts on President Plant from the perspective of the project. *I should not be so critical of Plant. His actions are consistent with the greedy and arrogant Americans who sell out America every day for profit. It goes back to a corrupted capitalistic structure that abandons the best interest of America. However, I should not complain about Plant. His actions were instrumental in bringing more partners to the project. He is so despised by so much of the world that his incompetence will serve to insure the successful execution of the project. Unfortunately, many innocent Americans will be hurt! Americans should have objected more strenuously to their leaders. Maybe their opposition could have changed the outcome. Just as many soldiers are dying daily for a spurious cause, so too all Americans will be hurt by the rampaging American capitalists. It could have been different!*

Todd Robbins is a man of extremely mixed emotions. As a man whose father was executed by greedy businessmen, he abhors the system which condones the destruction of anything or anybody that interferes with their insatiable appetite for profits. From this perspective, he is happy to be the founder of the project which will destroy unrestrained capitalism.

However, he is still an American and sometimes thinks he should have lead a different form of opposition. Perhaps he could have found a solution which would not be so financially devastating for America. He sought out alternatives over the years, but inevitably he was drawn back to the project. He just was unable to find a viable option against the power and influence of capitalism.

Todd is immersed in these thoughts when he is interrupted by the news announcer.

"And now to Washington, DC, where hoards of Americans from around the country have again descended on the offices of their congressmen. This is the 15th consecutive day of the protest with no end in sight. The Wake Up America group is insisting that the rules governing business pursuits be modified so as Americans benefit in the continued movement towards globalism. They claim that the loss of jobs, factories and industries is weakening America and destroying the standard of living for all Americans. What started out as 2000 protesters just two weeks ago has grown into a mob of approximately 350,000 people, and the number is growing every day. Members of the house and senate have promised action, but nothing has been done to date to persuade the growing throng to disperse and go home. Adding to the confusion are thousands of protesters who have camped out at the corporate offices of approximately 45 major multi-national businesses located around the country. The source of these demonstrations is David Paine, founder of Wake Up America, who less than six months ago began airing a nationally syndicated show which railed against many financial and political inequities before launching an attack on capitalism. The story is the group started about 18 months ago in a community room in Fort Myers, Florida. Where this movement goes from here is any ones guess? The word from Wake Up America headquarters is nobody is going home until a firm commitment to change is secured from the government and Americas multi-national corporations. In many circles, Paine is being painted as a radical with strong leanings towards nationalism, socialism, and even communism!"

Todd Robbins was listening carefully to the broadcast. Maybe there is another way besides the project. Americans seem to be responding. Perhaps, I could have better served my fathers memory by starting a similar movement. I will continue to watch the progress of David Paine and Wake Up America.

CHAPTER 65

▼

Amy Younger is at her home on Captiva Island. She is sitting on her lanai watching the blue expanse of the Gulf of Mexico. It's a calm and peaceful day. The sky is clear with just an occasional puffy cloud. Amy sees a pelican drifting on the air currents as it surveys the tranquil ocean for its next meal. Suddenly, the bird goes into an accelerating free fall and its large beak hits the water with a splash as his body temporarily submerges beneath the water. Within moments, the pelican surfaces with a fish dangling from its beak. The fish resists furiously as it flails its body in an attempt to escape. And then in a near effortless motion, the pelican raises its beak and gulps. The fish disappears as the large bird floats away on the smooth waters. Amy is reminded of life's frailties as she watches the pelican rapidly fan its wings and become airborne again. *The fish is here—the fish is gone. So it goes for all life. One never knows for sure when life will be snuffed out! We need to make the most of life while we are still able.*

Amy's thoughts are interrupted by the voice of her butler. "Amy. Paul Phillips is here to see you. Can I show him in?"

Amy was not expecting a visit from Paul and is immediately concerned. "Yes. Please have him wait in the dining room. I will be in shortly."

Amy reaches for her cane and pushes herself up from the wicker rocking chair. Amy's mind is racing as she seeks to account for the unexpected visit. So much has been happening since Wake Up America started the protests in Washington and around the country. For some time, she has been silently dreading the repercussions she was sure would come. She is not a fatalist, but she does pride herself on her judgment. She anticipates a very strong reaction. *We have really stirred up a hornets nest. I hope the news is not too bad!* Amy sets her chin and steels her resolve as she approaches the dining room.

"Hello Paul. What brings you here today?"

Paul is fidgeting in his chair and is uncomfortable as he replies. "I'm afraid I have bad news for you, and I wanted to deliver it in person."

Amy settles into a chair directly across from Paul. "Well. We've been expecting a severe backlash! How bad is bad?"

Paul Phillips is a seasoned businessman, but is unable to look Amy in the eye as he responds. "America Live Network is out of money. All but a few of the corporate advertising contracts have been cancelled, and the banks are calling in your working capital loans. We will have to shut down all operations within a week. The company is broke, and our attorneys are suggesting we file for protection under the bankruptcy laws."

Amy is somewhat relieved as she replies. "I have been expecting the financial crisis. I knew we could not go after the government and big business without the potential for major financial damage. I have over 125 million dollars in personal accounts. I want to use that money to keep the company going. I will have the cash available in 24 hours."

Paul interrupts. "Why do you want to use your personal money? You've done enough. Let the American people stand up for the rest of the fight! Besides, the extra money will only let the company operate for another month and then you would be destitute. Give it up Amy!"

Amy is a little disturbed. "I didn't start this just to quit. Use my money as long as it will last. I will contact some friends to raise some more money. I will not quit!"

Paul shakes his head disconcertedly. "There's more than the money! One of our few friends in Washington called me and said the FCC is in the final stages of obtaining an administrative order to stop all broadcasting of the Wake Up America show. The FCC is claiming the program is seditious and is inciting the people to rebellion! He claims the FCC will have an injunction within 48 hours. Amy, they have us boxed in. We have no choice but to give the effort up!"

Amy is angered by Paul's submissiveness. She raises her cane and pounds the dining room table that separates them. "I will not quit nor will you! We all knew the potential consequences of our actions. We will see it through as long as we can. Alert our attorneys of the FCC actions and have them raise the legal objections. We need to buy some more time."

Paul jumped briefly as the cane shattered some china, but he still failed to make eye contact with the enraged matron.

Amy notices Paul's meek behavior and empathetically addresses Paul again. "Paul. We have been together for a lot of years. I'm not asking you to take any personal financial risks! What's really bothering you?"

Paul sheepishly raises his head finally looking directly at Amy. "I need to resign. You're right! There probably is a short term way around all the money and regulatory problems, but I can't continue. Last evening I received another threatening phone call. This caller was very graphic in explaining how my wife and children would die. He told me they were under constant surveillance and any attempt to warn them or alert any authorities will result in their deaths. Amy. I can't do this anymore. He gave me today to cut all ties with you and Wake Up America. I hope you understand."

Amy is emotionally moved by Paul's dilemma. She gets up from her chair and walks over to Paul. She gently squeezes Paul's hand as she replies. "I do understand Paul. I'm sorry that I let this happen to you. I think I knew all along that you and David were both in danger, but I was too caught up in this thing. I should not have exposed you and your family to the idealistic madness that seems to have consumed me. You are free to go. I am grateful for your sacrifices. Both you and your family will be financially taken care of. I will have an announcement made within the hour of your resignation. Let me know if there is anything else I can do for you."

A tear trickles down Paul's cheek as he gets up. He reaches over and embraces Amy. "Thank you for everything. You have always been a special person to me. Please consider giving this thing up yourself."

Amy and Paul spend another few minutes together. Paul leaves and Amy returns to her ocean view on the lanai. She is deep in thought about the recent development. She will miss Paul and she realizes that the effort is rapidly drawing to a close. She looks toward the ocean and sees another pelican scooping up a fish. *How fast things change sometimes! I must call David while there is still time. I do not want to lose David!*

CHAPTER 66

▼

Todd Robbins is back in New York after his extended stay in Boca Raton. The rest has done him good. He feels more at peace with himself. During his vacation, he watched the progress of the Wake Up America movement. The number of participants involved in the protests in Washington DC continued to grow, along with the corporate protests around the country. Although nothing concrete has been agreed upon, he senses the movement is having a favorable effect on government officials and their big business partners. Based on the impact of Wake Up America, he has found himself rethinking the need for the project.

Todd is in transit to his New York office building. He is watching the news in the rear seat of his Cadillac limousine. Once again, the news is centered on the contingent of protesters in Washington. The newscaster indicates a break in the stalemate may soon occur as a number of congressional representatives have tentatively agreed to air the complaints in an open session of Congress.

The announcer goes on to explain in some detail the overall impact of the group. "Estimates are there are close to 600,000 protesters in Washington, DC. More are arriving every day as this movement has taken on a life of its own. The demonstrators have been peaceful, but are doggedly determined to have their government do something about their singular demand. The protesters insist the government must recognize the needs of its citizens in all its dealings with foreign governments and domestic corporations. Although the demand seems simple enough, there is tremendous amount of opposition. None the less, popular support for this movement is growing. Millions of phone calls have inundated switchboards. Approximately fifty million emails in support of the movement have jammed congressional web sites. Truckloads of mail are being delivered daily to congressional offices by an overwhelmed postal service. Americans appear to be in clear support of this initiative."

Todd changes channels on the television to get a different perspective from another station. He pauses briefly thinking of the potential impact people can have on their own government. *Perhaps Democracy does work! The people seem to be capable of bringing about change.* His thoughts are interrupted as he glances out the car window to a large group of people demonstrating at the corporate offices of CityFirst Bank. CityFirst is the largest financial multinational corporation in the United States. An endless line of marchers are walking their way around the block long perimeter of the immense building. A continuous chant from the multitude makes their point;

"America First—NOT CityFirst".

The chant is reinforced by the signs many of the protesters are carrying— **'America First—NOT CityFirst'**. The chorus echoes off the endless walls in the cavern of sky scrapers that is New York City. Todd's limousine is more than two blocks away and still the resounding sound overtakes him. *Unbelievable! I never thought the American people would stand up for their values. History is being made! I have to talk with Charlie about this!*

Suddenly, Todd's attention is captured by a news alert. The announcer is stammering as he blurts out the latest information. "America's financial institutions are under attack."

Todd smiles briefly believing the announcement was a judgment on the thousands of demonstrators he just viewed at the CityFirst Bank just minutes earlier. *More spin!*

The broadcaster continues. "The Chairman of the Federal Reserve Bank, Bob Mellon, has been killed. Just 15 minutes ago, at approximately 10 o'clock, Bob Mellon was exiting a car in front of the Federal Reserve building when he was cut down in a hail of bullets thought to be machine gun fire! Mellon was pronounced dead on the scene. Two aides were wounded in the gun fire which was purported to last for about 20 seconds. We have dispatched reporters to the scene, and will provide additional details as soon as we are able."

Todd Robbins sighs deeply as he digests the news. He is caught between a sense of euphoria and utter despair. *The murder of my father is finally avenged! What else do I have to live for?* Todd has patiently bided his time over the years in preparation for this moment of sweet revenge, and now it all seems so trite. For the better part of his adult life, he has been consumed with the thought of this very moment. *I am pleased with the death of Mellon, but I may have taken away my only reason for living!* He squirms uncomfortably as he continues to debate the avenging of his father with his own need for a reason to live. Todd's thoughts are once again interrupted by another news flash.

"And this just in to our news room. There has been still another blow against our financial institutions. Curt Davis, Chairman and Chief Executive Officer of Associated Bank Holding Company, was gunned down in front of the corporate headquarters in New York City. Davis is dead and his death is eerily similar to the death of Bob Mellon. It appears both men were killed at exactly the same time and in the same manner. Adding to the unlikely coincidence is the fact that Curt Davis and Bob Mellon had been partners at Associated Bank Holding before Mellon resigned his position to head the Federal Reserve. Associated Bank Holding is the parent company of some of the world's largest financial institutions, including CityFirst Bank. It appears there will be much more information forthcoming as this mystery unravels. There is already considerable speculation that these events might be part of a terrorist attack."

Todd is rather complacent with the announcement of Curt Davis's death. Upon hearing of the death of Bob Mellon, he knew that the news about Davis was imminent. *Charlie Bing is so efficient. He has never disappointed me!* Todd seems to have regained control over his vacillating emotions. He is happy that he is finished with his fathers executioners. *I will find new meaning for my life.*

None the less, Todd continues to be consumed with mixed emotions. Perhaps it was the suddenness of the events and the finality it represented. At any rate, Todd decides not to go into work. He orders his chauffer to return to his apartment. On the way back, he again notes the determination of the crowd that has gathered at the CityFirst building. The chants continue as the disciplined participants make their way around the structure. He directs his driver to pull over to the curb. He powers down a side window and motions to a small group of the protesters. A lone woman responds and approaches the limousine.

Todd asks the woman. "Why are you so much against this bank? What has it ever done to hurt you?"

The youthful woman is petite and appears frail. She looks over the lavish limo and is immediately suspicious of the inquiry. She slowly bends over and looks Todd directly in the eyes as she responds. "Sir, if you don't understand by now, I guess you never will. However, I will indulge you! This bank along with a lot of other corporations has forgotten about America. They and our government have decided that foreigners can work harder, produce more, and cost a lot less than Americans. We feel they are selling out the interests of Americans so they can show a bigger profit this quarter. Our movement is intent on letting our government and our corporations know that this is no longer acceptable. American interests must come first, ahead of foreigners and ahead of profits!"

Todd continues to bait the woman. "Young lady, do you assume we are all about profits and money? After all, this bank employs hundreds of thousands of Americans. Our corporations employ tens of millions. Our government employs millions more. This madness will only hurt Americans. Why can't you see that?"

The woman remains polite as she responds. "Yes, in America, we are all about profits and money. Unfortunately, the money and profits flow to a relatively few rich and powerful people, while the rest of us are left with the crumbs of trickle down economics. But, I judge from your chauffeured limousine that you fully understand the dilemma we are in today! I think we have wasted enough of each others time!"

Todd rolls up the window as the little lady walks away. *Feisty little girl! If this movement has more like her, success may be inevitable. Maybe I should talk to Charlie about modifying the project.* Todd has considered mentioning his thoughts on reconsidering the project, but was always hesitant. Both he and Chou have spent many years in developing and nurturing the strategies that would bring about change in America. As he has watched the progress of Wake Up America, Todd has seriously considered the project may be too destructive. *Now that my father's killers are dead, perhaps there may be a better way of dealing with the pervasive greed that infects American capitalism. I can help Wake Up America and still realize my objective. I am an American and do not want to needlessly hurt my country.* Todd is mentally wrestling with the events of the past hour as the limo pulls up to his apartment building. He reaches for the remote control to shut off the television when another news alert flashes across the screen. The commentator details the latest event.

"Approximately 15 minutes ago, David Paine the founder of Wake Up America, was shot outside a television studio in Fort Myers, Florida. Early reports indicate he had just finished a briefing with reporters outside of the studio. As he turned to go back to the studio, a single shot slammed into the back of his head. The head wound was described as massive and the information indicates he died at the scene. Again, David Paine the founder of Wake Up America is dead! This has been the third execution of high profile Americans in the last 65 minutes. The previously announced deaths of Bob Mellon, Chairman of the Federal Reserve Bank and Curt Davis, CEO of Associated Bank Holding have stunned the nation. And now David Paine, whose movement has an estimated 700,000 Americans picketing the nation's capital and a number of corporate offices around the country, is dead in Fort Myers, Florida. There is a tremendous amount of speculation that our country is under attack! President Plant has scheduled a 12:00 noon conference to address the killings of Mellon and Davis, but he will no doubt include the execution style slaying of David Paine in his comments. We will be covering the Presidential news conference and will continue to announce any new developments on this very sad day for America."

Todd Robbins face has turned an ashen white as he absorbs the information about the sudden death of David Paine. *Those sons of bitches killed him. He got too close to disrupting the powers that be, and they killed him! They killed him just like they killed my father—just like they will kill anyone who attempts to upset their great American monopoly game.* Briefly, Todd reviews his ill conceived notion that American citizens can make a difference. His age, experience and gut had constantly reinforced the need for the project, but the progress of David Paine and the Wake Up America movement had caused him to question his long held beliefs. *Now, I am vindicated. Only the project can change the greedy American capitalists. A severe dose of their own medicine is the only solution. Soon, they will share in the misery and desperation they so freely dole out to the rest of the world. Et tu Brute! I have been so foolish.*

He affirms his decision as he recalls the words of Jon Kenneth Galbraith who wrote: 'People of privilege will always risk their complete destruction rather than surrender any material part of their advantage'. He must fight the errant businessmen with their own devices. *Only capitalism can defeat capitalism.* These words had been his battle cry since the inception of the project. *Only capitalism can defeat capitalism!* Todd gets out the limo and proceeds to his apartment. He is drained by the recent events, but is now, once again, firmly resolved that the project must proceed.

CHAPTER 67

▼

Vice President Oscar Chimney is in his office having just watched the noon day press conference of President Plant. The President expressed outrage at the killings, while offering condolences to the family members and friends of the three murdered victims. The President had no information on the assassins, but promised to employ all the resources of the Federal Government to find and prosecute the perpetrators. In conclusion, the President said the timing and methods of the murders indicated a conspiracy of some sort. He mentioned the possibility of terrorist activity, but insisted the investigations will reveal the motives for the killings. He sounded a warning to any foreign countries that may have a hand in the murders.

Chimney is deep in thought as he ponders the recent killings of the high profile Americans. *Two were killed at the exact same time and in the exact same manner. The third victim, David Paine was killed about 25 minutes later. What's the link? Why were they killed? Who is responsible?* Chimney is busy penciling notes when his office phone rings.

Chimney picks up the phone and is greeted by the familiar voice of the President. "Hello Oscar. We have a real problem on our hands with these murders and no one seems to have a clue as to who killed these men. I've met with the heads of the intelligence agencies who have lined up task forces. My concern is that they will spend weeks or months chasing rumors, and come up empty. I think it's the damned terrorists again! The sons of bitches keep asking for it. I don't put it beyond the Iranians or Syria to make a move against us. If they're involved, God help them! I think we have to use some other resources to find the perpetrators quickly. I know you have an ace in the hole that you've used in the past. I think you need to put him to work again! I need some information as soon as possible. I need to make the military strikes within a few days! Our financial centers are severely shaken and we need to restore some order immediately. We need to send a message to the bastards that did this!"

Chimney responds. "Mister President, I was thinking the exact same thing about terrorists' activity. I have also checked with all the agencies and have drawn a blank. I have been working with my special contact on that explosion which killed Larry Yang a while back. I will call him and see that he immediately gets on these killings. If anyone can find these assassins, he can! I share your concerns about the rag heads. Some how they must be involved!"

"Okay Oscar. Do what you have to do. I need some answers soon. We have to find out what's going on! Call me as soon as you have some information. I'm placing the nation on alert just in case those Islamist bastards are moving on us! If they are involved, I'll bomb them into oblivion! One other thing Oscar. I know some of our friends have asked for our support in dealing with this Wake Up America thing. I hope none of our people are connected with David Paine's death."

Chimney replies. "The agencies have done what we asked. The IRS and the FCC have applied some heat on the broadcasting network. The FCC has issued a cease and desist against the Wake Up America show. I don't know of any other involvement. I'll get back to you as soon as I have some concrete information."

President Plant continues to ramble on, almost incoherently, as he searches for the means, methods and motivation for the recent killings. He hangs up the phone in a near frenzy after completing his tirade. President Plant is not a rational man when he feels pressured.

Oscar Chimney is well controlled after listening to the ramblings of his leader. Chimney, always the opportunist, sees a potential opportunity in the current predicament. He and Plant have been under tremendous strain from the public backlash of the recent elections. *Perhaps this is what we are looking for to justify our positions on the war in Iraq. I might be able to save his presidential ass after all.* He reaches for his secured phone and dials in the number for Preston Orient.

CHAPTER 68

▼

Amy Younger is at the Fort Myers studio of America Live Network. Following the death of David Paine, the Wake Up America show has been cancelled. None the less, hundreds of thousands of Americans were still protesting in Washington DC. The death of David Paine and the resignation of Paul Phillips left the movement without any visible sign of centralized leadership. Amy feels responsibility for Paine. *I tried to warn him, but he wouldn't listen. Now, he's dead! I should have never got into this thing. So many people will be hurt.* Amy is not only thinking of David and Paul, but also the millions of people who have been drawn into the movement. *There are so many who have set aside their lives because they believed they could make a difference. And now, they are a confused mass seeking direction. I must try to help!* It has been a heart wrenching week since Paine died, and the stress and hurt have taken a toll on the elderly woman. She has made a decision to air one final edition of the Wake Up America show in honor of Paine, Phillips and the millions of followers they so profoundly influenced. She is seated in the studio as the 30 second count down to show time is begun. *I hope and pray I can help!*

"Hello. My name is Amy Younger and I am the owner of this station and the many radio and television stations that comprise the America Live Network. My purpose today is to honor the memory of David Paine by airing this final segment of Wake Up America. I am fortunate to have witnessed David Paine build a movement of tens of millions of people. I first met him at a local library where he was addressing a group of 20 concerned citizens. I was astonished as he grew reaching many millions of Americans with the same simple message. David implored us to reach out to our government and our corporations and ask them to represent the best interests of Americans. He was accused of being a nationalist at best and a communist at worst. He accepted the title of nationalist if it meant that we look after our country and our people first! He did not disdain capitalism. He simply asked that capitalism be required to be responsive to the needs of our citizenry. His message was clear and concise, and it generated a movement unprecedented in American history. His greatest fear was that unrestrained capitalism was a form of American suicide."

Amy stopped briefly to clear her throat. She felt herself becoming emotional and forced back the tears and anguish that she was feeling. *It is important that I show resolve.*

Amy continued. "When David died, I thought the movement would die. I was wrong because the movement is not David. He was simply a catalyst for a disgruntled nation that is primed for change. Americans know in their hearts that our country is on the wrong track. David was a messenger who said that there are many of us that feel the sting of social, economic and political injustice, and we responded because we have waited so long for someone to reinforce what we already knew. The movement will only die if we permit it to die. If you are like me, it will not die because I remember too well the futility and frustration that used to grip me. Knowing something was wrong with our country, but feeling powerless to do something about it was my greatest despair. Today we are united in a cause to correct the ills of our government. We are tens of millions resolved to change America. Wake Up America will not die!"

Amy pauses for a moment. She sips some water from a cup. *I hope I am saying the right things!* She continues. "Having lost David, I feel obliged to issue a warning. The job of correcting the ills of America will get more difficult. Let me explain. David made the supreme sacrifice, but you should know that I as well as other members of Wake Up America have been threatened with physical and financial harm. My company is in a pending bankruptcy because the majority of our corporate advertisers have cancelled their contracts. Moreover, my accountants tell me the Internal Revenue Service has scheduled audits of our records. In addition, the Federal Communications Commission has issued a cease and desist on all further airings of the Wake Up America program. The FCC claims the show is seditious. Today as I speak, I am in violation of the FCC order. My lawyers have filed an objection, but even if we are successful in court, the damage will have been done. I tell you these things not to frighten you, but to make you aware of the severity of the reprisals that await our movement as we move forward. The forces that are aligned against us are significant. The large multi-national corporations with their lobbyists hold tremendous influence over our government. You can expect they will fight hard to retain their privileged but undeserved status. They will do whatever they must to hold onto their power. We will all have to be strong if we are to make a difference for America."

Amy once again pauses as she gathers her parting words. "I do not wish to leave you on a negative note. I feel we can succeed. We can triumph because we are tens of millions and we are in the right. Our opponents are comparatively few in number, but hold tremendous amounts of money, power and influence. The coming days, weeks and months will be trying, but we will prevail if we continue to believe in our movement. Failure is not an option for it will return us to the futility of hopeless inaction that has consumed us in the past. This will be the final program for Wake Up America. In fact, I fully anticipate that my company, America Live Network, will lose its licenses as a result of this unauthorized broadcast. However, I will be on the front lines of our movement in Washington DC tomorrow. I will join the active efforts of the hundreds of thousands of dedicated Americans to achieve our economic freedom. Please look to your local and regional coordinators for further organizational advice. If these people are no longer available, join us in Washington or at any of the corporate protests around the country. We can win if you remain dedicated to our cause. I repeat failure is not an option. We value the future prospects of our children too much to fail. Thank you for your kind attention. May God help us with our endeavor! Good bye."

Amy slowly rises and walks towards the exit. As she approaches the door, she hears the muffled sounds of people outside. Amy opens the door and is greeted by the wild applause of a few hundred supporters. Up front are the media reporters and television cameras. There are numerous questions all drowning out each other as the reporters scream for attention. Amy, cane in hand, walks through the frenzied crowd to her waiting car. The driver opens the door and she settles into the rear seat. The driver pulls out and Amy notices an official looking car on the edge of the lot. As she passes the car, she notes the FCC logo on the vehicle. Amy turns to look at the car as four men exit the car carrying signs, a roll of tape and a wrap of chain. She turns forward and recalls thoughts of her deceased husband. They both were strong advocates of change in America. *It looks like I lost the business Anthony. I hope I've not disappointed you! I pray I am doing the right thing!*

CHAPTER 69

▼

A month has passed since the deaths of Mellon, Davis and Paine. The stock market has gone into a freefall as investors panicked and initiated a sell off in the uncertain environment. There is no new information on the executions of Mellon and Davis. These men were kingpins in the economic marketplace and the conspiratorial overtone set by their murders has taken a toll on the financial markets. The Dow Jones has fallen by over 2500 points. Gold and the other precious metals are reaching new highs as investors seek protection from the financial onslaught. The value of the dollar is plummeting against the other world currencies. Add to this, the unrest created by the multitude of Wake Up America supporters protesting in Washington, DC, and one can understand why the economy is in gridlock.

President Plant is looking out a White House window at a large group of demonstrators on Pennsylvania Avenue. He can clearly hear the endless chant.

"America first—America first—America first".

These idiots can't see I'm all for America! Why can't they see how badly they are hurting our country? This movement has been a real pain in my ass! Daily, he receives calls from his corporate supporters urging him to disband the group. Recently, the calls have been more frequent and now sound of a desperate urgency. They are demanding that he take action to end the protest. The murders, the protests, the financial difficulties and the incessant phone calls have mentally worn down the President. He has become conducive to just about any action that might end the impasse.

Lacking any sort of new intelligence on the murders and in view of the countries fiscal problems, President Plant has been drawn to theories offering simple solutions. His mind has conjured up many possibilities, but he returns to a recurring solution that may be effective. *If a terrorist group wanted to create havoc in America, the murders of the FED Chairman and the CEO of our largest banking conglomerate would certainly be a desirable goal. The financial impact would be considerable. They might even have taken control of the Wake Up America group to gain popular support in order to position themselves to promote political discord. It is the type of intricate plan that our enemies have used in the past. The financial ramifications of 9/11 were far more destructive than the loss of the World Trade Towers. Yes. It's entirely possible that these events are part of an elaborate terrorist plot.* President Plant continues to build on his recently invented theory. The more he mentally reviews the circumstances, the more he becomes convinced of its legitimacy. *Who else could it be? We are at war with these conniving bastards now! Why wouldn't this be one of their plans to destroy America? I will discuss this with Oscar!*

President Plant telephones the Vice President. He feels a burning need to do something right away. He instructs Oscar Chimney to join him in his office. Within ten minutes, Chimney is seated across the desk of President Plant. Chimney has barely taken his seat when the President goes into his terrorist conspiracy theory. The President elaborates on the murders, the infiltration of Wake Up America and the resultant financial dilemma. He compares the financial similarities of 9/11 with the present fiscal dilemma. He asserts the need for immediate action to reverse the economic decline. Plant speaks with increased conviction as he lays out the plot for the Vice President. President Plant is convincing himself of the legitimacy of his invented theory.

He now begins to question Oscar Chimney seeking validation. "Oscar. What do you think? Do you feel the people would buy this explanation? Can the agencies or your special contacts find support for this premise?"

Chimney has been listening to the passionate presentation. "Mister President. It's a very interesting theory and I'm sure we can get the American people to buy it. We will need some irrefutable evidence for some of the Congressional hard heads. I believe we can develop the intelligence to prop up your theory. What would be your plan of action once everything is justified?"

"For starters, I will call a news conference that would expose the terrorists plot. I would then place blame for the murders on terrorists who were supported by Iranian and Syrian resources. I will use this issue to ignite the American people, and call for immediate economic sanctions against the two countries. Based on the terrorists' infiltration of the Wake Up America group, I will call for the removal of the protesters from the Capital, and the other locations around the country. I would also order the dismantling of the Wake Up America organization. It would be good if we can implicate David Paine in the plot!"

Oscar Chimney smiles shrewdly at the scheming inventiveness of the President. *To think that so many believe this man to be a dead head puppet. He might sometimes appear stupid with a lost look on his face, but he could sure teach Machiavelli a few things about politics and government!*

Chimney responds. "Incriminating Paine is out! The man is clean and I feel we would develop severe opposition if we attempt to impugn him. More over, I have some knowledge about Paine's murder that may open a hornet's nest if it were made public."

Plant interrupts. "Do you know who killed Paine? Why would there be trouble?"

Chimney responds. "You don't want to know who killed Paine! Let me just tell you they were business friends of ours. We need to let Paine keep his martyrs role. It is very critical that we do not stir up controversy about Paine. We need to support him as a hero! He has too much popular support and if somehow the names of his killers get out, all hell would break loose! We can't take that chance!"

Plant agrees. "Okay then—we will just claim the organization was infiltrated without his knowledge. At any rate, we must wipe out the movement. Find some scapegoats and shut them down! I want to use the regular army to get them out of the Capital. The army's involvement will attest to the seriousness of the situation and lend credibility to the charges against the group. If we do this right, we can get neighbor to distrust neighbor and hopefully stifle this type of movement in the future. These people need to know they can't bite the hand that feeds them!"

Chimney is nodding in agreement. "I do believe we would end the financial impasse with these actions. What's your timetable?"

Plant is feeling head strong. "We need to move quickly before this thing gets out of control. Line up your ducks. I will schedule a news conference in two days. The country will be placed on high alert, and I will implicate the Iranians and Syrians in the plot. At the same time, I will announce economic sanctions against the two countries. It will be an interesting prelude to a potential military action! I want to get the demonstrators out of Washington in four days, followed by the total dismantling of the movement. If all goes right, my guess is the financial markets will rebound inside of a week. Let's do it!"

President Plant and Vice President Chimney finalize their plans. They part company to pursue their parts in the nefarious solution.

Chimney will line up his insiders in the intelligence agencies to invent the people, circumstances and evidence necessary to convince a skeptical public of the terrorists plot. He is accomplished at reeling in the reins of government when it is necessary. He has a distinct ability to have his way in these circumstances. *I know where all the bodies are buried. I just need to call in a few favors and spread a little money around to get them to jump through the hoops!*

In spite of his totally invented scheme, Plant is convinced he is doing the best thing for America. His mind is racing and his thoughts are mixed as he goes through the ritual of the righteous. *These damn businessmen will get off my ass, and I will restore order to our economy. Sometimes one needs to bend the rules in order to get the right result. America will be stronger. Two wrongs do make a right! This could be the move that saves my presidency! I might just be able to justify military action in Iran: It has to be done eventually anyway. Our army is there now. My polling figures will grow once I get those whining liberals out of Washington. I know what's best for America!* President Plant is now determined to see his plan through. *There will be no turning back now. I have made the decision and it is final!*

Pres. Plant = Pres. Bush?
VP Chimney = Dick Cheney.

CHAPTER 70

▼

"Todd. You are brilliant. How did you know that the murders of your fathers' assassins would have such a favorable impact on the project? President Plant has assured us of victory!"

It has been six months since President Plant held his news conference on the assassinations of Bob Mellon, Curt Davis and David Paine, but the effects of his exposé continue to influence both domestic and international business. The financial markets found quick comfort in the presidential disclosure, and they quickly rebounded sending the various stock exchanges to new highs. Americans rallied behind the presidential decision to censor the foreign terrorists, and have once again embraced President Plant with rising poll acceptance. Iran and Syria are under broad international economic sanctions which have caused their fragile economies to rapidly deteriorate. None the less, the President has continued his verbal attack against Iran and Syria. In recent weeks, he has been calling for military action in order to preempt any future attacks on America.

On the domestic scene, the carefully choreographed attack against Wake Up America has caused the formidable group to disintegrate. The army was dispatched to disband the dissenters and made short work of the movement throughout the country. Lacking any sort of leadership, the hundreds of thousands who protested so vocally have retreated to the safe ground of their homes. Just as President Plant surmised, the lifeline of the movement has been severed with the fabricated tales of corruption and terrorist's infiltration. The members are frightened, disillusioned and confused. They are no longer a threat to business and capitalism. The unsoiled name of David Paine is a fading memory of another failed attempt to change America. Americans will not be as quick to come together for similar causes in the future. It appears President Plants fictitious scheme has resulted in a personal, political and financial victory.

Todd is deep in thought as he listens to his friend, Charlie Bing. Todd knew the eventual outcome of Wake Up America from the moment he heard of the murder of David Paine. He understood the death of the dynamic leader signaled turmoil for the movement that so deeply believed in Paine's mission. *Seeking solutions they were easily mobilized. Under attack and lacking direction, they were rapidly dispersed. They were the last serious hope for America. Now, the people must suffer with their leaders for failing to correct the ills that consume America!*

Todd Robbins acknowledges his friends accolades. "You give me far too much credit for our recent progress. My primary motivation was revenge. I have been obsessed with vengeance and thought only of the death of Mellon and Davis. In such a state, any additional benefits would have been beyond my ability to reason. If anyone is deserving of credit, it is President Plant. His fabrication of the events may have earned him the fearful respect of Americans, but it has also created the turmoil that has brought so many supporters to our cause. Thank the President for his inventiveness. He has committed suicide on behalf of the American capitalists who so eagerly accept his corrupted leadership!"

Charlie Bing responds. "I think you are too modest Todd. But the fact remains the project has been tremendously enhanced by the recent defensive measures of the United States. Much of the world is weary with the continuing arrogance and saber rattling of the American government. My Chinese contact tells me that the level of support for the project has increased substantially over the last year. What seemed for so long to be a dubious assault on the American system now appears to be certain victory. For the first time, I can envision the world without the negative American influences. It may be premature, but I feel positive we will prevail."

Todd replies. "I, too, am happy with the results. The position of the United States has been weakened by many situations. The housing and mortgage markets are in complete disarray thanks to the blatant overproduction of dollars by the Federal Reserve. This problem is going to get much worse as the full depth of the problem is realized. The trade deficit is close to 900 billion a year and growing thanks to the greed of Americas corporations. Foreign countries now control over 3 trillion American dollars owing to the continuing deficits. American factories and industries have been moved to overseas countries while the American people placate themselves with a deluge of cheap foreign goods. Americans have spent their savings and mortgaged their homes in order to sustain their living habits. The loss of good jobs and the government sanctioned policy of permitting millions of illegal immigrants to enter the United States have effectively castrated the earning power of the American people. Today, America is so weak that she can no longer produce for she lacks the factories. She can no longer consume because her people are deeply indebted. She can only print dollars and wage wars. Americas printing machines and military are her only formidable assets, and soon they will be made worthless."

Charlie acknowledges. "What you say is true. America is very weak, and her vulnerability is not due to any outside enemy or superior force. America has her corrupt government and greedy businesses to thank for her decline. The dollar used to be as seeds in a bountiful harvest. Now, the dollar is more like the weeds that would choke out the harvest. America has sought to make economic slaves out of the world with her dollar, while simultaneously making doting serfs of her own people. Her large multi-national corporations and a few privileged individuals dine at the table of prosperity while the multitudes fight for the crumbs which fall at the banquet. It is a system doomed to failure. But the beauty of her defeat is the method. Her obsession with capitalism will prove to be the weapon that will destroy her greatness. America will fall because of her unrestrained acceptance of an economic system devoid of any human interest other than the pursuit of profits. And I shall dance at the gravesite when the greatness that was once America is laid to rest!"

Todd is nodding in agreement. "I call it Kamikaze. It is economic suicide at the hands of a nation so engrossed with capitalism that it failed to recognize the needs of the people who built the country. It didn't have to happen this way. The very spirit of independence that propelled a fledgling nation into a world power has become the mechanism for her destruction. Over time, the powerful qualities of independence gradually turned into righteousness before morphing into superiority that subsequently changed into arrogance. It is this attitude of arrogance that insures that the American effort will culminate in the decline and destruction of a once great people. I feel sorry for the American people who will suffer when the end comes. Superiority and arrogance are slow to die when one is forced into dependency. The necessary change does not come in days, months or years as the image of former dominance is not easily erased from ones memory. Rather the change comes over generations when only history books are left to remind one of what was lost when the people lost touch with reality."

Charlie is stuck by Todd's discourse. "My friend, take heart. It is the way of mankind to build greatness only to see it falter and die as motivation and resolve changes. Every nation of the world has found greatness at one time or another. Every people have had the opportunity to drink from the cup of plenty. And all have ultimately shared in the pain and suffering when their lives are altered through their own indifference. Some countries have enjoyed their powerful positions for millenniums while others have only centuries and still others burn out like a shooting star. And through all of history, no country has proven worthy to hold onto the evasive reins of power. Time has shown that the future is built upon the ruins of the past. It is now time that America makes way for a new world. The hope is that the new world will have learned the harsh lessons of the past."

Todd has had enough of the philosophizing. "Let's get down to business. Here are the new quotas. Please note the increases in gold purchases. The continued acquisition of gold mines is extremely important. In this phase, I want to place increased pressure on the stock exchanges through a broad sell off. However, I want to continue purchasing government bonds. I know there are some conflicting objectives as is intended to confuse the financial markets. Can we get these things done in the next 90 days?"

Charlie is puzzled as he reviews the quotas. "Forgive me Todd, but I thought we were ready to begin the project. This looks like another delay. We agreed America is very weak now. We should strike while the iron is still hot! Perhaps you have lost the desire to see this through?"

Todd snaps back. "It appears you mistake my empathy for weakness! This is not the case. I will confess that I had second thoughts when David Paine was alive, but all that vanished when the man and his cause were put to death. If anything, I am more dedicated to the project. The quotas are not a delay. They are a reinforcement of the resources we need to bring America to her knees. Please understand. I see America as the largest ship ever to sail the oceans. This errant ship is running out of fuel and so she has had to cut back on her engines in order to conserve. Soon, this giant ship will have to stop her engines, and only the momentum of this lumbering giant will move her forward. That is the time we will strike." Todd looks at the papers and again questions Charlie. "Can we get these quotas done in the next 90 days?"

Charlie responds. "Yes. We can complete the quotas in time. We have plenty of dollars to accomplish this and much more. We all thought you would signal the go ahead now. I will have to report to my superiors and advise them of the delay. They will be annoyed, but I can convince them of the need to hold up at this time. We all have confidence in you and will support you in your decision. We are so strong now. I just do not want to lose any part of our advantage! I will——"

Todd interrupts. "Our advantage grows every day that President Plant is in office, and every day the American government and their business partners continue in their quest for globalism. Their greed and arrogance is our strength. We can only become stronger with time. The American actions will cause more to come to our cause. I respect your concerns, but bear with me in these final days. We will not have to wait much longer."

Charlie Bing and Todd Robbins complete their discussion on the quota and the project. They have dinner together before parting company. Chou will be off to China to confer with Liu Yen on the project. Todd Robbins has planned a trip to his Boca Raton estate. He is thoroughly exhausted with the events of the past year. He longs for a simpler life. He will be happy to be freed from the heavy burden of the project.

CHAPTER 71

▼

Chou Bing has flown to China to meet with Liu Yen. He is uncomfortable with his upcoming meeting. The thought of having to once again announce a delay of the project has been weighing on him. Liu was disturbed with the last postponement. *He will be angry today! I must convince him that the rescheduling is in our best interest.* He is still arranging his thoughts as he is being led into the study of Liu's home in Beijing.

As he enters, he notes Liu is in a conversation with another man who is partially hidden in a dimly lit corner of the room. Liu rises from his chair and bows respectfully to Chou. Chou bows and walks towards Liu. The two cohorts embrace and shake hands. Chou is stealing glances into the corner as he attempts to identify the man. Liu picks up on the distraction and proceeds to introduce the shadowy figure.

"Chou Bing, I am pleased to introduce you to Shentou Kong. He is here today to review our progress. He may have a few questions for you."

Shentou Kong emerges from the corner and greets Chou Bing. Shentou appears to be in his mid fifties. He has a slim figure of average height and is largely indistinguishable except for his piercing black eyes. The three men complete their greetings and take seats around a large circular table. Liu senses Chou is visibly uncomfortable in the presence of Kong and attempts to relieve his nervousness.

"Chou, Kong sits on the advisory board for the project. He is intimate with all the details of the plan. He reports directly to the Premier and he should enjoy your full trust and confidence."

Chou begins to regain his composure. "I understand Liu, and I apologize to Shentou for my reluctance. I can only explain that my sole contact has been with Liu, and that your unexpected presence surprised me. I am at ease now!"

Chou then proceeds with the update on the project. He recites the new acquisition quotas before nervously announcing the further postponement of the implementation date. As he looks up from his papers, the cryptic black eyes of Kong are imbedded into his twitching face. Chou finishes the summary under the intense glare of his recent acquaintance.

It is Liu who speaks next. "Chou. This is unacceptable. All our friends and partners are poised to act now! Another delay may cause some of the participants to waiver. America is on the brink. I think we should seize the initiative and act now! What would be the consequences if we were to act without your American friend?"

Chou is emboldened as he replies. "Todd Robbins has been correct in every phase of the planning. He feels the time is not quite right. He senses the victory will be complete and final if we postpone our efforts for a little while longer. In the meanwhile, America will continue to weaken her position with poor trade decisions, incorrect military campaigns and her overbearing and arrogant behavior. Time is on our side. I say we must support his request for the delay, and complete the new acquisition quota he has given us."

Liu responds. "I am not comfortable with this. I have been criticized many times for our reluctance to proceed. My greatest fear is that somehow news of the project might leak to our enemies, and the element of surprise may be lost. From this view point, time is an adversary which could jeopardize the project. I feel we must proceed now! What do you think Shentou?"

Shentou Kong has been busy reading the new quotas and scribbling numbers and notes while listening to the debate between Liu and Chou. He momentarily completes his calculations before raising his head. His forceful stare commands the attention of the dueling duo. He speaks slowly and concisely as he begins to comment on the project. "I have been amazed at the logical progression of quotas we have been receiving. They are designed to take control of critical resources without calling attention to the accumulated purchases. As a result, China and our partners around the world have a commanding control over those assets critical to the survival of the United States. We started many years ago with meager funds that we have built into a great fortune. We were able to do this because we adhered to the schedules of a man who had a plan to defeat the American economy. From the beginning, Todd Robbins said we would prevail without a war being fought or a bullet being fired. He warned we would not have to be aggressive, but may have to be submissive to the demands of the Americans. He believed the Americans would fall victim to their own system of capitalism. Robbins foresaw how American corporations would scour the world looking for ways to increase their profits, and he was right. When the Americans came to China, we gave them an abundance of cheap labor to exploit. They could not resist the profits despite the fact that our country is communist. It started with a few small ventures and in a period of 10 years, the Americans have made China into a rapidly growing economy. And still they come with offers of more jobs, more factories and more industries. And we oblige them with a ready supply of cheap labor and a compliant attitude. Just as Todd Robbins had predicted, the Americans started to make additional demands on our country. He cautioned that we be wary of their requests which are made to look attractive on the surface, but in reality are elaborate deceptions. They want to become partners with us in the control of our businesses. They want to buy our country so they can open their own businesses. They ask that we revalue our money so as they can further profit. They demand we buy more of their products which we don't need, or can produce ourselves. They insist we take sides against some of our allies in Russia, Korea and the Mideast. They seek to control us with their dollars, and have attempted to make China their puppet in their quest to control the world. In spite of the outrage of many of our countrymen, we have never refused the United States. Rather, we have tactfully considered all of their demands. We continue to procrastinate but we never refuse. This approach has resulted in still more American business coming to China. A few Americans profit while they strip the United States of more jobs and factories. Todd Robbins envisaged all these events many years ago. He has never been wrong. Perhaps we should continue to support him?"

Liu is the first to respond. "I agree the plan has worked flawlessly to date. What would happen if the project were compromised at this point? All we have worked for may be lost?"

Shentou replies. "I share your concern. The element of surprise is an immense advantage. But, I am not certain it would be a total shock if somehow the project is leaked to the Americans. Many Americans are aware of how much their country has been weakened while China has grown. There is much discussion of the potential jeopardy that has resulted as America has exported her industrial and technological prowess to the world. Fortunately, the discussions have fallen upon the deaf ears of the government and the large corporations. The affluent corporations and the rich Americans feel they can control the environment through globalism. Globalism is a metaphor for American financial control of the world.

This false logic depends on the continued acceptance of the dollar as the reserve currency of the world. Their theory is the world has so many dollars that any attempt to subvert the dollar would result in the collapse of the world economy. Todd Robbins foresaw the United States would attempt to enslave the world with the dollar! At this stage of the project, I do not feel there is a danger."

Chou is clearly in agreement with Shentou Kong. He has now grown comfortable with his new acquaintance. Chou now responds. "Many years ago when Todd and I were earning our advanced business degrees at Harvard, we were taught that the dollar was so universally accepted that no country could ever oppose it without risking their own financial welfare. It has proven true for many years. Countries have accepted large devaluations of the dollar so as they would not lose the full value of the dollar. It has been a ploy the United States has used many times through their control of the World Bank and the International Monetary Fund. The dollar has been manipulated and revalued to suit the needs of the American capitalists. America has so overproduced the dollar so as to make inflation a constant threat. America proved it is easy to be the premier capitalist of the world when you have enough printing machines to produce the capital. It was out of these concerns that the European Common Market launched the Euro to compete against the unchallenged power of the dollar. In less than five years, the Euro is contending with the dollar as a reserve currency. Todd Robbins expected this outcome when the Europeans first came together as a trading network. The dollar is extremely vulnerable because the American government still feels that mutual disaster awaits the world should the dollar ever come under sustained attack. This attitude persists due to a combination of naivety and arrogance that is historically prevalent whenever a great power is on the verge of destruction. American capitalism and the dollar are the twin engines of her defeat! America will die of her own devices."

Liu relents. "I feel you both have given me new perspective on the timing of the project. Sometimes, I get too anxious and tire of the unrelenting demands of the Americans. Many of our people not knowing of our plans look on the Chinese leadership as feeble and ineffective. This image of weakness causes me great heartache. I understand the need for the delays and will bide my time."

Shentou acknowledges. "We are of accord then! We will wait until we receive word to implement the project. In the meanwhile, we will fulfill the quotas within 90 days. I know there is a strong desire to act now, but I feel it prudent to stay in step with the architect of the project."

Chou is curious. "Shentou, I have many years dedicated to this effort, but I do not know our true strength. Liu has been my only contact for years. We agreed in the interest of security that one will know only what is necessary. Is it possible that you might share our preparations?"

Shentou looks across the table with his clear black eyes. He taps his fingers while gently stroking his forehead. Liu is clearly astonished with the unprecedented request. It has only been 10 seconds, but it feels like an eternity to Chou who is already regretting his question. The silence continues as Shentou reaches into his briefcase and pulls out an official folder. His black eyes betray a pending smile as he begins to speak. "You both have dedicated yourselves for years to making China into a great world power. I think it is time you both know of our specific plans."

Shentou opens the folder and begins his explanation. "China is joined by a consortium of nations who have agreed to co-operate with us. Our neighbors in Russia, India and Korea have joined with us. In the Mid East, we have commitments from Iraq, Iran, Syria, Lebanon and Saudi Arabia. Venezuela, Bolivia, Columbia and Cuba have pledged their support. We are also joined by three European countries and two African countries whose names I can not divulge. Many of these countries have been involved in the acquisition of gold, silver and platinum for many years. At this point, our syndicate holds more than 500 trillion dollars of these precious metals. Moreover, we now own and operate over 65 percent of all the metal mining companies in the world. These companies own 80 percent of the land with proven precious metal reserves. This aspect of the project is critical. These assets represent the support for a new world currency. China will have the only international currency backed by precious metals. The new Yuan currency sits in our vaults ready for distribution at the appropriate time. Gold backed money will be critical to restore financial order when the dollar fails."

Liu is fascinated and comments. "How can we be certain the dollar will collapse? The United States has over extended the dollar in the past, but it has always found a way to protect the dollar!"

Shentou replies. "Excellent question. Our group of partners control dollar reserves in excess of ten trillion dollars. Additionally, we own over five trillion dollars worth of stock in American companies. Moreover, the government debt of the United States is substantially owned by foreigners. Our partners have purchased about two trillion dollars of this debt. The first phase of our plan is to sell all our stocks in American companies in one week. In the following weeks, we will sell all of the government securities. Those proceeds will be added to our dollar reserves, and we will seek to make purchases of commodities and assets from countries around the world that are not in league with us. These actions will shake the financial world, and I estimate in less than one month, the United

States will come under tremendous inflationary pressures. The impact in America will be far more severe than the Great Depression. Wide spread financial panic will ensue and I anticipate the United States will default on their dollar obligations throughout the world. We expect the crisis to quickly spread to other fiat currencies that will create still more financial instability. The timely issuance of the gold backed Yuan will place China and her allies in a position of world economic dominance. It will take the United States decades to recover if they can! The basic plan is rather simple. Attack the dollar by selling our positions in United States stocks and government securities. We will then use the money to go on a spending spree. This spending spree of trillions of dollars at one time will be the impetus which will create hyper inflation in the United States. At the same time, China will issue the new gold backed currency to our partners to alleviate their dollar losses. Our consortium will be the nucleus of a new world order."

Liu is intrigued and has another question. "China and many of the partners you mentioned depend on the United States for a substantial amount of business. How can we survive when we destroy our biggest customer?"

Shentou answers. "It is true the United States has been our biggest customer for many years. We built many factories and employed millions of our people to make products for the United States. The United States paid us with their dollars which we invested in our growth. We are now at a stage where we can no longer efficiently use the dollars. In recent years, we have invested our excess dollars in United States stock, treasury bonds and acquiring American businesses. This was a part of the plan. American business is no longer good business because the dollar is no longer a fair unit of exchange. That is why the United States is after our leaders to revalue the Yuan. If we were to do so, we would fortify the dollar at our expense. China is not that stupid. Today, we continue to build our infrastructure adding new factories and businesses at a record pace. We know we will lose the American customers. We will use our people, our factories and our industries to satisfy the needs of our country, and then we will cater to the needs of our partners. Just in China, there is a population of 1.3 billion people who have been neglected for too long. With our partners, our coalition represents close to four billion people. I would think these four billion are a superior market to the people of the United States who already own too much and lack the ability to pay. Our coalition controls an abundance of oil and all the other natural resources necessary to provide for our continued growth. We will have no need for the United States! There will be a new industrial revolution for the new consumers of the world. We will provide for our own peoples. And we will stay constantly vigilant not to make the mistakes of America. The needs of our country and our people will always come before any profits. We will show the Americans it can be done!"

Chou Bing has been smiling approvingly. "It all sounds so exciting. China will lead the world in a new industrial revolution. It is as if I were dreaming! There is one thing that bothers me. The United States has a huge military and a tremendous arsenal. What if the United States were to launch a military attack in response to the financial coup? Have we crafted a plan to deal with that possibility?"

Shentou responds. "A long time ago, we began to consider the probability of a military attack. We know it is not above America to respond in such a manner. The Americans become irrational when their money and wealth is at risk. It is of no consequence that they created their own dilemma. President Plant made the issue quite clear when he said 'money trumps peace'. So in answer to your question, we have prepared mutual protection agreements for all our partners. If the United States should attack any of our partners, the consortium would be obligated to stand together to protect one another. We will disclose these agreements when the project is implemented to discourage any military action. However, we understand there are no guarantees and we will stand ready to protect ourselves should the need arise!"

The meeting continues for another hour covering additional details of the project. A code giving notification to begin the project was changed once again. The code **'hari-kari now'** will be used. They part company after discussing the scheduling of a future meeting.

Chou Bing will return to New York to meet with Todd Robbins. Chou is excited that everyone agreed to the project postponement. He was happy that Shentou Kong was willing to share so much detail on the status of the project. *The American collapse is imminent!*

CHAPTER 72

▼

The fight from Beijing to New York City is a tedious 14 hour trip. Normally, Chou Bing fills the time with a number of diversions in order to pass the time. Today, he has planned no such distractions. His mind is consumed with his recent meeting with Liu and Shentou. For more than 20 years, he has relayed messages from Todd Robbins to Liu Yen. He recalls the early days when Todd convinced him to go to China with just a concept of the daring project. He was quickly dismissed by his Chinese friends for being a dreamer. None the less, Todd continued to insist that Chou try again. It was his fourth visit to China that finally sparked an interest. Chou remembered being excited when he finally found an audience. He also recalled being somewhat ambiguous about the nebulous idea. *Americans are not that greedy or stupid that they would bring about their own destruction. Perhaps, Todd is so upset with his father's death that he has become consumed with the need to change America.*

At the time, Chou was young and ambitious. He was doing well in America, but ached when his country suffered under the criticisms, economic embargos and financial plight of the cold war years. The trips to China were an attempt to show his countrymen he cared. He wanted to help change the adverse conditions they lived and worked under. In the early days, Chou never dared to seriously think that the idealistic concepts that he and Todd discussed could ever be realized. *Only Todd believed that the project was possible. It was Todd's dedication that converted me to a true believer! Todd brought me full circle from an ambivalent dreamer to a hopeful thinker to the inevitability of success. And today, we are on the threshold of world wide change. It is true that it only takes one person to make a difference!*

Even though he has been the primary liaison on the project, Chou was surprised with the degree of preparation that Shentou presented. China is ready to set into motion the events that will impair the dollar and destroy the American economy. *The plan is so intricate and yet so simple! After the project is implemented, China and the consortium will continue trading with the United States, but only for Yuan, gold or other gold backed currencies. China will have the only gold backed currency in the world. The dollar will no longer be accepted. In a reversal of economic roles, it is the United States who will have economic embargos placed on their trade activity. The project countries will buy out all American owned interests in any of the project countries using American dollars. The United States will be offered the business interests of the consortium located in America. All payments will be made in dollars. Every aspect of the project has been managed so as to assure a torrent of dollars will be returned to the United States in the shortest period of time. The hyper inflationary impact caused by the unprecedented flood of dollars will be felt around the world. The dollar will be made worthless and the American economy will go into a frenzied panic.*

Chou is immersed in these thoughts of Chinese majesty. He can hardly wait to meet with Todd Robbins. Perhaps none of this will come as a surprise to him. None the less, *I must personally tell him the degree of our preparations.*

Suddenly, he feels uneasy. *What if China somehow permits itself to become tainted by the opportunity for greed and unchecked power? If that were to happen, China will follow the dismal lead of the United States and will also fail! After all, the United States was founded with an absolute belief in a government of the people, by the people and for the people. Over time, the corrupt accumulation of wealth and power has eroded the peoples hope for the future. Without the support of the people, Americas dollars are just paper and America's power is whimsical. We must recognize the potential fallibilities resulting from so much economic and political power. Laws must be enacted that severely punish those among us who succumb to the evils of unregulated capitalism. Policies must be adopted that force all to work only for the best interest of our country. We must agree to a form of capitalism that places the common good before profits and wealth accumulation. We have to always be on guard because greed and materialism will always seek to prevail! If we temper capitalism to the needs of the people, we will build a great and lasting nation.*

Chou continues to mentally dissect the future of Chinese leadership. *Todd has always instructed on the overthrow of a dishonest system. He said the system will defeat itself and it has. Now, he must speak out as to how to avoid the fatal mistakes of America. I will talk to him. This must be our new priority.*

Chou is deep in thought when he is jolted awake with an announcement. "Fasten your seatbelts and place your seatbacks in an upright position. We will be landing in New York in 10 minutes. It is 65 degrees and a light rain is falling throughout the metropolitan area. If you have a seat on the left side of the plane, you can see New York's stunning skyline coming into view."

Chou glances out the window and sees the faint outline of the city. As the plane drifts closer, the buildings become larger and the immensity of the burgeoning metropolis becomes apparent. Suddenly, a large statue with a torch in a raised arm comes into view. *It is Lady Liberty. She is such a beautiful expression to the world. If only the American government and businessmen were as true to the concept of freedom as this large bronze statue, the outcome may be different! Deny the people and you deny your future. China will not repeat the mistakes of America!*

CHAPTER 73

▼

"What have you learned Preston?"

Earlier Preston Orient had been surreptitiously led into the offices of Vice President Chimney. Orient has spent his career living and working in the back channels of politics and government in Washington. He has been around for 32 years protecting the confidential interests of the high government officials who could afford him. In spite of his longevity and his successful record with the political elite, he has never been invited into the White House. Today, he was urged to attend a clandestine meeting with the Vice President. As he was being hustled through a labyrinth of dark halls and locked doors, he thought himself more a secret agent than a guest. But the discreet entrance was in keeping with the persona of a man who intimately knew the entrails, organs and Achilles heel of every government agency. He has served both Democrats and Republicans in his long reign as the ultimate insider. Troubled officials appreciate Orients unique skills, and they pay handsomely for his tactful services. He has known Oscar Chimney through four administrations. He has worked for the Vice President frequently enough to be on a first name basis.

"Oscar. I'm afraid I do not have much new information. The murder of Larry Yang in Washington is as much a mystery now as the day it happened! My inquiries into the timed assassinations of Bob Mellon and Curt Davis have hit a brick wall. I can't find a single lead that warrants further investigation. Normally, there is some trail to follow when people with so much power die violently. But there is nothing! Not a suspect—not a motive—just nothing! I've come up empty."

The Vice President replies. "I would say that your lack of new information is not all bad. President Plant seems to think the Iranians had a hand in the killings. He claims to have an intelligence source that places the blame on the Iranians. The fact that you have not been able to find a suspect lends credibility to the Presidents indictment of the Iranians. Quite frankly, the situation at this point could get ugly if you did find a suspect!"

Orient responds. "That's the point Oscar. I have no idea how the President got his information, but I don't think the Iranians are involved!"

Chimney speaks. "I pay you to get solid facts—not for your thoughts. If you have not been able to find a suspect, then perhaps we will call it a day and support the position of the President!"

Orient snaps back. "I don't mind supporting the President on this one, but my gut tells me something is going on, and it's not the Iranians. The way the hits were made—the same day—the same time—the same method tells me someone wants to deliver a message. I just can't get a handle on this, but I think we should continue to pursue the issue. Something is wrong!"

Chimney acquiesces. "Okay, continue your investigation. But let me be perfectly clear. If you do find out who is responsible, the information comes to me and only me! Understood!"

Orient replies. "No problem Oscar. I understand the implications. I will use complete discretion when making my inquiries and I will report my findings only to you."

"Fine Preston. What about the matter of David Paine? Has everything been resolved?"

Orient answers. "Yes, the matter is finished. Your corporate friends acknowledge a debt of gratitude to you. Your retirement years will be comforted to the tune of 65 million dollars which has been transferred to the off shore banking account per your instructions. Your friends are grateful for your patience and consideration. The inquiry into Paine's murder is as dead as Paine himself. I don't believe we will ever need to discuss the matter again!"

Chimney smiles triumphantly as he speaks. "Well done. Paine was too much of a patriot. His death will save our nation from the inevitable turbulence that would have resulted from his movement. If they hadn't killed him, we may have had to do the job. Let's close the file on David Paine! Is there anything else?"

"There is just one more thing Oscar. When the country was going through the financial trauma following the murders of Mellon and Davis, there was a considerable amount of domestic and international speculation as to the strength of the dollar. The gloom and doom guys were predicting economic collapse as the dollar spins out of control. Everyone was rushing to buy gold. Fortunately, President Plant quieted their fears whenever he implicated the Iranians, but I can't help but be concerned. What if someone were making a move on our financial markets? It seemed the situation became so precarious that a follow up attack might have totally impaired the financial system. Are we prepared if someone were to make a move on our monetary system?"

Chimney laughs as he replies. "Preston, you are becoming a compulsive reactionary. I think you've spent too much time working in the pits. Let me ease your mind. First of all, there is not a person or country that is capable of severely damaging our economy. We take little hits as a result of incidents like 9/11 and the recent assassinations, but there is no power on earth that can financially impair us. The dollar is spread around the world like grass on a prairie. Every country in the world conducts business using the dollar. Everyone is so vested in dollars that they would not even think of taking an action against the dollar. In fact, whenever the dollar is devalued, the central banks of the world always act to protect the dollar with their own currencies. To move against the dollar is to invite a world wide economic catastrophe. The United States is in the driver's seat and the world knows it!"

Orient is still concerned as he replies. "Indulge a skeptic a little more. I agree we have been successful in making the world dependent upon the dollar. Judging from your comments, there are no new initiatives to protect our economy. I suppose we are left only with the old dollar support plan."

Chimney is caught off guard. "What are you talking about?"

Orient continues. "You recall Black Monday in October, 1987 when the stock market fell by 23 percent. It was the largest single day loss in the history of the exchange including the great depression. No one was able to reason the sudden drop. The economic conditions were much the same as today with stocks overvalued and the value of the dollar in decline. The impact of that day was felt by financial markets around the world. We thought we lost it all. When the decline finally abated, our brain trust got together and came up with a plan to protect America from future financial meltdowns. The plan was initiated in 1990 when the Treasury announced that all denominations of our currency, except for the one and two dollar bills, were to be remade. The Treasury said the changes would include a security thread and other protective devices necessary to prevent counterfeiting. In 1990, the new one hundred dollar bill was issued followed by the other denominations. By 1993, the program was completed. Again in 1996, another currency redesign was announced and by 2000, the hundred, fifty, twenty, ten and five dollar bills were all reissued. No sooner had those changes been made when the Treasury announced another change which would now add color protections to prevent counterfeiting. Starting in 2003, all the currency denominations above two dollars were again changed out. We changed select currency denominations a total of 15 times in the last 16 years all done supposedly to thwart counterfeiting. But, of course, that was not the real reason!"

Chimney is confused. "I'm aware of the money changes to prevent counterfeiting. You're saying there is some other reason. I think you had better explain yourself."

Orient is stunned. "But I thought you knew. The information is closely guarded, but I know the President and Secretary of the Treasury are aware. I'm surprised you were never informed. Well, here it is, but you never heard this from me. Counterfeit protection is only a fringe benefit. All the currency changes were done to measure the time it would take to pull old bills out of circulation, and inject new bills in their place. Through the years, we have become quite efficient. It is now estimated we could pull in old currency and replace it in less than three weeks. As we speak, there is an emergency supply of a brand new currency sitting in a secret location in West Virginia. If necessary, we could replace every circulating dollar in a three week time frame."

Chimney is still baffled. "Okay. So we can change out the money supply quickly! I still don't understand. What's the point of these exercises?"

Orient continues his explanation. "Black Monday of 1987 was a financial conundrum that no one has ever been able to explain. The theory behind the ability to quickly change the currency is our financial lifeline in the event we were to encounter a similar fiscal dilemma. Our government runs large budget deficits and continuous trade deficits paid for by dollars that we print in staggering quantities. In essence, we have overproduced dollars to sustain our position as a world economic power. To date, the American people and countries around the world have bought into and accepted our extravagances. The fear is someone may figure out how badly they have been screwed! A significant number of these dollars are held by foreigners and large corporations. The thinking is that at some point some or all of the institutional dollar holders may attempt to make a move against the dollar. If this were to happen, the United States would be unable to stop the free fall of the dollar and financial collapse would be imminent. The ability to get new money into circulation will prevent a total collapse. The new dollars would be issued to Americans, select corporations and friendly foreign countries on a favorable exchange basis. The United States then would default on all the other dollars. There would still be considerable financial turmoil, but the United States would be able to survive and rebuild its economy."

Chimney responds. "It sounds like a great plan—sort of like the Strategic Defense Initiative. You know, the Star Wars plan of the eighties. We invested a lot of money in that gimmick also. We didn't need Star Wars and I can't think of a good reason why we need a stash of new cash just in case someone challenges our economic superiority. Any one who comes against the American financial system would commit economic suicide. We have the world over a barrel and I can't see that changing."

Orient has been around enough arrogant government officials to know not to argue with their opinions. He decides to back off.

"Oscar, I know the scenario is highly unlikely, but someone in the 1990's decided we needed this protection and we have been doing it since. Like most government programs, it has a life of its own!"

Chimney continues to be negative. "I think the whole idea is superfluous. It's a waste of time, and God forbid this information ever became public. We would create our own financial downfall!"

The meeting is concluded with some final comments. Orient is exited through the secretive bowels of the White House. The day has been extremely profitable for Orient. Chimney pays well, and the confidential information he has acquired is priceless. Orients survival depends on the judicious control of sensitive information. None the less, his intuition tells him to continue his research on the recent killings. *Something is so wrong. I can't get my finger on it.* He is still fixated on Chimneys final comments as he drives away from the White House. *Financial downfall! Is it possible we have already created the means for our own financial collapse? Arrogance blinds the best of minds. Could we have underestimated our enemies?*

CHAPTER 74

▼

Charlie Bing and Todd Robbins are seated in the study of Charlie's New York apartment. Chou has been talking incessantly about the detailed plans of the project. His excitement is at a fever pitch since returning from China. As he completes the review of his China trip, he notices Todd is lethargic and somewhat complacent with the news.

"Is there something wrong Todd? I thought you would be excited to hear how well China has organized their end of the project."

Todd pauses a moment before answering. "Forgive me Charlie. I haven't been feeling well lately. I do not sleep well and I'm always tired. I'm quite happy with the news. It appears everything is on track. If I fail to share your enthusiasm, it is because I anticipated that China and our partners would be well prepared. The United States has invited the wrath of the world with its continued attitude of indifference and superiority. It has taken many years to achieve our current position, but it would have been impossible without the growing arrogance of a once great nation."

Charlie could not help but notice Todd's deteriorating physical condition. It seems he has worsened as the project nears its inevitable conclusion. Todd seems without purpose. *Has he lost the will to live?*

Chou attempts to bolter the spirits of his friend. "Shortly, we will be part of a new world. People everywhere will be encouraged to participate in the new economy. America and her few allies will be isolated out of necessity, but it will be a time of great opportunity for so many who have been beaten down. You have won a great victory. You should be proud of your accomplishments."

Todd responds. "America has been predictable for many years. She alone is responsible for her own demise. I have simply planned an economic alternative to a country that has lost its way. Time, patience and a financial option is what I have contributed. Unregulated capitalism has turned the American government into a greedy, self servicing aristocracy. This anal philosophy has fostered the growth of arrogance. America would have performed exactly the same with or without me."

Charlie retorts. "It is as you say. Nothing could have stopped the inevitable course of America. But, imagine that you never recognized the consequences and never acted to produce an alternative. The world would follow Americas lead and would be financially destroyed when the American economy failed. Today, thanks to your foresight and perseverance, the world will have an option."

Todd relents. "Thank you Charlie. You are right. America is destined to fail and it is good we have the alternative. I guess I sometimes hoped that it wouldn't have to come to this—that someone would have acted to save America from her infatuation with capitalism. Not so long ago, I thought that David Paine was capable of changing America. I admired the man for his ability to rally the masses. For awhile I thought he would succeed and that America could escape the death grip of her wayward government and greedy corporations. I almost approached you to change the project, but then Paine was murdered, and his organization was destroyed with spurious charges. At the time, I felt devastated. I was not anxious to act against my own country and David Paine gave me hope for the future of America. I should have known better, but I let myself hope nonetheless. The death of Paine has reinforced the need for the project. The need for the project is absolute. However, I can't help but feel sorrow for the hundreds of millions of Americans who will be devastated when the economy of the United States is brought down!"

Charlie is sympathetic. "I understand your predicament. I would feel the same if such a catastrophe would befall China. It is not the millions of citizens who caused the problem, but they must suffer. History rebukes the masses for their silence in the face of obvious transgression. Americans freely elected their leaders. They tolerated the vices of their leaders and encouraged them with their acquiescence. The masses are therefore part of the problem. Perhaps, your countrymen will rapidly respond to the crisis and their suffering will be decreased."

Todd replies. "It is true the people must suffer for the faults of their leaders. It has always been so. It just seems so unfair. Unfortunately, the people will be incapable of a quick response. I sense mass confusion and a lack of direction will plague the American people for a very long time. It will be a sad and futile time for America. I just can't feel good about it!"

Charlie and Todd complete the review. Charlie gives Todd the new pass word to implement the project—**'hari kari now'**. When the time is right, Todd will call Charlie and Charlie will relay the code to China. China will then initiate the project.

The two part company upon completing their business. Todd is in the private express elevator. Although he is comfortable with the project, he is still plagued by overpowering feelings of remorse for the destiny of America. He continues to convince himself. *America has brought this upon herself. I have just supplied another out for the world when America crashes. 'Hari kari now'—what a fitting code to end a country so bent on destroying itself?*

CHAPTER 75

▼

Todd is back at his mansion in Boca Raton. His health has continued to deteriorate and he finds himself unable to sleep. He does not eat properly and continues to gain weight. Todd lacks energy. He finds climbing the stairs a major task which robs him of breath. He is restless as he jumps from one matter to the next without resolving anything. His inability to concentrate has impeded his capacity to make decisions. At the heart of his problem is his ongoing struggle with the project. Todd knows he must proceed, but he secretly harbors a glimmer of hope for America's future. In his mind, he is convinced that the time is right to start the project, but he continues to procrastinate.

Todd has settled into the large leather chair in the library. It is the same chair his father favored. He is weary and lays his head back to rest for a moment. Todd shuts his eyes and soon a flood of distant memories of days gone by slowly come into focus. He recalls the carefree days of his youth when the world was a playground for him. Todd's rich and privileged heritage had isolated him from the typical worries of ordinary people. He was young, handsome, well educated and the son of a doting billionaire father. He deeply loved and admired his father, and had decided to build upon his legacy. Todd recalled thinking that he and his father could accomplish anything. His father preached constantly about the pursuit of excellence, and admonished him to always set goals that would achieve his objectives. *You are capable of anything your mind can devise—if you just do it!* Their business career together was cut short by the execution of his father. In the difficult years that followed, Todd took stock in his father's advice and built an immensely successful business empire. He accomplished every goal he ever set.

Todd is immersed in these memories as his mind drifts to his present impasse. *Why can't I do what needs to be done? I have worked on the project for close to 30 years, but I am unable to issue the final order. The timing is right and I should proceed.* Todd is once again fighting the internal struggle which has effectively immobilized him. He is ready to give into indecision when he looks up at his father's portrait. He looks into the painted eyes of his father and his concerns suddenly vanish. He can clearly hear the voice of the fallen patriarch. *You are capable of anything your mind can devise—if you just do it! Just do it! Just do it! Just do it!*

Todd picks up the phone and dials the number for Charlie Bing. Charlie picks up the phone and Todd whispers the words that will remake the world. "Charlie, this is Todd. **Hari kari now**! I repeat **hari kari now**! Good bye and good luck."

Todd hangs up the phone and again rests his head on the over stuffed chair. *At last it is done. Maybe I can find some peace now.*

Time races by and the economic ramifications of the project are felt around the world. Within 24 hours, the American stock exchanges are inundated in the largest sell off in their history. The unrelenting sell off of stocks by the project countries is soon joined by millions of private investors who are panicked into selling their own portfolios. In a little less than three weeks, the continuing rout has caused the overwhelmed Dow Jones index to plummet over 9900 points. The other indexes share in the gloom as they lose over 75 percent of their value. Trillions of dollars of paper profits and equity are lost. Phase one of the project has been implemented.

One week later, the Treasury bond market is besieged by the selling of huge amounts of treasury certificates. Project countries are cashing in their treasury bonds. Inside of four days, over one trillion dollars of treasury bonds have been liquidated. The United States Treasury has responded with a call to friendly nations to purchase the bonds. Interest rates on the ten year bonds have been bid up to 30 percent. Rumors are rampant that the federal government may shut down. State and local governments are under similar pressure as the interest rates change on a minute by minute basis. The housing market is completely shut down as mortgage rates approach 35 percent. Phase two of the project has been implemented.

Simultaneously with the implementation of phase one and phase two, the project countries flush with dollars are acquiring commodities around the world. Gold, silver, oil, agricultural products, livestock, minerals and other precious metals are in high demand as the buying spree takes hold. Prices for all commodities are quickly inflated in the buying frenzy that follows. Within two weeks, gold is priced at $18,000 an ounce; silver is getting $400 an ounce, while oil is over $2,000 a barrel. Prices on other commodities are commanding comparable prices. New highs are posted with every sale as the project countries are willing to pay just about any price in order to get rid of the dollars. The buying spree abates in twenty days when most sellers of commodities refuse to accept the American dollar. The project countries now purchase whatever they can at whatever price is asked in order to get rid of their dollars. Prices now begin escalating on just about any good or service that can still be acquired with dollars. The dreaded effects of hyper inflation are felt by every American household. A loaf of bread is $60, a gallon of milk is $95 and a gallon of gasoline is $85.

In the midst of all this turmoil, China has announced the introduction of a new international currency which is backed by gold. In doing so, China has become the economic safe haven for the world. China and the project countries will trade only with the newly issued gold backed Yuan. The dollar will not be accepted. The United States will have to pay for imports from project countries with either gold, the Yuan or acceptable commodities. All other world currencies will be valued against the price of gold and will be accepted by the project countries. The project countries have been issued the new Yuan so trading among them can remain undiminished by the economic chaos that surrounds them. The complete failure of the dollar is imminent.

At the same time, the project countries have announced a mutual military security pact. In essence, any military action against any of the project countries will be countered by the participating members. The concern is the United States may look upon the unified financial onslaught as an act of war. Subsequently, China is joined by Russia, India, Korea, Iraq, Iran, Pakistan, Syria, Lebanon, Saudi Arabia, Venezuela, Bolivia, Brazil Columbia, Cuba, Spain, France, Germany and South Africa in the pact. The United States is warned to act in a civil manner during it's time of economic challenge. The United States is also requested to remove all American soldiers and military installations from the participating project countries. The announcement makes it clear there is no desire for war, but any act of aggression will be met with an equivalent response. The hope is the world can be at peace during America's economic melt down.

One month after the implementation of the project, the cumulative effects in the United States have been cataclysmic. Unemployment is estimated at 75 percent. The exact figure is impossible to calculate as mass layoffs are announced every day. Those still employed are receiving pay increases daily in order to keep up with inflation. Inflation is rampant and prices on every conceivable good or service are increased hourly. The government at the federal, state and local level has furloughed millions of workers as they seek to find a way to remain solvent. Congress has been called into special session to deal with the escalating crisis. Armed robberies and burglaries are the new employment opportunities of necessity. The struggle to survive results in mass hysteria as the mayhem finds its way into every community. Sales of handguns, rifles and shotguns are widespread as people are eager to protect themselves in this period of uncertainty. Groups of neighbors have banded together in an effort to deal with the disorder. Internal conflict continues unabated.

Internationally, the ramifications are felt world wide. The dollar had been a reserve currency of the world. Many countries loyal of the United States initially attempted to support the falling dollar. As the situation worsened, many of the allied countries broke ranks and attempted to cash in their reserve dollars for anything of value. The stock exchanges in foreign countries were battered by the financial debacle and suffered losses averaging 80 percent. Unemployment and inflation hammered away at the deteriorating foreign economies. The only exceptions from the severe fiscal and social impact were the few countries who held small dollar reserves, and of course, the project countries.

Eight weeks into the abyss, millions of Americans gathered in Washington DC demanding to speak with their representatives. They insisted on a solution to the bedlam that has enveloped America. The mob grew unwieldy when government officials refused to meet with them. Then early one morning on the third day, the unruly crowd was greeted by 2 divisions of the United States Army. The army demanded that the multitude leave. The order resulted in cat calls and profanities from the assembly. The jeering soon turned to rock throwing as the crowd surged forward. The army responded with tear gas canisters which further infuriated the mob. A single shot rang out and a soldier fell wounded in the arm. The resulting volley from the army lasted for more than 2 minutes before a cease fire was called. Sheer panic seized the mob that rapidly retreated. The fleeing horde trampled over those that stumbled, fell or were shot. The crowd disbanded as it retreated leaving behind the casualties of the brief encounter. The toll was outrageous. 1850 people were shot and killed. Another 5200 people were trampled to death. Tens of thousands suffered serious wounds or injuries. And yes, one soldier had a bullet wound to his arm.

In the following days and weeks, hundreds of thousands of soldiers and police left their posts in protest to the massacre. The deserters elected to return home to protect their families rather than kill their fellow Americans. The diminished security forces were unable to peacefully control the enraged masses. Armed mercenaries, called in from America's foreign wars, were widely employed in an attempt to quell the uprising. Violence is met with violence as America descends into a protracted state of anarchy. The fighting rolls across the country in a series of local battles that astonishes the world. Neighborhood enclaves form their own militias. America has become an armed camp.

In less than three months, the United States has fallen from the heights of prominence to the depths of despair. No one is safe. Pitched battles between armed vigilantes and hired mercenaries are a daily occurrence. Government officials are shot on site. The poor rob the rich, and the poorest rob each other. Personal survival is now the only priority. America is doomed to a long period of decline.

The Federal government attempted to substitute the worthless dollar with a new dollar supply. The effort was short lived as civil unrest was too pervasive and confidence in the government was non-existant. Effective government control is impossible. The Dark Age has descended upon America, and no one knew how to deal with it!

Todd Robbins is in Boca Raton. He is gathering some personal effects to take to China. He has arranged passage on his personal jet. As he finishes his preparations, he hears the screaming of a mob coming up his driveway. Soon, the group penetrates his home and he can hear the screams of rage outside his library door. In an instant, the door is battered down and a young man wearing a black bandana appears. He is holding an automatic rifle which he levels at Todd. With a single burst, Todd is thrown back into the large leather chair. Todd looks down and observes the streams of blood coming from multiple chest wounds. He looks up at the shooter empathetically. The shooter grins and levels his rifle as he fires another burst directly into the face of Todd Robbins.

Todd contorts in response to the multiple wounds. He feels the pain of the intrusive bullets and screams out in agony. He opens his eyes expecting to see his own carnage. He feels for the wounds and the blood, but there is none. *I must be dead!* He looks around and everything appears normal. He hears an urgent knock at the library door. The door has been reassembled and the shooter is gone! He hears the voice of his maid as the door swings open.

"Mister Robbins. Are you all right? I heard your screams. Should I call the police?

It was all a nightmare. He had a fantasized look into the calamity that would befall America when he issues the order to implement the project. It had all been so real.

Todd acknowledges the concerned maid. "It was just a bad dream. I'm sorry to have bothered you. I am fine now."

Todd regains his composure and recalls his recent nightmare. It had all been as he planned, but it was more tragic than he had imagined. Regrets set in as he recalls the savagery and hopelessness that he had just mentally visited. *America does not deserve the massive destruction. Right or wrong, it is still my country. There must be a better way to solve America's problem. I will work at another solution while I diffuse the project. It is not too late. I can do it! You are capable of anything your mind can devise—if you just do it!* Todd rises from his chair and feels a familiar pain in his chest. *I will have to take better care of myself if I am to succeed.* The pain abates soon after he slips the nitro pill under his tongue. Todd has a new mission.

CHAPTER 76

▼

Life frequently goes by quickly. Days become months and months become years, and we all become older. Charlie Bing is in his New York apartment. Earlier he had placed a phone call to Todd but was unable to reach him. He left a message with the maid to have Todd call him back. Time and again, Charlie has pressed Todd for the start date of the project. Todd remained adamant that the timing was not right, and urges patience. Todd always left the impression the start date was imminent, but was evasive when asked for specifics. This unending procrastination has become a source of irritation for the two comrades.

Charlie is under intense pressure from his Chinese contacts. The understanding he reached long ago in Beijing has been over ridden by a call for action from the Chinese hierarchy. Everyone except Todd thinks the timing is perfect and have become demanding. *I must convince Todd that we must make our move now! It has been four hours since I called Todd. He should have called by now!*

Charlie sits down in front of the television and begins to watch the evening news. The opening piece is about the President. The broadcaster is somber as he reports the news. "The President is calling for the United Nations to authorize a military invasion of Iran. He claims that the international sanctions and the trade embargos have not worked, and the Iranians are continuing to develop a nuclear weapon. He has demanded the nuclear facilities be dismantled immediately. If Iran fails to comply in 3 days, the President is demanding an authorization for an invasion. The President has also renewed his verbal attack against Syria and Lebanon for their complicity in the murders of Bob Mellon and Curt Davis. Like his predecessor, the President has indicated a willingness to start World War III if it is necessary. Americans are clearly nervous as the leader of the free world continues to up the ante in this ongoing war of words and threats."

Bing snickers as he listens. *America has her hands full now in Iraq, Afghanistan and the mid-east. What makes this President feel America can handle another war? But this leader, like the predecessor seems too willing to invoke the threat of another World War. This country is out of control!*

Bing snaps to attention as the reporter mentions China. "The President is calling for trade sanctions against China. He is demanding that China devalue the Yuan and immediately tear down the trade barriers that have hampered American imports into China."

Chou silently reacts to the news. *What hypocrisy? American leaders have never cared about this issue because their corporate friends are making immense profits from the cheap labor China provides. For years, they have sought to increase their profits by demanding that China devalue the Yuan. I recall some time back when they attempted to discredit our products with health and safety concerns when we failed to do their bidding. The hypocrites acquiesced because they feared the loss of their profits. My country will continue to ignore the brash Americans. They are greedy and self-serving suitable for leadership in a corrupt and arrogant country. The end of your kind is near!*

Bing gets up to pour a drink. He goes to the bar where he drops a few ice cubes into a glass before pouring a generous portion of scotch whiskey. He briskly stirs the concoction and begins to drink the libation as he returns to the television.

The announcer completes his news presentation with a final comment. "And this just in. Todd Robbins, a billionaire real estate developer was found dead at his home in New York. He died of a massive heart attack late this afternoon."

Charlie Bing is stunned. He knew Todd was in poor health but had never anticipated his death. His grief is masked by the fond memories of their long relationship. From their early college days to the present, they have forged a loyal friendship that has endured throughout their lives. Together, they built financial empires based on mutual trust, and together they developed the plan to destroy America.

Charlie goes into a mental dialogue with his deceased friend. *We have accomplished much over the years. We have always been successful even under the most adverse conditions. But now you have left me on the eve of our supreme triumph. You will not be able to share in our greatest moment. You gave a lifetime and your life in pursuit of the project. Trust me my friend. All will be done as you have directed. I have never failed you and I will not fail you now. I just wish we could have cherished the victory together.*

Charlie wipes an emerging tear from his eye. He walks across the room to his computer, addresses an email and types in a brief message. **Hari kari now!** Charlie walks over to the phone and dials a number in China. A familiar voice acknowledges from the other end.

Charlie speaks. "This is Chou Bing. This is to confirm. **Hari kari now!** I repeat. **Hari kari now!**"

Charlie disconnects the call to China and immediately dials the number for the airline. He books a one way flight to China. The flight will leave at 8:00 AM the following morning. *America will not be a very pleasant place in a few days.*

Charlie sits down and pays a final silent tribute to Todd Robbins passing. *Rest in peace my dear friend. You are with your beloved father now. Take comfort now that your most cherished goal has been accomplished. America has committed suicide just as you predicted. I will forever honor your memory with this great victory. Good bye Todd.*

978-0-595-48226-9
0-595-48226-0

Printed in the United States
102387LV00005B/63/A